The Rise and Fall of a Jewish American Princess

A novel

Barbara Rose Brooker

Llumina
Press

ISBN: 978-1-62550-338-1
       978-1-62550-167-7

Printed in the United States of America by Llumina Press
Library of Congress Control Number: 2014911063

For my father Barney Rose,
My daughters Suzy Unger, Bonny Osterman.

You must be able to walk firmly on the ground before you start walking a tightrope--Matisse

1

It was June 10th, 1960. "Blue Moon," played on the radio. It was Dianne and Charley's wedding night. They were at the San Francisco Airport Motel, and the next day they were leaving for Hawaii. Moonlight fell on their naked bodies. They'd been kissing. She closed her eyes, waiting for the moment that would make her a woman, and no longer a virgin. But he suddenly stopped and moved away. Something had gone wrong. Maybe he'd say I love you, or something. Then there was the rustle of the cigarette package and the snap of his lighter, as he lit a cigarette.

"Can't we try some more?" she asked.

"Not tonight, Dianne ... I'm tired."

"But I can make it hard. I can."

She watched the smoke rings float to the ceiling and then fade. It couldn't be her fault. Maybe he wasn't feeling well? She touched his hand, but he moved it away and put out his cigarette in the metal ashtray on the table next to the bed. He turned to his side, and then there was nothing but the sound of his breathing.

She lay there, still as history, her arms by her sides. She closed her eyes, trying to remember every detail of their wedding, wanting to find what had gone wrong.

*

Only a few hours ago they had married in an evening ceremony at the Fairmont Hotel on Nob Hill. They took their vows underneath a Chuppah of white roses, promising to keep a Jewish home and to love, honor, and cherish each other for the rest of their natural lives. She smiled at Charley, but he looked away. Probably he was nervous, she'd thought. After all, everyone had said that he would never marry her. He was a "confirmed bachelor at thirty," they'd said.

"Do you Dianne Lisa Roseman take Charles Alan Berkowitz as your lawful wedded husband until death do you part?" Rabbi Goldman had asked.

"I do," she said softly, her taffeta gown rustling like paper.

"Do you Charles Alan Berkowitz take Dianne Roseman as your lawful wedded wife? Until death do you part?"

"I do," he said. He slipped a band of diamonds on her third finger.

They drank wine from a silver chalice, and then Charley stepped on the glass wrapped in a white linen cloth. It made a popping sound. Gently, he lifted her veil, and they kissed. His breath smelled like mint, and wine. There was applause, and the photographer took pictures. The flashbulbs hurt her eyes and she blinked them shut.

After the dinner dance, and wedding festivities, they had driven in Charley's car to the Airport Motel. She'd sat close to him, clutching her new leather monogrammed purse, thinking about the night to come, when they'd consummate their marriage.

When they had arrived at the Airport Motel, she'd said she'd get ready for bed first, adding shyly, "If you don't mind." In the tiny bathroom, she'd turned on the water so he wouldn't hear her rituals. Quickly, she changed from her going away suit into the nightgown she'd spent two weeks shopping for. From the next room she could hear him undressing, his shoes dropping, his light footsteps, as he moved about the room. She slipped on the nightgown and turned twice in front of the mirror, admiring the pleated white chiffon gown and the oval neckline decorated with satin rosettes. Yes, it was perfect and it wouldn't be worn for more than a second.

She sprayed a mist of gardenia perfume in the air and then she turned in it so that the scent would stick to her skin. It was quiet in the next room. She was ready. He was waiting.

As she crossed the room, she felt him watching her. She stood by the bed inside a slant of moonlight and in one quick gesture she shrugged the straps from her shoulders, and her gown floated to the floor, like a dropped handkerchief. For a second she hesitated, so that he could see her naked body, and then she got into bed.

Charley was lying still and she'd wondered if there was something she should do, or if she should wait? She touched his thigh, and slowly he moved on top of her, his body weightless, as if he were holding himself back. She pulled him closer, whispering how much she loved him, waiting for the moment of ecstasy to come. But he was moving away. Her legs moved back into position like embarrassed children caught doing something wrong.

"Not tonight," he'd said.

*

An overhead jet broke the stillness.
Was he really sleeping? What had gone wrong?

So as not to awaken Charley or be distracted by the light now spreading, she counted to one hundred so the panic would stop. Surely he would wake soon and tell her that he was sorry, would say something.

She looked over at Charley. Even in his sleep he looked handsome: his long mouth as if outlined by pencil, and his eyelashes like silk thread.

She tried to stop remembering the images of her wedding--her father walking her up the aisle, her brothers Mike and Bobbie, waving, her beloved Grandmother Nannie, blowing kisses, her mother smiling happily, and crossing two fingers in the victory sign.

Yes, it had been a beautiful wedding. For an instant, there had been sparkling laughter and music, and then in a few moments it had vanished, and her dream was left behind, just as her wedding dress was left on the chair in her bedroom for her mother to put away for her daughter someday. Something awful had happened. Something beyond making love. Or was she imagining that he'd acted …repulsed?

When the phone rang, she jumped. The rings were shrill in the silence of the dawn. Charley fumbled for the phone on the nightstand next to him, paused, as if listening, and then he hung up. "Wrong number," he murmured, and then slept.

Airplanes taking off from the airport dropped slants of light along the ceiling. She closed her eyes, and slipped into a dark, thick sleep.

When she awoke the next morning she had trouble opening her eyes. She felt disoriented like she would after waking from a nightmare and not knowing where she was. "Charley," she called, but there wasn't any answer. From the window she could see that his car was gone. She felt a wave of panic.

Naked, her arms over her breasts, she rushed into the bathroom but he wasn't there. The shower was still dripping and his comb and toothpaste were dropped in the sink, as if he had hurried. Not typical of him, as he called himself a "neat freak," and was fastidious about order. Then she saw the note on the corner of the bathroom counter. It was written in his tiny scrawly writing: *"I'll be back soon. I had to drive to the office. I had a business emergency."*

Emergency? She recalled the phone ringing at dawn, but he hadn't answered. Then again, even though they had been dating for almost a year, she knew so little about his work; only that he and his father owned one of the largest contracting companies in the country.

Yes, certainly it had to be business. Why else would he leave on the morning after his wedding? She felt relieved at that thought, but at another level she knew something was more than wrong.

She turned on the bathwater, and then locked the door. Quickly, she opened his leather-shaving bag, rummaging through his things--a small hairbrush with a leather top, deodorant, and breath mints---no condoms? He'd said he didn't want children because of his diabetes—so why didn't he have them?

One black sock was tied in a knot. She unfolded the knot and inside was a syringe about two inches long a half an inch wide, and a short thin needle encased in a plastic tube. She held it to the light. She thought it must be for his insulin, hidden like a young boy hides an imperfection and for a moment she felt compassion.

She folded the sock exactly as she'd found it and then she saw a pale blue envelope was folded on the bottom. She opened it and on transparent ice blue paper, dated almost nine months ago, was a short note about an office meeting. *Sign the document as soon as possible. Let's meet next week,* the note read. The letter was signed *Carol.* She took the letter and put it in her bag, and then closed his case.

Submerging her naked body into the hot bath water, she closed her eyes, trying to ignore the pervasive feeling that Charley hadn't wanted to make love to her.

She lay still, the palms of her hands turned up, her legs resting on the faucets, her head back, careful not to let the steam frizz her hair.

Then it dawned on her; at the wedding, Charley's parents and his sister Dorothy, had left right after the ceremony; the night before the wedding she'd called Charley at home to say I love you, calling all night, but he'd never answered. She had assured herself that he had fallen asleep early, as he'd said he was going to get some rest before the wedding. As usual, she'd pushed her suspicions away.

Still, the dawn phone call bothered her. She had the feeling that Charley knew who had called.

Or could he be …ill?

Assuring herself all would be well, she got out of the tub, reminding herself that they'd have three glorious weeks in Hawaii. Time to know each other. Then she'd ask him about Carol. When he returned from his business emergency she was sure they'd make love and then everything would be fine.

She slipped on the wedding nightgown and matching negligee. Next, she called room service. "Two cups and a pot of coffee to Mrs. Berkowitz…" she ordered, emphasizing *"Mrs."*

It was an hour later, and Charley hadn't called. Drinking her fourth cup of coffee, she sat on a chair facing the window so that she could see the cars driving in and out of the driveway. Her negligee surrounded her, like a puff of white air. Each time a car drove into the driveway, she held her breath. Twice, she'd called Charley's office but only the answering service was on, and she didn't dare leave a message. Rarely had he mentioned his work, except to repeat that he was a "work-a-holic." He had once confided that more than anything he wanted to please his father, and that he wanted to take over his father's empire. "I want to build the business internationally," he'd said.

Airplanes taking off from the airport rattled the window. Her legs were stiff from sitting in one position. Over and over again, she played back every detail from the wedding to her wedding night, searching for that tiny clue that made everything change, wanting to find it before nightfall.

Just to have him, she'd passed over so many little things that had bothered her. But never had she thought that he wouldn't want to make wild passionate love to her.

She recalled—two nights before the wedding, she and Charley were making out in his car. Johnny Mathis was singing *Misty* on the radio and they were kissing passionately and she'd slipped her hand down his pants and felt his warm soft penis. "Let's do it now Charley. I love you."

But he'd pushed her hand away. "Not now princess," he'd said. "Let's wait until it's right."

Charley's car stopped in the motel driveway.

She rushed to the window and watched Charley, necktie in his hand; wearing dark glasses, emerge from his dark blue Jaguar. He was tall, over six feet, with long lanky limbs and in the sunlight, his hair was so black it was blue. Relief poured through her body and her vow to act distant fell apart.

When the door opened and he came into the room, she rushed into his arms and she held him tight, slobbering how much she adored him, and missed him. "Charley. We have time to make love. Please, Charley—is everything all right? Your emergency?"

He nodded, then smiled like a patient parent smiles at a nagging child. "Fine. Now get ready and check to see that you have everything."

She paused, wanting to question him more, but instead she smiled, as if he was right, and hurried into the bathroom. She locked the door, and quickly began dressing.

Was she imagining that he had no intention to make love to her? Silly, she told herself.

Of course he was right...they'd miss their plane. Once they were in Hawaii for their three-week honeymoon, everything would be fine.

Quickly, so as not to keep him waiting, she dressed. She hooked her pale silk stockings to the garter belt, and changed into her white linen going away suit and matching leather pumps.

She rinsed her burning face, avoiding looking at her swollen eyes in the mirror, and brushed her hair so it hung loose. She opened the door, listening to Charley's low impatient whistle. She glanced at herself in the mirror, her face so pale, and her eyes dull, as though the night had clung like old dew, like some kind of bad memory.

"Dianne ... hurry!" shouted Charley.

2

They arrived in Hawaii later that afternoon. The white light was blinding and Dianne gasped at the rush of tropical heat as she and Charley walked along the ramp, and through the small airport. On the plane Charley had ignored her, and had read the *Financial Times*. Mostly, she'd stared out the window, imagining she was floating in space, and not feeling her increasing panic.

Outside, they waited for the limousine to take them to the Royal Hawaiian Hotel. Hibiscus scented the air, and boys wearing colorful Hawaiian shirts sang and played Hawaiian songs on ukuleles. Pretty hula girls swaying their hips to the music, dropped orchid leis around their necks. Everything was so beautiful, and suddenly Dianne felt optimistic. "Aren't the girls lovely, Charley?"

He folded a twenty-dollar bill between his long thin fingers. As the porters hurriedly put their luggage into the trunk of a black limousine, he complained: "You have enough luggage for three months, Dianne."

She pretended she didn't hear him. But she wanted to ask why he only had one bag for three weeks? She assured herself that once they got settled at the hotel, that later they'd talk about everything.

In the limousine, on the way to the hotel, he lit a cigarette. He looked straight ahead, as if his mind was on some fixed direction, while she looked out the window, admiring the low swirling sun, and the orderly rows of pineapple plants. Except for the sound of the soft motor racing to their destination, they sat in silence, and then finally the car ascended along a narrow road, past flowers so big they seemed to be exploding. At the top, the Royal Hawaiian Hotel was shimmering in the sunlight. It was pink stucco and tiered like a cake. Pink and green striped awnings dangled over the terraces protecting the perpetual light and the surrounding sea. The hotel was more beautiful than its pictures; it was a perfect place for honeymooners.

The car stopped on a large circular driveway and you could see the private beach below. Several porters wearing Hawaiian shirts greeted them, murmuring "Aloha." Efficiently, they stacked their luggage into metal carts, and then Charley and Dianne followed them into the hotel.

The lobby was rich with thick emerald carpets, rattan chairs, couches, and lush tropical plants. Huge wooden ceiling fans were spinning cool air, and the views from every window were magnificent. There, standing in line to register were the newlyweds from the plane. They were holding hands, their wedding smiles on their faces. While Charley signed the register Dianne stood next to him, her hand possessively on his arm, and her rings sparkling, as if showing everyone that she was his wife. Then they went upstairs.

The bridal suite was huge, and the air scented, as if all the flowers in Hawaii were in the room. The terrace doors were open, letting in the smell of the sea, and the white chiffon curtains were billowing like silk scarves.

The king-sized bed was on a raised platform, and orchids were sprinkled on the satin pillows, as though it were natural to sleep with flowers. On a rattan table next to a basket of fresh pineapples and fruit, congratulatory telegrams from family and friends were arranged in a neat pile. The realization that she was still a virgin came over her and suddenly the telegrams seemed embarrassing, as though they didn't belong. She'd read them later, she assured herself. Charley was still standing in the doorway, tipping two porters. Then the door shut, and she and Charley were alone.

"I'll just unpack a few things," she said with forced gaiety, as if everything between them was normal.

"I have important calls to make," he said with a quick smile. He sat on the edge of the bed, a leather book on his lap.

"I'll change," she announced, trying to sound cheerful, but wanting to ask what important calls.

"Do you want something?" he asked in a too polite tone. "I'm going to call room service."

"Just you," she said with a laugh, feeling suddenly foolish. "Anyway, I'm going to unpack. Three weeks is a long time." Her words drifted into the tense scented air.

Their luggage was side-by-side on the table. Carefully, Dianne unpacked her two large suitcases—first, the white cashmere sweater with the detachable fox collar, hanging it in the empty closet-- then the white backless cotton dress and the pink chiffon, the array of pastel dresses, matching sweaters, then arranging the dozens of dyed-to-match shoes in her satin shoe bag. "A dream trousseau," Mother had said. While her father had protested, citing too many expenses. A film distributor for Universal, he was on salary, and lived way beyond his means. He'd mortgaged his house to pay for the wedding. "A girl gets married once," Mother had insisted.

Carrying her overnight case and change of clothes, she went into the bathroom and changed to shorts and a halter-top.

When she came into the room Charley was still on the telephone, the receiver close to his mouth, speaking softly. Impulsively, she kissed him and sat on his lap. He covered the telephone with his palm. "Please, Dianne. Can't you see that I'm trying to do business?"

She stood there, feeling like a reprimanded child, looking at him. A part of her wanted to ask why he was so cold, and to tell him that she didn't believe for a minute that he was busy with clients. She pretended that she didn't notice, and she hurried outside to the terrace.

On the verandah, by the ledge, she admired the color of the sea modulate from turquoise blue to black. But then the harsh realization that she was still a virgin bride came over her like a smack and she wondered what had happened to make him so cold? From the moment he vowed till death do us part, to now, his eagerness to marry her had changed to forced tolerance. She lit a cigarette, inhaling deeply.

She watched a seagull float close to the edge of the sea, its wings out, it's feet down, and she wished she were that bird looking for a place to land, all alone but secure in her flight. At that moment she had the worst feeling that maybe she had been part of something ominous, something that she'd never know.

Feeling anxious now, she recalled that just a few hours ago, they'd cut the twelve-tiered wedding cake, Charley gently placing a piece of cake on her tongue as if it were a sacrament, while the orchestra played, "Love and Marriage." She had brushed the crumbs from his lips.

"Dianne! Be careful in the sun," Charley said, appearing on the verandah. "You're very pale," he said in a disapproving tone.

He stood by the ledge, looking at the sea. She loved the way his neck flowed into his long slender back, his small waist a graceful indentation. She put her hand on his back, listening to the waves rolling to the edge of the beach, crashing, and then rolling back. Finally she said: "I'd love to go for a walk and see the grounds, maybe walk on the beach. Would you like to?"

"You go ahead," he said with a quick smile. "I have to meet a client at the golf course. It's business." Slowly, he lit a cigarette. He inhaled deeply, blowing smoke rings hardly noticeable in the white light.

"You're treating me like I'm a bad date," she said with a nervous laugh.

"Honey, I'm sorry. I'm just—busy. I'm waiting for an important call, honey. Tonight, we'll go to dinner in the dining room."

But then as if he'd forgotten himself, he reached into his pocket and from his gold "B" money clip, stuffed with hundred dollar bills, he removed two one hundred dollar bills.

"Go shopping, or something."

She ignored his money and instead she fished in the big purse as though she were looking for something, trying to retreat from the flush spreading along her neck and face. Then she hurried across the room, aware that he was watching her.

She slammed the door, slammed it hard so he'd know she was angry, more than angry. She ran along the hallway towards the elevator, inhaling his scent drifting inside the still muggy air.

Outside, Dianne walked through the gardens, slowly, as though she were just enjoying her leisure while waiting for her husband, as though he had probably told her, "It'll be only a few minutes ... wait for me ... I have some calls to make ... I love you." Pretending she was an ecstatic bride and that her groom was making calls, she languidly walked past the families wearing shell necklaces and beach hats and carrying tote bags.

An important call? Golf? He didn't bring clubs, so why is he lying?

Though it could have to do with his business emergency—his money? She knew that he invested heavily in the stock market. Also, he gambled heavily, at a private club where only wealthy men were invited.

She walked faster, furious at herself for acting so dumb, so weak, until she stopped shaking. She stopped by a hedge of flowers, inhaling the perfumed air, and admiring the flowers lining the walkway. They looked like glass, almost transparent, or waxen in the sunlight, as if they were polished daily, and would never disintegrate. Only there to admire. She touched the coral-colored petals on a tall flower with a thick green stem. It was hollow inside, and it didn't have an odor. It was only beautiful. A yellow bee floated above her hand, and she moved back. Bees are beautiful, but treacherous. Like Charley, she thought. The bee floated to a flower.

On the edge of the lawn, overlooking the sea, she sat on a wicker love seat. Her hat and purse claimed most of the seat so that anyone looking would think she was reserving a place for her husband. The beach was white as a lily, curling along the sea like a pearl necklace.

She opened her tote bag and took out the notebook, and the pencil she always kept in her bag. When she was drawing, or writing in her journals, she could feel what she was really feeling. She sketched the cluster of birds flying low along the edge of the sea.

That call at dawn? Was it a warning?

Or was she imagining that some tragedy had occurred---was inevitable? She had a habit of dramatizing.

Stop it. They'd have three weeks. By then she'd know.

She drew the sun shrinking like a shapeless jewel, slowly falling into the sea. Slender shadows stretched lavishly across the expansive green lawns, and guests lounged on chairs, fanning themselves with straw hats.

She sketched faster, drawing the beach boys in their fluorescent orange bathing trunks, pushing sticks with nets on the ends, scooping debris from the sand, then drawing the surfers floating on top of the waves like shadows, the waves rising like lace. Hawaii was so beautiful, exactly as she had dreamed it would be.

Nor would Mother believe that she was still a virgin." It's up to a woman," *Mother would say.*

She shuddered at the thought of her mother knowing that she was alone. She'd never believe it.

Why had he been in such a hurry to rush the wedding?

She had wanted a winter wedding, but Bea Berkowitz had begged her not to wait. "If you wait, Charley will change his mind," Bea Berkowitz had said, explaining that Charley hated big events. Mother was only too happy to plan a wedding in three weeks. "Get him while you can," she'd said, happily. Eager to leave home, Dianne had agreed. Never had she seen Mother so happy, carrying lists, and shopping for Dianne's trousseau. "He's very rich," Mother had bragged to her bridge friends. Daddy had said little.

When dusk shadowed the lawns, and the sea turned mauve, she closed the notebook. By then she was sure Charley would be frantic. It was time to dress for dinner. Hurriedly, she walked back to the hotel.

As she waited for the elevator, she watched couples dressed for dinner, hurry to the Honeymoon Luau in the main dining room. The women wore pastel chiffon dresses, suntans, and the men wore white dinner jackets and joy on their faces. The sound of the orchestra playing *It Was Just One Of Those Things* cast liveliness through the lobby. The last of the sun had finally fallen into the sea and wicker lamps were flickering on.

Dianne got off the elevator, and hurried along the hallway. Her heart was pounding. Tonight at dinner she'd talk to him, just ask him what was wrong, and then they'd talk like a husband and a wife. It was time to be close. To grow up.

She opened the door to Room 704.

The room was dark except for the spotlight provided by the rising moon, and a breeze blew the curtains, like spectral things. He wasn't there. She turned on a wicker lamp. Fresh orchids were on the bed. His suitcase still wasn't unpacked. Red lights on the telephone flashed urgently, and Dianne wondered who had called?

Charley's blue silk shirt was dropped on a chair. She held it to her face, like an animal searching for its master's scent. Then she folded the shirt, placing it on top of the dresser and patting it as though she had performed something domestic. His suitcase was on the chair in the dressing room, and she was surprised that he still hadn't unpacked.

Deciding to dress for dinner, she bathed and began dressing. She slipped on the white organza dress with a low oval neckline, and a bell shaped skirt. Wanting to look especially beautiful that night, she arranged her hair into a low chignon and inserted a baby orchid in the side. Over her arm, she'd carry the white cashmere cardigan sweater with the detachable white fox collar.

Finally, she hooked the white stockings to her garter belt, and then she slipped into the white silk high heel pumps.

Completely dark now, she switched on the lamps. The verandah doors were open and Dianne could see the bonfires glowing along the beach. A full moon glowed in the dark like a baroque pearl.

At the small wicker desk with the glass top, she sat on the high wicker chair, and wrote postcards to her family and friends.

We haven't left the hotel yet except to go right outside to the beach. *I'm having a wonderful time.*" She underlined "*wonderful*" to give it significance.

By then it was past nine and she was hungry.

Where is he? Probably by then his business problem was worked out. Or is it business?

Really, she knew so little about him. And it was only four weeks ago that they'd broken up.

She'd been working at Saks, and frustrated that she'd dated Charley almost a year and he hadn't proposed, she'd called and asked him to meet her after work. They'd met at Compton Place in Maiden Lane. They'd sat at the bar and she'd blurted that she wanted to marry him. "I love you," she'd said. Gently, he'd explained that he had diabetes, and would never marry. He'd encouraged her to meet "a nice guy, who wants marriage, and children." For weeks he hadn't called, until four weeks ago, late at night he'd arrived at her parent's house and proposed, exclaiming that he couldn't live without her. As soon as possible he wanted to marry. Quickly, she'd agreed. It was the first time she ever pleased her mother.

Evening laughter drifted from the terrace, and the faint sound of bongo drums from the beach, pounded a sensuous rhythm.

She turned. How long had Charley been standing behind her?

"Oh ... hello," she said, getting up and kissing him lightly on the cheek.

"You're so—dressed up," he said, with a disapproving tone.

"I thought we'd go to the dining room for dinner. I made a nine o'clock reservation."

"I ate at the club. Sorry, honey. Order something if you want."

"I'll wait for you. We can order room service."

He emptied his pockets, dropping coins and keys on the dresser as if there was nothing unusual between them. Then he went into the dressing room, and emerged wearing black pajamas, yawning, saying how "exhausted," he was.

"I'm starving Charley. I'm going to order a burger—fries." She laughed. "You love fries. Remember when we'd eat fries? I'll order you fries? Crisp? We'll eat in bed like an old married couple. Tomorrow night, we'll go to the dining room. The menu looks wonderful."

He held the watch to the light, as if making sure that it was set to the correct time. He was always precise about time. Never early, never late.

She shuddered. "The wind is up. I'll close the doors."

By then the moon was full and she looked it in the eye, as if confirmation that change had occurred. Now it was time to consummate their marriage. Slowly, she pulled the curtains closed, the sounds fading, settling, the moon a blur.

"Dianne! Listen to me! We're leaving tomorrow. I made a mistake."

She gripped the curtain cord tightly as though if she let go of it she would lose her balance, would confirm Charley's words. The moon looked remote through the transparent curtains.

"Did you hear me Dianne? I made a mistake. I don't love you.' We're going home.'

When she turned around, Charley stood by the bed, watching her, his shoulders unnaturally back, like a soldier before battle. She stood by the closed curtains, watching his face, thinking that if she kept looking at him he would say it wasn't true.

"Tomorrow at seven, we'll leave. I'm sorry, honey. I made a mistake," he repeated. "That's why I couldn't ... make love to you. I'm sorry, honey."

"Mistake? What kind of mistake?" she said, her voice shrill. "A day ago we took marriage vows till death do us part! We're married! There are no mistakes! I can't go home."

"I'm sorry, honey. I tried to do the right thing. I wanted to do the right thing," he repeated.

"Right thing! I'm your wife. You can't do this."

"Don't make a scene, Dianne," he said with a sigh.

"Is it Carol?" Her voice sounded faraway. "I found a letter. I know it's someone else—"

He sighed. "Carol was my secretary for years. Until she and her husband moved to Chicago. It isn't anyone else, Dianne. I made a mistake."

As though it were settled, he got into bed, under the covers and turned on his side.

In the dark, she stood in the same place, her arms out as if trying to catch his words to squeeze them so they'd dissolve. She felt like she was in one of her dreams when she wanted to scream and no sound came out.

She undressed, dropping her clothes on the floor. She slipped under the covers, staring at the reflection of the sea floating along the ceiling. She moved in a prenatal position so she wouldn't hurt so much. Then time stopped. The only sound was the unfolding of the waves and Charley's soft, regular breathing.

Somewhere between darkness and light she must have closed her eyes and slept.

3

When Dianne awoke the next morning it was a little after five a.m. She blinked several times, trying to open her swollen eyes, and to adjust to the nightmare. He was still sleeping. She watched him sleep, his perfect face peaceful, as if he hadn't destroyed her life. When Dianne thought about a gun it was an almost a subliminal image. Her body was tingling and she felt as though she were sinking, slowly dissolving.

She got up, wanting to dress quickly, and hurried into the bathroom. Her reflection in the mirror shocked her; her eyes were dull, and her face was gaunt. Not bothering to bathe, she dressed hurriedly in her white linen going-away suit, and tied her hair into a ponytail. Quickly she packed her clothes, dropping the dresses and shoes into the suitcases. Not caring that she made noise she slammed her bags shut.

He sat up, rubbing his eyes. "What time is it?" he asked, and without waiting for an answer, he got up, and ran into the bathroom. Leaving the door open, he showered. "We'll have to hurry," he called out, his voice almost cheerful.

The drapes were closed but the ocean was loud, and bits of sunlight pushed through the opening in the curtains, making wobbling strips of light along the floor. She didn't look at the sun setting, or at the ocean. She didn't want to see its beauty.

Charley emerged from the bathroom, a towel around his slim waist. His hair was slicked back. She flipped through a hotel magazine on Hawaii, pretending she wasn't watching him dress, and imagining that she was aiming a gun at his face. That she felt panicked about what her mother would say. Would do. He buckled the narrow leather belt on his beige linen slacks.

"I'm hungry," she said, standing. "I'll be in the coffee shop."

"They'll have breakfast on the plane, Dianne. You can eat then." He smiled as an indulgent parent smiles at a too willful child.

"Are you packed?" he asked.

"Of course you are," she snapped. "You never unpacked because you never intended to stay. You set me up, Charley."

"Don't be silly, Dianne. Don't make a scene."

"Oh, sorry, Dianne. I made a mistake. Return me home like you return a sweater. And you expect me not to make a scene! What about my poor father? He mortgaged his house to pay for the wedding!"

"I'll talk to your parents. I'll explain."

"Explain that you made a mistake. Oh, sorry, I vowed to cherish your daughter forever, but oops I made a mistake so I brought her home after a day?"

She rushed past him, and went downstairs.

She sat at the counter in the coffee shop. She drank several cups of coffee, stretching out the time. She felt like she had been hit by something and the breath had gone out of her. She couldn't feel anything but her mind was a jumble of memories about Charley and thoughts.

Probably, Mother was home, on the phone, bragging about the wedding, and that Dianne had married a "millionaire." Daddy would be home relaxing after the wedding. He liked to be home on Sundays as during the week he traveled. Universal sent him weekly to the East Coast.

She smoothed the napkin under her cup. All sound had drowned out. She imagined she was underwater, fully submerged in that place she always went when trauma existed. The only evidence that she was upset was that her hands were shaking. Shaking so hard that she clutched the coffee cup. She was somewhere lost. Lost forever. Her dreams behind her. Lost.

What would she tell Mother? Oh, Mother. Sorry my wedding of one day didn't work out? She'd always been afraid of her mother. Easily, she could sense her mother's moods, and avoid her sudden slaps, and quick shrieks. She knew how to disappear into herself. She'd learned that well.

She had to do this now. To figure out what had gone wrong? So wrong. She had to find the reason he married her.

There had to be someone else. Something he wasn't telling her. Something he had used her for. Then she remembered: Shortly after her engagement was announced in the papers, Mother had mentioned that a woman had called, explained that she was a distant cousin of Charley's. The woman wanted to know where she could send a wedding gift. She'd asked Mother questions: how old was Dianne, and what kind of ring did Charley give her?

Charley tapped her on the shoulder.

"The limousine is waiting," he said impatiently, glancing at his watch. "Do you have everything?"

She drank her coffee, ignoring him.

"I checked out. I'll be at outside, waiting for you. Hurry," he said with an anxious sigh. He paused, as if he thought she'd jump up, and then he left.

It crossed her mind not to go at all.

Why couldn't she stay in Hawaii, get a job as a waitress, save money---disappear? Disappear forever?

Exhilarated at the thought of avoiding the impending tragedy that she knew was sure to come, she suddenly felt free. But then reality set in; she hadn't a cent. She didn't have an education. Beyond selling bridal gowns at Saks, she hadn't any work skills. She'd lived such an enclosed life. Already, she felt as though she had slipped behind the wall that existed in her, and she knew that she had to go home. She also knew that as soon as possible, she'd leave her parent's home, and find her own way. She had to. Or she'd end up like her brothers. Broken.

She left the coffee shop, crossed the lobby, hurrying past the honeymoon couple who waved, and went outside. The porter gave her a beautiful lei inside a cellophane bag, and said "Aloha.'"

As the limousine descended the long hill, she didn't look back at the sea surrounding the hotel, or at the sun expanding in the sky, or at the flowers blooming like lost jewels.

It was evening when they arrived at the San Francisco Airport. On the plane, Charley had been solicitous; he'd asked if she felt all right, assuring her that he'd explain to her parents that he'd done the wrong thing, and that it was his fault. She'd looked out the window, wishing she could float into the clouds and disappear forever.

Slowly, she followed Charley to his car. The *Just Married* banner was still taped to the back. He pulled it off, dropped it on the garage floor, and then loaded the trunk with their luggage.

The traffic was heavy. He drove fast, as if he were in a hurry to get it over with. She clutched her new monogrammed purse, and the orchid lei inside a cellophane bag.

A low fog floated over the City like a wool cloak, and the air was turning dark. By then Nannie would be setting the table for dinner, and helping Birdie, Mother's housekeeper in the kitchen. It was Sunday so Daddy would be home resting before probably traveling the rest of the week to the East Coast, and her brothers would be home. A talented golf pro, at seventeen, her brother Mike had left home and opened a stall at the flea market, trying to save money. Bobbie, only eleven, would be watching television.

He turned right on El Camino Del Mar, and stopped his car in front of her parent's house. He turned off the motor, and the sudden silence was final. Her parents' black Cadillac with the fins, and Mike's beat up van, were parked in the driveway. Foghorns made a lonely sound.

"Why, Charley. Why did you bring me all the way to Hawaii? Why did you marry me, when you knew you'd do this? Why?" Her voice sounded hollow. Faraway. He looked straight ahead, his hand still on the wheel. Then he said: "Dianne, you'll meet someone wonderful, live in the country, have dogs."

He got out of the car and opened her side of the door, standing politely, dutifully, and glancing at his watch. Slowly, she got out of the car. She watched Charley open the trunk and remove her luggage, and then she followed him up the long flight of brick steps.

At the top, the porch was surrounded by blooming camellia bushes. Charley dropped her luggage near the front door. He stood stiffly, his face chalk white, as if awaiting a battle. She looked at his blank face.

"Leave!" she said. "Don't ever come near me again or I'll blow your head off. Get out."

He looked surprised. He hesitated, as if maybe he wanted to say something. Then, like a boy let free from punishment, he ran down the stairs. He drove away, gunning his motor, the headlights blinking in the darkening dusk.

She slumped against the wall as though it would give her a place, gravity, and then she rang the doorbell.

4

After a long moment, she heard the sound of her mother's high heels clicking on the hardwood floors. Not calling who's there as Mother usually would, as if maybe she was expecting someone, the door opened.

Mother stood there, holding the door, as though the door could close out the shock; her gold colored eyes looked over Dianne's shoulder, as if to look for Charley.

"He's not here Mother. It's ... over."

Mother covered her mouth with her small hands. Then their eyes met, shocked, knowing, like sealed documents, understanding that, yes, something horrible had happened. Mother looked over Dianne's shoulder again, as if to make sure Dianne wasn't joking, or to make sure no one saw Dianne.

"He's not coming back—" Dianne whispered, watching her mother's shocked face. She kept her eyes on her mother's pale stoic face, as if waiting for acknowledgement that she was there.

"Don't just stand there. Come inside," Mother said, opening the door wider. Dianne stepped inside, her legs heavy, like she'd stepped inside one of her nightmares when she tried to walk and couldn't. She bent down to hug her mother who was only five feet one, and they exchanged an air kiss

"Your poor father. "Mother said as if to herself. "He's in the living room. Your poor father," she repeated with a heavy sigh.

Dianne followed her mother along the hallway, Mother's backless high-heel gold satin slippers clicking on the heavily waxed hardwood floors, her gold taffeta hostess gown rustling like paper. The air smelled of lemon wax and roast beef cooking from the kitchen. Stacks of unopened wedding gifts from Gumps were carefully arranged on the antique bench. Each package was marked with yellow tags, ready for the thank you notes Dianne would write on her new monogrammed lilac stationary.

The French doors to the living room were open. Daddy sat in the worn green velvet wing chair, "your father's chair," Mother always said. He was reading *Time* magazine. The chrome-reading lamp behind him revealed the pinkness under his thinning, silver hair. Next to him, on the antique end table, was his usual scotch and soda, "just one," he would always say.

"Lou ... Lou," Mother whispered again. It was almost like slow motion when he turned slowly. And then he turned back to Mother, as if he first needed her to acknowledge it really was Dianne, and then he looked at Dianne with confusion in his dark velvet eyes. He got up then, the magazine falling to the floor and came towards her.

"Daddy ..." Dianne managed to say, trying not to trip. They hugged with averted eyes, their bodies not touching. He pulled away. "Dianne dear," he said, softly. "Sit down."

Dianne sat on the edge of the beige velvet loveseat, her legs primly together, and her hands clutching her purse. Mother sat on the beige silk sofa, her pale artistic hands arranging the folds of her gown, murmuring, "My God, it's always something." As though the impact of what was happening finally was affecting her.

"Stop with the 'Gods' and let her talk," Daddy said, his voice breaking the anxious stillness.

Mother lit a cigarette, and inhaled deeply, the smoke spiraling into the high molded ceiling. The ice in Daddy's highball glass was clinking as it settled in the glass. Outside the closed French doors, Dianne heard whispering. Probably, her brothers, she thought. Mother's gown rustled as she moved closer to the edge of the loveseat. Daddy, next to her, cleared his throat and looked away.

"What happened?" Mother asked, her voice on the verge of shrill.

Dianne took a deep breath. "The marriage wasn't ... consummated." Her voice trailed into the stiff silence.

Daddy looked away, and Mother looked straight ahead, as if her frozen stare would maintain her composure.

"I've never heard of such a thing," Daddy said after a long silence." Never in my life!"

"He said he made a mistake," Dianne continued, nervously. "It wasn't my fault."

"Mistake? Mistakes like this don't happen to girls like you!'" Mother shouted. "There's no such thing a man like Charley brings home his wife after one day. Not unless you did something wrong!"

"It wasn't my fault," Dianne repeated, looking at her father for affirmation. "I mean I wanted to, I ... he said he didn't love me." Dianne broke into tears.

"Here's my handkerchief," said Daddy after a long shocked silence and giving Dianne a large white linen handkerchief. "You should always carry a handkerchief. All young ladies carry handkerchiefs."

"Dianne," Mother said in a low voice, as if it was only between them. "Don't tell this to anyone. I mean *anyone*. We'll make an appointment with Dr. Solomon. Some things take ... *adjustment*."

"What has Dr. Solomon got to do with it?"

"Well, you know," she said, looking away. "You never had... an *exam*."

"You think it's my fault! I was willing! He wouldn't. He set me up. I know it! He never intended to consummate. I know it!!"

"He wouldn't bring you home. Not unless you did something not normal. Something wrong!"

"I said stop it, Honey!" Daddy shouted, angrily. "Thank God she is a virgin. Thank God she's not with him. He's a bastard. Leave her alone!"

They sat in a frozen stillness. Dianne heard her brothers whispering outside the door, and then their footsteps as they scurried away.

"If you play your cards right, you'll get him back," Mother said. "Just tell everyone he was sick and that you had to come home——"

"I want a divorce, Mother. Do you hear me?" Dianne shouted, suddenly.

Her father demanded, "No more discussion!"

Mother lit another cigarette. "Go upstairs Dianne. Fix yourself up for dinner. You look terrible."

"Clean your glasses," Daddy said. His face was ashen.

Dianne pressed the damp handkerchief to her eyes, embarrassed that her face was red, and her stockings twisted and wrinkled. She managed to walk across the room. No longer was she the same girl who'd married only two days before, and had dreamed of becoming a different person faraway from her parent's house. She was back.

She ran up the stairs, into her room.

Upstairs, she closed the door behind her. Nannie's room adjoined her room, but Nannie was in the kitchen, helping Birdie, and she wouldn't come upstairs until after dinner.

She stood in the center of her room, looking at the canopy bed, the pink and green floral bedspread smoothed just so, the storybook bride dolls dusted and arranged in the tall glass case. On a metal table Mother had rented from *Abbey Rents,* wedding gifts were displayed: silver chafing dishes, tea sets, silverware and the gold and white China that she and Charley had chosen at Gumps. Mother had enjoyed showing the gifts to the steady stream of her bridge friends, whispering who sent what and how "expensive" the gifts were. Dianne's wedding dress stuffed with tissue, hung from a hook. Mementos, and ribbons from the one bridal shower that her friend Debbie had given her were in a box, tied like old love letters. "We'll turn your room into a sitting room," Mother had said. Already a lot of her things were gone--her jewelry box with the dancing ballerina, the Smith Corona portable typewriter that had been on the roll top antique desk. Vacuum tracks were on the dark green carpet. Never would anything be clean or neat enough for Mother.

She took her notebook from her bag, and a pencil, and went into her closet. In her secret spot, Dianne sat underneath the array of coats and rows of dresses that she had planned on sending to Charley's house. A heating vent was open and she could hear her parent's raised voices and Mother's dog Christopher, barking.

Soon, she stopped shaking. Sudden tears burning her face were a relief. She opened her notebook and drew a thin black gun. Over and over again she drew the gun until the image dissolved from her mind.

She sat still, trying to process her thoughts, just to get some semblance of reality, of order. She felt as though she'd landed in a strange dream and couldn't get out. Everything she had hoped for, had believed in, had suddenly evaporated. To survive her mother's rage she had to pretend that she was perfectly fine.

She closed the notebook and put it on top of the black notebooks with the white dots on their covers hidden behind a pile of old shoeboxes.

Her eyes closed, she sat in the dark, trying to absorb that she was back home, and that Charley had really happened. Or had she had merely a nightmare?

"Miss Dianne!" Birdie called, knocking on her bedroom door. "Miss Dianne, dinner's served in five minutes."

When she heard Birdie descent the stairs, slowly, she got up, smoothed her dress, and opened the closet door. She took off her glasses and put them away in the dresser drawer. "You're prettier without those thick glasses," Daddy always insisted. Next, she removed her diamond rings from her third finger, and dropped the rings like abandoned things, inside the tiny glass bowl on the glass dressing table. She combed her hair, smoothing it with her hand, and went downstairs.

At the dining room entrance, Dianne paused, watching her family settle in their chairs. Mother sat regally at the head of the table, her slim artistic hand on the glass dinner bell shaped like a swan, and waiting to signal Birdie. The Queen Anne table was set with candles and silver bowls of white roses Mother had taken from the wedding. A chandelier dangled crystals like pink jewelry, dropping a glow of apricot light along the apricot silk walls. It was a beautiful room: it was ornate but tastefully formal and reflecting Mother's tastes for opulence.

The impatient rustle of Mother's gown meant that she'd better go in, that it was time to start the evening dinner ritual. Mother's white poodle Christopher was on the floor, by Mother's chair, consistently growling and begging for food.

Dianne sat at her regular place next to Mike and across from Nannie and Bobbie. No one looked at Dianne, as if they'd been instructed not to. Bobbie, ten years old and known at "Punky," had carrot orange thick hair, a white pasty face, and pale sunken eyes, as if all the dreams were sucked out. He was the "late child," Mother always said laughingly. As always, he sat next to Mother, his chair close to hers, petulantly scraping a metal car along the apricot colored marble tabletop. Mike, on her right, squeezed her hand underneath the table. He was gorgeous. He had wavy gold hair, olive freckled skin and dark nervous eyes. Even with the tragedy that night, Mother's face was composed. As if she were hosting one of her many elegant dinner parties.

Nannie nodded several times, her lips moving and talking to herself, as if acknowledging something terrible had happened. She wore a thin brown hairnet over her tan short hair, a bobby pin holding each side.

The doors to the garden were open, blowing the scent of roses into the room. For a moment it was quiet except for Christopher's perpetual growl and Bobbie's truck scraping the table, and the clinking of ice as it settled in the tall crystal glasses.

"And tonight, Dianne, you say the blessing," Daddy said. As usual, he wore his jacket and tie. Before dinner, when he was home, he liked to always say the blessing.

Together, they intoned, *"Baruch Atah Adonoi, Elohenu Melch Hololom Asher Kidd."* Their voices sounded like a moan. Nannie was watching her through her bifocals, her false teeth clicking as she pronounced each word precisely. Christopher her mother's poodle, was growling, waiting to be fed. Daddy's voice raised above the moan, "*May our home be consecrated, O God, by the light of thy countenance shining upon us in blessing, and bringing peace, lingering on the word, "Peace."*

Dianne felt her mouth moving, and she held the prayer book tight so they wouldn't see her hands shaking. Daddy's voice was louder as he said, "Amen."

"Let's eat," Mother said. She rang the bell, shaking it several times. "We're ready," she called in her high baby voice. As he always would, Daddy then placed earplugs in his ears so he could listen to the baseball game or the fights. Already his eyes were distant, as though this was his way of not facing what was happening. He broke a piece of bread and then with a tiny spoon he spooned horseradish from a little jade green pot and dropped it on the china butter plate.

Right away, as he always would, Mike started bragging about his golf game, his insecure voice rising, laughing a gravely high-pitched laugh and then pausing, as if waiting for approval, and then escalating his story, going on about the antiques he was finding at garage sales and then selling for high prices.

"Just the other day, I found a famous Dutch painting at the flea, one of the most famous of its time, a general in Mexico is offering three million dollars and ..."

The door opened and Birdie, a tiny black woman with wiry arms and brittle eyes behind rimless glasses, her arms thin as pipes, came into the room. She balanced a huge silver platter, holding it as if it didn't have weight. Birdie stood by each family member, balancing the heavy tray, waiting patiently while each person helped himself or herself to roast beef, mashed potatoes, and string beans.

Dianne was grateful that Birdie hadn't welcomed her home or acted any differently. Birdie knew a lot about life. In her room off the pantry, Birdie always had a letter in progress and gold-framed photos of her family.

After Birdie went into the kitchen, everyone started eating. For a while it was quiet and only the tapping of their forks on the china echoed. Wax dropped along the candles like tears and Dianne kept her eyes on the tiny flickering flames. Mike's face was down as he ate hungrily, and Bobbie was scraping the plate with a table knife, and it sounded like a fingernail running down a blackboard.

Nannie's false teeth were making clacking sounds and Bobbie dropped his food to Christopher who was whining for more food. His feet were taped because of allergies, and were nervously scratching the floors.

Dianne kept her head down, her mouth closed so she wouldn't scream.

"Meat's tough," Nannie said as if to no one.

"I hate string beans," Bobbie whined.

"Eat what you want, darling," Mother said to Bobbie.

"I always knew Charley was peculiar," Nannie suddenly said, looking first at Mother, then at Daddy. "And a pretty penny you and Lou spent for that crazy wedding! You were in too much a hurry to marry the poor girl off."

"Enough!" Mother shouted.

"Made a bundle on Jed Cohn at the golf tournament," Mike continued as he bragged about his golf game. "He's a patsy—my handicap is below par and…"

"You're a golf bum!" Mother shouted, glaring at him.

"I play a good game of golf," Mike argued, his voice rising. "I make enough money to go to tournament. I'm working on a

Rembrandt. A General in Mexico wants to buy it! Found it in a garage."

"Shut up!" Mother screamed. "We're not interested in your lies."

"Enough!" Daddy shouted, not looking up.

Then it was quiet and everyone resumed eating. Christopher was yowling as Bobbie dropped meat into his mouth. "

Don't feed the dog!" Daddy ordered.

"I want everyone to meet my new girlfriend, Nelly. She's beautiful," Mike said, his eager eyes darting nervously.

"Meet a decent girl … not those Irish bums."

"Nelly's not a bum!"

"A drunk!" Mother screamed.

"What's all the commotion about?" Daddy yelled, removing the earplug. "Can't a man enjoy his dinner?"

Mother rang the bell. "Birdie, you can bring the éclairs now. We're ready for our dessert."

"Right away she had to get married," continued Nannie, as if to no one. "You had to show off with such a big wedding."

"Let's not talk about it," said Mother. "There's nothing to talk about!"

"How do you know?" Dianne suddenly said. "There's a lot to talk about!"

"Home one minute and she's arguing," yelled Mother. Who looked at Daddy, his head down. "Always arguing. Haven't you caused enough trouble? Drove a husband away in two days! A scandal now we have! Now you're damaged goods."

"Charley did this," Dianne protested.

"Men like Charley wouldn't bring his wife home of one day unless you did something wrong!"

"Can't keep a husband," Bobbie yelled.

"Leave the poor girl alone. You'll make her crazy," Nannie said. "I knew he was peculiar."

Bobbie leaned his chair back on Christopher's tail and Christopher howled a sound she'd never forget.

"You hurt the dog!" Dianne yelled. "I saw you do it.'"

"You're crazy!" Mother yelled. "No wonder Charley left you.'""

"He hurt the dog!" Dianne said, tears streaming down her face.

"Can't keep a husband!" Bobbie chanted.

She got up, and rushed from the room, past everyone yelling at each other, Christopher crying and on Mother' lap, Bobbie still chanting, "Can't keep a husband!" and she hurried upstairs.

Her luggage was discreetly in the corner of her room. Probably Birdie had been instructed to bring it inside. As quickly as she could she unpacked ... if she didn't, Mother would. She opened the lingerie satin case and removed the array of pastel panties and matching lace bras folded between thin layers of tissue, and placed them into her dresser drawer.

After she hung up the dresses in the closet and put away her things, she undressed for bed. Her head was throbbing and she knew that her headache would accelerate into a migraine. She took two aspirin, rinsed her face with cold water, brushed her teeth, and then slipped on the old frog nightgown. She unfolded the silk floral bedspread three times as Mother had always insisted, then carefully, so as not to muss the silk coverlet, she slipped underneath the matching floral sheets, moving her feet cautiously over the edge of the sheets until she found a cold spot.

She turned on the tiny radio on the nightstand, Mozart softly playing. She lay in a prenatal position listening to her parents' raised voices, arguing about her. "That girl is crazy!" Mother shouted. Then the back door slammed. Now her father was walking Christopher in the garden, his sad footsteps on the gravel—doors snapping shut, windows locking tight—fireflies hitting the window panes, Mike's van driving off into the night. Bobbie's ball bouncing--

Dianne's eyes closed. She wished she had an icepack for her head but she didn't want to go downstairs and face her parents again. She lay still, listening to the sounds of the old house as it creaked into the night.

Almost a year ago, they'd met. It was Friday afternoon. She'd modeled the Grace Kelly wedding gown in the *Saks Spring Fashion Show,* when she'd noticed a tall stunning man intently watching her. Charley introduced himself, and asked her to dinner. She was nineteen, and he was twenty-nine. Immediately, she'd been attracted to his smooth elusive manner. She'd always been attracted to boys who didn't want her, and repulsed by those who did. Closeness of any kind frightened her. Charley's gentility and elusiveness reminded her of her father, and she found herself waiting for his calls. "Older wealthy men can provide," Mother had said. Almost every Saturday night for a year, they'd dine at Ernie's Restaurant, or at Trader Vic's.

At the Fairmont Hotel, they'd danced to the Mills Brothers singing *Up The Lazy River.* He was her rescue, her prince charming. He was the one to take her away from her parent's dark angry house into his smooth world; then she could be who she wanted to be, and not who she was supposed to be.

Slowly she slipped into a dream where she was trying to trying to run on a beach white as pearls and a breeze blowing white curtains and a red light flashing on a phone—

*

5

The following morning Dianne awoke early. She felt strange and disconnected from all reality, wondering if she were caught in a nightmare; if she were really home? Maybe she had imagined Charley and the wedding and Hawaii? Maybe that's what shock feels like.

She forced herself to look at the metal table of displayed wedding gifts, and at the familiar morning light sweeping across the room and leaving bars of shadows along the walls.

She got up and quickly made her bed, careful to make sure there wasn't a wrinkle left or Mother would make it over, and scream that she was a "slob." And then she went into Nannie's room known as the "sun room," once a room above the garage.

Nannie sat on the edge of her narrow bed, cutting a recipe from a magazine. Dianne sat at her feet, light streaming from the windows, and birds chirping from the garden below.

Dianne buried her face in Nannie's lap and cried long deep sobs.

"Time. Time," Nannie said, her red-knuckled hands stroking Dianne's tangled hair. Nannie held her tight, rocking her like a baby.

"On my wedding night ... he ... he wouldn't ... 'I don't love you,' he said, 'I made a mistake.'"

Nannie sighed a long, tired sigh. "A terrible thing. Must be a queer."

"I gave up everything for him."

"Not everything, Dianne. He didn't take your dreams."

"Mother is acting like it's my fault. I hate her."

"Your poor mother," sighed Nannie. "She was born with a congenital heart ... an old heart, like Bobbie's heart. I spoiled her." She pressed her lips like Mother would, and sadness came over her face. "Oy, your Grandfather was ... a drunk. He left me when your mother was three. I waited for him to come back. I was penniless, and uneducated. Women then didn't have the chances you have." Nannie sighed heavily. "Look at me now, living with my daughter, playing bingo once a week, and taking an allowance from your father in exchange for chores."

"Mother always said I'm not college material. She said marry a rich man. Now I have no money, no car, no education, and I'm filing for divorce."

"Do something important with your life, Dianne. Forget the lousy men. They're good for nothings. Go to college. Oy, you're a talented girl. Let the bastard pay. Make sure he pays."

"I'm calling a lawyer, today."

"Make sure you do. Don't let Charley get away with it. "She paused, her eyes riveted on Dianne's face. "Get out, Dianne. Before it's too late. Or you'll end up like your Nannie. Now take a nice bath. I'll make you some sugar cookies."

In the small pink tiled bathroom Dianne shared with Nannie and Bobbie, Dianne bathed quickly, thinking about what Nannie had said: *Or she'll end up like your Nannie.*

After her bath Dianne dressed, and then applied *Erase* on the circles under her eyes. As soon as possible she'd contact her father's lawyer Howard Weinstein. Probably Charley didn't think she was smart enough to pursue his financial fortune.

An hour later, she went downstairs.

Mother was in the breakfast room, on the phone. A cigarette burned between her fingers. Dianne stood by the doorway, watching her.

"He had business to take care of, you know, he's a very rich man," Mother whispered into the receiver.

As if it were an ordinary day, Mother was perfectly groomed: her hair perfectly set, not a strand out of place, her coral lipstick and matching nail polish vivid next to her ivory skin. She wore a beige knit dress, beige leather pumps, and her usual strand of pearls.

A spiral of cigarette smoke floated in the air, mixing with the sweet aroma of fresh coffee perking inside a tall metal pot. Daddy's porcelain eggcup on the placemat at his side of the table was empty. Earlier, Dianne had heard the taxi arrive to take him to the airport.

The doors were open to the garden. Mr. Taki, Mother's gardener, was trimming Mother's bonsai trees.

Mother hung up. "That was Aunt Pearl," Mother said. "I told her you were home because Charley had to go to Europe on business." She averted her eyes, her delicate hand waving away the air as if there were a bug. "Have some coffee. You look terrible."

Dianne poured coffee into the tiny pink cup and stumbled into a chair, smiling, as if it wasn't the most tragic day in her life. A slow thin stream of steam curled from the cup.

"Dianne, I made an appointment at three o'clock today with Dr. Solomon. Just to see if something is---*wrong*? It's important Dianne."

"It wasn't like that, Mother. He never even tried."

Mother averted her eyes. "Things like that take time Dianne, it's an ... *adjustment*. It's up to a woman." She lowered her eyes, and slightly flushed. She then jotted a note on her monogrammed notepad, as if the discussion was final.

Suddenly, looking at Mother as she jotted notes on her pad, Dianne felt sorry for her. Charley had been Mother's dream. A dream of wealth, and social position.

My tragedy is her tragedy forever now.

"Mother, you didn't tell Dr. Solomon what happened, did you?"

She shook her head. "I told the nurse you need birth control. That you're home early from your honeymoon because Charley had a business emergency."

Desperately, she wanted to end her virginity. She'd need birth control as soon as possible.

"I need your car, Mother."

Mother looked relieved. "Fix yourself up before you go. Look pretty. Look happy. You never know who you'll bump into."

*

6

Dianne lay on the table in Dr. Solomon's office, her feet in the leather stirrups, and her fingers entwined tight. She'd never been examined, and she kept her eyes on a dark stain near the chrome ceiling light. "We don't want children for ... a while ... so, I thought a diaphragm," Dianne said, her voice wavering like faint lines.

"Knees apart," Dr. Solomon instructed in a baby voice. "That's right, Dianne ... knees apart. This will only take a second ... yes. Just relax. After all I delivered you... yes ... I'll break the hymen—there, a tiny prick. Maybe it'll help hubby penetrate. Sometimes an adjustment is needed, but one more pop. "

He mustn't see her crying. She counted to eighteen, squeezed her eyes shut, waiting for the blush to stop.

"Relax, let me break it a little more ... a pinch ... "

Her eyes squeezed tight, she imagined Charley's smug chiseled face, as she aimed the gun.

"All done! Now you can sit up. Sorry, I had to hurt you, but now you're ready for hubby."

Her face was burning. Her mother had betrayed her. She wanted to scream that she'd never be ready for Charley, and that she wanted birth control for someone else.

"Move to the edge ... further down ... we'll fit you for a diaphragm. Let me show you first what it is and how to use it."

Feeling dizzy, she adjusted the paper cover over her legs. He held up a thin rubbery thing. "You see ... you put jelly inside it here in the center and then fold it like a glove," he chuckled. "Yes.

Hold it like this—between your thumb and forefinger—yes. I'll turn my back and you do it. Just to make sure. You don't want babies. This will work."

Slowly, the paper gown crinkling, her hands shaking, her eyes closed, praying she'd do this fast, she inserted the rubbery slippery thing, and thank God, she felt the click as it snapped into place. "I got it," she said.

Dr. Solomon smiled. "Now insert two fingers and pull it out ... grab it by its rim ... careful not to tear it. I'll turn my back."

After two tries, she caught the rim, and slipped it out. Smiling, he dropped it in the sink, and then washed his hands.

"Fine. Everything's going to be just fine. I just want to help," he said, his voice like a parent appeasing a feverish child. Her paper gown rustled like wrapping paper. He patted her head and gave her a shiny white plastic diaphragm case. "Don't fret," he chuckled. "Greet hubby wearing something sexy." Then he left the room.

When he closed the door, she slid off the table. For a second she felt dizzy and her knees were weak. She dropped the case into her purse, and as quickly as her shaking hands could work, she dressed, avoiding her white shocked face in the mirror.

Dianne arrived home late afternoon. She parked her mother's car in the garage, and went inside the house.

In the hallway, Birdie was buffing the floor. The scent of lemon wax mixed with the sweet smell of Nannie's sugar cookies baking. Newly delivered wedding gifts were piled by the doorway.

Birdie turned off the machine, bending her tiny body over the large machine, waiting for its sound to trail off. "Miss Dianne,"

Birdie said urgently, adjusting her wire glasses, as if she wanted to focus closely to Dianne's face. "You get away from heah. Jesus prays for you honey." As though she hadn't spoken those words, she switched on the machine, her small body moving with the machine, buffing in circles.

"Dianne!" Mother called from the kitchen area.

Mother was in the pantry, ironing. She loved to iron. She pressed the small iron on the tiny edges of a white linen doily embroidered with lace flowers. Bobbie sat nearby, taking apart a clock. He liked to take things apart. His red hair was slicked back and his t-shirt was as white as his skin.

Mother looked up, the iron suspended in the air. "Well? How was your-appointment?"

Dianne shrugged. "You told him when I told you not to."

Mother pressed her lips tight. "I had to, Dianne. You needed to go. There's a *reason* a man like Charley...couldn't, you know."

Mother folded the doily on top of a pile of linen napkins, her artistic hands patting the doily twice, as though she were satisfied.

"A divorce after two days of marriage will do you in," Mother continued. "No eligible man will want damaged goods. Mark my words."

"I'm not damaged."

Mother frowned. "Stop shouting."

"I'm not shouting."

"You've disgraced us. Look at you! You look like a tired hag. Go fix yourself up."

Dianne ran up the stairs.

In her room, she called Howard Weinstein's law office and made an appointment for the next afternoon.

*

The next day at three p.m. Dianne was at the law firm *Weinstein, Weinstein, and Sons.* She wore dark glasses, a navy blue dress, and white short kid gloves with tiny flowers on the edge of the cuffs. She clutched her navy blue leather monogrammed purse.

After several minutes, a tall, thin, man appeared. "I'm Howard Weinstein," he said, shaking Dianne's hand. "You look like Lou. I can tell you that your father is a damned fine golfer." His eyes were small and gray, almost disappearing behind thick horn-rimmed glasses. "Let's go to my office."

She followed him along a gray-carpeted hallway, glancing at the shelves of old law books behind glass. She'd never been in a lawyer's office before. She couldn't feel her feet.

In his large office, she seated herself on a green leather chair in front of a large wooden cluttered desk. It was a warm day and he removed his jacket. A fan on a table blew cool air, rustling the papers on his desk. The cuffs of his blue shirt were frayed slightly, and three rubber bands were around his wrist. Framed photographs of famous golfers hung on the wall, along with framed law degrees, and photographs of his family. He was a well-known divorce lawyer.

"Make yourself comfortable," he said, his eyes probing her face. She sat on the edge of the chair, her legs primly together.

He tapped a pencil three times on the desk, as if a ritual. As she always would when she was nervous, she twisted a piece of hair around her finger.

Mr. Weinstein opened a yellow legal notepad, a pencil between his fingers, ready to write notes. "You were just married recently to Charles Berkowitz. Three days ago, actually? A fancy wedding?"

Dianne nodded. She crossed her legs and her stockings made a scratching sound. A large clock on his desk was ticking loudly.

"Okay Dianne, tell me the story. The real story."

"Charley refused to ... consummate my marriage." Her voice faded.

"Are you pregnant?

"Pregnant! Pregnant?" she repeated, incredulous. "I told you! He *wouldn't*. He said he didn't love me, and made a mistake. A mistake," she repeated, and burst into tears.

He stared at her. She fumbled in her purse, until she found her father's handkerchief. She held the handkerchief over the face until she stopped crying. Then she folded the handkerchief into a square, embarrassed about her tears.

"Okay, okay, okay. Calm down," he said with heavy sighs. "We're suing a very rich man here with considerable reputation. In 1960, things like this don't happen. Mr. Weinstein released a series of sighs, tossing the pencil across the desk to land on a stack of papers, as if he wanted to throw away the possibility of an untruth, and its complexity for the law. "I'll order coffee."

"I don't want coffee. I want justice. He set me up. I know it!"

"Whew! This is Jean Harlow stuff. Looking at you no one would ever believe it. And Charley Berkowitz! He's got a playboy reputation. Is he queer?"

"Why would he marry me if he liked men?"

"To hide."

"He took vows till death does us part, and then a few hours later he said he made a mistake. This is deception."

He listened intently, jotting more notes. She told him everything about the phone call on her wedding night, Charley's disappearance the next morning, his diabetes and the two days in Hawaii, and that he left her alone in the Airport motel, and in Hawaii. Nervously, her hands still shaking, she lit another cigarette, waiting while Mr. Weinstein wrote more notes.

Mr. Weinstein finally said: "What he did to you is fraud. It's extreme mental cruelty. I'll use it all. You'll sit pretty."

She reached in her purse and took out the pale blue letter from Carol, and gave it to Mr. Weinstein. "I think she might have something to do with it. She was his secretary, he said. She moved to Chicago with her husband. I think she's the woman who was calling."

He read the letter. "This means nothing. When did she move?"

"I don't know."

"Is he still in touch with her?"

"I don't know, but there were strange phone calls. He was always waiting for calls."

"So why did he marry you if only to dump you? Something sounds---odd."

"If you don't believe me don't take the case. I want to file for divorce as soon as possible. I want money so I can get my own apartment and go to college. He cost my father a fortune, and I'm returning the wedding gifts, everything, except for the rings. I can sell those. He needs to pay for what he did."

She opened a rumpled package of cigarettes, and put a cigarette to her mouth. He leaned forward and lit her cigarette with a gold lighter. She exhaled a stream of smoke, watching it rise slowly above the desk.

There was a frozen silence.

"I'll file the papers," he said finally. "Meanwhile, don't go near him. Don't talk to anyone. You're poor, uneducated, living at home. He'll pay."

He licked his forefinger and quickly turned pages in his appointment book. On one page he snapped a red plastic paper clip. As soon as I hear back from Berkowitz's lawyer, we'll take your depositions.

She nodded.

"A lot of money is involved, if we handle it right. As I said, fraud is a ... delicate matter ... this man has considerable reputation ... wait until he reads in the papers that he's a queer. This is a big case. You'll sit pretty. Believe you me."

She jabbed out her cigarette into the already full ashtray. She stood and arranged her purse over her arm, then turned to go.

He escorted her to the reception room where secretaries typed as if they had nothing else in the world to worry about. Dianne wished she were one of them. At the elevator, he patted her on the shoulder. "Say hello to Dad."

*

Ten days passed. Mr. Weinstein had filed the divorce papers. Charley had hired a famous socialite divorce lawyer. Mr. Weinstein was waiting for a deposition date. Mother told everyone that Charley was a "homo." Daddy never mentioned his name, and traveled more than ever. Her friend Debbie had said that no one believed it was Charley's fault, and that some of Dianne's former friends had even invited him to dinner. Dianne was shunned. Some of the family came to the house and treated her as though she were very ill. They had hushed voices and averted eyes. Mike had told

Dianne that he'd followed Charley after work, to a "homo bar," across the street from his office. He'd gone inside and punched Charley and left the bar. But Mr. Weinstein said that didn't prove anything. He was delving into Charley's finances.

Wedding gifts were still pouring in, and every afternoon, for hours, Mother would make her sit at the dining table while Mother dictated what to write on the thank you notes: Dianne wrote: *"Unfortunately, Charley is mentally ill and I must return your generous gift--"*

Except to criticize her, Mother rarely spoke to her. Except the other day: Mother told her that her friend Blossom Shapiro said that Charley was seen with a "gorgeous girl," at the museum fundraiser. Dianne had felt faint, and started shaking. Mother had frowned, insisting that if Dianne "played her cards right," she could have him back."

Mostly, the following days, Dianne avoided her mother's rage, and stayed away from her. Dianne hid in the basement, writing in her journal, obsessively tracing the exact dates she'd been with Charley, trying to connect words he'd said, phrases he'd used, anything, in an effort to prove his deception. On other days, she'd take the bus to the Legion of Honor, her favorite museum. For hours she'd look at the Impressionist paintings she loved so much. In her sketchbook she drew girls holding guns, or trapped inside boxes. Increasingly she felt a failure, and she retreated completely into her self. Her headaches were worse, and the anger she'd buried was deeper. If anyone looked at her she'd turn away. She felt completely as if she existed in a wide gray world with only butterflies and birds flying low.

That afternoon she was in her bedroom, lying on the bed, with a migraine, and Mr. Weinstein called. He said that he'd received papers from Charley's divorce lawyer. "He's filing for divorce," Mr. Weinstein said. "He claims mental cruelty and that you refused to consummate—"

"He's a liar!" Dianne interrupted.

"Now that's exactly what I don't want. You have to watch your emotions, Dianne. Or he'll wipe the floor with you. The deposition is set for next Friday, at Charley's lawyer's office. I'll be with you. Remember, Mr. Miller is a bastard. He'll try to rattle you. Just say yes, or no. We want to win this thing."

After she hung up, she freshened up for dinner. She tried her best to act "normal," as Mother would say. Daddy was coming home soon, and she didn't want him to see her upset.

Downstairs, Mother was in the living room, playing Chopin on the piano. Twilight played shadows on her oval beautiful face, the kind of face that belongs inside a cameo brooch, never to change. For a moment Dianne stood at the door, listening to the beautiful music. When Mother played the piano she was a different person, as if her soul played the notes. How sad that Mother never pursued her dream of becoming a concert pianist.

As if sensing a presence, her mother stopped playing. She frowned.

"Dianne. Stop creeping up on me."

"I just want to tell you that tomorrow is the deposition. I want to know if I can borrow your car in the morning?"

She nodded enthusiastically. "Be sure and look perfect. Wear the black suit, gloves…pumps. It's very important that you look perfect. Set your hair tonight in the electric rollers. It's too curly."

Dianne nodded. Mother blinked several times, smiling which meant she had something more to say.

"Freddy Krumpnick called twice. He sends his love to you. Ida Berman said he's asking everyone about you – and that his dental practice is thriving."

Dianne remembered Freddy's tortured face when she'd told him she was marrying Charley. He'd always desired her, and she'd taken him for granted.

"When Freddy calls, just tell him you're a virgin ... so he ..."

"So I'll be marriage material? So no one will think I'm not a virgin? Isn't that what you mean?"

Mother paused then, as if reflecting. Then she resumed playing.

7

The next afternoon she was ready to go to the deposition. Mother was in the living room, placing decks of cards on the walnut game table, ready for her luncheon bridge game. The room smelled of fresh coffee perking in the tall steel pot. Tiny shrimp sandwiches shaped like flowers, arranged on a silver platter, were ready for the "girls," Mother's bridge group. They were wives of affluent men. They were fragile pretty women, their voices like a symphony.

Mother turned around. "Dianne you scared me again."

"I need the car keys."

Mother pressed her lips. "Well, you look nice, Dianne." She reached in the pocket of her floral silk hostess dress, and gave her the keys. "Mark my words Dianne, when he sees you, he'll be sorry. Now play your cards right, and he'll come running."

"I did play my cards right, and I'm home."

Mother raised her hand, and Dianne jumped back. Mother's hand smoothed a curly strand that stuck to her forehead. "Your hair looks funny. That wave always falls in your eyes, Dianne."

"I'll see you later," Dianne said, hurrying from the room.

The traffic was heavy, and the air was muggy. The air conditioner in her mother's old Cadillac wasn't working, and beads of perspiration stuck to the tip of her nose, and forehead. She drove along California Street, passing the cable cars with tourists.

On Montgomery Street, she parked her car in a garage, and then walked briskly along the busy narrow street, until she went inside a tall, modern skyscraper.

The lobby was beige Italian marble, with abstract contemporary paintings and smooth leather benches. A guard sat at a wide desk, checking identifications. Good-looking men and women carrying briefcases, hurried in and out of the many elevators. Dianne identified herself, and then rode the elevator to the twentieth floor. She got off at the law firm of Miller & Miller.

"May I help you?" The receptionist was young with silky long blonde hair.

"Dianne Berkowitz," she said anxiously. "I'm waiting for Mr. Weinstein, my lawyer. We have an appointment with Mr. Miller."

She lifted the phone, and spoke into it. After she hung up, she smiled. "Make yourself comfortable," she said.

Dianne sat on a low, crème colored leather sofa. She pretended she wasn't anxious, that her heart wasn't beating so fast that she was afraid she'd faint. If only she didn't feel so anxious, her mouth tingling, and her hands shaking.

The elevator doors opened, and Mr. Weinstein appeared. He was wearing a dark suit, and red tie. He held a large worn leather briefcase.

"Now remember, Dianne. No emotions. Just yes or no."

The receptionist led them along a quiet hall, into a large conference room. Dianne blinked, as if maintaining her balance. When she saw Charley, she turned away. He sat between two men wearing dark expensive suits. He wore dark glasses, and didn't look up.

Mr. Weinstein shook hands with Charley's lawyer, Vincent Miller, a tall, strikingly handsome man wearing a dark pin-stripe suit and burgundy silk tie. He had a huge amount of dark shiny hair, and piercing dark eyes. Then Mr. Weinstein sat next to her and unpacked his briefcase, arranging several sharpened yellow pencils in a row along the marble table.

At the end of the table, a court reporter sat in front of a large typewriter. She had thin tan color hair and wore a tan suit with a white shirt and collar. Her hands were held high, as if at a piano, her fingers moving along the keys. She looked straight ahead, as if on a fixed point.

Mr. Weinstein placed a yellow legal pad in front of her, and gave her two pencils. "Don't talk, just write," he whispered. Charley was writing on his yellow pad, sunlight dropping on his blue-black hair.

She drank the water from the glass in front of her. A pencil was in Mr. Weinstein's mouth, like a dog with a bone. He patted the pile of papers beside him. She drew boxes on the yellow legal pad. She always drew boxes. She liked boxes. You never know what's inside them. She drew a flower with a long stem. Suddenly, she felt overwhelmed; a feeling like she'd won something big, and then lost it. She held the side of the table, her head down, assuring herself that she wouldn't faint. She couldn't faint here. Not in front of Charley.

Mr. Weinstein was twisting a rubber band around his fingers, as if unwinding a ball of yarn. Suddenly, after talking with Charley and the two men, Mr. Miller stood in front of Dianne, and Mr. Weinstein.

"Let's begin," he said. His voice was large and deep. The folder Mr. Miller held was marked, "Berkowitz," in red letters. Mr. Weinstein nodded.

"Mrs. Berkowitz, I'm going to ask you some questions. Only answer yes, or no."

Dianne nodded. She straightened her shoulders, as if it didn't matter at all, as if it wasn't that important, and was just a procedure. She lit a cigarette, exhaling a thin stream of smoke.

He began firing questions at her, one, by one: *"Weren't all the wedding gifts from Charley's family? Didn't she marry Charley Berkowitz for his family fortune?* His voice made her jump, especially when he asked: "Did Mr. Berkowitz insert his . . penis?" He looked at her with the stern expression, like a parent demands an answer from an unruly child.

"He wouldn't ... he ..."

"Yes or no!" he shouted.

"No."

"Is it true that you refused penetration?" And he looked over at Charley who was turned in his chair so that only his profile showed. Then, his voice sounding like a slammed door, he shouted, "Answer!"

"You're badgering the witness," Mr. Weinstein protested. "Isn't it true that you married Mr. Berkowitz for his money?"

"I object!" shouted Mr. Weinstein, on his feet now.

"I am trying to show, to illustrate," Mr. Miller said, his voice low, like a parent trying to be patient with a silly child, "that Dianne *refused* Mr. Berkowitz's penetration." The two lawyers argued a moment in legal jargon, and then Mr. Miller stood in front of her, his dark hostile eyes riveted on her face.

"Is it true you don't have a job? That you depend on Mr. Berkowitz for your living expenses?"

"Yes. He's my husband."

"Isn't it true that you are uneducated, have no job skills?"

"I worked at Saks," she replied.

He snickered. "As a model?"

"Isn't that work?"

He shouted, "Answer yes or no!"

"Yes."

He sighed. "Isn't it true that you wouldn't let Mr. Berkowitz consummate your marriage?"

"He ... he wouldn't."

"Answer yes or no!" he shouted.

"No!"

"No that he didn't touch you?"

"I object to this questioning!" said Mr. Weinstein.

"I am going to illustrate that Mr. Berkowitz tried to consummate the marriage but that she's frigid and wouldn't let him penetrate. Mr. Berkowitz gracefully tried to bow out of the marriage. All she wanted was Mr. Berkowitz's money."

"That's not true!" Dianne shouted suddenly. "He never intended to consummate our marriage! He knew he was going to leave me while he was taking his vows! He knew he had no intention of consummating! He knew! He set me up! He knew what he was doing!"

Mr. Weinstein's hand was on her arm. The room was silent.

"I hate him! I hate you!" she yelled, facing Charley who was smirking.

Untangling her arms from Mr. Weinstein's grasp, she ran from the room, past the shocked silence, to the hallway.

At the water cooler, she poured water into a Dixie cup but her hands were shaking and water was spilling onto the floor.

"Dianne," said Mr. Weinstein, rushing into the hall, and looking upset. "This won't help. Trust me. He'll settle. Come back into the room, take a big breath and answer the questions, yes, or no. We'll have our turn. I promise."

"He's lying. He set me up! I'm sure of it! Please believe me. I know it…the phone calls, the—I know it."

"Dianne … let him lie. Otherwise it's court and a hearing, nasty publicity. Expense. This way you can settle out of court. He has a fortune, and I'll find a way to get it from his father. His father, believe you me, won't want the public to know that his son is queer."

"I don't care if he's queer. I care about his deception. I want enough alimony to start a life. He's lying at my expense. Cheap bastard."

"Acting like this won't help. You'll get into trouble. Big trouble. Trust me. A hearing will not only be expensive, but it will be … painful. He doesn't know that I have testimony from one of his employees that he hangs out at a homo bar near his office. Trust me, if you settle out of court, I promise we'll get plenty of money. They're trying to scare you."

"Tell Charley's lawyer that his client's penis will be in every newspaper in detailed description and that he's impotent. I want money. I want my attorney fees paid. I want a million dollars. No more depositions. Call me when you have a court date."

Still shaking, she hurried along California Street, and went inside a coffee shop. She sat at the counter and ordered a cheese sandwich and a coke.

Why did he betray her? Blame her? Never would she make it easy for him. Did he really think she'd take a pittance? He took everything: her dreams, her innocence, and left her feeling weary and victimized. As soon as possible, she had to get away from her parent's house or she'd be stilted forever. Shaped to nothing, like Mother's Bonsai trees constantly shaped to suit Mother.

She fanned herself with the napkin, glancing at the people who sat at the counter. Men had their jackets off and women fanned themselves with menus, impatiently looking at their watches. She jumped when the waitress slapped down the plate with the sandwich.

Unfolding the crisp napkin and smoothing it on her lap, she began eating. She hadn't eaten for a day, and hungrily she ate the sandwich, the tiny-wedged dills, and chips. Little did Charley know that Mr. Weinstein had discovered his accounts in Switzerland and planned on publishing Carol's letter.

Is it possible to ever get over this, to be just like those women at the counter on their lunch hour, and not in terrible pain?

She ate slowly, eating around the crust, stretching out the time, and planning on not going home until evening.

An hour later, she left the coffee shop. She rushed to her car.

She drove into traffic, driving slowly, listlessly, not really knowing where she was going. All at once, she felt an explosion of anger inside of her. An anger she'd never felt before. Then she turned the corner and she was driving to Market Street, weaving the car in and out of the crowded lanes, around the streetcars sliding slowly along the tracks. She drove faster until she was on the seedier part of Market Street, and then she stopped the car on a side street, off an alley. She got out of the car and hurried into a gun shop next to a tattoo salon.

Inside, the shop smelled like grease ... like something charred. Shiny guns, all sizes were displayed in glass cases like perfume. As she looked at the guns she felt a strange excitement, as though she had traveled to some forbidden destination.

"Can I help you?" asked the salesman, his sleepy eyes scanning her body. He was Indian and he wore incredible Indian jewelry. His silky black hair was long to his shoulders. He wore a red headband and a single strand of turquoise beads gleamed bright against his dark slender neck.

"Just looking," she said. "... I had a robbery, and might need a gun ..."

"Nice gun," he said with a slow grin. "A Walther PK is nice ... has a sure fire reputation ... small enough for a purse ... a honey ... perfect for you."

He opened the glass case and placed the gun on the counter. He moved like a cat. Just the way he wore his jeans, tight, as if grown into his slim body. Everything about him exuded sex.

"This here gun," he said in a serious tone, "is our very best. A Walther PPK is the gun James Bond uses ... a gun with a sure-fire reputation," he added proudly. "Here ... hold it."

She held the gun, holding it as though she were afraid to touch it, trembling from fear and from excitement. The gun represented the rage she pretended didn't exist and in a strange way it was comforting.

"It fits your hand like a glove ... looks like you ... sporty and trim," he said, his sulky eyes watching her from under hooded lids. She moved backwards and aimed the gun at the salesman slouched against the counter, his hands tucked inside his Navajo belt buckle, and she pulled the trigger.

He grabbed the gun from her hand. "Hey … hey … hey," he said, clicking his tongue in disapproval. "Lesson one … never point at what you don't intend to shoot." In a parental tone, he began lecturing about the proper use of a gun. "Guns are to be taken very seriously," he said, shaking his head. "They're not a woman's whim."

"He lowered his voice. "It may not blow a man's head off … but it'll do a nice, clean job."

She didn't answer. Holding the gun, and turning it from side to side, Dianne chuckled and lowered her eyelashes.

"Now, I'll show you the little old bullets," he said. He opened the box, and the copper tipped bullets were nestled into slots like bees in a honeycomb.

"When you load this here Bond number," he said, his eyes closing like lines and moving along her neck, "you insert the buggers in this here magazine … see … just slide these here buggers into these here slots… then slide the magazine back into place.

He moved closer to her, so close she could smell the Dentyne chewing gum on his breath.

"Put your fingers in the trigger," he said, his voice lowering, and placing his hand over hers, she could feel his hot breath on her hair, and tiny shivers of heat poured through her body. "Now remember, first you load the magazine … slide it in," he said softly, his voice smooth as silk, "then push the safety catch… down … all the way down," he repeated, pressing his hand tighter over hers. "Then the hammer back … that's right, yank it all the way back," and his voice was almost a whisper, a caress, when he said, "And hold it tight … I repeat … when you push the safety lever down, all the way down, make sure ... always make sure it covers the tiny red dot ... see ... right there," he instructed, guiding her finger to the tiny red dot, so tiny she had to narrow her eyes to see it. "I repeat," he said ... "This here dot is important ... if the safety lever is one fraction of a millimeter away from the dot, and I repeat, one fraction, the gun could go ... POW ... blood ... and it's all over," and his breath was hot in her ear when he repeated, "POW!"

She gave back the gun. "I'll think about it," she said, averting her eyes from his stare.

"When you come back you'll have to sign a form. Then wait ten days to pick up the gun."

As she hurried from the gun shop she knew he was watching her, until she turned the corner, and ran to her car. She felt frightened. Threatened by something in her she didn't yet know.

*

The following days were lost in hours of self-reflection, writing in her journals, and pretending she was fine and not angry. Or that the slightest wrong look would set her off and she'd burst into tears. Or treated into the basement, until dark. Then Mr. Weinstein called and informed her the court date was set in two weeks. "It's going to be nasty," he warned. "Be prepared." He was ready to publish his findings about Charley. "I'm throwing the book at him."

Obsession starts slowly. Every day she wrote in her journals, obsessively going over the tiniest details about Charley, anything she could remember—the way he ate, swallowed, polished his shoes before he put them on, walked, his blank black eyes—

anything she may have forgotten. But no matter how hard she tried to rise above the Charley incident, the image of the gun lay in her mind like a rock buried in sand. She knew that she didn't always feel right. Something was wrong. Something was more than wrong.

She looked up names of psychiatrists. She'd told her mother that she wanted to see "someone," but Mother had been furious, shouting that girls like her don't need to see those "freaky doctors. To find a new husband."

More time passed. She got a job at Saks, this time selling lingerie. Seeing the women she'd once worked with was hard. She avoided their sympathetic eyes and questions about Charley. After work, she ate dinner at a nearby coffee shop, and then went home to sleep. Hardly ever did her mother speak to her, and their silence was full of unspoken resentments. Everything about her mother repelled her; her hands constantly waving the air, as if checking for dust, her little laugh at the end of her perpetual criticisms. Her hovering over Bobbie, insisting that he wasn't well, and that he had an "Old heart."

She decided that it was time to end her virginity. She desperately wanted to get out of the house. She returned Freddy Krumpnick's consistent calls. "I miss you," he'd said. They made a date for Saturday night.

*

8

Freddy Krumpnick would arrive in twenty minutes. Dianne turned on the water, and sat on the edge of the toilet seat, her legs spread. She squirted jelly in the center of the diaphragm, carefully folded it, then, her eyes closed, she inserted it, sighing relief when it snapped behind the bone.

After she bathed, she sprayed Shalimar perfume into the air, spinning in it until it clung to her skin like satin. Earlier, she'd gone to the beauty parlor and had her hair set in a pageboy, her natural waves smoothed with an iron. She applied pale white lipstick—just enough eye shadow and mascara.

Finally she slipped on the dress that she'd bought at Saks with her thirty percent discount. It was perfect—black silk, with a square low cut, showing just enough cleavage. Then she wore the pearl earrings, and the simple gold bracelet her father had given her for her sixteenth birthday.

Carrying the white cashmere sweater with the fox collar, and the black beaded bag shaped like a fan, white short kid gloves, she went downstairs. He was always on time, if not early.

"How nice you look," Mother said, approvingly. The French doors were open to the patio and just enough lamps dropped a glow of light along the living room. White Birds of Paradise filled the vases. Mother wearing a beige silk dress and beige leather pumps, was arranging chocolate truffles in the Steuben candy dish, their brown wrappers rattling. "I put ice in the bucket. Be sure and offer Freddy a drink."

"I'll see, Mother."

She pressed her lips tight. "The gossip, Dianne. Be sure and tell him—"

"I don't care about the gossip, Mother! Stop it!"

"Don't shout, Dianne," she said in a whisper. She pressed her small pale hand down, as if pressing down Dianne's voice.

"Freddy was always such a gentleman," Mother continued in her tiny voices. "Blossom Shapiro says that his dental practice is flourishing. Dentists are usually very reliable, settled."

At the Steinway, Mother suddenly played 'Beethoven's *Moonlight Sonata*, the melancholy music straining through the quiet. When Mother played she closed her eyes and swayed her shoulders, as if in another world.

The doorbell rang. Mother played louder.

Dianne opened the door.

"You're more beautiful than ever," Freddy said, puffs of peppermint mouthwash blowing into the air. He kissed her lightly on the lips. He was shorter than she and he stood on his toes. His hair was very black, and slicked back.

"Long time ... no see," Dianne said with a laugh.

"You look ... different." When he smiled his teeth were very white and even.

"Drink?"

"Well ... I have dinner reservations," he said, glancing at the large gold watch on his small wrist. "But I heard your mother's lovely music. Let me say hello to Mrs. Roseman."

Mother stopped playing, as though she was suddenly surprised. She waved her hand in the air, and said in a baby voice, "If it isn't Freddy Krumpnick. So nice...so..."

"Mrs. Roseman," he said, kissing her hand. "It's a pleasure. It's been too long," he said, looking at Dianne.

Before Mother could start one of her lengthy conversations about who was doing this or that, Dianne hurriedly kissed her mother. Freddy promised they'd all get together soon and to send his best to Mr. Roseman.

In the driveway, Freddy helped Dianne into the passenger side of his red MG sports car. She knew her mother was watching from the corner of the window and she wouldn't turn and look back. Freddy, looked at her again, as if to linger, to catch the moment before the intrusion of the motor. "I can't believe it. You're a beautiful woman now, not a girl anymore."

She looked away, remembering that they'd done everything but, in the back seat of his car, years ago. As they drove, he did most of the talking. Just about every other sentence, he kissed her fingers, and held her hand close to his heart.

"It's good to see you too, Freddy," she said, admiring how nicely his strong Semitic nose blended into his high forehead, and what strong bones he had. It'd been almost two years since she'd seen him and he looked better ... the kind of face that success and time would eventually make handsome. Driving to the restaurant he did most of the talking, mostly small talk about his recent trip to Europe, how great his practice was doing, the Chagall print he'd recently bought for his office. "We'll go to the museum. You'll love the Matisse exhibit. Have you been?"

Dianne tried to concentrate on what he was saying, but she didn't feel flirtatious like she used to be, she felt as if she'd been away for centuries, and was trying to wake up.

At Trader Vics, as they entered the dark elegant restaurant, he lightly held her elbow, his shoulders back, as though he were trying to make himself taller. "Dr. Krumpnick ... I called." The headwaiter led them swiftly to a dark corner table.

They sat close together on the silky leather booth. Waiters moved as if they were gliding. Candles and fresh flowers in tiny bud vases were set on the tables.

Freddy ordered vodka martinis, and prawn appetizers. Dianne opened the cigarette case Charley had given her the day they got their marriage license. It was engraved, *"Love always, Charley."* Freddy lit her cigarette with a gold lighter. As he lit her cigarette, his eyes didn't leave hers. She exhaled a slow stream of smoke.

He clicked the edge of his glass on hers, and they drank their martinis. The vodka immediately warmed her body, and she felt slightly lightheaded.

"I've thought about you a lot, Dianne."

She smiled. "I always liked you, Freddy. I'm glad to be with you too."

"You broke my heart, Dianne."

Over more drinks, Freddy talked about his growing dental practice, his travels to India, and to Africa. "I bought a home," he said. "I can't wait for you to see it. Hopefully, tonight."

"Maybe," she said, aware that she was flirting.

"It's good to have you back Dianne."

"You make it sound like I've been lost and found?"

"What happened with your marriage, Dianne?" he asked after a long silence.

"I don't want to ... talk about it."

"You need the *right* man. Someone to take care of you."

"I plan on going to college—studying art. I want to be ... independent."

He smiled. "I'll take you to Paris and you can see all the art you want. I've always been crazy about you."

"We'll see."

He laughed again, as if he couldn't believe that she didn't want him. "Let's go dancing."

At the Barbary Coast in North Beach inside a circle of light, Carol Doda danced topless on the small stage. The club was smoky and dark and the tables were close together. Carol had platinum color hair, and was making San Francisco history. The club was jam-packed. A sultry girl sang *The Man I Love*. On the small dance floor, Dianne and Freddy slow danced. Dianne slumped so she wouldn't be so much taller than Freddy. He held her tight, and sang in her ear.

In his car, an hour later, Freddy turned on the radio. He drove towards Nob Hill. A slow mist lay over the city and the moon was low in the sky. From the radio, Tony Bennett sang, "My Funny Valentine."

Their silence was an undeclared statement that they'd make love. It felt good to be with a man who desired her. At a stop sign, Freddy looked over at her, his eyes lingering on hers, as if to say, at last we're together; at last you'll say yes.

He stopped his car on Jones Street, in front of a Victorian house with an iron gate in front. Cable cars were sliding along Nob Hill.

He turned off the motor. "Drink?"

"Well, for only a minute. I'll have coffee. I drank too much," she said with a nervous laugh.

He turned off the ignition. He opened the car door and arm in arm, they hurried into his house.

The hallway was dark, and smelled of fresh paint. He turned on a lamp, and the light a dropped a pink glow on the living room. Wall-to-wall windows faced the Golden Gate Bridge. At a mirrored bar, he poured brandy into one large bowl glass.

Dianne kicked off her heels, and sat on the black leather sectional couch. "Your house is wonderful," she said.

He pushed a button, and records dropped slowly on a built-in turntable. Patti Page sang, "Who's Sorry Now." A large built-in glass aquarium glowed a florescent light, and exotic tropical fish darted back and forth. He sat next to her and they sipped the brandy.

"Really nice, your house…I mean. The fish are---exotic. My brother Bobbie has fish---"

He took the brandy from her and put it on the table. He kissed her passionately, gulping wet kisses, his eager hands on her breasts. "I'm crazy about you ... don't make me wait anymore, Dianne." He unzipped her dress and then he unhooked her bra.

"My God ... what breasts," he said, his small mouth sucking her nipples. "" God, you make me hot. Let's go to my bedroom."

She took his hand, and he led her to his bedroom.

The room was lit by moonlight. "Don't turn on the lights," she said, dizzy when she closed her eyes.

He undressed quickly, dropping his clothes to the floor. She unhooked her stockings from the garter belt, rolled off her panty girdle, leaving the underwear on the floor. Quickly, she got under the covers.

He got into bed naked, and sprawled on top of her. He felt thin, and light. She closed her eyes. She waited for that moment she had wanted so long ago.

"Touch it, touch it," he said, blowing his hot breath into her mouth, his hands squeezing her breasts. "It's for you."

His penis was hard and small.

"For you," he repeated. "All for you."

His fingers were probing, touching her body everywhere. Concentrating on the moon floating along the ceiling, she fought the urge to push him away. He tried to push her legs further apart, whispering "Relax." Closing her eyes, her hands fluttering along his hairy back, she was remembering Charley's cold smooth skin, the curtains blowing in Hawaii. Freddy was whispering that he was crazy about her. "I won't hurt you ... open wide ... give Freddy that beautiful body. God, I fantasized about this...."

Her arms fell flat by her sides, and her legs closed together. Freddy stopped moving. The sound of the wind rattling the windows upset her and she lay still.

"What's wrong, Dianne? Why are you crying? Did I upset you?"

"I'm not upset."

"You seem upset."

"Maybe I drank too much. The room is ... swirling. I want to go home."

Slowly, he got up. He thumped around the room, picking up his clothes from the floor.

"Do you want something? Can I get you something?" he asked, hopping on one foot, hurriedly trying to pull on his trousers.

"I'm sorry. I drank too much," she said, her voice hollow in the tense silence. She got up, and dressed. She rolled her garter belt and stockings and stuffed them into her purse.

He turned on the lights. His face was red, and his hair mussed. He concentrated on buckling his belt, dressing fast.

"Vodka," she laughed. "I'm not used to it," she said, smoothing her skirt and, blinking against the sudden blare of lights.

"Let's go. It's late," he said.

She followed him to the car.

On the way home, Freddy drove fast. The windows were open and a breeze blew her hair. From the car radio Johnny Mathis sang, "Chances Are." Dianne kept her eyes on the moon sliding along the sky. If she blinked, she'd cry. What had happened? Why hadn't she felt anything, and why had she hated him? Or would she ever feel sexual arousal again?

Freddy stopped the car. The motor was running. The lights blinked on in her parent's bedroom. Mother was waiting. She'd want a "full report."

"Well, thank you for dinner Freddy. It was ..."

"Lousy," he snapped. "You know something, Dianne. Charley is right. You're frigid. Everyone knows it. The whole town knows it."

She got out of the car, and before she got to the curb, he drove off, his car speeding into the night.

She hurried into the house, up the stairs, into her room. On her nightstand were a glass of milk, and a small plate with Nannie's sugar cookies. A note was next to it, written in her mother's slanted perfect handwriting: "Wake me, no matter what. I want to hear everything."

Dianne undressed in the dark, leaving her clothes on the floor, and without washing her face, or brushing her teeth, she slipped into bed.

Some minutes later, when she heard her mother tiptoe into her room, and stand by her bed, she pretended she was asleep. Until her mother sighing heavily, left the room.

Dianne slid into sleep.

The next morning, Mother was in the breakfast room, drinking coffee. Dianne poured coffee, and sat down,

"Well?"

"I'm not going out with Freddy again," Dianne said. "I'm not interested."

Mother pressed her lips tight. "You'd better be interested! You're damaged goods. Who do you think you are? Not interested? Thank your lucky stars he even wants to take you out. He's a catch. Everyone will know--"

"Know what? *Know* that Charley used me, set me up? Spread rumors that aren't true. Ruined my life. Know that I'm dead inside? And you don't believe me? I've done nothing wrong."

"You did everything wrong young lady. Now you'll never get a man. Never be married. Your wedding cost us a fortune! Do you hear me?"

Dianne hurried to the door, and left the house. She walked to China Beach. She walked along the edge of the tide. She sat on her favorite rock, watching the clouds turn dark, the ships like toys, bobbing on the high waves. She wondered if she'd ever feel right again.

*

9

The courtroom was hot. Mr. Weinstein and Dianne sat in the back. Charley and his sister sat in the first row. Only a few weeks ago they'd taken wedding vows, and now they were in court. Dianne stared at Charley's slender back, the back she'd pressed her face on during sleep, and for a moment she felt as though she was going to faint. Just then Charley's lawyer tapped Mr. Weinstein on the shoulder, and Mr. Weinstein and Mr. Miller went into the hallway.

The judge, a burly man with white hair, wearing full black robes, entered the courtroom and the bailiff shouted, "All rise!" After a shuffling of feet they stood and recited the allegiance to the flag. The judge pounded the desk with a wooden gavel, and they sat.

The bailiff called the first case to the stand. A young red-faced man, after taking oath, sat on a chair on a platform, and answered hostile questions. He spoke softly, and Dianne wondered if the pale young girl who sat in front, was his wife? If they had once said, "'til death do us part?"

The boy got off the stand, and soon it would be her turn. "Don't get emotional," Daddy had advised. Mother had told her friends that Charley was a "sick homo," and that Dianne was getting "a fortune."

Mr. Weinstein tapped her on the shoulder. "Come with me, Dianne."

When she stood, she felt dizzy. She followed Mr. Weinstein, papers hanging from his briefcase, to the hallway.

They stood by a long wood bench, away from the steady stream of lawyers and clients rushing in and out of courtrooms, their footsteps clicking on the gray marble floors. City Hall was a massive building, with real marble corridors, a circular stairway, and a gold dome.

"Good news. He made an offer," Mr. Weinstein said, standing so close that when he talked his breath blew her eyelashes. He smiled, as if he had a great gift to give her. "He'll give you an annulment."

"An annulment? That means the marriage never happened ... that it's null ... void. That I was defective. I don't want an annulment. I want a divorce."

"He'll give you twenty-seven hundred dollars. Cash. Plus, you keep the rings. They're worth a fortune."

"I told you! I want alimony, half of his estate!"

Mr. Weinstein sighed, looking at her like a parent looks at a ridiculous child. "Look, Dianne. His lawyer knows I have the goods on him. Knows that a divorce will result in a long dirty public case. This is 1960. Whoever heard of a husband taking a beautiful bride home after a day? A divorce will be a public scandal. They'll wipe the floor with you. They'll ruin you."

"I need more money."

He sighed. "He signed over his assets under his father's corporations six months before you were married. He doesn't show that he has any money. Take his offer and run, Dianne."

"Bastard! He set me up, and gets his father to bail him out. Something sounds fishy. Don't you see? He did that because he knew he was avoiding something, using me. He exploited me to save himself. I'll prove that he set me up."

"Dianne," he said looking grave. "He followed you to a gun shop. He wants to prove that you're---mentally unstable."

Just then Charley and his sister, who was smiling, and holding Charley's arm, and Charley's lawyer, came into the hall.

Rat what a rat, what a bastard. Any compassion she'd ever felt for him, had even thought that maybe he was ill, or maybe preferred men and couldn't help what he'd done, was gone. Watching his smug face, she felt her body move towards him, but Mr. Weinstein grabbed her arm.

"This isn't the solution. He's waiting for an opportunity to lock you up. You'll be the next Frances Farmer story."

"He set me up. He's getting away with it."

"You're a beauty," he said in a gentle voice." Move on. He'll stop at nothing. He's bringing in a shrink. He'll do you in Dianne. It could go on for years. Your father will have to foot the bill."

At that moment she felt beaten. Never would she put her father through her mess. She was furious, and at that moment she knew that she had to get out of it as soon as possible.

"I want the cash now," she said after a long silence.

He looked relieved. "I have it in an envelope Dianne. You'll see. You'll have a wonderful life and this will be just a short bad dream. Let's sign the papers and I'll give you the cash. Let me tell Mr. Miller."

She sat on a bench, watching as Mr. Miller and Mr. Weinstein huddled together, smiling and shaking hands. Then Mr. Weinstein took her into a small room. At a wooden table, she signed several papers.

Mr. Weinstein gave her a white envelope wrapped with a rubber band. She counted the cash.

"So he knew I'd take it," she said, bitterly.

Mr. Weinstein shrugged. "Good luck, Dianne."

She hurried down the marble stairway, past the security guards, and into the sunshine.

Forty-five minutes later she got off the bus on Van Ness Avenue. She walked along the wide street, past the car agencies, remembering her father looking at a red sports car spinning on a turntable in the window. He'd stood there, a shine in his eyes, holding her hand, murmuring wistfully, "Isn't that something?"

She went inside the Ford Agency. A shiny black 1960 Ford Falcon was displayed on a turntable. It was beautiful. Inside, it had red leather seats, and real wood paneling. She loved the car. A car would give her independence until she could leave home. Or maybe she'd drive far away and never come back. The car was $1,925.00. She'd have enough left over to start a savings account and eventually rent an apartment. *My payoff,* she thought bitterly.

"Can I help you, Miss?" said a man with silver hair.

"I'll take this car," she said.

His quick eyes glanced at her alligator monogrammed bag, and linen suit. She opened the envelope with the cash. "I'll pay cash."

"Come into the office," he said.

An hour later, she drove the car out of there. On the way home she turned on the radio. Bach's Brandenburg Concerto drowning the cat calls from the truck drivers, and she drove, fast, fast, faster through traffic. It was time now to stuff her anger into her imaginary box.

By the time she arrived home, it was late afternoon. The house smelled of Nannies' sugar cookies. She could hear the monotonous thumping sound of Bobbie's ball as he threw it against his bedroom wall. Mother was in the living room, shuffling cards. After her bridge games she always-shuffled cards, making sure they were still crisp and clean.

Mother turned around. Well?" Her lips were pressed.

"I'm officially Dianne Roseman." Dianne shook the car keys. "Look out the window."

Mother sighed, and reluctantly went to the window. "Whose car is that?" Her face was white.

"Mine. I just bought it. Now I won't have to borrow your car."

"How did you pay for it?"

"With my annulment money."

"Annulled like those Catholic girls?"

"Mr. Weinstein said it's better. A divorce would take a long time, years maybe, and the expense, and the scandal ..."

"How much did you get?"

"Twenty seven hundred dollars ... cash."

"You stupid fool!" Mother screamed. "No wonder Freddy Krumpnick hasn't called, and your husband left you! You're stupid. You settle for *nothing*. Disgrace yourself, and your family! Now you're penniless! You stupid fool! Your reputation is ruined! What do you expect us to do? Take care of you?"

"Nothing ... I ... will move soon."

Dianne didn't move fast enough, and Mother slapped her face so hard she shut her eyes.

"Give me your rings!' Mother screamed. "Your father spent a fortune on your wedding! Do you hear me? You stupid fool! You can't keep a husband for a day! Now go upstairs and get those rings!"

As Dianne hurried up the stairs, she didn't feel her feet. She didn't feel anything.

In her room, she removed the diamond rings from the glass bowl. She put them in a little satin case and brought the rings to her mother who waited at the foot of the stairs.

"You made your bed; now lie in it," Mother said. She put the case in her pocket and resumed shuffling cards.

It was night, now. Dianne closed the shutters. She kept her lips tight so that she wouldn't scream. Nannie was downstairs, helping in the kitchen. Dianne hadn't gone to dinner.

Until she stopped shaking, she sat on the edge of her bed, careful not to wrinkle the spread. The slightest wrinkle would put Mother into a rage. A box marked *Good Will* was in the far corner of the room. For days, when Dianne was at work, Mother had been packing her things into boxes, giving them away. This box was marked *Wedding* and inside were all the things from her wedding—place cards, menus, and satin matches with Dianne and Charley's names printed in gold, ribbons, and invitations. On the top was the wedding album. Never had Mother given it to her.

Dianne removed the book. It had a white leather cover. *Dianne and Charley Berkowitz, and the date, June 10, 1960,* were printed in gold on the cover.

She turned the pages; there she was, feeding Charley a piece of cake. Her smile seemed fake even in the picture, as if she'd already known they'd only exist in a photograph.— throwing the bridal bouquet--Aunt Pearl looks so funny in that bubble hairdo.

Nannie and Bobbie dancing the box step, Birdie dancing with Mike. Charley's eyes so empty and even in the picture she could see that he'd wanted out.

She dropped the album into the box and not even removing her clothes, she got into bed.

Her head was throbbing.

A door slammed. Daddy was home. Mother's shrill voice was raised and they were arguing. Bobbie's ball thumped louder, and she fell into a thick sleep.

*

It was October. The air was cold and the dark came early. Dianne loved this time of year, the sound of foghorns and leaves floating along the streets like pressed stars.

She was busy at work, trying to save money, but she hadn't enough to rent an apartment. Life at home was unbearable and Dianne had persistent headaches. She wished that she were like one of those brave women she read about, and admired; women who took chances, had purpose, and did anything to be on their own.

Since the annulment, Mother rarely spoke to her. Daddy was away all the time and when he was home, he reverted to his silent self. It was as though the incident with Charley, that one incident, had darkened the already dark house. So far, she couldn't find anything to prove that Charley had set her up. Recently, after work, she'd driven to his office. She'd waited until he emerged from his block long building, and then drove off in his car. She had followed his car to Russian Hill, watching as he hurried into a beautiful house. For several hours she'd waited, until he exited with a good-looking man with yellow hair. She wondered if the man was his lover? If that were why he'd go to any lengths, including destroying her, to hide that he loved men? What had he had at stake?

Increasingly, she craved being alone. On her days off from work, she went to the Museum of Contemporary Art, or to the Legion. She loved sitting on a bench, in the stuffy rooms, imagining what the artists were feeling when they'd conceived their paintings. When she'd seen an exhibit on Mexican art, she'd been thunder struck by Frieda Kahlo's self-portraits: her strange monkeys, and images from her dreams. She was interested in the artist's ability to paint her inner life. She read everything she could about Kahlo, fascinated with Kahlo's obsession with Diego Rivera. Fascinated with obsession. On her lunch hours, she haunted bookstores, buying art books, and literature. She read books by Jane Austen, Virginia Woolf, Sylvia Plath, and F. Scott Fitzgerald. Desperately, she wanted to educate herself. To rise above the petty conversations she heard at home-- who was buying what, Mother's bridge hands, Daddy sitting in silence. As if Daddy, a self educated man who read all the time, who'd worked himself up the ladder since he was fourteen, knew conversation about politics, or about the books he read, would be futile.

She read Freud's "Interpretation Of Dreams." She recorded her dreams in her journals, drawing images to match what she'd felt during the dreams. She'd dreamed that she'd shot and killed Charley, and then stuffed him into a box. She punched a hole in the box so she could study him.

Why was it that she felt so alone? Like some odd insect crawling flat on the ground, always in danger of being attacked? She knew it was time to get out of the house, to start socializing.

To find a way to get out of her mother's house. So when the family received an engraved invitation to Aunt Pearl and Uncle Maury's fiftieth Anniversary Party at the Fairmont Hotel, her parents insisted that she go. "You need to get out more," Mother had said, and she agreed.

*

10

It was Sunday afternoon, the day of Aunt Pearl and Uncle Maury's Anniversary party. Dianne and the family arrived at the Fairmont Hotel's Gold Room. Dianne wore a black mini-dress with a matching jacket with a white mink collar, a large bouffant hairdo, and white kid gloves. They stood in a receiving line and greeted Aunt Pearl and Uncle Maury. Aunt Pearl wore a gold satin low back dress, a rhinestone tiara in her dyed red hair.

"Oy, I'm glad you're here, Dianne. Go meet a nice man. Mingle."

After her parents, Nannie, and Bobbie went to their designated table. Dianne excused herself and went to the bar. She tried to smile at the cousins watching her. Not one of them had ever called her since the wedding.

She stood off to the side of the room, drinking her martini, and observing the party. The room glowed with candlelight, and a twelve-piece orchestra played fifties songs. Blown up photographs of Uncle Maury and Aunt Pearl on their wedding day, were displayed on stands set about the room. Dozens of tables were set with gold cloths and heart shape floral centerpieces. Dianne wondered what it would be like to live fifty years with someone? For some reason she didn't yet understand, she didn't feel that she would ever want to live with one man that long. Something was missing in her. She didn't know what.

She watched Aunt Pearl and Uncle Maury dance a fox trot to the orchestra playing *It Had To Be You*. Aunt Pearl was taller and larger than Uncle Maury, who was thin and wiry, but they danced like they were floating. Aunt Pearl followed Uncle Maury's series of dips and bends and twirls, his hand firmly on Aunt Pearl's fleshy back. They danced perfectly, their years embedded in their flawless synchronized steps. A spotlight soundlessly following them like a shadow.

The song stopped, and the orchestra played the *Anniversary Waltz*. Couples waltzed then, turning and spinning. Dianne's father tapped her on the shoulder.

"Put down your drink, Dianne. Let's waltz."

Feeling shy, Dianne followed him to the dance floor, and they waltzed. Daddy turned his head like a clock, his lips moving one, two three, her heels making a clicking sound on the parquet floor. As they turned, she saw Donald Perlman dancing with her cousin Fat Susan. She'd known Donald from her summers at Lake Tahoe with her parents. He was the only boy who had had a Chris Craft Speed boat. She recalled when she was sixteen, waterskiing behind his boat and self-conscious about her pale bulging thighs red from heat rash.

After the waltz, Daddy kissed her. "Go mingle. Pearl said Donald Perlman is here. His parents are swell people."

She watched him disappear into the crowd.

At the bar, she got a fresh martini, gulping it, and feeling lightheaded. She watched Donald Perlman and Fat Susan dance the twist to Chubby Checkers. Still handsome, Donald was tall, with dark curly hair and strong Semitic features. Moving his hips smoothly and hardly moving his feet, Donald danced gracefully, Fat Susan waving her pudgy hands. "Susan is a brain and she keeps a gorgeous house," Mother always said.

Then the orchestra played Glenn Miller's *Serenade in Blue*

and the dancers moved like they were floating.

"Dianne... Dianne Roseman."

She turned around. It was Donald Perlman.

"It's you," she said. "I saw you dancing."

He laughed, revealing even white teeth.

"I noticed you when you came in," he said with a slight drawl. "I asked Susan is that Dianne Roseman? Susan said you and she are cousins." He paused. "My mother is distantly related to Maury. My parents are in Palm Springs. They couldn't be here."

"It's been…"

"A long time," he finished, with a smile. He held a pipe and patted tobacco into the bowl of the pipe, his thumb patting it like a child pats sand.

They made small talk, what they were doing, where they were living, stuff like that. She told him she worked at Saks. "But I hope to eventually go to college and get my own apartment."

He nodded. His eyes were hazel, shadowed by dark thick eyebrows. He lit his pipe, and a sweet smelling haze of smoke floated over his face.

"That time I water-skied behind your boat," she reminisced. "Do you remember? I couldn't get up on the skis. I was so clumsy."

"Not anymore," he said. "What happened to your glasses?"

"I'm wearing ... contacts."

He told her that he lived in Happy Valley, an hour from Piedmont. "My house is set on five acres and I own two Arabian horses." He smiled, wistfully. "It's beautiful, far away from the city, noise, sirens, people."

Just then the orchestra played, "Unforgettable."

"Let's dance," he said, laying his pipe on the table.

She smoothed the wrinkles in her white kid gloves, and followed Donald to the dance floor. He held her close and danced gracefully, leading her in a maze of fancy crossover steps and spins. As they danced past her parent's table, Mother held up two crossed fingers. They danced every dance, and when the orchestra took a break, and everyone went to their tables for dinner, he said, "Let's get out of here."

During the applause, she grabbed her purse and jacket, and they sneaked out, hurrying past Fat Susan and a group of cousins huddled together watching them.

Donald's Chevrolet was cluttered with saddles, and smelled of horses. On the way to the restaurant, he talked animatedly about Happy Valley. "Five acres ... no neighbors for miles. It's the way I like it."

"I dream of yellow grass, dotted with pink flowers, clouds falling low."

"Sounds like a painting. I like the way you talk."

He parked at Fisherman's Wharf.

Holding hands they went inside Alioto's and were seated next to the window. By then it was dark and a full moon hung close to the water. The waves were so close they splashed the windows and seals sprawled on the rocks like flat black gloves. He ordered martinis and clicked glasses, as if they already knew their fates were locked.

He lit her cigarette, his face close to hers. As he talked about his horses, a light fell on his boy face. He loved nature, and the country.

"You have dreams. It's good to live your dreams," she said.

"You're different." He watched her through a maze of cigarette smoke.

"Jewish girls aren't supposed to be different. Bohemian, my mother calls it."

"I was supposed to marry Mimi Jacobs," he said. "Have babies, a mortgage. When I broke our engagement, I broke my Mother's heart." Narrowing his eyes and watching her through the film of smoke, he said, I'm going to retire by thirty-five."

"I understand." Dianne liked his ambition.

Donald inhaled slowly, holding the pipe gracefully like a musical instrument. "Susan told me you were married?"

"Legally... only two days. It was annulled," she said, her voice rising, wondering what else Susan had told him?

There was a discreet quiet. Donald patted the tobacco into the bowl of his pipe, this time faster, as though he wanted to get the ritual over with so they could continue talking. There was an unspoken understanding between them, like they both knew that they wanted each other for reasons not yet known.

"Children? So you don't want children?" she persisted.

"Maybe in time," he said, looking reflective. "I want to make a lot of money first. Build my properties."

They talked more about the things they liked—Donald loved Western music, horses, planting trees. In college he'd majored in business and then after his father retired he took over the furniture stores. He liked buying and selling furniture. He opened several stores in the East Bay, and planned on opening more.

"I want to paint. In college I want to major in art—maybe art history," Dianne said.

He smiled. "You always were the arty type."

Dianne was having a good time. He was innocent, vulnerable, and after Charley, refreshing. She knew that he was attracted to her. She felt alive again. It wasn't that she was attracted to him really, it was that he was so attracted to her that appealed to her, and she liked the idea of him. He made her feel that she had her youth back. Could rescue her.

After dinner, they walked along the pier. Boats tied to the dock made rocking sounds, and birds squawked low along the edge of the ocean. Lights blinked from the Golden Gate Bridge, and foghorns blew loud and lonely. Not wanting the evening to end, they drank Irish Coffees at the *Buena Vista Café*, talking and watching the moon slide into the water. And then they drove home. The car radio was on, and Elvis Presley sang *Love Me Tender*, and Donald sang along.

Fog covered her parent's house, and the lights were on in her parent's upstairs bedroom. Donald parked in the driveway and turned off the motor. Stretching out the evening, they continued chatting about the climate, movies, laughing for no reason. Suddenly, he kissed her on the lips. It was a shy, tentative kiss.

"It must be late," she said, gently pushing him away. She felt her mother at the window upstairs, watching. Waiting. Hoping.

"I'll walk you to the door," he said, quickly exiting the car to open her door.

They stood under the porch light. Dianne fumbled in her purse for the key.

"Tomorrow night?" he asked. "I'd like to take you to dinner. I want to spend time with you."

She nodded. She opened the door, went inside and ran up the dark stairway into her room.

11

The next morning she felt happy. She was actually giddy. She liked Donald. He was completely different from everything she was about. With him, she could let go of the past, and find a way to know herself, and who she really was. He adored her, hung on to her every word, but a part of him was like a secretive boy, and not feeling close to him, was perfect. Just enough. He could take her away from the Charley scandal that was spreading and she'd start a new life. One where she'd be free, loved, and could explore a new life. Yes, marriage was the only way she could get out quickly. She had to do it. She had to prove to herself, her family, to Charley, that they were wrong.

She finished dressing for work, and went downstairs. Earlier, she'd heard her father leave for a waiting taxi outside. Mother was already at the breakfast table, reading the paper. Dianne poured coffee into her cup, and sat at the table. She smoothed her hair, aware of the tense silence.

"Well, how did it go?" Mother asked.

"Donald is very nice. We're seeing each other tonight."

Mother smiled. "The Perlman family is ... *established*," she said, as if it were a necessary condition. *Poor Mother. Nothing meant anything to Mother but money.*

Dianne finished drinking her coffee. "I have to get to work. It's inventory today."

"Standing on your feet all day is no fun. Those poor women who have to work for a living. Old maids," Mother said with a sniff. "Pearl says Donald owns property. He's a very rich young man."

"I have to go, Mother." Dianne kissed her goodbye.

Mother folded the paper and blinked several times. "And Dianne ... there's no reason to ... discuss ... eligible boys like Donald don't come along that often. They marry *nice* girls."

"See you tonight, Mother."

When she got home from work, she hurried into her room. As quickly as she could she bathed and then dressed in a red woolen dress and matching bolero jacket. Carrying her white gloves and red silk fan shape bag, she went downstairs to the living room. Donald would arrive in ten minutes.

A silver platter of tiny shrimp puffs and cocktail napkins were placed on the black lacquer coffee table. Ice was in the Lucite bucket on the bar, next to the capix shell coasters and bowls of cashew nuts.

Daddy sat in the wing chair, reviewing papers, his briefcase next to him. She stood there watching him, wishing she could embrace him, talk to him, and confide that she liked Donald but she wanted to be alone, fantasized about to pursuing something extra-ordinary. But she wanted to please him and when she thought how in debt he always was and tired, she didn't. He seemed distracted and tired and his face was as gray as his hair. Earlier, from upstairs, she'd heard him arguing with Mother about the bills, and the high tuition costs of Bobbie's private school for problem boys, and Mike's recent arrest for stealing at the golf club.

"You look nice, Dianne," he said. "Mother tells me that Donald owns a home in Happy Valley." He placed several papers in his briefcase, and zipped it shut. "He seems like a nice boy. We saw him last night."

Dianne nodded. There was a shy silence. Bobbie's ball thumped on the wall downstairs in the garage. Christopher barked.

"Well, Mother wants me upstairs," he said, getting up. "But tell Donald hello." He paused, as if he wanted to say something, and then he left the room, calling to Bobbie to stop "making a racket!"

Donald was ten minutes late. This made her anxious—any sign of possible rejection gave her extreme anxiety. *Had he changed his mind?* She knew that she was becoming too neurotic, that deep down she felt fragile, so fragile that at times she'd thought she'd break or dissolve into nothingness. She had to stop it. As soon as she was safely away from her mother, she'd be fine, she assured herself.

At the piano, Dianne played the *'Moonlight Sonata,"* the moody melody soothing her anxiety. Since she was ten years old she'd taken piano lessons. Mother had made her. But she'd never felt the musical talent her mother had. The house was quiet now, as if Mother had warned everyone to be quiet, awaiting Donald's arrival.

The doorbell rang three chimes. Dianne pressed the chord a little longer, and then she stopped playing. Slowly, she got up, and answered the door.

Donald stood on the porch, holding a red rose wrapped in green tissue. He looked shy. "Sorry I'm late. Traffic was brutal."

"It's ... beautiful," Dianne said, inhaling the rose.

"I thought we'd get an early start," he said, clearing his throat.

Just then Mother made her entrance. She floated down the stairs, wearing an emerald green taffeta skirt with a long sleeve black top, and her double pearl necklace. "I just thought I'd say hello," she said, smiling at Donald. "I'm Honey Roseman."

She made small talk with Donald, smiling charmingly. He indulged her with his attentive smile, telling her a joke, and then giving her a compliment. She knew his parents, Mother told Donald. "Remember? We got together years ago, at Lake Tahoe? Isn't life funny?"

"Well, give my best to Mr. Roseman."

"He's upstairs dressing. We're having guests, but he sends his regards," Mother said with a charming smile.

No one could be more charming than Mother. She extended her hand one more time. "You kids have a good time."

"We will, Mrs. Roseman. I'll take good care of her. She's precious cargo."

"Come again," Mother said, going upstairs.

They dined at Vanessi's, Donald's favorite restaurant. Cooks wearing chef hats behind the open kitchen, made Italian dishes, and the room was festive. Over drinks and pasta, they talked about everything—her dreams, his dreams, movies and songs they liked, the mysteries of the ocean. Nothing too deep. Just the kind of chatter one animatedly exchanges when attracted. He was "excited," about meeting her. "You're different Dianne," he said approvingly, lighting his pipe.

"Do you want to know what happened with my marriage?"

He shrugged. "I heard he was . ...Ill?"

"Let me say that our marriage was never consummated."

He smiled and looked relieved. "I'm glad."

"Would it make any difference?"

"Let's just say it makes it more special," he replied.

After dinner they drove to Seagull Point. The sea slapped against the beach, roaring above the seagulls' haunting cries.

"So many stars tonight," she said.

"Bright like you, Dianne. I don't want you to be sad."

"I'm not sad, I'm happy with you, Donald."

He took her in his arms and kissed her passionately. "I want to make love to you but when we do it will be special."

"Let's walk on the beach," Dianne said, pulling back.

"You got it," he said.

Dianne unhooked her stockings and put them in her purse. They walked barefoot down the steps, to the beach.

The ocean was crashing along the beach and the stars were bright and so low she felt their light.

He rolled up his pants and they walked fast along the edge of the ocean, their bare feet making imprints in the wet sand. The wind blew her hair and the mist felt wonderful on her face. He took a stick and drew a heart in the wet sand. "Now we're here forever."

They kissed. And then they left.

*

Summer was over. Almost every evening since they'd met Donald drove to San Francisco to see her. After work he'd pick her up and they'd go to movies, the circus, comedy shows, dancing. Once again Mother was nice to her. She bought her little gifts--- perfume, a pretty silk blouse, leaving nice little notes on a plate with Nannie's sugar cookies.

The past weekend Dianne had met Donald's parents, Min and Harry Perlman. They lived in Piedmont in a modern glass house. They doted on Donald, their only child. Dianne had the feeling that they didn't approve of her. Around them she felt self-conscious, ashamed that she'd been married. She knew that Min had heard the gossip and a couple of times she had mentioned that there wasn't divorce in her family. But Donald had confessed his love for her. He invited her to see his home in Happy Valley.

Sunday afternoon, Donald and Dianne drove to Happy Valley. The country roads were quiet, and the air smelled of honeysuckle and horses and fresh hay. They drove along sudden twists of roads surrounded with umbrella trees, and fields of wild flowers. She felt the anticipation of something new, as though she were entering a new country, a new world. She felt happy, her past left behind.

Donald arrived at Happy Valley. He opened a gate and then they drove along a private road, passing acres of colorful flowers and sudden trees. His two Arabian horses Ali, and Baba were cantering along the hills like floating white shadows.

He stopped the car in a large driveway surrounded by tall umbrella trees. His low white brick house was ranch style, and set on top of five acres. It overlooked a spectacular view of the rambling Diablo Hills.

Hand in hand, they stood on the edge of the garden, admiring the view of the Diablo Hills below. It was a magical place. Private, and full of nature's beauty: odd sounds of owls, a sudden burst of blooms of screeching reds, vibrant light highlighting the wildflowers, and strange night creatures.

"So beautiful," she murmured.

An almost reverent expression lay on Donald's rustic face. He was in command of his land. He was someone else there. A king. He loved this place. She loved it too.

"Come on, let me show you around," he said.

He led her along a gravel path, into a large brick patio surrounded by an expansive smooth green lawn and surrounded by a large oval swimming pool with turquoise water. Fruit trees and flowers surrounded pathways and the garden.

"In the spring these trees will be full of apples and apricots," he said, pride in his voice.

"A wonderful place. No wonder you love it," she said.

He nodded, a modest expression on his face. "I bought the place six months ago. I bought it for a song. It needs a lot of work." He lit his pipe. "I'll show you the house."

Inside, every room opened to the central patio and pool area and view of the hills below. The country Mexican tile kitchen was huge, with tall oval windows facing the hills and Donald's Arabian horses. A stone fireplace reached the kitchen ceiling and there was a large breakfast area. Outside of a wooden table and a few Western style chairs, most of the rooms were empty. "Someday I'll fix it up," Donald said.

Donald made Bloody Marys, and they sat on the patio. Deer darted in and out of the bushes and insects darted in and out of the twilight. For a moment she felt as though she were just born, and was finally away from everything she'd ever known or had been. He planned on planting more trees along the driveway so that the trees would someday surround the house and "keep people out."

She laughed. "You are a hermit."

"I'm serious about that Dianne. I work hard, and I can't wait to retire, and live on the land." He told her about his plans to buy more property. When he talked about money and ownership of properties he became animated." I want to buy property that no one looks at because it's just sand," he explained, a serious expression on his tanned face. "Eventually the properties will be shopping malls, and hospitals, and towns."

"That's quite a dream," she said. "A big dream."

"They're the only kind," he said.

"I agree."

"You're one of my dreams, Dianne."

She laughed. Oh, you don't know me really well."

"I don't need to see how the clock works. I just know if it keeps time."

She laughed again. His homilies were hokey, but she told herself that underneath, he must be deep. More interesting. She was sure of it.

"I want to marry you, Dianne."

Even though he whispered it, his proposal startled her. Those words, the ones she needed, had expected, gave her a momentary shiver. At the same time she felt an enormous relief, as if all her anxiety about her future, her growing depression, suddenly evaporated.

"I…it's so soon…we've only known each other for two months. You don't know me, Donald. I'm not sure I can give you what you deserve. I have to be honest."

"I know that I don't want to live without you," he said, fervently. "You're what I've waited for. Trust me. Someday you'll love me. You'll see."

She kissed him then, lightly on the lips, enjoying the sweet smell of tobacco on his mouth. "I accept," she whispered.

He took a small box from his pants pocket. He opened it and gave her a diamond heart- shape engagement ring. "I've had this since I met you. I hope you like it." He slipped the ring on her finger. "We'll marry as soon as possible. Just the family."

She didn't know what to say. Part of her wanted to run. The other part of her wanted to hide in Happy Valley forever. After a moment, she told him she'd marry him. They'd marry as soon as possible.

On the way home, Dianne kept her eyes on the stars blinking in the sky like diamonds. Everything would be all right, she told herself. It was the only way.

*

Sunday, Mother invited the Perlman's and Aunt Pearl and Uncle Maury to celebrate the engagement, and make wedding plans. Mother was ecstatic. "Thank God she's still a virgin," Mother told her friends.

In one day, Mother had called the *Jewish Bulletin* and made sure that the announcement of their engagement, and their photos were published as soon as possible. Min and Harry Perlman, her brothers, her father, Nannie, Aunt Pearl and Uncle Maury, were in the living room, drinking cocktails, and discussing wedding plans.

Dianne and Donald sat on the couch, holding hands. Daddy sat in his wing chair, quietly, sipping a scotch and soda. He was leaving after dinner to fly to Los Angeles for a meeting. Mother, wearing a blue taffeta dress, and the diamond engagement ring Charley had given her, flitted about, serving shrimp puffs, and platters of smoked salmon and caviar. Bobbie sat next to Nannie, holding his tape recorder.

Mike bartended, slipping the silver ashtrays into his jacket pockets. Everyone had been talking at once, Harry Perlman shouting, "We're mashpuka now." Min shooshing him.

"This is some ring," said Uncle Maury, biting the ring, and then holding it to the light.

"Ssccch. Maury don't shout!" said Aunt Pearl. Her turquoise eye shadow matched the color of her dress.

"Donald only buys the best," said Harry Perlman. He had bright red hair, a very red face and tiny blue eyes. Donald called him "Red." He told perpetual jokes.

"A gorgeous ring," Min said in her deep gravelly voice. Min Perlman's hazel suspicious eyes watched Dianne's every move. She had lacquered jet-black hair, every strand in place, and worn high, like a Geisha girl. She was very slim, with over-size breasts, which made her look as though she'd topple over.

"Happy Valley is some place," said Harry, a cigar in his mouth, his eyes darting to each person. "Wait until you hear Donald play the horn. The boy's a genius."

"Red. Cut it out," Donald said.

Then everyone at once was talking about the wedding plans, Mother insisting they marry at her house, Donald emphasizing that he wanted a small wedding as soon as possible.

"So nu, what's the rush?" said Nannie in a thin voice. "You'd think the girl is pregnant."

"I agree. Why rush it?" Min said, narrowing her eyes at Dianne. "Second weddings aren't supposed to be big."

"Mother, enough!" Donald said, frowning at her.

"A marriage made in heaven," Aunt Pearl repeated, rapping her knuckles on the teak table.

So the wedding date was set for a week from Sunday. Everyone raised their glasses and toasted to Dianne and Donald.

"A marriage made in heaven," they said.

"A hundred years together," Aunt Pearl said.

Mike told stories about the fabulous antiques he was finding in garage sales, and that his golf game was on the verge of breaking records, Mother telling him to shut up. Daddy ignored the conversations, and spoke quietly with Uncle Maury about the rising stock market.

"Dinner!" Birdie called.

Dianne quit her job. She enjoyed days with her mother, shopping, and sorting clothes for Happy Valley. Once again in two weeks Mother planned a wedding. Efficiently she carried organized to-do lists and was constantly on the phone with her florist, caterers, and friends. So happy about the engagement, Mother was daily on the phone with her bridge friends and bragging what a wonderful man Donald was. "A real man," she'd emphasize. "Not like that homo Charley. And the Perlman's are very well off," she'd add.

Two days before the wedding, Mother's florist Yoko was at the house with workers who converted the dining room into a chapel with a Chuppah. Caterers set tables in the living room. Mother had hired a violinist to play for the guests. Daddy, looking exhausted, participated little and complained about the costs. He was upset about Bobbie who'd missed so much school he was tutored at home.

Once again Dianne felt optimistic and happy, even lunched with some old friends she hadn't seen since her wedding with Charley. At lunch, no one dared to mention Charley; they kept their conversations light and joyful, raving about her ring, and all eager to see Happy Valley. Pushing back her depression, Dianne concentrated on the joyful anticipation of her new life.

The night before her wedding, Dianne couldn't sleep. The light was on in Nannie's room, and the television was on. Nannie loved to watch the Ed Sullivan Show. Dianne got up and went into her room. Nannie sat in the wicker chair, pasting photographs in a red leather photograph album, brushing paste on the edge of the photograph, blowing it dry, before quickly pressing it on the spot marked with a red crisscross. She wore a thin brown hairnet on her thinning hair, the net held by two black bobby pins. Glass jars of lemon drops and a jewelry box with Nannies' few things were on the white wood dresser, along with a framed photograph

of an article in the San Francisco Times called, *"Artist in Ivory."*
At sixteen, Mother had won the Chopin award to Julliard. A fringe
of silky bangs flopped over her eyes.

"Can I have this?" asked Dianne.

Nannie looked up. "Keep it in plastic. So it won't fall apart."
Nannie sighed wistfully. "She could have been a great pianist. But
she wanted to marry a rich man. Turned out your father isn't so
rich, but a wonderful man."

She continued pasting photographs, pointing to photographs
of Mother as a child, Nannie at sixteen singing at an audition. She
wore a long dress and a bow in her hair.

"I was chosen Dianne, to sing Carmen for the San Francisco
Opera. But my parents were poor, and I married your Grandfather.
A drunk," she sighed, closing the album. She placed the album on
top of the other albums on her nightstand.

"He's only a boy, Dianne. You don't need to marry him. You
need yourself."

"He's three years older, and he is successful, has a home,
money, and I can go to school. At last pursue my dreams. Also I
want a child."

"For what? You're a child yourself."

"Then everyone would know that I'm not frigid, and that
Charley lied. He set me up." Dianne fought the urge to tell her
she was always meddling. But the sight of her swollen fingers,
her tarnished wedding band grown into the skin, made Dianne
suddenly sad. "Donald loves me, Nannie."

"Why shouldn't he love you? Charley married you on a
rebound, and then you marry Donald on a rebound, oy ... a mess."

"I want a normal life. A happy life."

"You want to show Charley that another man wants you," Nannie answered simply.

Dianne stood there a moment. And then she went to bed.

.

12

It was Dianne's wedding day, a cold November day. Dianne was in her room dressing. Twilight dropped shadows along the walls and foghorns blew lonely bellowing sifts of sound. After the wedding Dianne and Donald were driving to Carmel for three days, and then directly home to Happy Valley. The week before Mother and Birdie had helped her move her clothes into her new home.

At her dressing table, Dianne smoothed her pageboy hair. She applied rouge to her too-pale face. She'd lost a great deal of weight and her face was gaunt. As she went through the motions of getting ready for her wedding she felt faraway, as if she were watching herself in a dream. Finally she applied a pale pink glossy lipstick just right against her dark hair.

The door opened. "Time to get dressed Miss Dianne," Birdie said. She wore a blue silk dress with a white spray of orchids pinned to her belt. "Comon, hurry up. Your guests are arriving. Let's get dressed, child."

Birdie unzipped the cellophane bag and removed the dress. Dianne had bought the dress with her discount at Saks. It was more of a cocktail dress than a gown. Birdie slipped it over her head, carefully pulling it over her body, and then zipping the back. Dianne loved the dress. It was blush pink. Mother had insisted it wouldn't be proper to wear white on at a second wedding. It was to the knee, with a low oval neckline, and a puffy bell-shape skirt. The narrow waist was hand embroidered with flowers embedded with seed pearls, and the dress accentuated her small waist and long legs. She wore dyed-to-match silk pumps.

Next, Birdie helped her clip the matching ice pink silk band of silk flowers attached to a tiny veil that went to the tip of her eyebrows.

"Mighty beautiful," Birdie said. "Like a pink cloud."

Dianne turned in front of the mirror, satisfied with the veil.

"You're a pretty bride," said Birdie, her hands on her hips and tears in her eyes. "Now you be a good girl," she said, hugging Dianne.

"I will, Birdie. You'll come visit. You promise?"

Birdie shrugged her narrow shoulders. "'Everyone gets over everything in time." Birdie had been at the house since Dianne was a child. She adored Birdie and felt suddenly sad that she was leaving her.

Just then the family and the photographer came into the room, and everyone was talking at once, circling around Dianne, and complimenting her dress.

"Smooth your hair, Dianne," Mother said, with a frown. Mother wore a green print chiffon dress, and her face was very pale. She'd been ill, "Her heart," Nannie had confided. Daddy stood by the doorway, watching.

"Schmaltzy dress," Mike said, laughing his Donald duck laugh. He wore a dark suit that Mother had bought for the occasion. His golden hair waved back from his head and his black eyes darted about the room. Bobbie wore a dark custom tailored suit oddly making his eleven years look distorted. He aimed his tape recorder at every conversation. Then Min and

Harry came into the room. Min wore a yellow lace dress with a matching bolero, and yellow dyed to match silk pumps. Her hair was combed in a high beehive.

"Look at the ring!" Harry shouted to everyone. He held up Dianne's hand for the photographer. "My son knows what he's doing."

"Say cheese!" instructed the photographer, a thin man holding a huge camera.

They posed for pictures. Bobbie held two fingers behind Dianne's head and Mike was laughing the Donald Duck laugh.

"Now the bride alone. Dianne pull up the skirt ... show the garter... give us that million dollar smile ... that's right...."

Harry's hand was on Min's breast as the camera went off and Min slapped his hand. "Behave! We're the Mashupka. "

"Oy, another fortune this wedding cost," said Nannie.

"Mother! Stop it!" Mother glared at Nannie.

From downstairs, the violinist played the first chords of the *Wedding March*.

"Time. The wedding is starting!" Min announced.

Then, one by one, the family descended the staircase—Bobbie holding Nannie's arm, Min and Harry, Mother and Mike.

Holding the bridal bouquet of white roses, Dianne stood next to her father, waiting their turn. The music rose louder. "It's time," Daddy said.

Dianne took her father's arm and they slowly walked down the stairs, Dianne avoiding the tear in the carpet on the second stair, the one Mother was always saying had to be replaced. As they passed the antique mirror Dianne caught the somber empty expression in her perfectly made-up eyes, and her father's tired face.

Downstairs, they walked along the narrow white runner in the dining room, past the tall candelabras lit with white candles. The guests whispered "Congratulations."

At the end of the runner, in front of the Chuppah, Donald moved forward, his eyes shining like a young boy accepting a prize. Daddy kissed her lightly, and then she took Donald arm and he led her under the flowered Chuppah where Rabbi Goldman waited. The room settled into a hush and they took their vows quietly.

After they vowed, 'til death do us part,' in his bellowing voice, Rabbi Goldman shouted, "I pronounce you man and wife! You may kiss the bride!" To robust applause, Donald grabbed her, and kissed her on the mouth so hard she almost tipped backwards. "I love you, Princess."

Then everything was a blur. The hundred guests hugged and kissed them, raving about her ring, her dress, exclaiming what a "gorgeous couple," they were. The relatives whispered, "Mazel. You made it. Good for you."

While the musician played love songs, the guests sat at tables set with pink cloths, glass bowls of pink baby roses and pink-lit candles. Dianne and Donald and the family sat at a U- shape table and ate squab and wild rice. Everyone gave speeches, Harry going on about what a "catch," his son was, and that Dianne was a "beauty," Min poking him to sit down. Donald kept his arm around her waist, whispering that he loved her. For a moment, Dianne wished she were in a dream, would wake soon, and hide in her closet. Quickly, she told herself it was just the excitement.

"I love you, Princess," Donald whispered again, his eyes imploring hers for a response.

"Me too." She kissed his eager lips, aware that Min was watching her.

"May they live to be well and happy forever," a guest shouted.

"Forever!" the guests reiterated, rapping their glasses with their spoons.

"Time to cut the cake," the guests jubilantly shouted. The caterers wheeled in a serving cart displaying a tall strawberry and whipped crème cake, Donald's favorite, with a replica of the bride and groom on top.

As they cut the cake, the violinist played *I Love You Truly.* Like mannequins, they posed for the photographer. Donald kissed cake from her lips.

And then it was time to go. Dianne threw her bouquet to Nannie's open arms, and everyone cheered. Then she and Donald, the family following them and throwing rice, ran outside to Donald's Chevrolet covered with banners that said *Just Married.*

As Donald slowly drove away, Dianne turned and looked back. Mother was waving her handkerchief, Nannie blowing kisses, Daddy's sad tired face fading, Bobbie throwing rice, and Mike laughing and waving. Like figures in a tragic play, always in the same place, she had already duplicated them; something like the pattern in the rose bush that was growing crooked along the side of the house.

She waved one more time and Donald sped faster to their wedding night destination.

When they arrived at the Carmel Valley Inn, it was ten p.m. The room was half lit by a fire in the fireplace, the logs turning softly. The windows faced the turbulent dark sea and the white caps were rising like lace. Donald closed the drapes, and then the room was quiet.

"I'll change," she said.

"Okay, Princess. Don't take too long."

In the bathroom, she locked the door and turned on the water. Quickly, she slipped off her wedding dress, hanging it on the hook. Quickly, she changed into a pale pink nightgown. She rinsed her face, and brushed her hair, rice falling to the floor. She wouldn't use the diaphragm. Probably, she wouldn't get pregnant for a long time anyway. If ever.

The room was dark. A fire was rising in the fireplace, and the wind howled. Donald was in bed. "Hurry, Princess. Don't let me wait any longer."

Dianne got into bed and Donald quickly moved next to her.

"Take this thing off," he said hoarsely.

He fumbled with the gown and slid it off, and then they embraced.

"Princess, you're .... beautiful. "

She moved closer to his naked strong body, and their faces bumped as he kissed her.

His eyes were closing, but hers were wide open. This time she'd make no mistakes. She kissed him the way she'd kissed him at Seagull point, sucking his lips, and kissing him hard. His hands were warm, almost sticky, and hesitant as he explored her body, and then like a boy rushing a new game, his hands were faster.

He was on top of her and quickly went inside her. He was making moaning sounds. Their skin made suction sounds.

"You're mine, always. You're mine forever, my princess," he murmured.

He was clumsy like a boy learning the four step his body making jerky movements. His breath was hot on her face and he was blowing love words, into her mouth. She tried to move her body like he did, waiting for her delicious orgasm but she felt like she was underwater holding her breath. She felt frozen.

As his lovemaking became more passionate, she concentrated on listening to the sound of the logs settling in the fireplace, fighting the urge to push him away, even feeling slightly repulsed. Then he was yelling like a proud boy winning a race, "I'm coming! God! I'm coming!"

He lay heavily on top of her, his body damp. She kept her eyes closed, as if in ecstasy. So that he wouldn't see the disappointment on her face. And then he rolled off her, and lay on his back.

The fire was fading into ashes. Donald's hand was damp on her thigh, pressed there, as if waiting for her move.

"Did you come?" he asked.

"Of course."

"But you're crying," he said, anxiously, touching her damp cheek.

"That's because I'm so happy."

He sighed, and then closed his eyes.

She watched him sleep. His handsome face was almost coy, like a child who had stolen cookies from the cookie jar. There was a settled half-smile on his face, his fingers spread into contentment.

As the waves retreated, her eyes closed. She listened to the shrill gulping of the seagulls, and then she slid into a soft sleep.

Three evenings later they sat on the hotel deck, talking, and holding hands. The sea sounded like a roller coaster tumbling down tracks, and seagulls were suspended in the sky, hardly moving. Donald patted tobacco into his pipe, watching her like a proprietor guarding his store. Other couples and families sauntered along the beach.

They'd been lovely days. They'd taken long walks. They had collected shells, stopped at cafes and ate fresh fish, observing the seals lying on rocks like shiny black gloves. They acted like newly weds; they called each other "honey," and kissed at the end of each sentence. But when they made love she still felt numb. Hoping that he didn't know this, she learned to fake desire and to pretend she was joyful. Constantly, he told her he loved her and even in his sleep he murmured loving phrases and held her tight.

They were leaving the next morning. She was glad. Perpetually, he talked about his properties, horses, and the "importance of saving money." A few times he'd spread his money on top of the bed, counting it twice, and then placing it into his large leather wallet.

But now it was time to get their life started. Besides, marriage takes time to adjust, she assured herself. And she had a lot to learn.

"I can't wait to be at Happy Valley," she said, her voice rising above the sound of the waves crashing along the beach.

He sucked noisily on his pipe. "You'll have plenty to do there Princess. We can ride ... do things together."

"I discovered there's a small Junior college in Walnut Creek."

He frowned. "As long as you spend most of your time with me, and our home."

"Yes, of course."

"Let's call it a night," he said, stroking her bare leg.

*

Section Two: Happy Valley

1962 to 1969

13

It was spring in Happy Valley. Apple blossoms covered the hills like pink chiffon.

Dianne was in the kitchen preparing dinner. From the window, she watched Donald riding Baba, cantering gracefully along the hills. At the top of a steep crevice, under the fading sunset, Donald sat on his horse. As if he was surveying his land.

She tossed the salad in a wooden bowl. She hoped that Donald would be in a good mood. Often he was sullen, and would drink too much. Trying to be a perfect wife, and to please him, she'd taken a series of cooking lessons. She'd loved preparing meals and dinner parties and decorating the house. "A showplace," Min raved. Mike had helped her stain the wood floors to a high polish, and install white wooden shutters. She'd re-finished old antiques that she found at flea markets. She had sprayed wicker furniture white and covered the chairs and loveseats with colorful fabrics and pillows. Harry had given her an upright piano. She loved the house.

At first, Donald was romantic—bringing flowers, going out to dinner, but then very quickly, their marriage had settled into routine: Donald up at five in the morning before leaving for his office, brushing his horses. At seven he'd arrive home, ride his horses, take a swim, eat dinner, and early to bed. Gradually, their marriage had changed from eager anticipation, to settled resignation.

Recently, she'd enrolled at the Civic Arts Junior College in Walnut Creek. She loved her classes, and her paintings were developing into larger paintings of women inside boxes. School was opening a whole new world. She'd turned the tool shed behind the pool, into her studio. There, she spent a great deal of time, writing in her journals, and painting the flowers bursting along the Diablo Hills. Donald paid little interest in her work, calling her painting a "hobby."

The world was changing. It was the beginning of the Woman's movement, and Dianne wanted to be a part of it. She loved President Kennedy, and followed closely the Bay of Pigs Invasion. She believed passionately in racial equality. She admired Jackie Kennedy's confident intellect. Now that she was free, away from her past, she found herself interested in more than life in the suburbs; she wanted to be a part of the changing generation, and not stuck in the past.

Often, she'd drive to Berkeley, watching the confident students march in protests, or hurrying to classes. She admired their purpose, to pursue education and professions. For hours, she'd hang out at the Berkeley Museum, studying the artist Eva Hesse's massive sculptures, and her use of materials: hospital tubing, balls inside nets. Dianne craved her own identity as an artist. She began exploring construction sites, collecting odd things to later use in her own work. Contemporary art inspired her. It contained it own special world.

The door bounded open.

"Honey ... what's for dinner?" Donald clumped into the kitchen, his boots heavily marking the shiny waxed floors. He sat at the table, and took off his boots, socks, and dropped them on the floor.

"I ... thought we'd have dinner on the patio ... it's a lovely night ... you can see the moon."

He dropped three ice cubes in a tall frosted glass, and poured a hefty amount of scotch. "To us," he said, raising his glass.

She kissed him lightly on the mouth. He put his hand on her breasts, and she was careful not to let him know that she felt slightly repulsed. Whenever he touched her, a dread came over her, a feeling she didn't understand. Kept secret.

She placed the roast chicken on the silver platter she'd decorated with orange slices and asparagus.

Donald made another drink, explaining in his slightly Western drawl, how Baba was frisky and had to be handled just so. She hated it when he drank. Every night at dinner, after drinking several highballs, he'd drink a jug of wine. Slurring his words and crying, he'd tell stories about how his parents always made him play the horn, perform, and tell jokes.

"Princess ... I'll hop in the shower," he said with a frown. "Then we'll eat—make sure the ice doesn't melt—I like the skin on the chicken burned."

She nodded. He'd take a quick swim, and then change for dinner. She finished roasting the vegetables the way he liked them. Crisp. But he was a man of routine, she reminded herself. He worked hard. He was busy expanding his furniture stores. His *Red Barn Furniture stores* were known for wagon wheel coffee tables, oversized leather chairs, and Western style tables. "I'm making a fortune," he bragged. On Sundays, he took her with him to collect rents from his properties. She waited in his truck while he collected the rents, and then he'd return with a sack of checks and cash. "I bought the properties for a song," he'd brag.

At Min's insistence, they'd joined the Temple, and to please Donald she went with Min to Hadassah teas. Dianne hosted coffee klatches by her pool, the suburban ladies talking about their "help," husbands, and recipes for Jell-O molds. On weekends, they gave barbecues for friends and neighbors.

On the patio she lit the candles inside the glass bug jars. The table was set perfectly—yellow placemats, wildflowers inside the blue glass vase—sterling cigarette holders filled with cigarettes, jade pots filled with salt and fresh pepper. A spray of fireflies hovered over the garden and deer rustled the tall bushes along the side of the patio. A turquoise light glowed in the pool that Andy the pool man kept clean.

Dianne lit the candles inside the glass bug jars, and poured ice water into the glasses. Dinner was ready.

As they ate dinner fireflies lit the dark, and wind-bells rattled with the breeze. Donald was drinking red wine, ranting about the economy, and that he wanted to buy more properties, and to build an empire. "A penny a day is a penny saved," he repeated.

Dianne picked at the steak, trying to smile; to be attentive. To please him always.

"Wait till you see my land in Concord, Princess. It's sand fill now, but just wait till the shopping mall builds up. It will be worth a fortune. Old Donald isn't so dumb."

"Hardly dumb. You're very smart," she said, smiling at him.

He sighed. "Princess, we have to tighten our belts. Your painting classes, college tuition, art supplies, cost a fortune. You need to cut down on the classes. I give you a nice allowance for all your needs, and I want us to be filthy rich by the time we're thirty. We'll live in Concord, on a thousand acre ranch without neighbors, only us and our horses ... what's wrong? You're so quiet..."

"I ... haven't felt well. "

"Flu can be a bitch," he quickly said with a frown, his hand on her forehead. "Go to bed. I'll do the dishes."

"I'm pregnant."

He stared at her. He held the glass of wine. "Tell me you're kidding?"

"I'm five weeks."

"Your diaphragm? You weren't using it?"

"I thought you'd be happy. I thought ... you'd said that someday you wanted children ... I ..."

"You tricked me!" he shouted. "We talked about not having children! You *agreed* we'd wait! My mother told me not to marry you! I should have listened! Everyone told me not to marry you! No wonder Charley left you. You're a cold fish, and a liar!"

He got up, carrying the jug of wine, and ran into the hills.

By then it was dark. A wind blew out the candles. She sat there, trying to absorb what had just happened. Deep down, she knew that Donald had a right to be angry; she had agreed that they wouldn't have children, at least for years. Of course she had to have children. In 1960, that's what married women did. Children gave women an identity, and a role in their marriage.

No wonder Charley left you. Everyone told me not to marry you.

All along Donald's parents didn't believe her innocence. They believed the scandal that Charley continuously kept alive.

The melancholy sound of Donald's horn, echoed along the hills. The air was full of fireflies.

The moon was fading, and the wind was up. He wouldn't come to bed for hours now. Feeling slightly nauseated, Dianne cleared the table.

In the kitchen, she rinsed the dishes, placing each dish carefully into the dishwasher, making sure that the plates were upright between the tiny rubber slots. Or Donald would be furious. He hated broken things, and waste. He was always checking to make sure she didn't throw anything out that was half full.

Next, she prepared the coffee for the morning, and set two cups next to the pot. She set the breakfast table with Donald's favorite yellow ceramic cereal bowl. She folded the yellow linen napkin like a flower.

She turned on the dishwasher, relieved by the sound of the dishes thumping against the door. She then made peanut butter and jelly sandwiches for Donald's lunch the next day, slicing the crust, as he liked it.

The horn stopped. She finished cleaning the kitchen. She turned off the lights, and then she went to bed.

*

It was summer, and the valley was hot. She was seven months pregnant, and had gained a great deal of weight. Donald adjusted to being a father; he'd even helped her decorate the nursery. At the San Francisco Furniture Mart, together, they chose a white wooden crib, a play table, rocking chair, and a bright red shag rug. Dianne painted a circus scene on the nursery wall. But whatever had been between them, was now gone. They were polite with each other, entertained at barbecues, dinner parties, did the right things, but their marriage had settled into pretend tolerance. Dianne was sure that once the baby arrived, their marriage would grow.

Mother hadn't been as thrilled as Min was about the baby. "A child is a lot of work," Mother had said, disapprovingly. But she'd made sure a baby announcement was published in the Jewish Bulletin. "Now that rat Charley can see," Mother had said.

As the summer grew hotter, and Dianne grew larger, to please Donald, she was only taking one painting class. Voraciously, she read books on art history, and literature. She spent hours in her studio, drawing, and painting. Fascinated with women artists, she read about Georgia O'Keefe, Mary Cassatt, Lee Krasner, Berthe Morisot, and other woman artists she admired. She was in awe of their independence, and their strong commitment to their art. These were women who inspired her and made her realize what a sheltered environment she lived in. These were women who took risk and didn't follow the mold. Just as medicine or God or parenting or the land calls some people, art is a calling and is a way of being.

*

A few weeks later on a hot Friday afternoon, Dianne arrived at her painting class.

The large room smelled of turpentine and linseed oil. About fifty students stood at their easels, setting up their palettes. Dianne took her place at her easel in the back, and unpacked the fishing tackle box that contained her array of palette knives, tubes of oil paints, brushes, and pastel crayons. Carefully, she chose the brushes and palette knives she would use. Next, she mixed the colors she'd use, on the glass palette.

It was hot in the room, but the doors were open and a soft warm breeze filled the room.

A model, a young girl with flowing yellow hair, reclined naked on a Persian rug set on a raised wooden platform. A radio was on and Janet Joplin's sensual voice rose above the students' animated chatter. A haze of cigarette smoke floated along the room.

"Thirty minutes to paint the model," Earl announced. A cigarette dangled between his fingers. His long silver hair was tied by a beaded clip. He knew a lot about painting. She felt connected to him, and knew that she had a crush on him.

The model took off her robe, and arranged her slender body in a classical position. Her hair hung past her waist, like a drape. Her eyes gazed straight ahead, as if on some destination, or place that only she knew. Dianne felt her solitude.

First, with a charcoal stick, Dianne drew the model's arms dangling like stems. Slowly, she shaped the model's body. She worked fast, wanting to catch the model's isolation, rubbing the charcoal with her hand, wanting the lines to smudge so that the figure was a blur. Next, she dipped a brush into the peach colored paint mixed with white, letting the paint drip along the canvas, and form is own logic. Quickly, she painted now. Except for the sounds of palette knives scraping canvas, or water running in the sink as someone cleaned their brushes, it was quiet.

Dianne painted the hair orange, scraping the paint with her palette knife until the hair seemed almost faded. Shivering from excitement, she painted a fuchsia color moon.

"Time is up!" Earl called.

Everyone was talking to each other now, wishing they had more time. Dianne lit a cigarette, and stood back observing what she had painted.

The figure was elongated, distorted. She felt frustrated that she could only see from her imagination, and not as the model was. Next to her, Joanne, an older woman, painted the model exactly as she looked…the proportions perfect. Joanne always painted an apple perfectly, while Dianne's apple was always crooked and floated in the middle of the canvas.

"Interesting palette," said Earl by her side. His lonely intense eyes observed her painting. He lit another cigarette, never taking his gaze from her canvas.

"Your line is energetic, but hesitant. What you've captured is a sense of isolation in the figure, and I like that. It's emotional."

Dianne was excited by his critique. She'd seen his paintings of women, and they were sensitive.

"I like your work," he continued. "…it's unformed, but your paintings disturb, and the color is luminous. Keep going. This painting has potential." Then he moved on to the woman next to her.

Potential, he said. She'd record his critique in her journal, and later study it.

During the break, she and some of the students sat on the lawn outside, eating their lunches. Most of the students were young, but there were several women her age and older who were enrolled at the college. They called themselves "Re-entry" women. She watched Earl open the trunk of his car, and then go off by himself, his slender figure fading down the lane.

"Just the way you apply fuchsia is wonderful," sighed a woman from her class. "I can't paint with imagination, but my husband hangs my paintings in his office."

"You have a college degree," Dianne said. "It'll take me years to get a degree—then a masters."

"My mother made me go to college to meet a husband," said the woman. "I wanted to be an illustrator, but then children got in the way—marriage." She took a bite from her chopped olive sandwich. Dianne thought the woman's paintings were well done, and she seemed happy.

"I've been reading about the Bloomsbury group," Dianne said. "I read the biographies of women artists. They're brave, and take risk. But they're hidden. Only the men seem to make it as artists. You hear about De Kooning, Picasso, Stella, Pollack, Hoffman, but you don't hear about Eva Hesse, or Eva Gonzalez."

They ate their sandwiches, quietly talking about artists and exhibits they wanted to see. After smoking one more cigarette, it was time to go back to Happy Valley.

Later that night, Dianne and Donald were in bed, watching the Jack Paar show. Earlier, Donald had been drinking, and the room smelled of scotch.

"Did you shut the window?" asked Donald.

"Yes."

"If the window is open the air conditioner won't work. You have a habit of leaving the window open," he persisted. He put his leg over her legs.

"I don't know what my headache is from. Maybe too much sun. Or the oil paint in class today."

He sighed, and removed his legs from hers. "You're a cold fish, Dianne."

"It's just that I'm not feeling well," she insisted. "A migraine, I think."

"After the baby comes, I don't want you hanging out at that college with those beatniks. You're going to be a mother. Act like the other girls in Happy Valley."

"Donald, they're artists, they're intelligent women. They want to be more than a hostess."

"Good night," he said, pulling the covers over him.

As he snored heavily, Dianne lay awake, watching television. Her mind was on her next painting. She wanted to paint a woman crawling from a box.

*

14

It was a steamy August day, and near Dianne's due date. Nannie came to visit. Just having her around comforted Dianne. And Nannie loved being away from her chores at home. She spent hours picking fruit and making jams and pies. In the afternoons, Dianne and Nannie picked wildflowers or lounged by the pool. It was heartwarming to see Nannie so relaxed and happy.

That late afternoon, Dianne was lying on a Chaise on the patio, watching Nannie pick fruit. Bees floated in the air, and the sprinklers had soaked the lawns. Nannie wore a pink sundress with thin straps, a large straw hat, and her white legs were streaked with sunburn. As she picked the fruit, saying aloud to no one, "What waste," sorting the bruised fruit from the good, she dropped the fruit into tin buckets.

Dianne fanned herself with her hat, feeling heavy and bloated. During her pregnancy she'd tried to feel excited, but she felt faraway from the baby, like it didn't belong to her. As though she were someone else watching. She assured herself that as soon as she gave birth she'd feel joyful and present, like her other pregnant friends.

The past months, Min's Canasta friends gave Dianne a flurry of baby showers—the tables decorated with paper umbrellas, and colorful rattles, everyone applauding when she opened her gifts: a years diaper service from Aunt Pearl—a buggy from Min and Harry, a sterling silver rattle from Mother, a tall stuffed giraffe from Mike.

Nannie set the tin buckets in the shade. "These apricots will make nice pies. Oy, such waste," Nannie repeated, her thin voice floating in the air.

"Donald loves apricot pie," Dianne said.

"He loves booze! Oy, you need a drunk like a hole in the head. I was married to a drunk. Your Grandfather left me high and dry to raise your mother."

"Mother told me that her father died."

"Your mother is crazy. She believes in fairy tales, that's her problem. Like an arranged marriage, she pushed you into marriage. First Charley, a good-for-nothing, and now you're married to a drunk. Now you're stuck."

"Nannie, I'm married, and soon to be, a mother."

Nannie continued to drop apricots on sheets of newspaper, her swollen red fingers sorting which ones she wanted for her pies.

Dianne closed her eyes under her dark glasses, trying not to think about what Nannie had said. Of course she knew that Nannie was right. She d married Donald on rebound. She'd thought that she'd forget about Charley, but obsessively, every day she wrote about him in her journals, searching desperately for the reason he'd married her. She wanted justice. She wanted to make Charley accountable.

When the air turned hotter, she and Nannie went into the kitchen. Nannie boiled apricots in big pots, and made pie dough. Dianne sat at the kitchen table, watching Nannie's swollen fingers scallop the dough along the edges of the pie pans. The aroma of boiling apricots sifted throughout the house.

As Nannie worked, she told Dianne stories about the 1906 earthquake in San Francisco. She'd lived in her parent's house on

Castro Street, raising Mother. At sixteen, Mother won the Chopin piano award, and a scholarship to Julliard. Nannie had insisted that Mother go secretarial school.

"Then she met your father. He was fifteen years older, handsome, and on his way up at Universal. They bought a house, and they insisted I move in with them."

Nannie sprinkled flour on the dough. A sadness lay on her sweet intense face.

"How is Bobbie?" Dianne asked after a long silence.

Nannie sighed heavily. She confided that Bobbie had been expelled from his private school for fondling boys, and that Mike had been once again arrested for stealing cars.

"I warned your mother when Mike was a child to stop hitting him. She couldn't stop hitting the poor boy, oy, he'd go to school with welts on his body. Sighing, Nannie made a design on top of the pies with a fork, and then she placed the pies into the oven. Dianne remembered Mike howling from the basement, while she had hid in the closet, covering her ears.

Donald's truck bumbled up their private road and stopped in the driveway. It was exactly six o'clock and still hot.

The kitchen back door opened and Donald, his shirt open, and carrying his jacket over his shoulder, barged into the kitchen.

Dutifully, he kissed Dianne on the cheek. "Getting fat," he said, patting her stomach. "I suggest you cut out the chocolate bars."

"Dinner will be ready soon," she said, trying to sound cheerful. "Nannie is baking apricot pies. Your favorite."

He frowned. "I told you to turn off the sprinklers. The water bill is huge," he complained. "Paint is all over the sheets, Dianne.

Christ. You're going to be a mother not a beatnik artist. Act like it! Make sure you don't use the water so much. The water bill is too high."

That night, Dianne slept on her side. Donald slept with most of the covers pulled over him. During dinner, he drank a lot of wine, and Nannie had seemed upset. Dianne had helped her wash the dishes, and then they sat at the kitchen table and ate a slice of her wonderful apricot pie.

Dianne closed her eyes, trying to sleep, but she had a stomachache.

Maybe it's from the pie, she thought.

She sat on the edge of the bed, and the pains were coming faster. Her water broke, forming a puddle around her bare feet.

"Donald. Donald. It's time to go to the hospital."

He turned on the light and got up, dressing quickly and lecturing that he hoped it wasn't a "false alarm." Hadn't she had a false alarm before? She was in terrible pain.

She went into Nannie's room, and woke her. "I'm going to the hospital Nannie."

Nannie hugged her. "Oy, you'll be fine. I'm going to call your mother, now go. Nannie loves you, darling."

The hospital corridors were empty, and a light stretched along the shiny green linoleum floors. A nurse helped her into a wheel chair; she was doubled over from pain. She kissed Donald, and left him in the reception area for new fathers.

After she changed into a hospital gown, the nurse helped her into a narrow bed. The metal bars were up, and her legs up in the examining position.

"The doctor will be in soon," said the nurse. It was hard to see her over her stomach. The pains hurt so much she could hardly breathe. The faint sounds of babies crying carried down the hall.

Dr. Howard came in and after examining her he said. "Let's get this girl to the delivery room. She's going to have a baby."

Everything was moving fast, as if it were upside down. The delivery room was green tile and the nurses voices echoed. An orderly slid her from the gurney, onto a narrow table.

There was a lot of noise in the room, and her pains were coming faster.

Dr. Howard came in. He patted her hand. "Give her some gas," he ordered.

A nurse put a rubber mask over her face, and it smelled like ether, like when she had had her tonsils out. Watching the overhead lights fade, she struggled to keep awake, and then it was only dark.

"It's a girl! A girl! Wake up. You had a girl. A daughter. A healthy girl."

"A girl," Dianne murmured, blinking, the ceiling lights fading in and out. Her daughter's warbled cries sounded like they were underwater.

A nurse held the baby wrapped in a pink blanket, in front of Dianne. Her daughter's face was like Donald's face. Dianne felt the thrill of giving birth, the miracle of it. She felt as though she were floating.

Her legs were wrapped in sheets and still in the stirrups. Dr. Howard performed an episiotomy, and she felt the pinch.

"Had to take a lot of stitches," he said.

Still groggy, after what had seemed hours later, Dianne was placed on a gurney, and she was wheeled to her private room.

By then it was early morning. Donald wearing a cowboy hat was waiting with a bouquet of red long stem roses. They kissed lightly on the lips. Several cigars stuck from the pocket of his red plaid shirt. He looked so innocent, and for a minute, she felt a rush of love. "Red roses. Thank you. Isn't our daughter beautiful?"

"She's funny looking," Donald said, biting back a chuckle. "But she has ten fingers, ten toes."

"I'd like to name her Sara, after my great grandmother. She was an opera singer. "

Min and Harry arrived. Harry carried a huge teddy bear with a pink bow. Min, dressed in pink, raved that Sara was "The image of Donald." She couldn't wait to baby-sit. The nursery is all ready," she repeated.

"A chip off the block," said Harry, a cigar in his mouth. "Some kid," Harry repeated, between puffs of a thick cigar.

"Same nose as Donald's," Min said.

"Some kid," Harry repeated.

Donald passed cigars to the doctors, telling jokes, Harry and Min laughing before he finished.

Mother and Nannie arrived. Mother carried gift boxes from I. Magnin. The room was filled with flowers inside pink ceramic shoes, and hats, and gift baskets of pink rattles and bibs.

"I hope you hired a baby nurse, Dianne," Mother said. She wore a beige knit dress, beige shoes, and her face was white.

"I'll be helping out," Min said, happily. "I'll send Buster to clean, and cook. I'll babysit."

"She needs a baby nurse," Mother insisted. Her lips were pressed tight.

After an hour, everyone left.

Later that day, a nurse wheeled Dianne in a wheel chair, Donald by her side to the nursery. In front of the glass partitions, parents waved at their babies and took pictures. Sara looked so tiny, and Dianne wondered why she wasn't acting like the mother next to her, who was kissing the glass partition? Why she felt as though she existed behind a wall, peeking out?

The next morning, when Dianne opened her eyes, she was surprised to see her father standing by her bed. The bars were still up, and she was embarrassed by her tangled hair, and half-open hospital gown. Smoothing her hair, nervously, she sat up. "I thought you were ... in Portland?"

Daddy nodded. "I caught the first plane out. I wanted to meet my granddaughter. The nurse let me see her. She's beautiful. Just like you."

Dianne smiled, feeling self-conscious, as she always would around her father. Even that early in the morning, he looked elegant, ready for a long day of work; his Shriner diamond pin was carefully attached to his jacket lapel, gold monogrammed cufflinks on his French cuffs, and his impeccable tailored custom gray suit was perfect. He was known for his style.

"Maybe you can come back soon, Daddy. Stay a few days at Happy Valley? Get to know Sara. You and Mother can stay in the guest room."

He shrugged. "Your mother is busy with Bobbie. We're looking for a new school." He sighed. "He has those migraine headaches."

He looked at his watch, and Dianne averted her eyes from his sad face. He kissed the top of her head. "I flew here this morning, but I have to get to the airport and catch a plane to New York." He paused. "Take care of yourself, Dianne."

Dianne watched him gracefully cross the room, carrying his worn leather briefcase, the faint scent of his cologne lingering in the air.

The door shut. She closed her eyes. She loved her father so much, and what was between them was unspoken.

She remembered when she was ten, clunky and it was her tenth birthday. A screening room was in the back of her father's office on Hyde Street, and every year, he screened a movie and gave her a birthday party. She was tall, and awkward. She was wearing a pink organdy dress and it scratched her bare legs. She wore black Mary Jane shoes and white silk socks and pink plastic barrettes in her too curly dark hair. Nearsighted, she wore aqua color plastic very thick eyeglasses. During the movie she sat next to her father. She sat very still, fearing she'd breathe too hard, and her nose would run. "Do you have a handkerchief?' he'd asked. "Ladies carry handkerchiefs. Desperately, she'd wanted to hold his hand.

She closed her eyes and slept.

That afternoon, the nurse brought Sara wrapped in a blanket, and placed her in Dianne's arms. "I'll be back in ten minutes so you two can be alone," she said. She left the room and closed the door.

Please don't go, please come back, Dianne wanted to scream. She was afraid to hold Sara too tight, afraid of the tiny mottled face, the wandering gray eyes looking up at her. She was feeling so faraway, as though Sara belonged to someone else. She didn't know what to do. She wondered if that was the way she was supposed to feel, or if she had completely internalized her mother?

She pressed her face closer to Sara's face, blowing her breath into Sara's little open mouth and whispering that she would try her best to be a good mother and that she loved her. Maybe if she said the words she'd feel the joy she knew she was supposed to feel.

She felt panic that she'd pass her mother's coldness, to her daughter. Quickly, she rang for the nurse. When the nurse took Sara from her arms, Dianne felt relieved.

Five days later, Dianne went home with Donald, Sara, and the nurse Mother had hired. In the car, on the way to Happy Valley, Miss Ek sitting in the back seat held Sara wrapped in a blanket. The nurse smoked, and complained about the summer heat. Miss Ek's face was as white as her uniform, and she incessantly smoked. Dianne's stitches hurt, and she sat on a rubber tube, wondering if she'd know what to do with Sara? Finally, Donald's truck ascended the private road to Happy Valley, past Baba galloping along the hills, and they were home.

For two weeks, Dianne followed Miss Ek around, watching carefully, as the nurse diapered and bathed Sara.

On Miss Ek's last day, Dianne bathed Sara in the tiny rubber portable bath. The doors were closed to keep the room warm, and the bassinette was half filled with warm water. Holding Sara in one arm, Dianne rubbed the tiny bar of baby soap along Sara's pale, slippery body.

"Be careful of the soft spot on her head," warned Miss Ek. A cigarette dangled from her prim mouth. "You young princesses. You give birth and you don't know what you're doing. Now soap her little body... there in the creases ... yes that's a rash, honestly, you young girls." After drying Sara, Dianne wrapped her in the blanket, closed the top of the bassinet, and diapered her. As she pinned the folds, her hands shook.

"Careful not to stick her skin," repeated Miss Ek with a frown.

Later that day, Donald drove Miss Ek to the train station.

After Miss Ek left, Donald installed an intercom in Sara's room so that they could hear Sara's every sound.

Dianne loved sterilizing the bottles, boiling the nipples, pouring the formula into the bottles, and then arranging the bottles in rows, in the refrigerator. Sometimes, she'd sit next to Sara's crib, watching her sleep, touching her tiny hands, wishing that she could love her the way she had always wanted her mother to love her, love her in a way that Dianne knew she didn't know.

As the days passed, and then the weeks, rarely was Donald home. When he was home, he barely looked at Sara. He'd drink his wine, or ride his horses, and gradually, spent more time at his office, or fishing for salmon. He planned on by buying a fishing boat. "He needs time to adjust to being a father," Min always said.

That night, Dianne kept the intercom on in the bedroom. Donald was sleeping, and Dianne lay awake. At one a.m. Sara's wobbly cry echoed on the intercom. Trying not to wake Donald, Dianne put on her eyeglasses, and quickly got up, shuffling along the hallway in the red furry slippers Min had given her.

After she changed Sara, she heated the bottle of formula and tested it on her wrist. Then she went into Sara's room and sat on the white rocker by the window, feeding Sara and listening to the silence.

*

Winter came and the trees were bare. Three days a week Min happily babysat Sara, while Dianne went to school. Sometimes, Min would take Sara to her house, where she'd decorated a nursery with toys, a crib, playpen, swing, and a full baby wardrobe of clothes. "Everything Sara needs," she'd say.

At school, Dianne's paintings were developing, and getting special notice. "I think you'll be an important artist," Earl had told her.

Giving birth had given her a new awareness. As if her sensory experiences came full force. Sunlight was brighter, food tastier and everything seemed more than it was. In her journals she listed colors that affected her and words came faster. The sight of a blooming rose made her feel breathless. Every free moment Dianne would go to her studio and paint, letting the images evolve from her unconscious. Through her paintings, like a jigsaw puzzle, she began to see glimmers of who she really was and what she felt. It was still difficult for her to feel her feelings all at once. But she knew she was going through change. Her clothes changed from matching outfits, to clothes she bought at

Bazaars, and painted with flowers, and decorated with beads. She grew her hair long and didn't wear makeup. She felt alive in a way she never had before.

At school, her painting of a lady sitting inside a box, holding a baby, had been chosen for an exhibit at the college. A known collector had bought the painting for two hundred dollars. With the money, Dianne opened her first savings account.

On Sundays, Min and Harry came over, bringing toys for Sara. While Donald barbecued, Min carried Sara around, or held her while they sat on the big swing Harry had installed on the patio. "Some place the kids have. Donald's a good provider," Harry repeated.

Occasionally, Mother and Nannie came over, but Mother spent her time sweeping leaves, complaining that Dianne's house wasn't neat enough. "Nothing is more important than cleaning your house and taking care of your husband, Dianne. He's a good provider."

Nannie had confided to Dianne that Bobbie was tutored at home, and was stealing her medications. He had perpetual migraines. "He has an old heart like mine," Mother would say.

*

It was November 22, 1963, and the world was exploding. Martin Luther King gave his *I Have A Dream* Speech. President Kennedy was helping to change the world. The art world was busting with new ideas and movements. With Earl and the class, they'd gone to see Andy Warhol's pop exhibit. Dianne felt inspired by new ideas. "A bunch of old soup cans and crap," Donald had said.

That afternoon it was raining hard. Dianne was in the den, folding laundry, and watching the afternoon news on television. The President and the first lady were in Dallas, and the crowds were going crazy. Sara was next to her, sitting at her play table, placing pegs in the myriad of tiny holes. A howling wind snapped the windows and blew the trees covered in red berries. Earlier, she'd made a meatloaf, Donald's favorite, and the smell of the cooking meatloaf floated into the house.

Just then she saw the President lean forward, and then all hell broke loose the President had been shot by a sniper, and the motorcade sped to the hospital.

All day, Dianne sat there, between feeding Sara, and when the announcer announced that the President was dead, Dianne cried. Why? What was wrong with human beings?

When Donald came home at his usual time, she ran into his arms, sobbing. "I'll try harder. I love you and my family. I don't mean to be cold."

"Even worse. You don't know how to be sexy or warm. Something's wrong with you. I should have listened. Everyone said you were a frigid bitch."

"Donald, please don't say that. I'm sorry I've hurt you." She moved closer to him. She wanted to comfort him. She knew his pain. But he pushed her away. "Clean up, and let's have dinner."

*

The days, and then the months passed. Dianne tried harder to please Donald, but nothing changed. You can't force love. And things were terrible in the family; Nannie had told her that Mike had gone to prison for a year, for stealing black bugging boxes.

Mother never mentioned it, and when Dianne asked about Mike, Mother would say, "Oh he's doing fine. He's playing golf. He'll be home soon."

At fourteen, Bobbie was tutored at home, and he was always ill with migraines, or was having tests for brain tumors. "Something is wrong with the poor boy," Mother would say. Never would Dianne understand why her mother kept Bobbie at home, never to live life, but to stay with her. Increasingly Mother became angrier, always yelling at poor Daddy. When Mother rarely visited Happy Valley, no matter how thoroughly she had cleaned the house, Mother would find some tiny thing---a broom out of place in the utility closet, a dish in the sink, anything, she'd scream that Dianne was a "slob," a "loser," and that she'd "lose Donald too if she wasn't careful." Dianne's migraines would rage, and she'd lie on her bed, an icepack on her head, feeling worthless. She knew that her mother would never forgive her for Charley.

15

It was a Saturday night. Donald and Dianne were driving to the Berman's dinner party. The window was open and a breeze snapped her hair. Haystacks were piled like yellow spindles along the roads, and the air smelled like hay and honeysuckle. A million stars sprinkled the sky. Earlier, Donald had complained about the constant round of barbecues and dinner parties. He was quiet that night. He'd bought a large fishing boat and had been fishing on the bay all day.

"Last night you forgot to turn on the air conditioner," Donald complained. "It's hot. When it's hot, I need the air conditioner on all day! You don't listen, Dianne."

He continued to complain about the heat, the lawns turning brown, and Dianne's indifference to her chores. Dianne knew his complaints well, and she'd learned not to argue with him. She didn't want Sara to see that part of them.

Twenty minutes later, they arrived at the Berman's sprawling ranch-style house in Walnut Creek. Donald held a salmon he'd caught, and had wrapped in a newspaper.

The hostess gave Dianne an air kiss, exclaiming how much she loved Dianne's white cotton mini dress. On the skirt, Dianne had painted a large yellow rose with a long green stem curling to the waist. "It's so arty," she raved. Donald gave Dolly a wet kiss and gave her the salmon.

"Wally will smoke it," Dolly said with a pleased smile. She wore a see-through tiny mini yellow dress, and yellow shiny high heel shoes. Falls were installed in her big hair, and false eyelashes curved up, giving her small eyes a squinty look.

The guests stood around an Olympic-size swimming pool surrounded by fake palm trees, and Japanese rock gardens. The women wore mini-dresses, glitter, and big hair. The men wore bright silk shirts, and sideburns. From speakers set around the pool, the Beatles sang *I want To Hold Your Hand.*

"There it is!" Dolly said, leading Dianne and Donald into the living room, and pointing to Dianne's painting of children lying by an ocean. It was framed in an ornate gold frame, hanging above a gold brocade sofa.

"We love it," she told Donald. "It's the *exact* yellow in our sofa. Our decorator Moosie Franklin raved."

"Cost me ten thousand dollars," Donald said, laughing hard, as if he'd said something funny.

At the bar, Wally Berman was telling jokes, and making drinks. Lamps in the shape of hula girls jiggled, the breasts lit up in red lights.

Dianne sipped her vodka over ice, and joined the group of ladies clustered around the pool, like bouquets. They talked about their "help," their children, and their decorators.

"Jonathan is very gifted," lisped Patsy, a thin red head wearing a turquoise strapless dress, and a huge bouffant hairstyle.

"Zachary is in a pre-*gifted* class," said Myra Levin. She wore pink hot pants, and white leather boots. Pink fake flowers were arranged in her huge dark hair.

"The Schwartze has been cooking all day," said Dolly, lowering her voice.

"*They're* wonderful," said Bunny Katz, smiling, "... Warren won't hire anything else."

"Dianne. We want to commission you," said Francie Kay, not moving her mouth. She wore a sequin mini dress with balloon sleeves. "We want something like Monet's gardens in Giverchy."

"Giverny," Dianne corrected.

"Dianne's paintings of flowers are ..."

"Emotional," finished Holly.

"Dinner!" called Wally, ringing a cowbell.

Like a herd of cattle, everyone rushed to the tables, looking for their names on nametags by each place.

Quite drunk by then, Donald told sick jokes, laughing before he finished the punch line. Dianne picked at the lasagna layered by mounds of thick cheese.

"The stock market took a dive. The Vietnam war is fucking up the market," said Larry. He was thin with a huge head of wiry curly hair. He wore white pants, and a floral silk shirt with parrots on it.

"Did you hear the Goldman's filed bankruptcy? Evelyn has to go to work. Wally says they tried to keep up ..."

"What's wrong with work?" Dianne said. "Read Betty Friedan's book The Feminine Mystique—suburban housewives are going back to work. The feminist movement is growing."

The men laughed, slapping each other on their backs. "A woman's work is at home. With her children."

"Larry thinks it's fabulous that Dianne is selling art," said Joanne, smiling at Donald.

"Dianne's overhead costs ten thousand a month!" said Donald, poking his finger down his mouth, the men laughing and poking him.

After coffee was served, canasta tables were set up. Donald and "the boys" played gin rummy, slamming their cards, and yelling,

"Bazooka!" And the girls gossiped about who was donating to the Temple. Finally, the evening was over.

Donald drove home in silence. The radio was on, and Sonny and Cher were singing, "It's You Babe." The long dark roads were quiet, and the moon was full blown.

At home, Dianne slipped on her old seersucker nightgown, and splashed cold water on her face. Sara was at Min's house, and she looked forward to sleeping later in the morning, and then spending the day in her studio.

Donald was already in bed. The room was dark, except from the moonlight touching the windows. The air reeked from Scotch, and Dianne was glad the air conditioner was on, pumping cool air. Moonlight made patterns on the aqua color walls.

Careful not to wake him, Dianne got into bed, curling in a prenatal position at the edge of the bed.

When she felt Donald's hand on her bare thigh she didn't move. If she didn't move, he'd stop. Usually, he would.

"Are you sleeping? Dianne? Talk. I know you're awake."

"I have a head ache... I drank too much tonight...."

"Take that thing off." He pulled at her nightgown.

"My... diaphragm ... I didn't put in my... diaphragm."

"I'm tired of your excuses. I'll pull out."

On top of her, he pulled her legs apart, and roughly he entered her. While he pushed deeper into her, she kept her eyes closed.

"Act like you like it, Dianne. God damn it, I can't stand it when you're so quiet. Tell me you love it. Now!"

He pushed his penis into her mouth.

"Suck it now. Hold your lips open ... don't bite! How many times do I have to tell you not to bite!"

Quickly, he came. So she wouldn't gag, she let the warm sticky semen run from the side of her mouth. Satisfied, he got off her and pulled the covers around him.

"Did you swallow it?" he asked after a long while.

"Don't I always?" she replied.

*

"We're having a baby," Dianne told Donald, several weeks later. They sat on the patio. Donald had been talking about a new property he purchased in Concord. He pressed the tobacco down with his thumb. She waited for his reaction.

"You tricked me again," he said after a long moment.

"Donald, I didn't. It was that night after the party. I'd told you I didn't have my diaphragm on. That was the last time we had sex."

"Tricked me again," he repeated.

"You knew. I told you."

"I can't get ahead!" he continued, his voice rising. "Bills. Your bills are killing me. You're ruining my credit. You hide the bills."

"I don't get enough allowance for extras. I'm trying to sell my paintings and…"

" My credit is ruined," he interrupted. "I give you everything; a pool man, gardener, and my mother takes care of Sara. How are you going to take care of another baby?"

"I will do better. I promise, Donald. We both will."

He continued to complain: paint was on everything--he hated her friends. She never went riding with him. She'd tricked him into marrying her. As she always would, she sat still, numb, watching the stars spread along the dark sky. *Once a marriage deteriorates, it's dependent on civilities. There is no turning back. She had to try harder. Or had she duplicated the emptiness and sadness between her parents and her brothers?*

"You're cold, Dianne," he continued. "A cold fish. When I come home after a long day's work you're on the phone with your hippie friends, or in the shed painting. You wear beatnik clothes and never fix yourself pretty. You don't think I know that when I make love to you, you cry."

"It isn't you," she said. "I don't feel cold. I can't express myself. I don't know how to love, Donald. I'll try harder."

He looked at her with narrowed eyes. "I should have listened," he said. "I should have listened."

Dianne shivered, pulling her sweater closer over her shoulders. Poor Donald. He was right. She was cold and except when she was painting or writing in her journals, she couldn't feel her feelings. She'd have to try harder.

"Monday, I'm having a vasectomy," Donald said after a long silence.

He got up and went to the hills. He played his horn until far in the night.

*

Two days later, Donald had a vasectomy. It was a hot Monday morning, and Donald had just arrived home from the hospital.

Min arrived, carrying Tupperware containers of Donald's favorite foods: tuna and egg, olives, and potato salad. Sara hung onto Min's skirt, Min whispering, "Grandma Min is here."

Dianne went into the bedroom. Donald lay on the bed, compressing ice between his legs. The air conditioner pumped warm stale air, and the shutters were closed.

"Can I do anything? Dianne asked.

"Leave me alone," he grunted.

"Tonight, I'll make meatloaf."

"Don't strain yourself. Close the door, and keep the noise down."

Dianne sat on the lawn, watching Sara cut her paper dolls with a child's red scissors. Carefully she placed the paper dolls in a shoebox.

A lovely child, Dianne thought. Deeply, she resented Min acting like Sara was *her* child.

But you created that, she thought. She'd worried that Sara would internalize her inability to be loving, like her own mother was to her, but ironically that's exactly what she'd created.

Do mothers unconsciously pass their horrors to their daughters?

Even though she had always tried not to emulate her mother in any way, so much of her was like her mother---just the way she'd press a napkin twice on the table before using it, or solemnly press her lips---repeat, "Thank your lucky stars."

Dianne opened her book on Georgia O'Keefe, admiring the pages of flower paintings. She loved the colors, the personal vision.

Min was folding Sara's laundry, blowing kisses to Sara. "Grandma loves you," she repeated in a singsong voice.

Every fifteen minutes Donald blew a whistle Min had given him, and Min would rush into the bedroom. She was a doting mother, Dianne thought, and meant well. Dianne knew that Min still didn't approve of her. It was in her too quick laugh, averted eyes, and her eagerness to push Dianne away. "Go paint. You have plenty to do," she'd say, happily taking Sara.

When the sun subsided and a breeze blew over the valley, Min finished folding Sara's laundry, and placed it into the plastic laundry basket. "Everything is spic and span," she said. "I'll take Sara home with me. Donald can rest, and you can concentrate on school."

"I'd rather Sara stay home," Dianne said, emphatically.

Sara cried, hanging on to Min's skirt. "I want to go with Grandma Min," she said, narrowing her eyes.

"Well, all right. But I want you home tomorrow. Mommy misses you, too."

"Donald can't be *disturbed*," Min said, disappointment in her eyes. "Tomorrow, I'm taking Sara on a picnic at the duck pond. We have an early dinner at our favorite place by the merry-go-round. After dinner, I'll bring her home."

Dianne hugged Sara goodbye. Anxiously, Dianne watched Sara carry her Mary Poppins purse, and her favorite doll, and eagerly climb inside Min's' wood paneled station wagon.

As the car descended the narrow road, Dianne waved, watching the car slowly drive past the rows of pine trees Donald had planted, and finally disappear into the fading day.

Donald blew the whistle, and she hurried inside.

*

It was 1965. Jenny was born January 7th, on a stormy night. She was an adorable child, with jet-black hair, and black curious eyes.

Immediately, Dianne and Jenny bonded. Never would she let Jenny out of her sight. Sara spent more time with Min and Harry, going on weekend vacations to Carmel, or to Lake Tahoe. Not wanting to ignore Jenny as she had Sara, Dianne took a leave of absence from school, and spent her days with Jenny.

As the months passed, Dianne took Jenny wherever she went. Often, she slept next to her. She took extra care cleaning her house, and cooking better dinners for Donald. Determined to improve their marriage, she'd even gone with Donald on his fishing boat. But quickly, she'd felt seasick. Twice, she'd gone riding with Donald, but she was terrified. They were just different people, with different talents and interests. She even attempted to flirt, at night greeting him in a skirt, and snug sweater. But her flirting was more an act, and it always ended with Donald angry, and half-drunk, while she'd promise to do better.

As Jenny got older, Dianne hired a baby sitter, and on those days, she returned to classes. Determined to earn enough credits to eventually transfer to a University, Dianne doubled up on classes, studied art history, and English literature, and printing classes. When she read Virginia Woolf's *Room Of Your Own*, she fantasized about living alone. She wondered if marriage was ever for her? If maybe she and her mother were those women who should live alone, content to do their art? Or if some women are born without maternal genes? She tried hard to be the perfect wife and mother, but she always felt something was missing.

No matter how they tried, things weren't well at home. Donald spent long days at the office, or on his new fishing boat. It was an elaborate boat. He'd hired a Captain to navigate the boat. He was becoming very rich and had often asked Dianne to sign papers. "It's for us. Just sign here," he'd say. Dianne never questioned him. She was taught to believe that the husband took care of everything.

*

On a dark foggy day, Min took the girls to the park, and then to her house for dinner. Dianne decided to drive to San Francisco and meet a friend for lunch, and later go to the San Francisco Museum of Contemporary Art.

At the museum, Dianne sat on a bench, studying *Woman In Hat*, Matisse's painting. The vibrant colors, indifference to rules, the lyrical brushstrokes, every-thing, inspired her. She took notes in her journal, carefully recording details about the painting. "*Paint what you feel, not what you see,*" she wrote.

She wandered through the over-heated rooms, taking notes on the Rothko paintings, De Kooning, the elegance of Barnett Newman, and other contemporary painters she'd never seen before. When she was looking at art, she felt a connection, an excitement that she'd never felt with people.

After she left the museum she drove to Chinatown, and parked her car near the cable car line. She walked along the bumpy streets cluttered with narrow crooked shops, with red slanted roofs, inhaling the delicious aromas of soy sauce, rice, Chow Mein, past open grocery stores with bins of fresh vegetables.

At a tiny shop she bought rubber spiders dangling from strings, and painted fans made of rice paper.

By then it was getting late, and she hurried along Grant to where her car was parked. When she saw Charley, she hid in a doorway. She watched him and a bawdy looking blonde woman wearing a fake leopard fur coat, cross the street, and enter the Red Dragon Restaurant. Mother had told her that she'd heard that Charley had bought a home on Russian Hill. Dianne took a deep breath, her heart beating fast. Seeing him brought the unfinished trauma to consciousness. Still, she didn't know why he married her, only to dump her.

She hurried to her car, wondering if the woman was Carol?

*

16

It was 1967, Saturday afternoon, and a late September day. Jenny was two years old, and Sara was going on five.

The sky was streaked like chalk, and the air was still, and warm for that time of year. Dianne and her friends were lounging by the swimming pool, watching their children play in the pool. Jenny bobbed in the water, a rubber seahorse attached to her small shoulders. And Sara, already a good swimmer, was throwing a beach ball to her friend Susie, the ball spinning in the stagnant iridescent air. Andy the pool man stood on the end of the pool, maneuvering a long pole with a net on the end of it, removing leaves and dead insects from the surface of the aqua blue water. His arms were bronzed, and his white hair was yellowed from the sun. Splashing children and their laughter echoed along the hills.

Dianne lit a cigarette, the smoke curling into the heat. Butterflies floated in the air, and the hills were full of wildflowers. The women, their bodies shiny from baby oil, were talking at once about recipes, their decorators, and the Vietnam War.

"Things are changing," said Misty Blumberg. "Women are going back to school, and to work."

"Women from the fifties were expected to marry, have babies, and never want anything again," Dianne said. She exhaled a slow white circle of smoke into the hot static air.

Between anointing their bodies with more baby oil, the women talked about Hadassah luncheons, Dr. Spock, and the

Kinsey Report. They chain smoked, and drank cokes in tall frosted glasses.

Dianne wondered if there was a world outside of this soapy perfect world? One that wasn't about only about Dr. Spock, Sara Lee pound cakes, all white nursery schools, pool parties, and diets? And would she ever not feel like she existed inside a box, peeking through a hole? So far she'd watched life from afar. She'd seen Kennedy shot on television, and the march at People's Park.

"Women are in psychological pain. They're chattels," said Beverly emphatically. Her mane of black wavy hair surrounded her tanned face, like a halo. She wore a white two- piece bathing suit.

"Benny! Don't go near the water!" screamed Misty Blumberg, rushing to the crying Benny. A pale sickly child, poor Benny was constantly crying. Misty had black hair cut in an "artichoke cut," and she wore Jackie O dark glasses that covered most of her small face.

"Warren wants me at home," said Polly, pressing her lips. She wore pink foam rollers on top of her head, her tanned thin arms shiny from baby oil.

"Donald! Don't go near the water!" screamed Toby Meyers, as she grabbed her screaming child, and then spanked him. His piercing screams invaded Dianne's reverie.

All at once children were crying, demanding cokes, a glass of water, a potty seat, a graham cracker, and various tearful demands.

"Catch! That's right," called Dolly, "Good boy!" The beach ball slowly revolved inside the iridescent stagnant air.

"I have to go pops!" screamed a three-year-old child.

A cigarette in one hand, Dianne jumped up, her rubber thongs slapping the wet cement, picking up towels and toys, shouting through her orange megaphone: "Everyone out of the pool! Lunch!"

Dianne passed on a tray, peanut butter and jelly sandwiches, and mini bags of chips, and cold drinks. The children sat on towels under the umbrella trees, eating. Except for the rattling of wax paper, and a coke can rolling on the hot cement it was quiet. A slight breeze caught the blossoms quietly drifting and covering the pale green lawns.

As the afternoon heat heightened, and there were less shadows, and sleepy children squabbled, Dianne called: "Nap time. Everyone home."

Sounds of the children's rebuttals and cries reverberated from the hills, as the station wagons drove away.

Suddenly, it was quiet. Only the sounds of the sprinklers could be heard.

Dianne put the girls down for their naps. Listening to the soothing sounds of the sprinklers, she sat underneath the apple tree, and read a book about Georgia O'Keefe.

When the girls woke and played on the lawns, and shadows dangled like games, it was time to prepare dinner.

When Donald came home, Dianne was on the patio setting the table. The girls sat on the merry –go-round that Harry had put together, spinning around the garden. By the scowl on his face, Dianne could tell that Donald was in a bad mood.

"Dianne, there's paint on my clothes—did you pick up the cleaning?"

She nodded. "Dinner is almost ready," she said, trying to smile.

"I had a hard day," he said, his voice rising. "Put the girls to bed," he ordered.

Not wanting to argue, Dianne took the sobbing children to their room. Jenny sobbed herself to sleep in her crib, and Sara dutifully got into her trundle bed, and looked at her beloved books. Dianne turned off the light, and kissed them goodnight.

Donald was at the barbecue cooking steaks, and smoke curled into the air. Jenny's pacifier tied by a string, lay on the grass. Dianne held it a moment, close to her heart, feeling a sudden sadness. Owls hooted from the valley below and the flowers lit the garden like jewels. Happy Valley was the most beautiful place on earth, but static. As if they were caught inside a photograph, and no one could get out.

"Steaks are ready," Donald said. He wore cutoff shorts, and his skin was very tanned. His hair was bleached from the sun.

A handsome man, Dianne thought.

At dinner, Dianne feigned interest in Donald, trying not to show her fury that he was drinking. She knew the routine and it always started with the economy. "I work hard for my money," Donald repeated, uncorking the second bottle of red wine. "You don't budget properly; you're not good with money," he said.

"I sell my paintings. I started a savings account, and I'll help pay the tuition. Earl said that a patron he knows is interested in buying *Childhood Box.*"

She felt the blow so hard she fell off the chair. Dazed, she held her swollen eye with her hand, a warm trickle of blood flowing from her nose.

"I've had it. You're a curse!" he yelled, with a sob.

He locked the bedroom door and she slept on the couch in the living room. An icepack on her eyes, most of the night she didn't sleep.

She felt sorry for Donald. Just as Charley had used her for something she didn't know, she'd married Donald on rebound, deluding herself that marriage would make her whole, would dissolve her past. She'd used denial well, learned it from her mother. Once again, she'd failed. When you're rejected you lose a piece of yourself.

Whatever had been between them left on their wedding night and just as on her wedding night with Charley he'd taken a piece of her. Never to be regained.

The crickets were loud. The sound of the horses and the valley lulled her to sleep.

In her dream she stood behind a tall door, watching her mother play Chopin's Minute Waltz, her pale artistic fingers floating over the keys. She moved closer to her and just as she touched her, she dissolved....

*

The seasons passed. As her paintings developed, she wanted to find more clues to herself. Who she really was.

Obsessively, she wrote in her journals, writing every detail of her life, crossing out words and replacing them with new words, new observations, and new images, trying desperately to reach deeper into herself and to find answers, and new questions. At times she felt as though there was a wall between her heart and her soul. To penetrate this wall, she drew constantly, pushing her line and her images to the utmost.

Between Jenny's naps, she went to the shed, and painted women diving into the ocean, or lying on rocks, or flying. She Often, when Min babysat the girls, she went to local gallery openings, studying the art, and dreaming of showing her work in a gallery. Earl had sent her a note, encouraging her to keep painting. He'd written: *" Every few years I meet one student who should take their art seriously. You are one. "*

Dianne saved that note. It was pasted in her journal.

A month ago, she'd received an announcement that Earl was having a show at a small San Francisco Gallery. Donald refused to let her go to the opening. But she wanted to see the show before it was taken down. So she'd asked Min to babysit the girls.

"I'll be home before dinner," she'd promised Donald.

The gallery was inside a swank building on Grant Avenue. It was full of light, the large room quiet like a church.

The receptionist was a young girl wearing a black mini skirt, black stockings, and high heel boots. A table was set with plastic glasses, and a young boy wearing black, served wine.

Dianne tiptoed into the main gallery, her heels clicking on the shiny parquet floors. Earl's paintings surprised her. Gone were the lithe nudes she'd seen before. The paintings were painted on small square boards. They were of odd female faces outlined in thick black paint, in the tradition of the German expressionists. The backgrounds of the paintings were in bright colors. One portrait of a young woman with sad eyes, sitting on a chair and looking straight ahead, moved her. Her face was featureless, but conveyed isolation, and a deep inner strength. "Transform all your feelings into your art," Earl always said.

. They were mature paintings, and Dianne wondered how many layers one must go through to achieve self-awareness? If the past could be obliterated?

She bought *Woman In Yellow*, for two hundred and fifty dollars. She wrote a check.

Because the show was would be taken down the next day, the receptionist wrapped the painting in brown thick paper tied by a thin string.

By the time she left the gallery, the day was turning dark. She had to get home before Donald arrived home. The painting under her arm, she hurried into Union Square Garage. She had to take the elevator to the fifth floor where her car was parked. When she got into the elevator she was stunned: Charley's sister Dorothy was the only person in the elevator.

"Hello, Dianne," Dorothy said. She was very tall, and exotic looking. She wore an expensive dark mink coat.

Dianne nodded.

"How are you, Dianne?"

"I'm fine. I'm married and I live in the country. I'm fine," she repeated.

"That's nice," Dorothy said in a patronizing tone.

The elevator wobbled slowly to the third level. She felt Dorothy's eyes on her, the elevator filled with their silence.

When the door opened, Dianne rushed to her car, and quickly got inside.

She turned on the motor, and cried, wanting to run back to Dorothy and demand to know why she and her parents left the wedding early? Had shunned her? To ask if they'd known exactly why Charley had married her?

She drove out of the garage, giving her ticket to the man in a tall partition, and then drove to Happy Valley. The car radio was on and the Supremes sang Baby, Baby, Baby.

That same night, after the girls were in bed, Donald and Dianne were watching Jerry Lewis. Donald was laughing.

He turned off the television then. "How was the show?" he asked, lighting his pipe.

He was in a good mood so Dianne decided to show him the painting she bought. "I'll show you."

She unwrapped the paper from the painting. "Look," she said, holding the painting to the light. "Isn't it ... wonderful? Earl is on his way up. It will be worth much more money soon."

His pipe made a whistling sound. "How much?"

"Two hundred and fifty dollars."

"You're kidding."

"It's ... an important painting. It's an investment."

"I do the investing!" he shouted. "Understand, pal? I'm cutting your allowance."

"I used my savings."

"Even worse. That school made you nuts. Do something worthwhile! Take the shit painting back tomorrow. It looks like one of Sara's drawings! Take it back immediately."

"It's mine. I earned it. I sold paintings to buy it. I'm keeping it."

He started yelling a diatribe of complains: she didn't take his shirts to the cleaners on time, her cooking was lousy, he couldn't trust her with the lawns and they were turning brown. "Your beatnik friends hang around our pool, eat our food. Bums."

She stood there, wanting to tell him that she hated him, that they had nothing in common, and that he treated her like a slave. But she was married to him forever, and if she did, what good would it do? They'd taken vows for life and this time it had to be true.

He got up. He held her face with both hands. She could see the pain in his eyes. "What makes you so cold? You're more excited about that shit painting then you ever are when I touch you. You're frigid. Charley was right."

"Stop mentioning Charley. You don't know what I went through. Stop it."

"Stop nothing. Everyone knows. I'm a laughing stock for marrying you. I should have listened."

He got into bed. "Get out. I want to sleep," he said.

Dianne went to the shed, following the light from the moon. There, she hung Earl's painting. At last she knew that she was an artist too and that she wanted to spend the rest of her life making art. When the owls hooted and the crickets burst a cacophony of sounds she closed the shed and hurried into the house.

By then Donald was snoring. Her back turned to his, she watched one star break loose and soar down the dark.

She closed her eyes, and slept.

*

It was 1968. Dianne had enough credits in school to transfer to a University. But Donald refused to pay tuition, and she still didn't have enough money to pay on her own. "You have children to raise," he said. "You wanted them. You raise them."

Determined to save enough money to transfer to San Francisco State University where she wanted to get a masters in Art History, she began going to galleries and asking the owners if she could sell art for them. Many gave her prints to take home on consignment, for a commission.

She set up a studio in her shed, and sent announcements that she was private dealing prints. Word spread and affluent women in Happy Valley came to the shed and bought prints for their homes. Dianne loved selling art. She also sold paintings by students she'd worked with. Soon, her business began to grow, as did her savings account.

"I don't want my wife working," Donald would protest. But she ignored his protests. Also, she exhibited her paintings in gift shops, and in small local galleries. She read everything she could about the growing art market and subscribed to all the art magazines. She used her savings to buy larger canvas, and art materials.

Though richer than ever, Donald doled out a modest allowance for groceries, household expenses and a few of the girl's needs. Min and Harry paid for the girl's private schools, and for most of their clothes. Never was there enough money for Donald. He hoarded his money, always citing, "A penny saved is another property bought."

Mike had given her a used Smith-Corona typewriter, and she'd started typing pages from her journals. She loved highlighting the areas of the journals about Charley, transforming them into scenes, and dropping the pages into a box.

At three, Jenny was a rambunctious active child. She went to the Happy Valley Nursery School, and Sara went into the first grade.

Dianne adored the girls. But Sara only responded affectionately to Min. What did she expect? She hadn't given Sara love? But it was different with Jenny. Dianne had hovered over her. At night, Jenny would climb into their bed. Donald complained that she had spoiled Jenny "rotten."

Donald bought a larger fishing boat called *The World* and got his Captains license. On weekends, he took his boat on long trips. His furniture stores had expanded and he'd bought more properties. Often Dianne signed papers, Donald murmuring, "It's for us. For the kids. I'm rich. But I'm going to get richer."

Dianne was selling more art and her client list was growing. When she could, she sent Mike cash. Her family was a mess: Mother leased an expensive Porsche for Bobbie. Poor Bobbie. He lived an unlived life, with no purpose, no education, nothing, but expensive clothes, and things. While Daddy complained incessantly about his rising "debts," he seemed withdrawn. Jewish men like Daddy didn't divorce their wives, but Dianne felt he was deeply troubled. Trapped.

Nannie had confided that Bobbie was taking heroin, and that Mother drove him to the Tenderloin, and waited in her Cadillac while Bobbie bought the heroin. "It's his medicine," Mother would explain. "He needs it for his old heart."

Dianne hated her mother for what she did to her sons. To live without education and purpose, and triumphs, is a dead end. To explain her mother, Dianne felt that her mother was mentally ill. But Dianne also knew that her mother was from a generation of women who didn't recognize mental illness.

It was a terrible year. Martin Luther King was assassinated and then Bobby Kennedy. This made Dianne determined to expand her world, and she joined a feminist group in Happy Valley. They met every two weeks to discuss the growing feminist movement, and the political unrest. A lot of the women were married, and protested life in the suburbs. Many did not believe in marriage. Dianne wasn't sure if she did either.

Life was changing. Some days Dianne felt misplaced, and yearned to live in the City.

*

17

It was a scorching August day, and Sara's sixth birthday. Dianne invited the family for a swim and barbecue. Early that morning, wanting everything perfect for her mother, Dianne hosed the patio, making sure that everything was clean. It had to be, or Mother would be furious.

The girls, wearing matching pink floral sun suits, hats, and white sandals, were in the driveway, eagerly awaiting the family. From the speakers Donald had set around the pool, the Rolling Stones sang. Mother had said that Nannie wasn't feeling well, that she had "the flu," and wouldn't be there.

Sara was riding her new bicycle around the driveway, ringing the bell on the handlebars, and Jenny was riding her Crazy Car, a wooden car with huge red and white striped wooden wheels. Donald, wearing a Harvard tee shirt, and cut-off jeans, kneeled at the barbecue, preparing the coals for the spareribs and steaks. A haze of black smoke floated over the gardens.

Past noon, Harry and Min's station wagon, followed by Mother's Cadillac, chuggled up the hill. The cars stopped at the far end of the driveway.

Two giant-size teddy bears were tied to the top of Harry's car. Jenny ran so fast her sandal caught on a rock, and she fell. She was screaming and Sara was blowing a large gold whistle hanging from a long cord around her neck.

"Christ!" shouted Donald, waving his arms. "Dianne. Don't just stand there! Get a Band-Aid! Make her stop screaming!"

The cars parked. Doors opened and slammed, cameras clicked, and trunks opened, disclosing pink pastry boxes, toys, and brightly wrapped packages. Harry, a cigar dangling from his mouth, held the two huge teddy bears. "Look what papa brought you!" he shouted. Everyone was kissing everyone at once.

"Welcome to Happy Valley," Dianne said, giving her Mother a quick kiss. She wore a beige linen dress, beige pumps, and her dark gold hair was set in waves close to her head. Her hand waved the air, as if waving aside bugs.

Dianne's father looked tired. His face was tanned but his arms were thin and white. A Nikon camera dangled from a strap around his neck. Bobbie had gained a lot of weight. He wore tan shorts, loafers and argyle socks to his knees. His face was as white as his bare legs and his small mouth was pressed tight. He held his tape recorder, and seemed uncomfortable.

"God, it's hot!" Mother complained, her pale hand waving away a tiny bug. "Dianne, you should always have bug spray."

"Give papa a kiss," said Harry. He wore maroon pants and white shoes and a big straw hat. He carried a pink cake box.

"Harry! Put the cake in the shade," said Min. "It cost a fortune!" She wore a shocking pink sundress with a heart cut out in the middle, and high-heel pink clogs.

"I want the rose!" said Sara.

"My rose," Jenny said, crying again.

"Christ! Put her down for a nap," Donald said, back at the barbecue.

The girls sat on the lawn, opening gifts.

"Dianne, you're too tan," Mother whispered, with a frown. "You're going to ruin your skin. You mark my words ... and you need a better bra, you bobble."

"Let Papa Lou take pictures!" instructed Donald.

"Stand straight," ordered Daddy.

Jenny stood rigid, sobbing. Her arms were stiffly at her sides. A bee perched on her nose.

"Come to Grandma, my piece of face," crooned Min to Sara who wanted to go swimming.

Finally everyone settled in chaise lounges around the pool. Min changed the girls into their bathing suits, and the girls happily went into the pool.

Sara was showing off her swimming lessons, and Jenny floated on a rubber raft with an umbrella on top. Harry sat on a chair next to the pool, applauding and repeating, "Some kid. Smart kids. My boy is some provider." While Daddy slept on a chaise under a tree, a newspaper on his head, his arms dangling over the sides. Frowning and complaining that the patio was "dirty," Mother swept leaves into a plastic bin. While Bobbie sat on a chair under the tree, recording everyone. Dianne felt sorry for him. He'd never been away from mother---gone to camp, had friends. Mother was always insisting that he had an "old heart," or that he might have a "brain tumor." Constantly he was going through medical procedures.

Donald kneeled at the barbecue, preparing the grill. Min sat at the edge of the pool, repeating, "You can never watch them enough."

"Some place the kids have here! Donald's a moneymaker," Harry said to no one. "Donald tell the new sick joke you told me."

"Okay, Dad, that's enough!" Donald said. He dropped ice into a glass, and poured scotch. Then he sat next to his father, drinking, and telling princess jokes, Harry laughing before the punch line.

"Donald, play the horn. You should hear the kid play!" shouted Harry.

Sara sat on the edge of the pool eating a Popsicle and crying because Donald had yelled at her. Daddy slept, and Bobbie stayed near Mother.

When the heat subsided and shadows played over the lawns, the barbecue was ready.

"Steaks are ready," Donald said. He plaed a platter of ribs and steaks on the table Dianne had set under the awning.

The girls exhausted from the day, sat on telephone books, while Min cut their meat.

After Dianne cleared the table, she carried the Mary Poppins birthday cake to the table and everyone sang Happy Birthday Dear Jenny.

"I want the rose, "Sara called.

"I want it," Jenny said, her face red from the sun.

Deer rustled in the bushes and the sound of Baba cantering along the quiet dark hills echoed over the impending night. It was time to go, Daddy said. He had an early flight the next morning.

"Daddy, I want to show you my studio—what I'm doing at school."

Quickly, he followed her up the steps.

When Dianne turned on the lights they made a popping sound. The studio smelled of turpentine. Her collection of dried leaves were in baskets arranged on a long wooden table next to the miniature hand painted boxes she collected in China Town. Her collection of movie scripts that her father had sent were arranged by alphabetical order on the built in shelves. Her large paintings leaned along the walls. Several hung above the table.

"Your boxes are marvelous," Daddy said exuberantly looking at the papier-mâché box poked with holes. Smaller music boxes dangled from rubber cords she'd found at construction sites.

He studied her sketches, and then the paintings. His hands were folded behind his back and she could sense that he was impressed.

He turned and looked at her, wistfully.

"Pursue your education. Never stop learning. And don't listen to your mother," he said, lowering his voice. 'She doesn't... understand. You're a talented artist."

He paused. "I'm leaving in the morning for Los Angeles, but I'll be in San Francisco on Wednesday. We'll have lunch at Joes. Noon?"

"Yes. I'll drive to San Francisco," Dianne said eagerly. "It's a date"

He glanced at his watch. He looked sad. She wanted to tell him she adored him, that he was her hero. That she knew Charley had devastated him, but that she was fine, and knew where she was going.

"Time to go," he said.

Before he got into the car, she hugged him again, and this time he held her close. It was the happiest day of her life. More than anything she wanted to establish a close relationship with her father.

When the last car descended the driveway, Dianne felt as though she were watching them disappear forever. But she was especially happy that she and her father were meeting on Wednesday. She'd tell him then that he had provided structure, and a work ethic for her and she wouldn't let him down.

The following tuesday afternoon, Dianne was in the kitchen, making sugar cookies. The girls were home from school, in the playroom, and Dianne could hear Jenny's favorite Mary Poppins records playing. When she saw Donald's truck ascend the driveway she was surprised. Most days lately, he never came home before nine pm. It was only three p.m.

The kitchen door banged open. Donald stood still, his unlit pipe in his hand, as if a prop to hold on to.

"Hello. You're here early. I made a meatloaf. We'll have dinner early tonight—they say it might rain. I 'm tired of the heat. I'm making Nannie's sugar cookies…"

He moved closer.

"Your father passed away."

She stared at his face, making sure he wasn't telling one of his sick jokes. She felt as if the floor slipped from under her and she held on to the kitchen counter. She held on tight. Her world just collapsed.

"He couldn't have—he was here on Sunday. We're having lunch on Wednesday at Joes. Noon, he said. He couldn't have."

"He was at the Brown Derby in LA, today, at a business luncheon. His manager said he suddenly slumped over and that was it. It was quick."

Donald lit his pipe. She watched the sweet-smelling smoke rise.

"He couldn't have," she repeated. Shock stopped all emotions. All she could think about was that the meatloaf was burning, and that Sara needed to take her asthma medicine.

"Get dressed," Donald said. "My mother is on her way to take the girls to her house. The funeral is tomorrow. Your mother wants it that way."

An hour later, Dianne and Donald arrived at her mother's house. Florists were delivering flower arrangements. Many cars were parked in front of the house.

The door was open. Mother, like a hostess, wearing a beige dress, greeted the steady flow of Daddy's colleagues from Universal, friends, and relatives. "So sorry Honey. Lou was the greatest," they murmured.

Dianne quickly held her mother tight. "I'm sorry, Mother. So sorry." Mother kept her arms by her sides. "Dianne. Put on some lipstick. You look like death took a holiday. There are a lot of important people here." She turned and hugged one of Daddy's friends.

Dianne found Nannie in the kitchen, helping Birdie, and the array of caterers from Nate's Delicatessen. She placed cold meats on silver platters. Caterers carved turkeys and roast beefs. Nannie looked devastated. She'd adored Daddy.

"Oy, your poor father. Your mother's spending and Bobbie's shenanigans, put him in the grave."

The rest of that day went in a fog. Dianne couldn't believe her father was gone. Over and over again she recalled her father lying on a chaise lounge under a tree and a newspaper over his head.

Little had she known that day was the last day she'd ever see him. One never knows when one's last day is, but she felt that her father had sensed his time was near and that was why he wanted to be closer.

More people flowed into the house. Relatives she had never liked and had hardly seen hugged her. Bobbie wearing a dark formal suit, held his tape recorder, recording pieces of conversations. Mike wearing his old beat up navy suit, stayed in the background. Sadness in his dark darting eyes. Daddy had never been close to Mike.

Donald made drinks at the bar. With each drink he made, he told a joke.

After a while, Dianne and Donald drove home. On the way they didn't say a word.

That night Dianne dreamed she was waltzing with her father.

The next day Dianne and Donald arrived at Mt. Sinai for the funeral.

Daddy lay in an open coffin lined in puffy pink satin. He wore one of his custom gray suits, and a nice navy Sulka tie with tiny white dots patterned on it, His lovely hands were folded on his chest. He looked as though he were sleeping. Dianne stood there, trying not to breathe too loud, feeling somewhat odd that she was looking at her father's face so closely. She felt as though she were invading his privacy.

The coffin was surrounded by huge wreaths of flowers and the air was muggy and still. As if death had a special privacy. As she bent over the coffin, holding her breath and looking at her father, she wondered why she didn't feel grief? Or maybe grief is not feeling it?

She touched his hand. Just the top where a few dark hairs curled along the slim knuckles. The skin was cold like granite, and she pulled her hand away. A red gash was on his forehead where he'd fallen, when he had died. She was afraid he'd wake, and see her staring at him. He'd say "Dianne. Do you have a handkerchief? All young ladies carry a handkerchief."

Behind a faded velvet curtain, the family sat on wobbly folding chairs. One by one, Daddy's colleagues from Universal, men with slick hair, wearing pin stripe suits, paid their condolences; they whispered to Mother. "Lou was a prince."

Bobbie sat next to Mother. His face was pinched like that of an old man. He snapped a thick rubber band around his wrist. Nannie wore a black veil held by two black thin bobby pins. Birdie pressed a large handkerchief to her small withered face. Mike sat in the back.

After the Rabbi spoke, a lovely woman wearing a big hat with silk roses on the brim, gave a eulogy. She praised Lou Roseman for his work at *Variety* and his special work for blind babies. She was president of a garden club and presented the "Lou Roseman" rose; a delicate peach-colored rose that she'd planted in the park. As she spoke Dianne recalled when she was eleven and lost the sight in her right eye. She'd had a detached retina and the doctors didn't have proper treatment. How upset her father had been. Since she refused to think about it.

And then it was over and Mother asked everyone back to the house.

A long black limousine drove the family to the cemetery. There, they stood in the light drizzle while Daddy's coffin was placed inside a marble wall. Fountains spurted water and Dianne shuddered at the gardeners digging fresh graves, and coffins being placed in walls.

Back at Mother's house, hundreds of people came to pay their respects. Daddy's golf partners, poker groups, colleagues paid their condolences to Mother who stood regally in the hallway, her scented handkerchief dangling from her pale hand, murmuring, "Thank you. Lou loved you too."

Not once had Dianne seen her mother cry. If anything she was trying to comfort Daddy's colleagues with tears in their eyes, told little stories about Daddy's golf, or poker games.

Nannie stood at the dining table, helping Birdie and the caterers serve the growing crowd. While Bobbie stole change from the coat pockets hanging on metal coat racks in the hallway, and Mike stuffing sterling ashtrays in his oversize pockets.

The relatives sat in rented chairs set along the wall, eating.

"No wonder Lou died. His son is a goniff," Uncle Maury said to no one, stuffing potato salad into his mouth. "The kids gave Lou trouble."

Fat Susan and her husband, a cardiologist, bragged about their art collection. "We know what we like," Fat Susan said. Their three-year-old daughter "Missy" rode a toy truck with big wooden wheels, screaming "Poo Poo!"

"The doctors opened him, closed him," Uncle Buddy was saying with a double shrug. He looked as if he were about to cry.

"He don't know the difference!" Uncle Maury shouted.

"Don't scream Maury!" said Aunt Pearl in her mans' voice. "Put on your hearing aid."

"Dumb fuck," Bobbie murmured under his breath, taping the conversations.

"Lou said you paint, Dianne," said cousin Zoe. "He was very proud of you."

"We bought a Pollack print. Lavender Mist," said fat Susan's husband. He popped a nut into his mouth.

"Mist, schmist!" said Uncle Maury. "He gets plenty for his mist!"

"Poo poo!" screamed Missy.

"Susan take her potty!" said her husband.

Wanting to be alone, Dianne went upstairs, her knees weak as she hurried along the familiar hall.

Her parent's bedroom was painted beige. Beige silk bedspreads were smoothed tight on the antique twin beds. Daddy's pillow was already removed, and the plastic covers on the beige headboards made a crinkling sound.

On the nightstand next to his bed, the book *Nixon* was open. His reading glasses were on their side. Dianne touched the glasses, wanting to touch him.

In the closet he shared with Mother, she touched his custom-tailored suits, inhaling his special scent. Poor Daddy. He'd worked hard all his life and never bought a red sports car. He'd chased the American dream, providing Mother with a lifestyle he couldn't afford. His electric shoe polisher was on the floor next to the neat rows of his expensive shiny shoes. A tie rack held his Sulka ties.

She opened the top drawer of the double built in dresser. Mother's stiff girdles were neatly rolled next to a pile of wire bras. Their rubbery smell mixed with her scent. Oddly, out of order, in the second drawer were loose photographs ready to paste into her many albums. A blue spiral notebook, the kind you buy in dime stores, was neatly labeled 'Miriam Roseman's Diary. Dianne read the first page: '*I was born April 19th, 1913, the daughter of Edith and Fred Scheideman. I can only recall one day at the circus, in my father's arms and then one day I never saw him again.*

She read pages of beautiful writing, descriptions of music salons on Sundays, and fun loving uncles who lived with them. It was her Great Grandparent's house. "*A grand house,*" Mother wrote.

Dianne closed the diary and put it back exactly as it was. Then she opened her father's drawer, noting the neat pile of monogrammed handkerchiefs. She held one to her face. She recalled the day Charley took her home, the pain in her father's eyes, and thereafter the pain in his silence.

She put the handkerchief in her pocket and went downstairs. It was time to go home.

Downstairs, she said goodbye to Nannie. "I'll see you soon."

"Oy, your mother needs me now. Your poor father. He left a mess in this house. Dianne, you don't know the half. A mess," she repeated.

She found her mother standing by the window, in the living room. She held a large brown paper bag. Confusion lay in her eyes.

"The coroner brought your father's gorgeous suit in a bag. A paper bag, Dianne."

She blinked several times.

"We had an argument the night before he went to Los Angeles. I was angry with him for traveling so much. An argument," she said again, biting her lower lip.

"I—I just want you to know, I'm here for you, that I love you, Mother."

Mother blinked several times.

"Put some lipstick on, Dianne. That white lipstick makes you look like death took a holiday. Your father thought so too. Your husband is waiting. We'll talk tomorrow." Then she turned to talk with a guest.

That night Dianne dreamed she was inside a glass bubble, slowly dropping through darkness and landing on a meadow of tiny lilac flowers and rainbows exploding and she went looking for her father. She wanted to find him. To tell him that he'd meant everything to her. He was her foundation. Please let me find him, she said as she hurried along the meadow ....

*

Mike opened Mike's Antiques, a tiny store in the Haight. Dianne spent more time in her studio. She painted an oil portrait of her father's face. She drove to her mother's house, and gave her the portrait. Dianne leaned it against the wall.

"He looks dead," Mother said with a frown. "He doesn't have blue hair! Take it away!"

"It's an impression of Daddy. Of his essence."

"It's freaky. Your dress is too short, Dianne. You're too old to wear such a short dress."

Dianne missed her father so much and she realized, he was the one man she'd loved. But she'd also loved him from a far. What was sad was that he'd died broke, leaving huge gambling debts. To keep her house, Mother and Nannie were sewing beautiful silk and velvet tablecloths, and selling them to Rhoda's Gift Shop.

Bobbie was running up debts and smashing cars and charging expensive clothes in expensive shops. Mother gave him money to go to expensive restaurants. "The poor boy. He needs some fun," she'd say. Dianne would never understand her mother's devastating parenting. Only doom and failure was left for the boys.

Mike was arrested by the feds for selling marijuana behind his store. Mother didn't have the money for a good lawyer and so he was sent to Lompoc Prison for three years. Mother never mentioned him except to say, "Mike is away."

Dianne was glad that her father didn't live to see the deterioration of his sons. Though she believed that he had known what was going on.

It was afternoon. The girls were at Min's house and would be home soon. Daddy's death had exacerbated her anger at Charley. More than ever, she wanted to avenge her father and to prove Charley's deception. When did Carol move to Chicago? Dianne wondered. And why?

This question bothered her. Donald checked the phone bills, underlining her calls. So that afternoon. Dianne drove to a phone booth and dialed Charley's San Francisco office.

"Berkowitz & Sons," answered a woman's curt voice.

"Hello. I'm looking for a secretary named Carol? She used to work there? I'm a relative."

"You want Carol Moore. She moved to Chicago, in 1960," the woman replied.

"Could I have her number? I'm trying to locate her?"

In a few minutes, the woman gave her a number in Chicago. "It's the last number we have of hers."

Dianne jotted the number, thinking 1960 was the time she and Charley had married.

The phone call on her wedding night—the next morning—could it be?

She dropped several dimes in the phone, and dialed Carol's number. After several rings, a man answered.

"Is Carol there?" she asked.

"She's busy. Who's calling?"

Dianne felt panic and she hung up. She was shaking.

She drove home.

The following days she couldn't stop thinking about Carol. Why had she moved before they were married? Something had gone on, something that Charley had needed from her. But she had to stop. Her migraines were worse. She'd been depressed. She called her friend and neighbor Shirley. She loved Shirley who was older and divorced. She had children and sold real estate. They'd often talked about many things, and Shirley was sympathetic to Dianne's confessions that she was depressed. Shirley gave her the name of Dr. Stockford in San Francisco.

Not wanting Donald to know, Dianne took the money she'd saved and placed it in an envelope. Then she called Dr. Stockford and made an appointment.

*

18

She arrived at Dr. Stockford's office in the Height Ashbury. Pretty hippie girls, barefoot with flowers in their hair, lounged on the park lawns. Dianne parked her car on a hill, and then she hurried along a narrow cobblestone street.

Dr. Stockford's office was in a blue Victorian with white trim. She rang a bell, and the door opened.

Up a narrow staircase, at the top, there was a reception room with stained glass windows. The ceilings were high and faded Persian rugs covered the wood plank floor. Several ferns inside macramé baskets, dangled from the ceiling. Paintings that appeared to be painted by patients, hung from the pale yellow walls.

Dianne sat on a wicker chair, holding her purse. A red light flickered on the wall, and a door opened. A somber looking boy about twenty, rushed past the reception room, and ran down the stairs.

Dianne lit a cigarette, exhaling nervous streams of smoke. Soon, a tall, lanky, pale man with long, tan hair, wearing leather boots, and jeans, came into the room.

"I'm Dr. Stockford." He extended a thin hand. He had intelligent gray eyes. He wore a beautiful Navajo Indian bracelet on his thin wrist, and a large turquoise ring on one finger.

Dianne followed him along a narrow hallway, into his office.

It was a large room. Sunlight streamed from the skylights, and sunlight dropped flickering bars along the large Persian rug. Ferns dangled from hanging macramé nets.

Dianne sat in a brown leather chair, and Dr. Stockford sat across from her. She took a cigarette from her silver cigarette case.

Quickly he rose, and lit it with a flat silver lighter.

"Thank you," she said.

"An ashtray, and a box of Kleenex are next to you," he said with a smile.

He crossed his long legs, and lit a thin brown cigarette.

"I like your plants," Dianne said after a long silence. "So healthy looking—my plants die. I like roses mostly. Plants die on me," she repeated. "Things—die. People die."

He sat very still, his intelligent eyes on her face.

"I don't have a green thumb," she continued nervously. "I don't take care of things so well. For days, I didn't change Sara's cat Anny's litter box—I ignored Sara. I knew she was unhappy but I gave her away to my mother-in-law. Men don't love me. They leave."

He nodded, his eyes riveted on her face, and on her hands as she moved them back and forth.

After a long moment, she said: "I've never been to a shrink. My dreams are –strange."

"How are they strange?"

"Well, I float a lot, and I'm always holding a gun." She laughed nervously. "Anyway, it's just a dream. A stupid dream."

"What makes you angry?"

"Charley."

He nodded. Waited.

"Anyway, when I was barely twenty, and a virgin, I married Charley. He was the town catch. On my wedding night, he wouldn't … have sex with me. He took me home two days after our wedding. He made a mistake, he'd said … then he got an annulment on the grounds that I was frigid. My mother blamed me. Everyone blamed me."

She lit another cigarette, her hand shaking. "Maybe I am ... frigid. My husband says I am. I don't feel anything during sex. I don't feel my feelings. My husbands lay in my dreams like dead soldiers. I don't feel anything much."

She held a Kleenex, rolling it into a ball. Silences made her nervous.

"In my dreams, I kill Charley. It feels good. I avenge my father." She paused until the feeling she'd cry, passed. "Not that I would kill Charley, "but it's how I feel. Not that I would. No, of course I— wouldn't."

He put out his cigarette in a metal ashtray.

"He messed me up. I'm always wondering what is wrong with me. I'm like one of those broken dolls you glue up. It's fine as long as it sits on a satin pillow."

A red light clicked on the wall.

She dabbed her eyes with the Kleenex. She didn't talk and she wouldn't look at him staring at her.

"I'm afraid your time is up," he said after a long silence.

He opened a brown leather book. "I want to work with you. Help find the real you. We have a lot of work to do. It's like peeling back an onion, layer by layer. You've been through a lot. To start, I want to see you twice a week."

He smiled, as if reassuring her. He turned the pages in his date book. "Next week, same time."

"I don't know how to pay. My husband Donald won't pay. He doesn't believe in … shrinks. If I told him he'd be … furious. But I sell my paintings and I'll pay on installments. I have some cash today."

He smiled. "We'll work out a payment plan. I don't want you to worry about money now. It's important. Let's talk about making some appointments."

*

The winter was cold. Red berries vividly surrounded the driveway like jewelry.

Twice a week, Dianne hired a babysitter and drove to San Francisco to see Dr. Stockford. She found therapy exciting and painful, but she felt herself slowly more aware of her feelings, and motivations. She realized that though she wasn't in love with Donald, and never had been, she'd treated Donald with cold indifference; exactly what Charley had done to her. "You didn't know what love is. You never experienced it at home," Dr. Stockford had said.

Therapy was like an enormous jigsaw puzzle and she'd only started putting together a few pieces. The journey into the self is a long and arduous one and filled with cluttered dreams and murky images. Often she found herself in her past, watching herself and horrified by her actions. She didn't want to be that person. But the past doesn't lie. If only she could pass her past and become as she wanted to be.

Dr. Stockford encouraged her to paint. "There, you'll see your truths," he'd urged.

At home she tried hard to be more attentive to Donald. At times it felt like she was trying to be someone else, squeezing out new words and new actions. When he'd be moody-angry, she didn't react, instead she'd bake a cake he liked, or took extra time with her appearance. She'd even invited him into her studio and smoking his pipe, he'd looked quietly at her work. But as time went on he was home less and less. He spent most of his time on his boat and with his horses.

He bought three thousand acres in Concord and was excited about starting a horse ranch.

"It's fabulous," he said. "Sign your name on the marked pages. This is for us, Dianne. For our family."

The next afternoon, Dianne was in her studio, working on a painting. The girls were at Min's house for the weekend and Dianne planned on catching up with classes and her work. She'd doubled up on classes so she would graduate the following year and she wanted to catch up on work, graduate and get her BA at the end of the year.

Quickly, with her spatula, Dianne scraped the layers of white paint until light shone through the surface of the canvas. Next, she dipped a large brush into turquoise color paint, dragging the brush along the six-foot canvas and letting the paint flow over the woman lying on grass. She wanted to capture the woman's solitude and at the same time the beauty of the landscape. As she worked, owls hooted and deer scrambled in and out of the bushes. *Let the emotions follow the line,* Earl had said. She'd seen the paintings of Joan Mitchell and had been greatly inspired by her use of color. She worked faster now. She wanted to somehow input more emotions into the figures of the women, but she felt as though her emotions were stuck. As if they lagged behind.

Donald's pickup truck rattled anxiously along the long driveway. She stopped working, and quickly locked the creaky wood door and hurried past the pool, to greet him.

"Christ Dianne! Do I always have to trip on some goddamned toy?" he growled, throwing Jenny's favorite doll, the battery hanging out of its back in coils. "I want to eat soon. I'm leaving at five a.m. to go on my boat."

During dinner, Donald seemed distracted. After dinner, he moved boxes some boxes to his truck.

Late that night, she tiptoed into her bedroom. Donald was already sleeping. The television was on mute and its light flickered circles of light. She turned off the television and slipped into bed. Quickly, she slipped into sleep.

At dawn, she awakened. Donald, wearing a plaid woolen shirt, tall rubber fishing boots, stood by the bed. The light was barely up and the night fading. "Oh…I didn't hear you. I …"

He stroked her hair, looking at her with the gentlest expression. He kissed her lightly on the lips. "Take care of yourself, Princess."

And then he hurried from the room.

The rest of the day she was busy. Later Dianne planned on picking up the girls and bring them home for dinner.

Near evening, after going to a local gallery and bringing home a portfolio of new prints to sell, she stopped at the Happy Valley Bakery to pick up Donald's favorite angel food cake.

By the time she arrived home it was turning dark. She went into the kitchen to prepare dinner. Min would bring the girls home soon.

She noticed a note taped to the front of the refrigerator. She pulled it off and read: *Dear Dianne, I'm not coming back. Get a lawyer, Donald.*

She was stunned. Quickly, her mind flashed to that morning, when he'd said, *take care of yourself, Princess.* The past two days that the girls were at Min's house, Min never had called. Then Donald had seemed distracted; it dawned on her that the day Min had picked up the girls for their visit, she had helped them pack extra things. "We're going to be very busy," Min had said, stuffing their clothes into a larger suitcase.

Dianne ran into her bedroom and opened the closets. Donald's clothes were gone. She opened his dresser and the drawers empty—his things gone from the bathroom.

Had she been in such denial that she hadn't noticed that the night before he'd moved boxes into his truck? Nothing was left of his, except some pipes.

She held on to the side of the sink, dizzy, wobbling on her feet. The day before she'd signed several papers. Just sign your name," he'd said impatiently, shaking the pages. Not to mention what she'd signed the past years.

Panic overcame her, realizing that she'd spent her savings paying Dr. Stockford and Donald hadn't given her, her allowance. As soon as possible she needed money for groceries.

She called the bank where she and Donald had their accounts. She asked to speak to the manager. After a long moment the manager came to the phone. She asked what her balance was.

"Insufficient funds," he snapped coldly. "Mr. Perlman closed your account."

Before she could say anything he hung up.

Shaking, she called Donald's office. His father answered. "Harry, I need to talk to Donald."

"He's not here," he said, coldly.

"I don't have money, Harry. I need money for groceries, and for the girls."

"Tell your lawyer!" He banged the receiver down.

Next, she called Min. When she answered, Dianne told her she'd pick up the girls. "I want them home, please Min."

Min hung up on her. She'd heard Jenny crying in the background.

Not knowing what to do next, she called her friend and neighbor Shirley Maxwell. Dianne told her exactly what had happened and by then she was hysterical.

"Dianne. You need a lawyer immediately. Call Cha Cha Berman. She's my divorce lawyer and a ball buster. She got me the max alimony. She won't let the bastard get away with what he's doing. She'll get the kids back immediately."

As soon as she hung up, Dianne called the lawyer's office, and made an appointment for the next morning.

Outside of the cake she'd bought, she hadn't any food in the house. She decided to go to the Happy Valley market where she had a charge account. Until she got money, she'd stock up on food.

She rushed to her car, glad she'd filled her gasoline tank earlier that day.

It was raining. She drove slowly on the slippery roads. When she arrived at the market she took her time, filling her basket with canned goods, frozen dinners, fresh produce, packages of spaghetti, and household items she needed.

At the check-in counter, the clerk who'd helped her for years bagged the groceries, all the while chatting about the rain. The total came to two hundred and five dollars. "Just charge it," Dianne said breezily.

"Of course, Mrs. Perlman. I'll take the groceries to your car."

He helped load her car with the boxes of groceries. He slammed the trunk shut.

"Thank you, Roger," she said.

"Sure thing, Mrs. Perlman."

But just as she was about to drive off, he came running to the window. His face was very red. "I'm sorry Mrs. Perlman. I have to take the groceries back. My boss said Mr. Perlman closed your account."

She pressed the button so the windows went up, placed her foot on the gas pedal, and before he could say anything more, she drove out of the parking lot to the freeway, not turning around as she heard Roger yelling for her to stop.

She drove faster, furious now, and telling herself that no matter what, she'd get the girls home.

*

"Schmuck!" said Cha Cha Berman the next morning. She exhaled a thick layer of smoke, looking at a sheaf of papers. "Stop crying. He can't take the children. I'll have them home by tonight."

"We've been married almost eleven years. He can't do this without taking care of the children."

She sighed heavily. "Henny penny the sky is falling. This morning I ran a check on him. His assets are listed under his corporation and he's the only owner listed. Last year, he mortgaged the house so he'll look poor, kick you out, and then buy back the house. Fuck his phony tax records! He owns millions of dollars worth of properties all bought after you were married. Shit! What did you sign? Don't you read? You signed away everything."

"He said they were properties he bought after we married. For years, I signed papers. I thought I—"

"Hey, it's 1970! The women's movement. A man landed on the moon. Marjorie Morningstar is old news! These Jewish princes graduate from potty training to Harvard to Mommy! Learn to be smart. Smart is in for women. Haven't you heard?"

Dianne lit a cigarette, sheepishly shaking her head. Cha Cha was about forty, with short red hair and suspicious dark eyes. Everything about her was decisive, even the way she lit a cigarette, quickly, then snapping her light back into place. Her desk was covered with folders, empty coffee cups, and packages of Marlboro cigarettes. Law degrees from Stanford were displayed on the wall behind her desk.

"For God's sake, now lay low. I'll try to get temporary alimony. I'll find out who his lawyer is. "Get a job. Show that you're poor, and that you need money. Work, eat, sleep. You've been married ten years, you're, going on thirty-one, have two kids. Hey. I'm going for the jugular vein. Big alimony, property, lawyer fees! I'll get the schmuck on income tax evasion!"

As if remembering Dianne was there, she lit another cigarette, her cheeks puffing out as she exhaled the smoke. Anti-war buttons were pinned on the lapel of her tobacco-stained jacket.

"So Dianne... my love, where were we?" She sipped coffee from a yellow cup stained by red lipstick. "I can't stress enough to lay low ... be a good girl until the *interlocutory* is over. Which means for six months, you *don't* do anything. He'll use anything you do wrong."

Dianne nodded.

"Shit!! You pretty princesses with tits haven't learned there's no rainbow in a man's penis. Don't you know men are worthless? Get a job! Take responsibility for yourself! Stop sniveling! I'll set the dogs on the Perlmans. Your girls will be returned today! Now go home, be a good girl. Be smart."

Two evenings later Min brought the girls home. Dianne waited in the driveway and when Min's station wagon stopped in the driveway, Jenny jumped from the car and ran into Dianne's arms. Dianne held her to her heart, kissing her full cheeks, whispering that she loved her. Min and Sara stood by the car, Min holding Sara's hand, and talking softly to her. Frowning, Sara walked hesitantly towards Dianne.

"Sara. I'm so glad you're home. I love you, Sara." Tears ran down Dianne's face, but Sara walked past her, carrying her pink ballet bag, into the house. Min placed their bags in the driveway. Although Min was dressed fastidiously, every hair in place, there were circles under her eyes and she looked sad.

"Min, thank you."

"I don't want you to take them away from me." Min's lip quivered.

"Of course not. They love you."

"Dianne. You did wrong by my son. During the years he told me *everything*. You used him. But I love the girls. I'll be here when you need me."

Dianne watched her get into her car, wobbling slightly, and then drive away.

*

The valley was cold and the dark came early. Dianne got a job at *Mendelsons Furs*, a shop near her house and from eight till five she was selling furs to affluent ladies in Happy Valley. Donald didn't send temporary alimony, but she had new clients and was selling art. She studied the rising art market and familiarized herself with galleries in San Francisco.

She'd hired Terecita, an older woman to babysit the girls. Desperately, Dianne tried to be closer to Sara but it was too late; to Sara, Min was her mother. Just as Nannie had always felt like her mother, Dianne sadly.

Dianne hated her job, lugging fur coats into the fitting rooms, aware of Mr. Mendelson's beady eyes watching her every move. "Sell, sell, sell," he'd say, patting her hip.

Thursday afternoon Dianne was on her lunch break in the "employees lounge," really the boiler room. She sat on a canvas wobbly chair, eating her chopped olive sandwich. She ate fast as she only had thirty-five minutes for lunch. The sales ladies sat on deck chairs, their shoes off, and their swollen feet resting on boiler pipes. While they ate, they compared sales, commissions and complaining about their long hours and small pay. Some days Dianne's headaches were so bad she'd go into the bathroom and press cold paper towels to her throbbing forehead.

"Dianne, you look tired," said Miriam, in a thick German accent. She was an older lady who'd worked at the furriers for almost thirty years. She was about sixty-six, wiry thin, with bright red curly hair and dark brown tired eyes She'd been a victim in the holocaust, and often showed the numbers burned into her arm. Dianne admired the pride she took in her work-- the careful way she'd hang the fur coats, her red hands lovingly smoothing the fur. She carried her book of clients with her everywhere. "My livelihood is here. I'll get a pension," she said proudly. She made huge commissions.

"Dianne will get a huge divorce settlement and then forget us," said Zoe Klein. Her gray hair was arranged in a chignon, her gaunt face too rouged. She wore support hose for her varicose veins. She still hoped to find love. "And he'll buy me one of these fur coats," she said.

"Dianne is pretty and young," Miriam said wistfully. "She still has a chance for love."

"I don't want any more men," Dianne said.

"Don't bank on a man for anything," advised Mildred Nickels. She wrapped the rest of her chopped egg sandwich and put it in a bag. She was a widow and had worked there ten years. Everyday she wore the same black dress, and her gold wedding band. She was a top saleswoman.

Dianne was struck by the ladies' pride, and work ethic. She admired that they worked hard and earned a steady paycheck.

A bell rang. It was time to go back to work. Dianne put her shoes back on, slipping her blistered feet into the plain black pumps that Mr. Mendelson insisted she wear. It was time to make sales. She looked forward to taking the girls that night to Bud's Coffee Shop for their favorite hamburgers.

Upstairs, Dianne took her place at her station by the rack of mink coats.

"Look pretty. Sell! Smile," Mr. Mendelson hissed as he passed by.

He was a short slight man with a beak nose and tiny dark eyes. At the end of the day Mr. Mendelson tallied up their sales. If they didn't meet a quota they were "let go."

"Dianne Perlman. My God. What are you doing here?" Nancy Kleinberg was a wealthy Happy Valley socialite. She was on the board of everything. Tall, model thin, with silky black hair, she and her surgeon husband had often been to Dianne's home barbecues.

"I'm working here. I'm getting a divorce," Dianne said.

"Tch Tch Tch," she said, averting her eyes. She wanted a mink coat. She was going on a cruise to Europe. "It's cold in Italy," she said.

Dianne helped her into a beige mink coat. "It's perfect for you. Especially for traveling."

Nancy twirled in front of the mirror. She twirled several times. She tried on several more coats and twirled in them, gossiping about women they knew in Happy Valley. "The Bermans filed for bankruptcy," she whispered. "Debbie Lynn is getting a... divorce."

She removed the coat. "I'll think about the coat, Dianne. Good luck."

Dianne watched her hurry from the store, knowing that she'd never buy a coat from her. No longer would she be accepted. She was now a divorced woman.

At the end of the day, avoiding Mr. Mendelson's glares, Dianne hurried to the basement to get her things from the locker.

She stood in line, punched out, and then she drove to Happy Valley.

As she drove into the driveway, Jenny ran towards the car, her pigtails standing out in the breeze. "Mommy, mommy," she said, between sobs. Her arms grabbed Dianne's waist. "Sara hit me."

Sara stood on the porch, holding her doll, her eyes narrowed, watching.

"We're going out to dinner," Dianne said, trying to sound cheerful. "First, Mommy has to soak her feet. Dianne took off her shoes and stockings, and sat on the edge of the pool, dangling her swollen feet in the cool water. And then they went to dinner.

*

19

A month to her interlocutory, Dianne decided to have a potluck party. She'd invited friends from art school and people she'd felt close to. It was Saturday night and summer vacation. The girls and Terecita had gone to Carmel with Min and Harry.

Dianne wore a white silk mini dress with no back. She brushed her hair so it hung loose. She wore silver open sandals, and silver rings on almost every finger. She felt free.

It was evening and a moon glowed light along the gardens. Hanging lanterns dangled from the trees, dropping a blue glow. From speakers, Janis Joplin records played, her fabulous voice booming. She lit candles inside glass jars and placed the jars on tables she'd arranged on the lawns. The garden looked like a fairyland.

Her friends began arriving, parking their cars, vans, and motorcycles in the driveway. They brought platters of homemade salads, breads, and jugs of wine. A rubber raft filled with flowers and lit candles floated in the pool. Soon, the party was going full swing, their laughter echoing over the hills.

Standing in a stream of light by the pool, Dianne was talking to friends from art school, when she noticed a medium height, man with pale blond hair to his shoulders. Even in the dark she could see the blue in his eyes. She felt his gaze.

"Fabulous house, Dianne," Earl said. His girlfriend had long red hair, and a pale beautiful face. She wore a beautiful flowing dress.

Everyone was drinking, lying on the grass, smoking, and dancing to the throbbing sound of the music. For the first time in years, Dianne felt alive, present, confident, and happy. Everything aroused her. This night represented the years she'd worked hard at school.

"Dance with me," said the blonde stranger.

She took his hand and he led her to the patio where couples were dancing to the moonlight. They slow danced, their bodies moving in perfect rhythm, as if they'd danced for years. It wasn't necessary to ask his name, to ask anything, to know anything beyond the moment. She felt like she was floating on a raft going nowhere.

When people were leaving, they sat on the lawn, under the moon. He said that he was a sculptor. Earl had told him about the party. That was all she knew, and all she wanted to know.

"I think you you're beautiful," he said.

She laughed. He said it so honestly, so without seduction, so without motive.

"I think you're beautiful too," she said.

After the last guest left, and the records stopped, he followed into her bedroom.

They undressed quickly. There was no hesitation. Hardly had they said a word, not even when he went inside her and for a long moment they lay still, quietly, so they could enjoy the wonderment of their bodies together. Never had she felt so sexually aroused. Heaven, this was heaven. They breathed soft words into their open mouths. Slowly her orgasm came, so naturally, so easy, and she held him tight, her body shuddering. When the bedroom door crashed open, she thought it was thunder. But Donald stood in the doorway with a burly man with a big camera. He yelled, "Take pictures of the whore!"

Flashlights went off, blinding her eyes, and the stranger tried to cover her with his body but it was too late. Donald was repeating that she was a "whore." And then Donald and the burly man left, their angry footsteps heavily retreating into the night, and finally it was dead quiet.

"My God," the stranger said. "My God."

"That was my husband."

"I didn't know you were married."

"We're getting a divorce. Obviously, he's been following me."

"I'm sorry," he whispered. "Do you want me to stay with you? I'm worried he'll come back."

"No, it's best to go," she said.

He dressed hurriedly in the clothes he'd dropped by the bed. He kissed her on the lips.

"I'll call," he said.

"Please don't say that. It's best not to call."

When she heard his car descend the driveway she sat on a chair in the living room until the light came. And then she called her lawyer and said she had to see her immediately.

The next morning she was at her lawyer's office.

"We're fucked!" Cha Cha screamed. "A week to go! All my work down the drain. We're fucked! For God's sake, buy a vibrator."

"It ... wasn't like that ...." Dianne lit a cigarette.

"I know, I know. It the moonlight and you had hot pants!"

202 | Barbara Rose

"It was more than that, it..."

"Grow up Dianne!! It's 1969! Sex is in! You're not Doris Day in the suburbs! You're Dianne Roseman fucked over by schmuck! Your husband has you on adultery. Now he has a custody suit! No alimony, no child support! *Comme ca?*"

Dianne sat there, feeling ashamed. Once again she'd acted on impulse. Not to mention putting her children in jeopardy.

"Look, Dianne," Cha Cha said, moving her eyeglasses to the top of her bubble hair-do. "The judge doesn't know from hot pants. You're right or you're wrong. You're a good wife or a bad wife. Your Donald schmuck is shrewd! You want Happy Valley? You want alimony? Child support! Come to the party! Comme ca?"

She jabbed the cigarette into a big metal ashtray. "I'm going to bargain with the bastards. His lawyer Suren Abjian is a tough mean bird. So that means never seeing the guy again. I'm sure you won't have to worry about it anyway. Men think with their pee pees! Lay low. *Comme ca!*"

20

Dianne missed her period. She was pregnant. It'd been five weeks since the night of her party. Once again she made herself a victim. She paced back and forth, not knowing what to do, what doctor to call. Abortions were illegal, and if Donald found out, she'd lose her children.

She couldn't go to Dr. Howard, but she recalled that Shirley Maxwell had once confided that she'd had an abortion. She called Shirley, and Dianne confided that she needed an abortion. Shirley promised that it would be confidential. She gave her the name of a doctor in San Francisco. Next, Dianne called the doctor and made an appointment for the next day at three p.m. Then she called work and said she was sick and wouldn't be in for a few days.

The next day, Dianne parked her car in a narrow alley near Chinatown. Following the directions she'd written on a piece of paper, she hurried along the narrow bumpy streets. Aromas of pork buns, and cabbage, floated with the fog. She turned into a narrow alley, and went inside a very old building painted yellow, with a slanted red roof.

She went up a flight of narrow stairs, into a small reception room. A nurse was typing.

"Dianne Roseman? I have an appointment."

The nurse came led her into an examining room. She took Dianne's blood pressure, and then instructed her to undress and to put on the paper gown folded on the table.

"Dr. Wang will see you in a minute," she said. "Undress from the waist down."

After the door closed, Dianne undressed, remembering painfully, undressing for Dr. Solomon.

The door opened. Dr. Wang was older, with a stern, kind face, and gray in his thick dark hair. He wore a white coat. When he examined her, Dianne kept her eyes on the ceiling, assuring herself that this would be over soon.

"You can sit up now," said Dr. Wang, sighing. At a tiny sink, he washed his hands. Then he turned to her. He looked grave.

"You're about six weeks pregnant. Your uterus is slightly crooked. You have very high blood pressure."

Dianne nodded.

"Where do you … do the procedure?"

"I can't do it. I don't want to put your life at risk."

"Please … I'm married. If my husband finds out I'll lose my children … please Doctor. A D&C is surely legal? You did a D&C on my friend Shirley Maxwell, so why not me?"

"I don't want to go to prison. It's not worth it for me, or for you. Have your child."

He left the room.

At a phone booth, on a windy corner, she called Shirley. She told her that Dr. Moore refused to do an abortion. "This is confidential," Dianne emphasized. "If Donald finds out … "

"Calm down," Shirley snapped. "Dianne, go home. Stay by your phone. I'll find another way." She paused. "On one condition. When you sell the house I want the exclusive listing."

"Of course. But I'm going to fight for the house."

Later that evening, Shirley called. She made a contact in El Paso, at an abortion clinic, and the abortion was set for the day after next.

"El Paso? How can I get away? The girls are coming home today."

"Tell your baby sitter that you have to go to LA for a job interview, and that you'll be back the next day. Tell her not to say a word about it. Do you understand? Neither one of us wants to go to jail."

"Okay … I'll do it."

"We need fourteen hundred dollars, pronto," Shirley continued in a tense voice.

"I don't have any money left.'"

"Give me your diamond engagement ring. I'll sell it right away."

The next morning, Shirley arrived. Shirley's *Clinique* perfume clouded the hallway. She was very tall and slim, and had very green suspicious eyes. Her short auburn hair was waved close to her head. She wore a green wool plaid suit, green stockings, and green eye shadow.

"Here's the ring," Dianne said, giving her the ring inside a satin case.

Shirley held the ring to the light, squinting her eyes.

"Donald has the ring insured for thirty thousand dollars. I have the insurance papers. It's worth a fortune."

"Look, Dianne. You're in a bad place. Let's get this done. I can't promise."

She dropped the case with the ring into her brown alligator bag. "I'll call you. Stay home. "

Later that afternoon, the storm was worse. The driveway was flooded with deep puddles, and the wind was so strong it blew a tree over. The girls, home from school, played in the playroom, their laughter reverberating through the house. Feeling ill, Dianne prepared dinner. When the doorbell rang, she hurried to the door. It was Shirley.

"I'm in a hurry," Shirley said, impatiently, coming into the hallway. "I came straight here. I made a quick deal at Nathan's Jewelers for fifteen hundred dollars. Enough for the abortion. I had to buy your airline tickets," she said, giving Dianne the airline tickets.

"Fifteen hundred dollars?" Dianne said. "I'm sure that the ring is worth more that. . , "

"Look, Dianne. Nathan said the diamond had a flaw in it." She patted her tightly set hair. "Thank your lucky stars I could get anything."

"Sure." Dianne wondered how much money Shirley had kept, but didn't dare argue with her at that point.

"You're leaving tomorrow at noon," Shirley said. "I'll be here at ten a.m. pronto, and take you to the airport. When you get to El Paso," she whispered, "your contact will find you. He'll say *Chino* and then you say the password, *"freeze."*

Dianne nodded.

"Can you remember?"

"Yes."

Shirley's eyes scanned the living room, the tall glass doors overlooking the garden and pool. Bright silk pillows scattered the couches, and vases were filled with wildflowers.

"A nice house," Shirley said, with her evaluating eyes. "You're lucky. It's worth a fortune. Not like the dump my ex-husband left me with." Then she left.

The next morning, it was storming. Dianne watched the girls go on their school bus. Then confided to Terecita that she had a very important job interview in Los Angeles and would be back the next day. "Don't answer the door or let anyone in the house, and don't tell the Perlmans where I am. I want the girls to stay home. Their dinner is in the frig, and you know about Sara's medicine."

At ten a.m. Shirley, wearing a tan raincoat and hat and rubber rain boots, drove through the Caldecott tunnel, and over the bridge to the San Francisco Airport. The rain had subsided but streaks of lightening crossed the darkening sky. Shirley ranted about her ex-husband, what a "louse," he was, and that he left her and her son penniless, and how she had to fight for alimony. "You have no idea Dianne what it's like out there. I have to work my balls off to keep my kid in college. I'm not a pretty princess like you."

As Shirley ranted about her hardships, Dianne looked out the window, assuring herself that everything would be fine, and that the girls were safe.

"I haven't sold a property in a year," Shirley continued. "I need the money. You're younger than I am, and you're pretty. The men want younger women. They don't want a forty-three year old woman."

At the airport, Shirley double-parked her car.

"Now remember," Shirley said in a tone like a teacher lecturing her class. "When this is over, get birth control. Christ. You're almost thirty-one. Grow up. The party's over."

Dianne watched her car drive into traffic, and then she hurried into the airport. As he boarded the plane, she prayed that somehow she'd be safe and home soon to her daughters.

21

The El Paso airport was small and crowded. Men and women wearing black, and crucifixes around their necks, waited in line, holding crying babies. Still shaking from the turbulent flight, Dianne waited by the ramp, holding a small overnight bag.

A very short man wearing a brown crinkly leather jacket with fringe on the bottom, and cowboy boots, appeared in front of her. "I'm Chino."

"Freeze," Dianne said.

"Come with me. I'll take you to the hotel."

Dianne followed him to a small yellow cab parked in a "reserved" zone.

Dianne squished into the backseat, sitting between three visibly pregnant airline stewardesses. During the ride, Dianne looked out the window, at the wide, dusty, unpaved streets, and at the low thatched houses. Chino drove slowly, the car radio loudly playing Elvis Presley songs.

"Don't worry, honey," said a blonde girl about twenty, with white lipstick, and huge hair. "Here, have a cigarette."

"I'm nervous," Dianne confided, accepting a Marlboro cigarette. The girl lit Dianne's cigarette. "Don't worry. This is my third time. You'll be all right. It's a good place."

"You lucked out," said a dark Pan Am stewardess, chewing bubble gum. It's a wonderful clinic. A lot of famous people come here. "

"We're going to cross the border," Chino announced in a heavy accent, and turning off the radio. "We'll be at the hotel soon."

In fifteen minutes, Chino stopped in front of a one-story red adobe building in the middle of a dusty barren road. A sign read: "Hotel Clinica."

The hotel lobby smelled of heat. Large ceiling fans blew stale air. Several girls played cards at a wobbly card table. A thin black cat slept on a shabby chair.

"Be ready at five a.m.," Chino said, dropping their bags on the floor. "I'll escort you to the clinic."

Up a few stairs, the room was small and stuffy, and the bare windows were streaked by dirt. The bathroom was so tiny that when Dianne used the John, she had to leave the door open. After washing her face in brown cold water, she lay on top of the narrow bed covered by a brown blanket. Exhausted, she closed her eyes and dozed into a heavy thick sleep with no light and cracked moons.

She awoke to a dog barking. A thin light straggled across the room. She rinsed her face with water, brushed her teeth without swallowing water, and then she sat by the window, watching the morning light spread into the sky. A small brown bird was pecking at crumbs on the unpaved street, and a lovely looking child with long black hair, rode a wobbly bicycle along the sun-streamed street. Dianne pictured Jenny sleeping, her hair spilled over her pudgy face, and Sara's deep-set sad eyes. What a mess she'd made.

At five a.m. on the dot, Chino arrived. Downstairs, the girls were already in the lobby. Chino drove them to the clinic.

The clinic was small and airless. Girls were lying on gurneys in the dank hallway, their faces covered by sheets. A Hispanic nurse with a kind face, led Dianne into a small, windowless room. A narrow bed was neatly made up with clean white sheets, and a tall wood crucifix hung above the bed.

"Get undressed, pretty girl," the nurse said in a thick accent, pointing to a blue cotton gown on the foot of the bed. She gave Dianne a pleated cup with three orange pills. "No water," she explained. "Swallow the pills and they will make you drowsy."

Dianne undressed, put on the gown, and got into the bed. The sheets felt rough on her bare legs. From the hallway, she could hear girls chattering, laughing, and waiting their turns. The screech of gurneys wheeling down the hallway mixed with the nurses' soft voices and accents.

Drowsy now, she thought about the tiny person forming inside of her, and squeezed her eyes shut, surprised by the tears falling down her face.

Two tall male doctors wearing masks, and green gowns, came into the room. The doctors had dark eyes, and strong brown smooth arms and big metal watches on their wrists.

"Cash," said one of the doctors in a heavy accent.

Dianne gave him the envelope of cash. He counted the cash, and then gave the envelope to a nurse, saying something in Spanish. When he talked, his mask puffed out.

"We'll inject you with sodium pentothal. Your face will be covered. This never happened and you never saw us. Do you understand?"

Dianne nodded. They left the room.

The nurse helped her onto the gurney and covered her face with a sheet. As the nurse pushed the gurney down the hallway, she felt dizzy, and then she heard doors close.

The nurse removed the sheet from her face. The small room was empty with a narrow table with stirrups. Rows of instruments were arranged on a high metal table.

"Move to the edge of the table," instructed the nurse. Knees apart ... move down pretty girl, come on, knees apart ... okay pretty girl, feet in the stirrups, that's right. The nurse strapped her arm to a board and injected her arm and she felt instantly dizzy, like she was falling and then she heard the doctors talking in Spanish and she couldn't open her eyes, and she was praying that she wouldn't die and promising to be a better mother, and she was counting nine ... eight ..."

She awoke in a small recovery room. Slowly she opened her eyes and placed her hands on her stomach. She was in a narrow bed, in a small room. Relieved that she was alive, she let the tears come. She hadn't expected she'd feel grief.

She sat up, feeling cramps. A nurse came in and gave her a Coca Cola in a green glass bottle. "Here, pretty girl. Drink some."

The cola tasted good, and then the nurse helped Dianne dress in her clothes. Next, she gave Dianne a Kotex Pad, and a packet of pills, instructing her when to take the pills.

She led Dianne to the reception area where Dianne waited for Chino to take her to the airport. Several girls waited on benches.

Chino arrived with a taxi full of girls, and after they went into the hotel, he took her, and two other girls, to the airport.

When Dianne arrived home, it was late at night, and a blanket of rain soaked Happy Valley. She hurried into the house, stepping over Jenny's doll buggy.

The light was on in the living room and she crept into the girl's room. Sara's trundle bed was slightly lopsided, and she slept on her back, her mouth half open, breathing noisily. Jenny slept on her side, clutching her rag doll, "Rags." Terecita slept on the cot in the middle of the room, her head a mass of pink foam hair rollers, and her rosary beads wound around her wrist. Dianne kissed the girls, Jenny murmuring, "Hi Mommy."

In bed, Dianne wrapped the blankets around her, and she slept.

*

Three days later Cha Cha called and excitedly told Dianne that Donald wanted to settle before court. They would meet the next day at Suren Abjian's office in Oakland.

"I worked my balls off to get you the house and alimony and child support," Cha Cha said. "Don't fuck it up."

22

"Let's get started," said Donald's lawyer. Suren Abjian was a burly man with hostile dark eyes and styled gray hair. He had a reputation for being ruthless and for favoring the husbands. Donald sat across from her, smoking his pipe. He'd kissed her hello. He looked happy, she thought. She felt optimistic.

"Okay, Suren. Let's get the show on the road. Get this baby settled," said Cha Cha, opening a folder of papers.

Mr. Abjian sighed heavily. "For the sake of his children, my client is willing to make a settlement. Otherwise, there will be a custody suit."

"You don't have evidence for a custody suit," Cha Cha snapped.

He opened a manila envelope, took out several photographs, and spread them like a fan on the table. They were blowups of Dianne at the El Paso clinic, and several of the stranger on top of her, her legs wound around his neck.

There was a stunned silence. Cha Cha lit a cigarette. Donald pressed tobacco into his pipe.

"Photographs aren't admissible court evidence," Cha Cha said.

"Believe me. After Judge Brown of the Martinez court, sees pictures of Dianne at the El Paso abortion clinic, he'll be unhappy. He's a well-known advocate against abortion, and he's for children's rights."

"Enough!" said Cha Cha, after a long silence. "Cut out the crap. Let's hear your terms."

"Adultery charges are enough for a custody suit. Abortion can send her to a prison term. Also, we're aware that Dianne has been seeing a psychiatrist in San Francisco. Obviously, she's unstable. She hangs out with hippies."

"My client has been married legally for ten years and they have two children. She deserves alimony and child support. Cut out the drama."

Mr. Abjian lit a cigar, and the thick smoke floated a circle in the air, and then evaporated. Donald leaned back in the chair, smoking his pipe. He looked satisfied. He'd made a deal, Dianne thought. He was a businessman. Only money mattered to him.

"My client Mr. Perlman, and his family, want to settle this *amicably*," continued Mr. Abjian in a hushed voice. "*Avoid* a nasty custody hearing … pictures in the papers … witnesses … messy."

Dianne looked straight ahead.

Cha Cha spoke: "Mr. Perlman has considerable assets under his corporation. I have documents showing when Donald Perlman purchased the named properties, *after* they were married. That's community property. Under duress, Mr. Perlman forced her to sign papers, Dianne relinquishing all claim to what should have been half hers. Prison time for this."

"Unfortunately," said Mr. Abjian with a long sigh, there are records from her first marriage that she was sued for fraud, for trying to exploit money from a very wealthy man."

"Hearsay evidence," said Cha Cha. "Not true."

"My client has agreed to pay attorney fees, and grant Mrs. Perlman full custody of the girls. He has made arrangements with a realtor to sell the house and from the sale, he will kindly give your client fifteen thousand dollars. He will not pay alimony, or child support, and the house bought before their marriage, is legally his." He paused. "Otherwise it's court, a long custody battle, and we'll win."

"I'll sign the divorce papers," Dianne said into the sudden silence. "I want my children."

"Let's get the show on the road," Cha Cha said after a moment. Then there the scratching sound of the pen as Donald and Dianne signed the many pages of the divorce agreement, Mr. Abjian, repeating, "Initial there ... that's right dear," and then it was over, and she had custody of her girls. Cha Cha closed her briefcase and looked disgusted.

Mr. Abjian, trying not to look pleased, sighed. "Good move. Now you can be friends and good parents," Mr. Abjian said.

Outside, in the parking lot, Cha Cha lit a cigarette, and glared at Dianne. "You fucked me over! You got knocked up, and didn't tell me. I could have bargained. You made me look like a fool! Stop being the victim, and grow up!"

"I'm ..."

"Don't say you're sorry!"

"I am sorry."

"Now you're poor and single and penniless. You bought into the penis promise. "

"I'm sorry," Dianne repeated.

"Look Dianne," she sighed. "You went through this with the first bastard. Stop repeating the patterns. Get smarter. Don't marry so fast. Buy a vibrator. Find yourself, and finish college. You don't need these assholes."

Dianne watched her drive away, her Volkswagen bug bouncing along the bumpy driveway. The court drama with Charley flashed in her mind, but this time she caused the drama. It was time to start her life in a new way.

*

The next day Shirley placed a 'for sale' sign on the front of the house. They'd nodded to each other but they didn't speak. She knew that Shirley had snitched to Donald about the abortion, and made a deal with him to sell the house.

A week later, Shirley sold the house to a couple with three children. Mr. Mendelson called and fired Dianne on the grounds she missed too much work.

When Dianne received Donald's check for fifteen thousand dollars, she rented a two bedroom flat in San Francisco's Laurel Heights District, two blocks away from a good public school, and from the Jewish Community Center where the girls could enjoy after school activities. Dianne paid her landlords, the Pons, who lived upstairs, a year's rent in cash. Then she'd enrolled at San Francisco State University, planning on going to night classes. She'd work from home, selling unknown art. She designed postcards announcing her business, *New Artists*. She sent the cards with her new address, and telephone number, to every gallery in San Francisco, and to former clients.

She was ready to leave, but she had to tell Min about her plans. They agreed to meet at the Happy Valley Coffee Shop for breakfast the next morning.

When Dianne arrived at the Happy Valley Coffee Shop, Min was already there. It was early in the morning. They hadn't talked in a long time, and at first, the tension was thick.

Min lit a cigarette, her hand trembling. As usual, she was impeccably groomed. She wore a white knit dress, every hair lacquered and in place. Dark circles lay under her eyes.

Quickly, Dianne told Min that she'd found a flat in San Francisco. "It's perfect for the girls Min. They can walk to school, and to the Jewish Community Center and take after school classes. It's perfect, Min," she repeated.

"My poor babies," Min said, dabbing the tears in her eyes with a paper napkin.

"You're always welcome in our home," Dianne continued. "I want you to be with the girls. You're the most stable, loving person in their lives."

Min clutched her purse. Her long oval manicured nails were polished silver to match the silver eye shadow. Dianne felt sad and guilty. She hadn't been nice to Min, and she regretted this. At the time, she'd been hurt that Min hadn't approved of her, and had blamed her for Charley.

"You can still take the girls on weekends to your house, and on weekend vacations," Dianne said. "Especially, Sara. She'll need you more than ever."

Min lit another cigarette, and exhaled a stream of smoke. Her eyes were narrowed. "What a mess you made, Dianne. What a mess," she repeated. "You used my son. You never loved him. You married him on rebound. He told me how …cold you were. He tells me everything."

They sat in stony silence. A jukebox played the Beatles singing *Let It Be.*

Min stirred three sugar cubes in her coffee, the spoon making a tapping sound on the cup. Dianne wouldn't argue, nor tell her that Donald drank too much, was spoiled, immature, and that they weren't ever a match. No, she wouldn't because Min was right. She had never loved Donald.

"You did him in, "Min continued. "He's very angry."

"I think Donald will be fine," Dianne said after a long silence. "I'm sorry, Min. Sorry that I caused pain. Pain to you, Donald, Harry, Sara. Sorry about everything. Sorry I am the way I am. I'm working on changing and well, so many—things. "Dianne burst into tears. Then they both cried.

Min lit another cigarette, as if to cover up her tears. "Well, as long as you let me have my babies," Min said, trying to smile. "Don't take them away from me, Dianne."

"Never. I promise, Min. Please accept my apologies for all the times I resented you."

Min held Dianne's hand. They looked at each other, as if for the first time.

"Let's order pancakes," Min said after a long moment. "I'm hungry, and I want to see the girls today."

As they ate, Min chattered about the places she planned on taking the girls, showing Dianne the latest photographs she'd taken of the girls. They didn't discuss Donald. She knew that Min had little power over him, and that Min also knew that Donald wasn't interested in spending time with the girls. Always, Min covered up for Donald.

Later that afternoon, Dianne told the girls that they were moving to San Francisco. The girls cried, and said that they didn't want to go.

"Grandma and Papa will visit often. We'll ride the cable cars, and our new house is near your school. Sara, you can walk to your ballet and gymnastic classes. Jenny you can ride horses in Golden Gate Park. You'll see."

Two days later Dianne had a garage sale. She sold furniture, silver, old toys, and she made over a thousand dollars. Only a couple of her former friends and neighbors had showed up and wished her well. Dianne was starting over now. Her life was like a tapestry woven with ups and downs, and it was time to pursue her truths.

Finally, she called and told her mother that she was moving to San Francisco.

"Now what will you do?" Mother asked.

"I'm starting a business. It's called *New Artists*. I'll go to college at night, and work from home so I can be with the girls."

Mother sighed heavily. "Two divorces Dianne. You're damaged goods. No man will want you now. You made your bed. Lie in it."

Then as if she hadn't said something cruel, she told Dianne that she'd met Max Perlman, a wealthy widower.

"Wonderful, Mother."

"He's wealthy, and can help poor Bobbie. We're going to elope, Dianne." She giggled. "We're going to Carmel, just us, no children. Max has four children, and two grandchildren." Dianne was happy for her mother, and relieved that now her mother would have enough money to stop making tablecloths, keep her house, and maybe find joy.

Life was changing.

*

Moving Day:

The girls, wearing yellow slickers, and hats, holding their favorite dolls, watched three men load boxes into the giant size moving van.

Jenny's Crazy Car, and Sara's old tricycle were still in the driveway. Folded yellow leaves floated on the pool, and the lawns were brown and faded.

"Okay, Ma'am. We're ready," said the man.

Dianne and the girls hugged Terecita, who would stay behind to finish her packing. She wouldn't be coming with them. She was going back to her country.

After a tearful goodbye, Dianne strapped the girls into the back seat. Then she got into the car and drove slowly down the driveway, past the pine trees Donald had planted and now covering the house until Happy Valley was shrinking into a dot and now only a part of the past.

*

Section Three: San Francisco

1975-1981

23

Four years passed. It was 1975. Vietnam was ended and the Watergate burglars were arrested. Dianne and the girls loved living in San Francisco. Except in her dreams, Happy Valley seemed another lifetime.

It was an October evening. Dianne was home in the dining room she'd turned into a studio, sorting prints she'd show her new client the next day. The girls were sprawled on the living room floor, watching The *I Love Lucy* show. Heat was hissing from the old radiator, blowing Jenny's wind-bells dangling from the window. Dianne loved this time of day when it was quiet and dark and the world was shut down. The flat smelled of chocolate chip cookies, and kitty litter.

The four years had gone fast. After taking night classes, she finally got a BA in Art History. She'd loved the classes, the endless papers, reading, and especially meeting other women who were also single parents working, and her age. They were called "Re-entry Women." On the nights she had gone to school, her landlords the Pons, cooked Chinese food for the girls, and babysat until Dianne returned home. Dianne felt indebted to them. The girls loved the Pons and their families.

She finished tagging the prints she'd taken home from Carsons Print Gallery. Later, she'd pay bills, and go over her accounts.

At least once a week, she'd resumed seeing Dr. Stockford. Therapy was like working on a massive jigsaw puzzle— taking herself apart one piece at a time. Who am I? Can someone damaged become someone new?" she'd ask Dr. Stockford.

"We're hungry," Jenny said.

"In a minute," Dianne said. "Dinner will be ready."

"Not spaghetti again," Jenny said.

"With clams."

"I'll set the table," Sara said.

At thirteen, Sara had grown tall, and was extremely thin. Her chestnut thick hair was worn in a bun at the nape of her neck. A serious ballet student, Sara had dreams of going to New York University on a ballet scholarship, and studying ballet at the New York City Ballet. While Jenny, at eleven, hated school and preferred to ride horses at Golden Gate Park. Also, she was boy crazy.

Dianne put the prints into the bin drawer, and went into the kitchen. She made sauce for the pasta, chopping tomatoes on a wooden board. She and the girls had loved decorating the rooms. Wicker chairs she'd sprayed white, mixed with her old loveseats.

After Dianne prepared dinner, they ate at the kitchen table. Sara ate little, and Jenny talked nonstop about a horse Misty she loved. Wistfully, Jenny hoped to someday ride Donald's new horse Midnight. "Grandma Min said it's a beautiful horse."

"Fat chance," Sara snapped, clearing the table. "Daddy never sees us, anyway."

Since they'd moved to San Francisco, Donald rarely saw the girls, and had never sent money or a gift. A few years ago, he'd married Conchita, thirty years younger, and who had taken care of his horses. But the girls loved seeing Min and Harry, who generously paid for many of the girls' needs and clothes.

Mother had married Max, and outside of going to their home for an occasional dinner, they rarely saw the girls. Mother had had a heart attack, and bypass surgery. Shortly afterward, Bobbie had had a triple heart bypass. "We have the same heart," Mother had said.

After the girls went to bed, Dianne sat at the kitchen table, paying bills. The bills she couldn't pay, she kept in a red folder.

Though *New Artists* had grown, she made barely enough money to keep up with her bills. Her car had conked out, so she'd gone to a used car agency, and spent the rest of her savings for a down payment on a brand new Chevrolet station wagon. It was perfect to hold her canvasses, and to carpool the girls.

It was late. She stretched her arms. She finished paying the bills, and she turned out the kitchen light. She wanted a good night's sleep. Early the next morning she was driving to Marin and showing a Warhol print to a wealthy new client. She needed the money.

When the doorbell rang, she was surprised. She tiptoed to the door. "Who's there?"

"Joe Brenner. Brenner Motors."

She peeked through the peephole. A tall man holding a black umbrella stood on the porch. She waited. Maybe he'd go away. She was used to bill collectors.

"Lady, you've missed two car payments. I'm just doing my job."

"Please, sir. I have two daughters and I have to drive them to the doctors, and to school. Please, sir, I'll get the money."

The sound of the rain on the porch was heavy.

"I'll be back tomorrow at noon, lady. If you don't have the money, I'll have to repossess the car."

From the window, she watched a tall man get into a dark car, and drive away.

She turned off the light and went to bed. She left her door open so she could hear the girls, and soon slid into sleep.

She dreamed she was conducting an orchestra. She stood on a podium, her arms out, the baton loose in her hand. The musicians looked at her expectantly, and then she waved her baton, and the Brahms Concerto began—

The next morning, her client called, and canceled her appointment, citing the flu, and she'd make another appointment.

Dianne had to have her car—yes, she'd post-date a check for one hundred and fifty dollars. She'd learned all the tricks of survival—sending post-dated checks, or sending envelopes without the checks, then later, saying she forgot to mail the check.

Exactly at noon, the doorbell rang. "Joe Brenner," he called.

She opened the door, the chain rattling a metallic sound. "Come in."

Joe Brenner was at least six feet two, slender, with silver hair, dark skin, and eyes blue as cornflowers. He looked more like a movie star, than a car salesman.

She gave him the envelope. "I postdated a check but I'll have the money next week. I have to drive the daughters to their classes—I'm an art dealer, and I need the car to deliver paintings."

He placed the envelope in the pocket of his tweed jacket. He pointed to her painting of a girl on a swing. "Did you paint it?"

She nodded. "Yes. I'm a painter."

He looked reflective. "I bought a Richard Diebenkorn drawing, years ago," he said. "I'm looking at a Diane Arbus photograph."

"She's my favorite. I admire her photographs of unusual people. She makes freaks ordinary, and ordinary people, freaks."

"My friend Sam West is an important collector," he said. "He buys art when it's unknown, then donates the art to the museums. He takes me to the artist's studios." Then, as if remembering why he was there, he glanced at his watch. "Where's the car?"

"Outside."

"Let me see it," he said.

She grabbed her leather jacket, and Fedora hat. She led him across the street where she'd parked her car.

He walked around the car, graceful as a cat, his fist pounding the top, like a doctor checks reflexes. There was elegance about him. Even the way he wore his snug jeans, and brown tweed jacket.

"It's in poor condition," he said.

"I promise by next week you can cash the check. As soon as I can, I'll fix the dents," she continued.

He glanced at his watch. "Have you eaten?"

"Well—no…"

"Let's go for Japanese food," he said.

"I've never had Japanese food," she said, surprised by her willingness to go.

He drove a metallic blue Cadillac with fins on its back. All the way to Japan town, he drove slowly, stopping to admire a garden, or the rain lingering on the trees. He talked non-stop, in run-on sentences from growing orchids, to cooking fish just right. But if she listened carefully, he had a lot to say about a lot of things.

At the restaurant nestled behind a cobblestone street in Japan Town, surrounded by Cherry trees, they sat at a green Formica table in a booth underneath two Japanese paper lanterns. Japanese music, strangely sensual, played from an overhead net speaker. Joe ordered the lunch—hot Saki for two, platters of seaweed and sushi and other Japanese dishes.

As they drank the Saki, he pontificated about the importance of good nutrition, lecturing not to eat white bread, sugar, and unhealthy food. He was Norwegian and had been raised on fish balls, and good health. His smooth olive skin glowed and his eyes sparkled when he talked. "It's easy to live well and be healthy without pressure," he added. He smiled. "There' s something beautiful about simplicity."

Two Japanese women wearing traditional Japanese dress, their expressions somber, brought the array of dishes he'd ordered.

In one swoop, Joe swallowed a whole egg. They drank rice soup from a bowl. The soup was warm and delicious, and tasted like rice candy.

"Bring the lady a fork, please," he ordered, as he watched her struggle catching a piece of eel.

He maneuvered his chopsticks like knitting needles. He talked about country cross skiing, and the beauty of Norway.

He'd married, and divorced, and then came to San Francisco and opened his car agency. Every free moment, he went to museums, gallery openings, and collected contemporary art.

"Art is life's thumbprint," she said. "It tells the story of generations."

She sipped more Saki, enjoying her conversation with him. Underneath his rambling style of talking, he had depth, and sensitivity He was sincere and his plain talking and homilies defied his extreme good looks. She hoped they'd be friends.

"I like your paintings, Dianne." He nodded as if confirming his statement. "Sam West should see your work. He knows all the dealers and museum curators. He could help you."

"I would like that."

"Sam's not afraid to take risk," he continued. "He collects new California artists before they make it. Christ," he said, his eyes flashing, "He took me to William Wiley's studio before anyone had bought his work. We paid fifty dollars for each painting, and loaded a truck with his paintings. Sam won't buy from dealers. He goes right to the studio." He paused. "Tell me about yourself."

Easily, as if she'd known him for years, she told him about Charley, her rebound marriage to Donald, the divorce, the subsequent years selling art, going to school, and her dreams of becoming financially independent as an artist.

He folded the napkin into a square, smoothing it with his hands. After a moment he said: "You've been through a lot."

"Like an airplane crashing. It hits so hard you don't feel it," she said with a series of laughs. "I was supposed to be a Jewish American Princess, married to a rich man and to forever give dinner parties. I was bought and sold to the highest bidder—like an arranged marriage." She was embarrassed that she'd confessed so much.

"The rise and fall of a Jewish American Princess," he said softly. "Only you're on the rise."

"Based on my past, I'm not sure I can ever feel love again. I've made so many mistakes. The past shapes us."

"Yesterday it a bucket of ashes," he said with a sigh. "Use your pain for your work. Not for your life."

By then, it was late afternoon, and shadows lingered over the room like guests. They drank jasmine tea, and ate rice cookies.

He held the cup of rice tea close to his face, the steam puffing around him. "Next Sunday, I'd like you to join me, and Sam West. We'll have brunch at the Fairmont. Would you like that?"

She nodded. "I'd like that."

That night after the girls came home and went to bed, Dianne noticed a white envelope slipped half under her door. She opened it. Inside the envelope was her check torn in three pieces.

*

The following Sunday the City was full of light, shimmering like a Monet painting. Dianne and Joe were walking up the hill, to the Fairmont Hotel where they'd meet Sam West.

She'd dressed in gray woolen knickers, gray stockings, and a fitted black velvet jacket she'd found in a thrift shop.

The wind was blowing hard and Dianne held her Fedora hat close to her head. Joe's stride was fast, and she held his arm. From St. Patrick's Cathedral, the bells were ringing, competing with the vibrating sound of the cable cars sliding up Nob Hill.

The Fairmont Hotel always made her nostalgic. In the lobby, tourists lounged on ornate red velvet sofas, and a harpist played Vivaldi. When they passed the Gold Room, Dianne averted her eyes.

They got into a glass elevator, and Dianne kept her eyes shut until the elevator clunked to a stop. The doors opened to a large room drenched in light.

A short man with a box-like body greeted them.

"So you're Dianne Roseman. I'm Sam."

He bowed ceremoniously. His Gatsby manners were incongruous with his eccentric dress. He wore a baggy green suit, green shirt, and green necktie with a cable car painted on it. He carried a walking stick with a brass head. Immediately, Dianne liked him.

"Joe has told me wonderful things about you," she said, smiling.

"Lies," he said with a mischievous grin. "Lies make controversy! All artists need controversy!" he said, with a series of laughs that sounded like bullets. "Say! You're elegant. You should always wear a strand of perfect pearls and Chanel #5 perfume."

A waiter seated them at a table next to the window facing a view of the entire City. Sunlight slid up the buildings, turning them half gold. They drank Ramos Fizzes, and began talking about the art world.

Sam spoke carefully, as if his words were edited. His nut-colored eyes sat on the edge of his head much like a frog's. His hair was dark and curly and cut close to his rather large head.

Dianne was impressed by Sam's intellect, his quick references to literature, and philosophy to elucidate an idea.

"People are afraid of what they don't know," Joe said. "Afraid to take risk."

"Some of my clients buy prints by famous artists to hang in their bath rooms. They use the art like they buy designer labels. They don't care about process, only product."

"Fools," said Sam with an exasperated sigh. The rich socialite ladies sit on museum boards, deciding which artist is right, or wrong. They wear nametags and big hats and pay high prices for a Wiley drawing. When they could have bought the same drawing before it was known."

"Let's go the buffet and eat Pancake Oscars," Joe said.

The buffet went clear around the room. Chefs wearing aprons and puffed up tall white hats, carved roasts and ducks and chickens. Sam heaped Dianne's plate with caviar, pancakes layered with cream and strawberries, the pancakes so light they floated. "A thin, nervous girl like you has to eat." Sam laughed the bullet laugh.

As they ate, and drank another round of fizzes, Sam told more stories about the art world. Sam had bought many California artists before they were known, and most of his art was stored in Joe's warehouse along with Joe's collection of antique Cadillacs. Sam spoke in a staccato manner, pausing at the end of each sentence, as if to let you absorb what he was saying. When he spoke about paintings, a light fell over his bulbous face.

"Joe tells me that you sell art by unknown artists?"

Dianne reached into her purse. "Here's my card."

Without looking at it, Sam slipped the card into his pocket. "He tells me that you're a good painter. What do you paint?"

"Boxes."

"Boxes?" He spread caviar on a small round of toast.

"Women caught in boxes. They represent entrapment."

"Interesting. I'd like to see them."

"It's hard to sell art," Dianne continued. "To make it as an artist you have to be dead. Stick your head in the oven like Sylvia Plath, or put rocks in your pocket like poor Virginia Woolf. Or be the wife of a famous painter so you can be labeled wife of."

"Dealers are sheep in chic's clothing." Sam laughed at his pun. As quickly as he had laughed, he looked suddenly morose. "David Noel, the former curator for the Levi Strauss collection, has recently opened a gallery. He's a phony horse's ass, only shows celebrity New York minimal art. But he owns a very important collection and a wide stable of artists. He may be interested in letting you sell for his gallery on consignment. You should contact him and ask to see his collection." He paused. "Join the Docent ladies at the San Francisco Museum of Contemporary Art. They're like Red Cross volunteers in fancy clothes, but they will buy art."

She was enjoying Sam's ideas about art patronage. He envisioned a museum to exhibit unknown artists.

"Patrons gush over dead artists," Sam continued, indifferent to the stares from people sitting next to them. "All they know is Van Gogh's fucking ear!"

"Van Gogh's ear is the art world's Resurrection," Dianne said.

Joe laughed.

"If an artist is famous they'll buy a handkerchief of snot," added Sam, his long mouth sliding over his slightly yellowed teeth like a zipper. "They'll salivate over a piece of string or a brick."

Say! Let's get out of here," said Sam, waving impatiently to the waiter. "I want to show you some excellent art. Maybe you can sell Janet's paintings."

They piled into Sam's beat-up Chevrolet with a crunched in door. He drove fast, his dented Chevrolet weaving in and out of lanes, the doors rattling. Art catalogues were open on the shabby seats, along with boxes of teeth, and X-rays of gums. He cackled. "Artists have rotten gums. I call them *gooms*. I fix their rotten *gooms* in exchange for art."

He drove along a hill so high Dianne wouldn't look out the window.

He stopped the car in front of a long crooked stairway surrounded by lush trees.

They climbed up a maze of flat steps to a small red cottage. Sam knocked on a tall red door, three times. And the door opened.

A thin man about forty, with a hawk-like nose, holding a black cat with yellow eyes, invited us in. "Janet will be glad to see you," he said, giving Sam a hug.

They went inside a large room with high ceilings. Light streamed on the massive paintings of clouds so precisely drawn you could cut them out.

Janet was a tall woman about Dianne's age. She wore a long, loose skirt, and her light brown hair was simply plaited around her head. She hugged Sam. She was charming, direct, and her face devoid of makeup shone as if a light was under her skin.

"Dianne sells art," Sam said, tapping his cane. "She is a painter. And Joe collects art. "

"Take your time looking," Janet said, leading Sam to a long wood table in the kitchen area.

Joe moved slowly in front of the paintings, his arms behind his back and looking at the paintings. Dianne admired the detailed line, the simplicity and the beauty of white clouds suspended in space or touching the edge of a building or floating over dark streets with odd lights. The paintings conveyed movement and emotion and sound.

An hour later they sat at the wood table, drinking berry wine, and eating Janet's homemade banana bread. Sunlight was falling from the skylights, and a large yellow cat slept in Janet's lap. Her husband, a well-known photographer, showed his photographs of empty streets. They were black and white with lavish gesture and shadows.

"Dianne, feel free to bring clients here."

Dianne smiled. "Your work is important and very beautiful."

"And I'll be back. It takes me time to buy," Joe said.

Janet smiled. "You're welcome any time."

As they discussed Janet's cloud paintings, and her husband's photographs, before answering a question about their work, Janet and her husband looked at each other as if they were having a private conversation, their devotion through their respect and quiet.

Sam insisted they go to his apartment and see his collection before going to dinner at the Presidio Officers Club. "Sam was a Colonel in the army," Joe explained. But Janet and her husband said they were tired. After more hugs and promises to contact each other soon, they left and drove to Sam's apartment.

Sam opened the door and they went inside his apartment.

Paintings and sculptures leaned along the walls, hung from the ceiling, or were free standing. William Wiley's orange and silver panels of airplanes soared off the walls, and Joan Brown's mural-size paintings of haunting brown women with protruding bellies and huge eyes peering behind jungle trees. Wesselman's airplane mural soared from a wall, David Parks, many bay area unknown artists, and Manuel Neri's white plaster life-like human size figures were placed in doorways; Robert Hudson's metal stars dangling from cords.

Everything was alive ... crooked, reflecting California's colors, landscape, and indigenous art world. Sam's bold elegant tastes in art were incongruous to the ordinary low-ceiling apartment: the beat-up few chairs scattered around the room. As if only the art mattered. Books spilled from bookcases, and were piled along the edge of the floor.

"Fabulous," Dianne said.

Joe sat on a chair, looking through an art catalogue.

"This calls for a very chilled martini," Sam said.

In his plain kitchen that didn't look used, Sam took a package of Marlboro cigarettes from the freezer, explaining they tasted better frozen. And then he made cocktails. She loved his eccentricities. He was unique.

They sat on the floor, talking about the art world, Warhol's Factory, and abstract expressionism.

"I love the artists," Sam said. "Everyone is classified like a plant. If you're different, they say you're eccentric; if you act on it, they say you're crazy."

"Like Timothy O'Leary. Or Van Gogh," Joe said.

Sam waved his arms. "Fools! Religion talks about God and faith, and brutally excludes those who don't agree. My God is Mozart. "

"I'm starved," said Joe. "Let's go to dinner now."

The officers club was in the Presidio, set amongst vast lawns, and army bungalows.

Inside, the club was like going into another world. The room was dark, and the air smelled of expensive scotch and after-shave. Thick carpets were inlaid with gold crests, and officers wearing uniforms, saluted Sam. "Good evening Colonel West," they said.

A full orchestra was playing Glenn Miller tunes. At the bar, officers with medals rolling up their jackets, played liars dice. Their wives wore lacquered hair and rhinestones and pastel chiffon dresses. And then their table was ready, and they went inside the dining room.

At a buffet, chefs wearing white coats, and tall hats, sliced roast beef, and fresh turkeys. Sam heaped her plate, murmuring, "A thin nervous girl like you must eat."

The dinner was delicious and the room festive. They talked non-stop about art. It was as if they'd known each other for a lifetime.

When the orchestra played *Moonlight Serenade*, Sam asked her to dance.

Smoothly, like gliding, his box-like body effortlessly led her into perfect step. She was strangely attracted to this Quasimodo man.

After the dance they went to the table. By then she was giddy and high from the day, tapping her foot to the music.

After she danced *Goodnight Sweetheart* with Joe, they said goodnight, and Joe brought her home.

By the time she got home it was midnight. He came in for coffee. The drapes were drawn. It was cold in the flat. Joe put logs into the fireplace and made a fire.

"Who's that?" he asked, pointing to the framed article about her mother.

"My mother. She was sixteen, accepting the Chopin Award to Juilliard. She was a concert pianist."

"Interesting," he said. His face was close to a photograph she'd taken of her father.

"This is your father?"

She nodded. "He worked his way up at Universal Studios. He died."

He looked at her, and then he looked at a small painting she'd painted of an empty house.

"I like this," he said. "It's haunting. Sad. Beautiful."

"It's yours. Please take it. You've been kind to me." She took the drawing off the wall. She gave it to him.

He held it gently, and then placed it under his arm. "I'll take good care of it. Thank you, Dianne. It's late. I've worn out my welcome."

At the door, he paused. "Don't forget, call David Noel."

On the last step, under the light, he looked back at her. "You know what I think? I think you're ready for some fun."

She watched him, the drawing under his arm, hurry to his car, his tall frame receding into the night.

She closed the door, and went to bed.

That night she slept with the moon on her face.

*

The March winds came.

Dianne had joined the Docents at the San Francisco Museum of Contemporary Art. Twice a week she'd taken classes at the museum, taking copious notes on the paintings. She didn't believe in telling people what to look for in art. She wanted the viewer to come to their own conclusions. So she didn't take tours. But she'd met a lot of Docent ladies, who bought art from her artists. She brought bringing the Docent ladies to see the artists' studios, riding shaky freight elevators to the top floors of abandoned buildings. The ladies wore silk blouses with bows, and bought a lot of art. Her business was expanding.

Almost every day, Sam called. Or he came over for dinner. He brought her Chanel #5 perfume, and sent notes on green stationary, and articles about artists, architecture, film, the notes signed *SW,* with three little stars. While Joe cooked fabulous dinners for the girls, Sam and often his artist friends sat on the floor, exchanging stories about the art world. Dianne felt close to Sam. She felt a special connection with him.

That evening, Joe and Sam were at her flat. Joe was in the kitchen making spaghetti, and Sam was watching her work on a twelve-foot painting of a lady climbing from a box.

The girls were playing jump rope on a rope they'd made from rubber bands, and attached across the hallway.

"I like that painting," Sam said. "It's strangely perverse. It's exciting."

"I told you," said Joe, emerging from the kitchen. An apron was tied around his waist.

Sam said: "Someday you'll be an important painter, Dianne. But you need controversy. Or your paintings will end up over a Docent ladies' sofa."

Dianne laughed. She dropped her brush into the coffee can, and then she covered the painting with a thin plastic sheet.

"I want to buy all the box paintings," said Sam with a cackle. "One hundred dollars each."

"I'd love you to own my paintings."

"Your work will be in the Samuel West Wing."

Joe said: "We'll put the box paintings in my warehouse with the antique cars."

Sam clapped his hands, as if it were settled. "Excellent. Someday people will stand in line to see the box paintings, and the Cadillacs. He let out a series of cackles. He wrote a check for nine hundred dollars. He bought nine box paintings.

"Thank you," Dianne said. "I'm thrilled."

Joe said he'd make arrangements to pick up the paintings. "Now, let's eat."

They ate at the kitchen table. The fresh salad with Joe's home grown vegetables, and the spaghetti were marvelous. The girls enjoyed Sam's outrageous stories about the art world.

It was a wonderful night. Sara and Jenny loved Sam and Joe. After dinner Sara danced for us, and Jenny did magic tricks she'd learned with cards.

After everyone left, and the girls went to bed, Dianne sat by the window, observing the moon. She believed in fate. For the first time in her life she knew that she was on the right journey. Something was happening. If you stay on your dream, never give it up, you'll find your way.

She closed the drapes, and then she went to bed.

Two days later, Dianne watched as two movers wrapped the box paintings in bubble wrap, and one by one, loaded them into the back of Joe's warehouse truck.

A week later, Dianne rented a small studio on Alabama street. It was a garage, but it had a sink, a bathroom, and the last artist who'd rented it, had built slots for canvasses.

She loved working in the studio. Sam continued to introduce her to new artists, and her client list continued to grow.

Sam had taken her to William Wiley's loft. A sensitive, interesting man, Wiley had introduced her to corn whiskey, and showed her his marvelous map paintings.

Afterwards, Sam had taken her to dinner at a restaurant in Sonoma. They ate corn chowder, and danced to songs on a jukebox. He was exposing her to a new world.

But still, even though her business was growing, she took small commissions, sometimes even not taking any, and she was barely making ends meet. She needed to sell more expensive art, and to expand her knowledge. Taking Sam's advice she called

David Noel, and introduced herself. "I would love to sell art for you. To see your gallery, and your art collection?" Her voice trailed.

"My gallery is being renovated," he said in a deep impatient voice. "Be at my house tomorrow, at three o'clock. Don't be late."

He gave her the address, and before she could thank him, he hung up.

*

24

The next afternoon, Dianne arrived at David Noel's house on Nob Hill. It was set high, as if hanging on the edge of something. Trees dropping like umbrellas shadowed the narrow wood house in sudden darkness.

She took a deep breath and rang the bell. Plantation shutters folded over the tall arched windows. She rang the bell again, wondering if she had the wrong time. Just then she heard fast impatient footsteps.

The door opened.

Her breath was taken away. Immediately, she was attracted. He stood there like he owned the world. He had long auburn hair, and a short auburn beard framing his narrow face. Just the way he dressed was different. He wore full tan trousers, a belt buckled in silver, and a silver cuff on his narrow wrist. His intense gaze made her feel like she was in her dream, caught naked in a crowd of dressed people.

"I'm in a bit of a rush," he said, glancing at the Rolex watch on his narrow wrist. "I'll show you my collection."

She followed him into a narrow hallway with tall angled skylights letting in spasms of light. He walked on his toes, like a young boy, his spider thin body toppled forward. A very young girl was lying on the living room couch, her jet-black hair dangling over the edge like black satin.

He led Dianne along a hall, pointing out paintings by Agnes Martin, Richard Serra, Dorthea Rockburne, Brice Marden, Ellsworth Kelly, paintings she'd seen in art books.

Each painting was minimal, perfect, austere, no misses. Even the furnishings--a Corbusier chair, a Mies Van Der Rhoe glass dining table, a perfect hybrid orchid inside a square glass vase, were perfect. Everything was white, chrome, minimal. As if he lived inside the art.

He paused by a Richard Tuttle pale blue rectangular cloth. "Notice the narrative, its quintessential line. You see, less is more," he sighed.

He continued lecturing about minimal art, as if there were no room for opinion.

She thought he was arrogant and slightly ridiculous, but she admired his confidence, his absolute passion. Everything about him aroused her; the way he suddenly touched the side of a painting, then sighed.

"Tuttle is pristine," he said, gazing at a blue hexagon cloth. "He's elegant."

"Tuttle is ...cold," she said. "The work lacks emotion."

"Tuttle is clout. Class!" he snapped. "His paintings are about ideas and intellect. Not about gaudy images to hang over gaudy sofas and to evoke gaudy emotions." He paused. "Do you have a client list?" He adjusted a Tuttle drawing that'd tilted slightly on the wall.

"Not with me. I've sold mostly new artists to new collectors. Sam West introduced me to a lot of new artists."

"Sam West collects schlock! A dreadful little man who trades art for dental services!" He frowned unpleasantly. "He buys low, donates high."

"Sam takes risk. He buys art that no one else is buying," she said. "He'd bought Christos' curtain, Joan Brown, Diebenkorn."

"All minor artists," he snapped. "There isn't any decent art in the San Francisco Bay Area. New York is the only place that has decent art. The better collectors are in Los Angeles."

He spoke as if there were no room for any discussion or opinion. She wanted to tell him that he was wrong, that art has no gender, no place.

"I hear your gallery is showing art that no other gallery is showing."

He frowned. "My shows are too good for the Bay Area," he said, petulantly. "I'm in the business of selling serious art to serious collectors for serious money. I'm showing *important* art: Chuck Close, Joel Shapiro, Flavin's neon light paintings, Sol LeWitt-cutting edge—*major* artists."

"I'd like to work for you," she said. "Here is my resume. I also paint. I have a degree in art history."

He dropped the resume on a table. His appraising eyes lingered on her burgundy silk vest, lace-up ankle boots, long silver earrings.

"Tomorrow ... late afternoon, around three, stop by the gallery. I'll show you the inventory."

"I'll be there," she said.

"Next Thursday night," he said, dropping his voice, as if extending a precious invitation. "I'm opening the gallery with Tuttle. I'll put you on the mailing list." He said it reverently. As if the mailing list was a private club.

"I'll try and be there," she said.

An arrogant, nasty man.

But there was something about him, some odd sexual glow, some edgy thing that made him unique. Like a dream dressed up.

"Well, thank you. I'll see you tomorrow."

He shut the door.

She ran down the stairs. The fog was thick and the clouds were fading into dots. Her heart was beating fast and she knew that something significant had happened. Something that only happens once.

The next afternoon she arrived at the David Noel Gallery on Fillmore Street.

The industrial modern building smelled of fresh paint. Dianne followed a freshly painted black arrow that pointed to the *David Noel Gallery*.

At the top floor, she went inside the gallery. It was huge, at least five thousand square feet and tall industrial windows.

Her high-heel black leather boots clicked on the gray concrete floors. Workmen were installing track lights, and the walls were empty, ready for the next show.

Careful not to step on the maze of cables, and ladders, Dianne tiptoed across the gallery to David Noel's office. She stood by the open door.

He sat behind a modern white lacquer desk, typing. He sat slumped over the typewriter, typing on two fingers. His shirt cuffs were perfectly folded over the edge of his gray cashmere sweater. David's Semitic nose, pointed chin, and beard reminded her of Van Gogh's memorable face. Several small grid paintings hung from the wall next to his desk. The paintings were sparse, but like the repetition of pure melody, they had a force.

"Excuse me, Mr. Noel?" she said after a moment.

He pulled the letter from the typewriter, read it, and quickly folded it, his hand smoothing the crease. As if remembering she was there, he turned, and looked at her.

"I don't have much time," he said. "Richard Tuttle is coming to town and I have to pick up him up at the airport." He glanced at his watch. "I'll show you the inventory. Follow me."

He walked ahead of her, bent slightly forward, stopping to yell at a workman that a track light was off a fraction of an inch. "Incompetent!" he said, as if to no one. "The workmen in this country should have their wrists broken."

He unlocked the storage room, turned on a switch, and track lights slowly flickered on, making popping sounds.

The stockroom was piled with sculptures and paintings she'd seen in art books and magazines. He moved like a shadow between paintings and sculptures, explaining the origins of each piece. As she listened to him pontificate in a didactic tone about minimal art, repeating, "Less is more," she knew that underneath his arrogant tone and stern demeanor, was a passion so strong, so emotional, that she shuddered.

"A beautiful Hunt," he said wistfully, his artistic hand stroking the steel cone-shaped sculpture. "Sell it for twenty thousand, and I'll give you twenty percent."

He moved to a magnificent bronze sculpture. "Joel Shapiro's 'Running Man,' is a masterpiece. Sell it, but not a penny under forty thousand. If you sell it you're a genius. It's too good for the Bay Area."

He brushed a speck of dust from the sculpture, his hand touching it as gently as a parent touches his child.

"Joe Brenner ... he's an interesting collector, and he might like the Mangold circle painting. He buys a lot of different works. I'll bring him to the opening."

He slouched, looking at her with an unpleasant scowl. "If you can sell Bay Area dreck to yenta Bay Area collectors, you can sell anything. Every night I pray that medical science will find a cure for menopause. Every rich doctor's wife in this town calls herself an art consultant."

Dianne stifled a laugh. "I believe that there are all kinds of collectors," she said. "I met a garbage man who rides the truck by day and at night he goes to gallery openings and buys wonderful Bay Area art."

"There is no wonderful art in the bay area. Only ceramic frogs, and curtains."

"But art is art," she protested, irritated by his blanket statements. "You never know where it comes from. At the Armory show, people threw eggs at the Fauves," she said. "'Green Hair,' they laughed. Gertrude Stein said to Alice B. Toklas, 'Let's buy it.' It was a Matisse."

"I like your spirit, Dianne. You have style and energy. Sell these pieces, and we're in business. I'll give you twenty percent."

She stood so close to him she could see the tiny silver flecks in his beard. He turned off the lights, as if their discussion was ended, and then he locked the door. "I'll give you slides of the artists I want sold."

She followed him into his office. He gave her a manila envelope of slides. The envelope was marked *Dianne Roseman*. His phone rang, and as if she'd been dismissed, he answered it. He turned his back, holding the receiver close to his mouth, and talking low. She knew it was the girl and she felt jealous. She paused a moment, and then she left.

It was past midnight and Dianne couldn't sleep. She couldn't stop thinking about David Noel. Something about him affected her in a way she'd never felt. It was his undying passion for his own beliefs that moved her. As if the passion she felt as an artist had connected to his. He was more than just an interesting man. He was a force.

The sound of foghorns and the rain pattering on the windows slowly lulled her to sleep.

She dreamed that David Noel was in a box, the top poked with holes. She studied him; his nose was long and thin, bumped at the bridge, and slightly red at its tip. Tiny creases sagged along the edge of his small and prim mouth. His forehead was wide and his auburn hair curled at the neck. His temperamental eyes were gazing at some distant point. She wanted to go into the box and touch him.

*

"I'm going to sell art for David Noel," Dianne told Sam the next night.

Sam was at her flat, lying on the sofa, his bare feet perpendicular.

"Excellent! Sell his constipated art and make a lot of money. Then you'll make a fortune and can concentrate on your paintings."

"I found David Noel … interesting. He invited me to his Tuttle show."

"Don't fall for him. He's engaged to Gloria Simmons."

"Yes, I met her," Dianne said, pretending that she'd known he was engaged.

"He chooses his women like he chooses his art," Sam continued. "A classic narcissist. Art defines him. He's a tin man with no heart."

During the week, Dianne made cold calls to clients, asking if they'd like to see a masterpiece "From David Noel's Gallery," she whispered into the phone. She studied patron lists on the back of art catalogues, and located their phone numbers and addresses. She sent her business cards, and made more calls, introducing herself, and letting them know quickly that she was working for David Noel. "The Hunt is one of a kind," she said. "David Noel won't show it to just anyone. He told me to contact you."

She'd made several appointments to show the art.

And then it was the night of David's Tuttle show.

25

Dianne, Joe, Sam, and his new girlfriend Teresa, arrived at David Noel's Tuttle opening. The gallery was packed. After Joe, Sam, and Teresa had disappeared into the crowd, Dianne stood by the entrance, observing the show.

The crowd was a mixture of affluent collectors and art groupies and artists wearing bell-bottom jeans, hot pants, tie-dye shirts, and leather jackets. Pale thin women—wealthy art world goddesses with tight eyelids and fluttering hands, were wearing Halston mini dresses and Elsa Peretti silver bean necklaces. Their men wore dark navy blazers with brass nautical buttons and silk handkerchiefs folded in their pockets like flowers. They moved like slinkies, barely looking at the art. As if their glances would make or break art history.

The installation was perfect, with just the right amount of light. The Tuttle paintings were strategically hung; one on a wall, as if too precious to mingle. The cloth constructions were indeed minimal, a hexagon cloth attached to two nails, the configurations titled "Magic" or "Paladin." Studying each painting, she thought that the configurations were really elegant, but self-conscious; as if the artist had maybe started to get inside himself and then stopped, letting virtuosity take over.

And then she saw David, and her heart pounded. He was talking to a group of men wearing pin stripe suits. He was wearing a brown velvet jacket with wide lapels, and two flaps that dented into his narrow waist. A tiny white rose was in his lapel. Transfixed, she stood there watching his dramatic presence, imagining what it would be like to kiss his prim mouth, reminding herself that he was engaged. Their eyes caught and embarrassed that he saw her staring at him, she moved closer to a group of collectors.

She lit a cigarette, eavesdropping on the group discussing the show.

"I don't like string," said a red face man. His head was bald, with a fringe of dark hair floating along its edge. He had tiny eyes under double folded lids, and a wide fleshy nose. Dianne recognized him as Harry Nathan, president of Nathan's Cement companies, and a big time collector. She'd seen pictures of his collection in Art Forum Magazine. He bought one of everything.

"Tuttle is ... so Kafkaesque ... so ... poetic," his wife, a bird-like woman lisped, her small hands tugging at a yellow silk shawl with dusty fringe.

"Kafka Schmasque!" he shrugged. "Poetic prices! David Noel sells me a Schnabel painting with broken plates on it. And now you made me buy a rag stretched over a nail."

"It's an investment, Harry," she whispered.

"What about the painting by the Mexican broad who got a pole up her yang-yang? You made me buy that picture of her holding a monkey."

"Kahlo, darling," said the woman, poking his arm.

"A fortune I spent on a dented soup can! I have dozens in the kitchen cupboard. What did I have to buy that shit for?"

"Warhol, darling."

"Hello, Dianne," said David, appearing by her side.

"Hello, David."

"I love your outfit," he said, his appraising eyes on her black velvet man's suit, and white satin necktie. A black thin feather was on the side of her hair. "You've got style, kid."

She smiled, taken back by his sudden compliment. "This is a great crowd."

He frowned unpleasantly. "The show is *major*. I put two away for myself. Charles Saatchi bought two Tuttle paintings. Mimi Plotkin bought one."

He glanced at his watch. "I have to run. I'm giving a dinner for Tuttle, and Gloria is waiting. Keep trying to sell. I'll be in New York for the next two weeks."

"Sure. Soon. I've made some good contacts. I'll let you know."

But he'd already turned his back and she watched him hug the girl she'd met at his house. She was no more than twenty, drop dead gorgeous. She was wearing a red cape, tall boots, and her hair draped her shoulders like black satin.

"I've been looking for you," Joe said, suddenly appearing by her side. "I like the show, but I don't like David Noel," Joe said. "He's an arrogant bastard."

"I have to get drunk to look at these rags. Designer art," Sam said, with a wave of his hand.

"C'mon Sam. Let's go to dinner," Teresa said, giving Dianne a warning look, like a parent does when their child is misbehaving.

"Be careful," Sam said to Dianne. "He's using you. He knows you can sell, knows that you're hungry ... talented. If you don't sell, he'll throw you out. He's a star fucker."

She nodded, pretending she agreed. "I'm starved," she said, taking Joe's hand.

*

26

It was almost two months since she'd seen David Noel at his opening.

Dianne hurried into a tall building on Montgomery Street. She was on her way to meet Lori May, a well-known art consultant, and the president of *Art Beat*. Lori sold expensive art to corporations, and Dianne had met her at a Docent meeting.

She rode the elevator to the twentieth floor, and got off at a quiet reception hall. Prints by Warhol, Serra, O'Keefe, Picasso, and other famous artists, framed in sleek chrome, hung from the walls. Shiny art magazines, and huge art books still shrink wrapped, were arranged on little chrome tables.

"I'm Sky, Lori's assistant," said a very young girl with hostile gray eyes, and wearing a black poncho. She led Dianne down a quiet hall into a large beige room.

Lori May sat behind a huge glass desk. Quickly, Lori extended a tiny smooth, hand. Her dark curly hair was shaped to her teeny head, and when she moved, her long silver earrings made clanking sounds.

"Make yourself comfortable," she said, pointing to a huge red chair shaped like lips. She shuffled aside some papers strewn about her desk. "I ordered lunch." She waved her tiny hand towards a black lacquer tray of sushi and with artificial flowers. She sighed. "It's been busy ... going wild."

Dianne opened her briefcase, and arranged the slides along the desk. A projector was set up. Lori cleared her throat and leaned forward.

"I want *important* art," Lori said. "I have *important* clients." She wiggled her fingers over the top of an eel wrapped in seaweed. She took a dainty bite.

"I have several pieces from David Noel's Gallery," Dianne said. "He's very select about who he sells to."

Dianne loaded the slides into the projector and began showing slides and explaining each painting. "The Richard Arschwagger is elegant, isn't it? ... notice the use of space ... then of course the Jo Baer."

"I know what I like," Lori said in a hushed tone, blinking several times. "I'll know it when I see it."

"Of course. Note Harriet Korman's beautiful white painting— Agnes Martin is pristine-- Douglas Cramer ... surely, you've heard of Douglas Cramer? He bought a Martin grid painting. Here's a Bryan Hunt sculpture. A major artist. David Noel handpicked these pieces to show you. He doesn't show them to ---anybody. The Chase Manhattan has a hold on the Hunt sculpture," continued Dianne. "I think you should buy the Hunt."

Dianne ate a piece of salmon sushi.

Sell the Hunt and you're a genius, David had said.

Lori looked at the image of the Hunt seven-foot metal sculpture.

"As you can see," Dianne explained. "Hunt's line is exquisite. The lightness defies the heaviness of the steel."

Lori squinted her eyes at the image.

"I see a ... stain on the steel," Lori said. "At these prices I can't place art with a stain on it."

"It's not a stain," Dianne emphasized. "It's the grain in the steel. Just as Serra has grains in his steel sculptures."

Lori laughed, as if unsure whether or not Dianne was joking.

Dianne said: "Have you read Harold Rosenberg's piece on the Hunt? Also, Pincus? Robert Pincus, the critic?"

Lori nodded. "How much?"

"I'll have to give up my commission ... not a penny less than twenty thousand."

"Are you sure that's not a ... stain?"

"Anyway, don't worry about it," Dianne said, placing the transparencies into her briefcase. "David wants to send it to the Guggenheim."

Lori opened a leather checkbook with "Art Beat" printed on the top in gold letters. She wrote a check payable to the David Noel Gallery, for twenty thousand. Her hand smoothed the crease on the pink check.

"You won't be sorry, Lori." Dianne slipped the check into her briefcase. She put on her gray fedora hat, and shook hands with Lori. "David Noel will call and make delivery arrangements. I look forward to doing more business with you."

An hour later Dianne arrived at David's gallery. He was in his office, on the phone, his velvet arrogant voice echoing over the gallery. She'd read in *Art News* that he and Gloria had eloped.

Her heart beating, she tiptoed across the gallery, waiting by his office until he was off the phone. He was talking to some poor artist, yelling that the artist's work was not developed, and that he was an "important dealer," and didn't have time for such "incompetent work!" "You should have your wrist broken! Don't bother me again!" He banged the phone so hard that Dianne jumped, and then he threw a telephone book across the office, the book landing with a loud thump.

"Excuse me, David?"

He turned. As if he hadn't just destroyed some artist's life, he smiled. "Dianne, I was going to call you. See how you're doing with the transparencies." He glanced at his watch. "I have an appointment in Sausalito. I only have a few minutes."

"I thought you might be interested in this," she said, giving him the envelope with the check. "Lori May bought the Hunt sculpture."

He opened the envelope, and removed the check. "You're a genius kid. She's a yenta."

He paused, looking at her intently. "You could make a lot of money selling art." He nodded, as if substantiating his statement. On his desk was a pile of books wrapped in plastic. He removed one. "I bought this for you in New York."

"Me?" she said, holding the book on Picasso. She was surprised.

"The Picassos were fabulous," he said, pressing two slim fingers to his lips, as if a kiss. "New York was lovely. Wait until you see the Schnabel paintings. I'm going to open with Schnabel in LA."

"You're moving to Los Angeles?" She tried to sound casual.

"I'm looking for a space there. LA is where the major collectors are." He glanced at his watch again, and then buttoned his cashmere jacket.

"May I have my check?"

He sighed. Then brushing a speck from the sleeve of his cashmere jacket, and frowning, reluctantly, he wrote her a check.

The check was for one thousand dollars instead of four thousand. "It's supposed to be twenty percent," she said.

He shrugged. "I lost money on this deal. I had to give up my commission. I didn't make anything, so I had to give you less commission. Sorry, kid."

She fought the impulse to leave the check on his desk and walk out but she needed the money. She folded the check and put it in her purse.

"I'm meeting John Block, a *major* collector. He's selling his collection. I think it might be good to see what he wants to sell. I'll make the commission up to you."

"I have to get home ... the girls' babysitter ... "

"Another time," he said. "Thanks, Dianne. I have to get going. Try and sell the Shapiro."

"I'll call my babysitter," she heard herself say. She called Sara and told her she had an appointment to sell art, and would be home later.

The sun was coming down and a dark fog lay over the bay. David drove his Honda fast, and his hands barely touched the wheel. He told her about the two Brice Marden paintings he'd recently bought, and about the art he owned and kept in a warehouse. "The Marden paintings are pristine. Perfect," he said with a series of satisfied sighs. Underneath his snippy tone there was a child's yearning for something extraordinary. Everything he described was either great, or poor. There was no middle ground. Only a top.

Half shadowed by fading light, the Golden Gate Bridge dropped an apricot glow on the darkening sea.

"The Clementes, and the Jasper Johns, are phenomenal," David continued. "Post Modernism at its best." He continued to rhapsodize in intellectual phrases about Raushenberg, Marden, and Mangold. "I put a Mangold away for myself. Also Marden."

They arrived in Sausalito at a suburban style house overlooking the bay. John Block greeted them. David introduced her as his "new employee."

A somber man, John had the dazed look of someone who spent his days collecting stamps. Kids rode tricycles through the house making whooping sounds, and his wife, a shadowy figure, gave hostile looks.

John's collection was vast; minimal paintings by New York artists from Carl Andres bricks, to Jasper John's flag painting, and Lynda Benglis, and Richard Artschwager, and a wonderful Roy Lichtenstein and Barnett Newman's *Yellow Painting*. Each piece he explained in animated detail. He spoke in a low monologue, answering his own questions. As if he existed alone inside a special world.

"I need to sell the Mangold, and the Jo Baer," John continued. He patted his perspiring face with a folded handkerchief. "The jewelry business is bad. I need the money as soon as possible."

"I'll sell whatever you want," David promised.

In the living room, they sat on a faded sofa, drinking wine. John and David gossiped about who was collecting what, David ranting about the lack of patronage in the bay area. "Los Angeles is where it's at," he repeated.

As John and David discussed art, their voices passionate, their knowledge vast,   John's children were screaming, and his wife, a small red head woman, looked irritated.

"I have to go, or my wife will kill me," David said, looking at his watch.

In the car, on the way home, the radio was on and Diana Ross sang "My Man."

"You're very good at sales," he said after a long silence. "You have a gift, an energy that's necessary to be a good dealer. I'll move Block's work, but I'm inundated with New York collectors, and trying to find a space in LA. I'll tell you which collectors to call. Run any collectors you come up with by me first."

"Sure thing," she said.

He was driving on the Golden Gate Bridge. Moonlight skimmed gold lines along the black water below. And then they discussed John's collection.

"John has to sell a lot of his collection. He's in financial trouble and on the brink of divorce," David confided. "His wife keeps him back. John is a great collector, and that's all he likes to do."

"How's Gloria?" she asked after a long silence, surprised by her impulsive question.

"Great. She's great. She's studying fashion photography," he said with a laugh. Then he got quiet.

She opened the window, as if the gesture of opening it covered up that she'd asked such a personal question.

Then their talk turned to the art market, and the art they loved. Dianne said that she especially loved Eva Hesse's paintings and drawings. "She uses grids, and boxes and sterile materials, but her work goes beyond her ideology, into humanity. It's just so human. So emotional."

"Yes. But Tuttle is pristine. Perfect," he said with a series of sighs. "Tuttle's vibrating wires with their graphite shadows have an air of delicacy, but it commands attention, respect, and power. His invisibility leads the mind into great vistas. Give me Tuttle and a Richard Serra and a Marden, and I'm happy."

Off the Golden Gate Bridge now, David drove his cluttered car in jerky movements, weaving in and out of lanes. After a long silence David mentioned that Joe Brenner came into the gallery and put a hold on a small Mangold drawing. "He seems like a nice man. He has a good eye," David said, approvingly.

"Yes. He's special."

"Are you with him?"

"He's a close friend."

"What do you paint?" he asked for the first time.

"Right now, women inside boxes."

He drove faster along Lombard Street. Their self-conscious quiet was embarrassing. She was struck by that inevitable disaster of unexplained chemistry and for a moment she couldn't breathe. Just being next to him aroused her: his scent, the sound of his voice, his sudden sighs. She couldn't wait to get home.

He stopped the car in front of his gallery where her car had been parked, his foot remaining on the pedal, gunning the motor. He looked straight ahead. His hands were tight on the steering wheel. She fumbled in her purse for her keys and then got out of the car trying not to clump or drop things.

"Well ... I enjoyed seeing John's collection. I'll see if I can find a client for the Baer."

"Goodnight, Dianne," he said formally, his hands tight on the steering wheel. She was hardly out of the car when he sped up the hill, a trail of smoke puffing in the dark.

27

It was two months later. Since that night at John Block's house, David Noel had sent her slides and detailed notes about the pieces he wanted sold. She had called the collectors David had referred, explaining to them that she was working for David, and that he wanted them to see certain pieces as soon as possible. "The Agnes Martin is *major*," she said into the phone. She met the collectors in their fabulous homes, and offices. She'd sold several pieces from John Block's collection. Immediately, David paid her and for the right amounts. With the money, Dianne was able to pay Jenny's tuition, Sara's ballet lessons, and Dr. Stockford. She loved earning enough money to live on her own. She'd grown up in a household where her mother had preached that a woman working was a tragedy. Dianne's business success gave her a confidence that she hadn't had.

She spent more time in her studio, painting on larger canvas, and exploring new images. Often she stopped in at David's Gallery check the inventory. She'd watch him sell art to chic, trendy, looking couples, David pontificating arrogantly about the value of owning "serious art." She admired his passion, his artistic manner, and she couldn't stop fantasizing about him. She even confided to Joe that David Noel fascinated her.

"Stay away, Dianne. He's dangerous. He'll hurt you."

"Of course not. He's married."

*

Summer passed. Her business *New Artists* was making money. Her own paintings were developing, but they weren't where she imagined them to be. She struggled with trying to connect the images of the women she painted with the emotions she wanted them to convey. At times, though the women were exciting to paint, she felt as though she couldn't catch the emotions. Making art is a process, and requires introspection and a consistent probing of the psyche. She was frustrated with her paintings of half-formed women, her hesitant line, and she had a long way to go. She spent long hours in her studio, writing in her journals, highlighting images that came from her unconscious.

Sunday night, Dianne sat at the kitchen table, typing pages from her journals. The girls were sleeping and the flat was quiet. Earlier that day, Jenny had gone to a birthday party and Min had taken Sara shopping for new clothes, and to dinner. But Sara had come home early because Min wasn't feeling well. Upset that Min was ill, Sara had gone right to bed.

She typed faster, the words, as if writing themselves floated along the page. Dianne typed: *If he wanted to leave me why did he bring me to Hawaii? In 1960, a man with a man was a dangerous situation for a Jewish Prince like Charley? I wish it were a man and then I'd know that it wasn't my fault ---*

The phone rang. Quickly she answered it so it wouldn't wake the girls. It was *Peralta Hospital* in Oakland. A nurse informed Dianne that Min was in the intensive care unit. She'd had a stroke. She was on the critical list. They'd call as soon as there was a change.

Dianne hung up the phone, when Sara, rubbing her eyes, in her long nightgown, stood by the door. "I heard the phone," Sara said. "Was it Grandma?"

"It was the hospital. Grandma had a stroke, but she's resting." Dianne got up to hug her but Sara pulled away.

"I want to see her.'"

"Not tonight, the nurse said. Tomorrow, I'll bring you to see her…"

"I want to see her!" she shouted. "Call the hospital. I want to talk to her. Now!"

While Dianne called the hospital, Sara, in her bare feet, stood anxiously next to her. Dianne asked the ICU nurse if Mrs. Perlman's granddaughter Sara could talk to her. The nurse said no, but she would talk with Sara.

Dianne gave her the phone. Sara's face was white. She held the phone close to her ear and repeated, "Give my Grandmother my love. Tell her that Sara loves her and that I love her more than anyone in the world." She hung up then. Tears streamed down her delicate face.

"Would you like … some hot chocolate? Or …"

"As soon as you hear anything wake me up. Not that you ever cared. You were mean to Grandma and to Daddy and to Papa. They hate you."

"I'm sorry, Sara." Dianne tried to hold her, but she pulled away, went into her room, and slammed the door.

Dianne couldn't breathe. She felt regret. She and Min had become friends, but since the divorce, rarely had she been with Min alone.

Dianne buried her face in her hands. If only she could go back and start all over, hold Sara close to her heart, loving her, spending time with her, doing so many things with her so that she'd have wonderful loving memories. Instead, she did nothing. She'd used the excuse that she'd been deathly afraid of being like her mother, and ironically, she'd behaved just like her mother had with her—unloving, cold, distant. Self absorbed. How foolish. How selfish she'd been. How cruel that she'd taken Sara's memories of a loving mother away. Then poor Min. So many times she'd blamed her for Sara's devotion to her, had accused her of taking Sara away from her. But the past was gone and she couldn't go back.

Dianne sat by the window, the phone next to her, awake until dawn streaked into the sky. Past five am, when the phone rang, she quickly answered it. The nurse said: "Mrs. Perlman passed away. I'm sorry."

Dianne was stunned. The words were so final. She got up and she went into the girl's room. They slept in twin beds and were asleep. Jenny's cat Moonlight lay next to Jenny, the cat's gold eyes glaring at Dianne.

She stood by Sara's bed, her heart beating fast, knowing that Sara wasn't sleeping and had been waiting. "Grandma passed away Sara. I'm so sorry. So sorry," Dianne whispered. She moved closer to the bed, her hand out to touch Sara, to hold her.

"Get out," Sara said in a dead voice

Jenny sat up, confusion on her face. "Grandma died?"

Dianne nodded. Jenny rubbed her eyes. Then she got up and went with Dianne into Dianne's room. She got into Dianne's bed, under the covers, and sobbed into the pillow.

"I love you so much Jenny. I'm so sorry. I'm so sorry. Sleep and I'll make you pancakes."

All day, Sara kept her door locked. She was inconsolable. Dianne left a bowl of hot soup by her bedroom door. Jenny brought her sandwiches and drinks but she refused to eat and told Jenny to get out. Dianne tried to call Donald but he wouldn't take her call. She called Harry and when he heard her voice, he hung up. Dianne loathed herself. Min was the only love Sara had ever felt. But the past was gone. Only there for reference. Never to live in.

It rained all day and Dianne never went out, even to get her mail. Later that day, near evening, Donald called and said he'd pick the girls up the next morning and he'd bring them to the funeral.

"I'd like to go to the funeral," Dianne said on the phone.

"You're not welcome. Have the girls ready at nine and tell them to wait outside."

The next morning, the girls dressed in their best dresses, and holding bouquet of flowers they'd picked in the garden, sat on the porch. Dianne felt so sorry for them. They hadn't seen their father in years. He'd never answered Jenny's constant letters telling him how much she loved him and wanted to see him. "It's too painful for Donald," Min would always explain.

When Donald's truck arrived, with his wife in the front seat, Sara tentatively walked to the truck, but Jenny ran. From the window, Dianne watched as Donald got out of the car. He wore Western style cowboy boots, snug jeans, and a dark blue jacket. His hair was very silver. He didn't hug the girls, and she watched them climb into the back seat.

What happens to make a father turn against his children? So embittered? Had she done that too?

All day she felt sorrow, a kind she'd never felt before. She sat by the window, watching the fog, remembering the days in Happy

Valley, when she'd been numb and had gone through her life like a robot. Yes, she'd created so much damage.

Near evening, Donald brought the girls home. Before they opened the door he drove away. Their faces white and sad, and without a word, they'd gone right to their room.

The days following, in her room, next to her bed, Sara built a shrine to her Grandmother—the needlepoint ballerina Min had made for Sara hung on the wall next to Sara's bed, the gold heart locket Min gave her, her gold charm bracelet, and the silver ballet slippers, were carefully arranged on a velvet cloth on the table next to her bed. Dianne realized then, that Sara's capacity for love all came from Min.

Jenny clung tighter to Dianne, at night, climbing in Dianne's bed and sleeping closer to her. Sara spent every extra hour she could at ballet class, excelling in her grades at school. Not once had she mentioned Min.

Two months later Harry died from a brain aneurysm. The girl's loss was devastating and Sara's eyes were filled with silence.

Min and Harry left their wealthy estate to Donald and a dollar to the girls. Dianne thought that Min probably assumed Donald would help the girls. But they never heard from him again.

*

Six Months Later:

New Artists was making more money and she'd taken out an ad in *Art Forum Magazine.* Her client list grew and she'd sold more of her box paintings. In a year, Sara would be going away to college, and she was applying for New York University. Dianne was putting away most of the money she earned for Sara's college tuition.

The art market was rising and clients were clamoring to buy New York art. David continued to have monumental shows, but few patrons showed up. He'd stand in the middle of the gallery, dressed in an elegant Armani jacket, a flower in his lapel, pontificating the "importance of buying monumental art.'" She admired his steadfast dreams and hard work. His reputation was growing and articles about him appeared in national art magazines.

Her paintings were developing from women inside boxes, to impressionistic style mothers lying in the grass with their young daughters. She was interested in color and expressing emotions and characterizations. She didn't know where she was going with her art, but through her paintings, she could see the beginnings of her new birth and transformation.

"Someone different from the way I was," she said to Dr. Stockford. "But who? I wish I could extricate the anger in me."

He nodded.

"I transferred my anger at Mother, to Sara."

She cried. He waited.

"Like my Grandmother and mother, I'm not supposed to be angry. Women are supposed to be tranquilized or married."

"You're used to hurt," he said after a long moment. "Be careful not to choose it over joy."

"Oscar Wilde says. 'There is only one real tragedy in a woman's life. The fact that her past is always her lover and her future invariably her husband.'"

"Let Charley go."

"It isn't Charley."

"What is it?"

"I don't know yet."

*

Time was passing so fast. Dianne could identify the seasons by the colors of the leaves floating along the streets. She was painting a lot, and often showed her paintings in local art shows, and small galleries. Her paintings had evolved into twelve-foot canvasses and her figures were emerging from women in boxes into women wearing erotic dresses and standing in the corners of the canvasses like shadows.

Christmas came. The girls decorated their tree with paper ornaments they'd made and strands of pearls they'd bought at the five and dime. Dianne had made a star and painted it silver and it wobbled on top of the tree.

Sara had danced the part of Clara in the *Nutcracker Suite* and she was so beautiful. While Jenny was winning blue ribbons for horseback jumping and riding.

But Dianne felt a void and she wanted to be closer to her family. She decided to visit Mike who was home from prison again. He had moved again. She had always loved him.

The next day she drove to a small area in Marin. She arrived at Mike's house. He lived in a small rented house. Tires and broken antiques were strewn about the front yard.

Mike waited on the porch, in front of a tiny crooked wooden house. His once golden hair was almost white and hung to his shoulders. He'd put on a great deal of weight.

"Good to see you, sis. You look great. He wore turquoise jewelry: rings, a squash necklace, so beautiful, but the scent of dust and perspiration exuded from his clothes.

"So good to see you," she murmured.

He smiled. Two teeth were missing. "I heard you're selling your paintings to a lot of fine people. Come in."

The small living room was stuffed with antiques he'd found in flea markets and had refinished. Each piece was carefully arranged. A tiny kitchen counter with a hot plate for cooking, and a curtain separated the kitchen from a tiny area for sleeping. His dog Maggie slept in the middle of the floor.

Mike made grilled cheese sandwiches, and he ground fresh coffee beans. They ate at a small wooden table set with china plates painted with pink roses. Everything was lovely, as if he were replaying the opulent things that he'd grown up with.

Mike poured hot steaming coffee into two antique cups. He bragged about his "big deals," about how he was making a "golf comeback." She felt sorry for him, remembering Mother screaming that he was dumb, "no good," she'd say.

She wanted to shout: *Why didn't you protest, and why didn't you get angry, and why are you so content to forget your golf career? Why are you dying?*

He stirred two sugar cubes into the coffee, the spoon tapping the side of the cup. He sighed. "Nannie used to put sugar cubes in our coffee."

"With pet milk." Dianne smiled.

"And sugar cookies," he said, laughing.

"Remember you and I hid in the basement, then when we'd hear Mother and Dad going out, we'd run up to Nannie's room and have a party."

"She made paper boats from newspaper." Mike blinked several times, as if blinking back his sadness.

"And the diving bell at Ocean Beach," Dianne continued. "When it hit bottom, you held my hand. You wore a cap with a windmill on top."

They were quiet then. She remembered Mike as a beautiful blonde boy curious about everything, and always hiding from Mother. She winced at the memory of the sound of Mother's strap on his bare buttocks.

"Bobbie has a plan to kill Mother," Mike said after a long while. "He's dangerous."

Mike smoothed the napkin on the saucer, so the coffee wouldn't spill.

"We had a hard childhood," Dianne said after a long moment.

He blinked. "I had a great childhood."

"We were criticized. You were beaten ..."

"I was a bad kid." He shrugged.

He got up. The conversation was ended. It was too painful, Dianne thought. From a narrow shelf, he removed a thick bound folder.

"Here are my depositions. Hundreds of hours. Recorded. It's quite something. I thought you'd like to see it."

She turned the pages of depositions, police reports, reading about the marijuana heist.

"Agent Dunbar said it was the biggest heist ever ... twenty six grams of heroin is no small amount ...you should have seen, Dianne... . Helicopters ... dogs. It was something."

"It must have been something." She smiled. He was so vulnerable. So sweet.

His eyes nervously darted.

"I have something I want to give you," he said after a moment.

He opened a wrinkled brown paper bag and took out a rubber band ball and a brass circular stand. It was intricately laced with thousands of colored bands.

"It's beautiful. Thank you. You're a wonderful artist," she said, moved by the intricate ball.

He shrugged. "Not like you are."

"No. Because you're you. How do you do this? It must have thousands of rubber bands?"

He shrugged. "You start with one and keep going."

They sat on the porch, and he played the harmonica. He played *Autumn Leaves*, and other songs. He'd taught himself to play. He played beautifully. While he played song after song, he closed his eyes, and his shoulders swayed.

On the way home Dianne felt sad. Mother always referred to Mike as a "bum." "Why doesn't he get a job?" she'd rant, not understanding that without an education, a prison record, he didn't have a chance to get a job. She didn't realize that she'd destroyed him completely. Never would she understand why her mother had hated him so? Why she had destroyed any ego, or potential that he'd had? Why she preferred failure instead of triumph? Her mother had tried to do the same with her, but luckily she'd sensed danger, and had learned to feel safe within herself. Still, she constantly tried to overcome her pervasive sense of worthlessness.

She drove past the farms with grazing cows. She felt sorry for the cows, wondering what they were thinking as they looked over the fence? As the sunlight dropped shadows along the roads, she thought about Bobbie's plan. She'd always worried that Bobbie's rage would surface and that he'd kill Mother. He was on heroin, and recently he'd smashed his car and Mother had replaced it with a new gold Porsche. Arrested several times for drunk driving, he wore a monitor around his ankle and everyday Mother drove him to a private methadone clinic. "He can't take those dirty busses. He has an old heart like mine," she'd say.

She drove over the bridge, into the San Francisco fog. She was home.

28

It was Sunday afternoon, a foggy gray day. Sara sat on a chair in the living room, sewing laces on her ballet slippers, and Jenny was on the floor, working on a large puzzle of horses.

Sam was lying on the couch, his bare feet perpendicular, and drinking corn whiskey. Joe was cooking spaghetti sauce, every few seconds bringing in the sauce on a wooden spoon for them to taste.

In a morose mood, Sam began talking about art world gossip--which dealer was losing money, which artists were cheating on their wives.

"The latest is that David Noel is divorcing Gloria. She doesn't suit him anymore." He cackled then.

Dianne buried her face in the *New York Times,* pretending that she hadn't heard, but her heart was beating fast. She recalled a month before, wanting to see if he had any more art for her to sell, she'd gone late in the afternoon to the gallery. She'd sat in his office, looking at slides. When her hand touched his, she'd pulled it away. When his phone rang, he'd answered it quickly, and she got up left.

"I want my mommy!" Sam said suddenly. "You don't know how sick I am, how lucky you are to be healthy." He gulped the corn whiskey.

"You need a vacation," Dianne said. "We should all go on a vacation."

"Everything is an effort," Sam complained in his Truman Capote voice, waving a pale hand. "One big fucking effort—

taking clothes to the cleaners, standing in line for prescriptions, cleaning the toilet bowl. All those fucking proletariat chores are an effort. I want to ride a merry-go-round and eat candy floss at the circus. I want my mommy. I never had a mommy. I want a mommy."

They had dinner in the dining room. Sam barely ate, and Joe talked exuberantly about his Mangold. Sam said little.

After dinner, Joe and Sam left early, and Dianne and the girls went to bed.

Deep in her dream, Dianne watched herself at twelve. She was wearing an ugly organdy dress with puffed sleeves. She was at her cousin Donald's Bar Mitzvah. No one had asked her to dance. She pretended she was searching for her napkin. When a waltz began her father asked her to dance. Blushing, she followed him to the center of the dance floor. She tried to follow him as he counted, a one, two, three, trying not to step on his feet, and praying that he wouldn't see the yellow wax in her ears. The music suddenly stopped. She awoke crying and it was dark.

She lay in bed, listening to the leaves blowing along the hills, like feathers, staring at her father's photograph.

*

The next afternoon, Sam called. He was at the Veteran's hospital. "I want to see you," he said. He sounded like it was urgent.

She drove to Veterans hospital, wondering if his diabetes was acting up again. A lot of times Sam had had insulin attacks. He'd sounded strange on the phone.

She tiptoed into the private room. It was shadowed by late day. Sam, wearing a red plaid robe sat on the narrow bed, peeling an orange. Pale, he was so pale. Why hadn't she noticed that he was so thin? The hatchet Wiley had signed and given Sam to cut trees was on the nightstand next to his bed. Sam loved that hatchet.

"Hi," she said, kissing him lightly on the mouth.

"Don't just stand there. Cat got your tongue? Pull up a chair."

She sat on a metal chair next to his bed. "You look ... fine."

He peeled another orange, his delicate fingers digging into the skin.

"Rain ... it's really raining," she said.

"What are you going to do about Joe?"

"I ... don't... understand?"

"He's in love with you."

She looked away. "We're friends."

"David Noel will hurt you. Don't go near him."

"I work with David." She looked away.

"David is emotionally limited," he continued. "He's only interested in who and what will serve him. At the first crack or flaw he'll drop you."

"Stop worrying. I'm making money with David."

He sucked the tip of the orange slice, and then dropped it into the newspaper. "And make sure your box paintings stay in my collection. As soon as you're famous the fools will try to take them away from you."

"Why are you talking like this?"

He sighed. "I have pancreatic cancer."

She couldn't talk. She couldn't process what he was telling her. Why hadn't she noticed how very thin he was? At her house just two days ago, he wouldn't eat. Had wanted his mother. She felt horrible that she hadn't seen the signs.

"I have six weeks to live."

"No one knows when someone is going to die. No one knows Sam. The doctors don't know. We'll get a second opinion. "You're not going to die."

He opened a manila envelope next to his bed and held the X-rays to the light. "These are my bones," he said. He put them into the envelope. Then he closed his eyes.

She felt as though she was in one of her dreams and was calling wake up, wake up, trying to get out. She couldn't believe this was true.

"Don't fuck it up, Dianne. You're talented, and I expect big things from you. Don't fuck it up," he repeated. "Don't give in to your demons."

She lay next to him on the thin bed, her head on his shoulder, listening to the sounds from elevator doors opening and closing, doctors paged on intercoms. She stayed there until the room got dark, and Sam was sleeping.

At the door she turned. "I love you, Sam."

He didn't open his eyes, but he nodded. And then she left.

The next morning, she called the hospital, and the nurse said Sam had gone home. She called Sam's apartment but the line was busy. She was just about to go to Sam's apartment when the doorbell rang. It was Joe. He looked stunned, like he hadn't slept.

"Come in, Joe. I tried to call Sam at the hospital. Have you talked to him?"

"Sam shot himself."

Joe's voice was far away as he repeated "He's dead, Dianne. He shot himself."

Dianne held on to the door. She felt as though the floor was coming up on her. "I saw him yesterday."

Joe explained that during the night Sam had called him. Sam had been agitated and was threatening to kill the nurses with the hatchet. The doctors threatened to commit him to the psychiatric ward. He'd called Joe and asked him to pick him up, and take him home. Sam refused to stay in the hospital. So Joe had picked him up, and driven Sam to his apartment. He'd stayed with him until he slept. Sam hadn't told Joe that he had pancreatic cancer.

"He told me that he had some tests. That he was fine."

Joe was tormented. He cried.

"It wasn't your fault, Joe. You didn't know," Dianne said, holding him tight. "How would you know?"

"If only I hadn't left him."

"He wanted to go."

"There's more, Dianne. Sam left a note. It reads that he wants the box paintings by Dianne Roseman and his collection to go to the Samuel West Wing at the Oakland Museum."

"My God. I can't believe this."

"Funny," Joe said, unfolding a white cotton handkerchief from his pocket. "He wanted controversy. He got it."

Joe made phone calls and funeral arrangements. He cooked a huge pot of spaghetti. Janet and her husband and other artists who'd known Sam, came over. They sat on the floor, and ate and told stories about Sam. Dianne and the girls made a fire in the fireplace, and they talked until after midnight.

The next day, the *San Francisco Chronicle* published Sam's suicide note. In Sam's scrawly handwriting, it was written on a page torn from *Art News* magazine. It read: *Goodbye cruel world. I leave my entire collection, my David Parks painting, and Dianne Roseman's box paintings to the Samuel West Wing for New Artists. My collection is to be moved to Brenner Motors Cadillac warehouse. It can be seen there until it is moved to the Samuel West Wing at the Oakland Museum.*

It was signed *SW* with a drawing of three tiny stars. Next to the note was a picture of Dianne. She was standing in front of her twelve –foot painting of a woman inside a box. Underneath the picture, the caption was "Mystery Woman."

It was the picture of her that Teresa had taken one night at her studio.

Within hours, Dianne received phone calls from collectors and dealers who asked to see her paintings. Controversy, Sam always said.

Now she knew what he meant. Hypocrisy was more the word.

The next few days, Joe planned the funeral. It would be at the Officers Club in the Presidio, and a full military funeral. Sam had loved pomp, and performance art. When Dianne had called Teresa, she'd hung up on Dianne. Joe said that Teresa had a lawyer and was suing for Sam's collection.

The day of the funeral it rained. Stretch limousines brought dealers and curators with solemn faces to the *Chapel Of The Chimes.*

The small chapel was packed. Artists Dianne recognized, and other artists from all over, stood along the walls, holding babies and cameras. Garish flowers shaped in Sam's initials were set on tall wood stands.

Joe and Dianne and the girls sat in the front row near the casket draped with an American flag. Baby faced soldiers surrounded the casket. They wore helmets with thick brown leather straps under their chins, and they held rifles. Artists Dianne recognized stood in line and single file passed the casket, dropping flowers or notes on top of the casket.

The chaplain, a man with a huge face and a tiny voice, gave the sermon. He exalted Sam's accomplishments at West Point, his expertise as a periodontist and his devotion to the arts. "A brave soldier and an art historian who gave his life to art," the Chaplain continued. He was careful not to mention how Sam had died.

So what if he chose to die? Dianne thought. Cats and dogs are put to sleep when they're in pain, why can't people do the same?

Sam had lived his life his way, Death had not been something he'd craved, but was his suicide was a way out of the inevitable. It's what he wanted. Again, he had created controversy.

When the sermon was over, the soldiers shot their guns twelve times into the air. Then, the soldiers folded the flag into a triangle, and marching in place, they gave Dianne the flag. It was still warm. She felt deeply honored.

The soldiers carried the casket up the aisle and d then she and Joe and the girls, ignoring the stares and whispers, followed the soldiers to the gravesite.

*

Teresa pursued a lawsuit. Three weeks after the funeral, Dianne and Joe took a deposition. The suicide note had been dated and signed. His will specifically stated that his collection would be moved from Joe's warehouse to the Museum for the Samuel West Wing. Teresa backed off and arrangements were made for the collection to go to the Oakland Museum. Officially, she donated her box paintings to the Samuel West Wing.

Curators and gallery owners called and clamored to see Sam's collection and her box paintings at the warehouse.

Wanting to raise money for the Samuel West Wing, Dianne and Joe decided to have a fundraiser at the Cadillac Warehouse, and charge twenty dollars a person, to see Sam's collection. The proceeds would go to the West Wing.

The Oakland Museum sent invitations to Bay Area collectors, announcing the date, time, and exhibit.

The night before the exhibit, Dianne was at her neighborhood pharmacy, xeroxing flyers for the show. She held her nose away from the sickly odor of the fumes from the Xerox machine, catching the flyers as they fell through the slot.

"Hello, Dianne."

She turned and faced David. His pale skin was white under the yellowish light. Airline tickets stuck from the pocket of his dark green cable knit hooded sweater.

"What are you doing here at night?" She hoped he didn't know how flustered she felt. She hadn't seen him since Sam had died.

He sniffed. "I'm leaving for New York in the morning. I have a cold. I picked up my medications." He paused. "I could ask you the same?"

"Actually, I'm Xeroxing flyers for a show of Sam West's collection at Joe's Cadillac warehouse. I sent you a flyer."

"I read about it, kid. Sorry, I won't be there. Sounds like a circus. Someday I'd like to see your box paintings."

He coughed several times. She wanted to laugh at the way he kept feeling his forehead and was clutching the bag of medications. He looked at his watch. "I'll be back in a couple of weeks. I'll call you, kid."

She nodded.

She watched him hurry away, his shoulders slumped forward, coughing, and sniffling. She went on Xeroxing, reminding herself that David Noel wasn't a man to fall in love with.

*

The show at the warehouse was a mob scene. Curiosity seekers, hopeful artists, and on- the-fringe art consultants came in droves to see the exhibit. Mimi Plotkin brought several of her friends. Former Docent ladies Dianne had known, and had once ignored her, fawned over Dianne. They asked to go to her studio and see the rest of her work.

During the exhibit, Dianne felt Sam's presence. She could hear him say: "See! All artists need controversy."

A local gallery owner invited Dianne to have a show. Dianne didn't think her work was quite ready and wanted to wait, but the gallery owner seemed nice and young and eager. Dianne agreed to show a few paintings on consignment. Meanwhile she was building a stronger body of work. But she promised the gallery owner she'd be in touch soon.

Sara and Jenny wearing long Granny skirts and hats had a great time. With their friends, they passed out flyers. Wiley played the banjo, and served corn whiskey. Pretty young artists served guacamole, and chips. Speakers recorded the Rolling Stones and people were dancing.

If you stay on your dream something will happen. She was glad Sam was getting the recognition he deserved.

Artists Sam had known had provided vintage cars decorated with paintings and beads and flowers. The cars glowed like sculptures. They were fabulous.

The show ran for four days and they'd raised over twenty-five thousand dollars. The curator of the museum was planning more exhibits at Joe's warehouse, with new artists. Dianne loved this idea.

Dreams do come true, Dianne thought. *But you have to be ready for them.*

As the days passed, Dianne worked hard selling art. She'd sold several of her own paintings. Happily, she put the money away in Sara's college account.

But it was time to visit her family. Since Mother had been so ill she hadn't seen much of her. Mother had invited her to the house the next night to have dinner. The girls were going on an overnight camping trip with their school and wouldn't be home. Dianne's car was in Joe's shop getting new brakes, so Max had said he'd pick her up.

29

The next evening at six on the dot, Max picked her up in his red Volvo. The traffic was heavy and as Max drove across town they made small talk about the humid weather. She liked Max. He lived by simple values and a hard work ethic. He loved sports, and though he was short, he was a champion skier and tennis player.

He drove fast, almost recklessly. A scowl was on his face. Dark curly salt and pepper hair framed his fleshy face and bulbous nose, but his eyes were beautiful, and he was smart.

"Your mother's crazy!" he said suddenly, jerking the car faster. "I pay her mortgage off! Bobbie gets arrested for drunk driving and I bail him out. The only job he's ever had is community service. Slick Mike steals us blind. Every time he's at the house there's something missing—silverware, money. Next time, I'm not bailing him out. He can fry."

"What does Mother say?" Dianne carefully asked, saddened by her mother's troubles, and by Max's obvious pain.

"She cries." he replied, with a tired sigh. "Bobbie has a hold over her. He's a faggot on top of it."

"That part is good," Dianne said emphatically. "At least he knows who he is."

"He's still a faggot."

Dianne recalled Nannie telling her that Mother had had Bobbie's boyfriend Mark arrested for stealing her jewelry. Then, Bobbie had set a fire to the basement. Poor Mother. She thought that money would create her sons, but without love and values and purpose, she'd created broken people.

Max stopped the car in front of Mother's house. He parked behind Bobbie's gold Porsche.

Mother was wearing a long emerald color hostess dress, matching slippers, and pearls. As usual she was beautiful, but since her heart attack, her face was bloated, and her body was heavier. The sudden smell of lemon wax made Dianne suddenly sad. Everything was the same. As if kept in place forever.

"The family will be here soon," said Mother in a baby voice. "Mike is arriving soon, Dianne, and Nannie is upstairs waiting."

"Where's Bobbie?" Dianne carefully asked.

"In the tool room," Mother said in a coy voice." He's *fixing* our toaster. He's so clever."

"Fixing nothing!" scowled Max. "He's taping our conversations."

"Max! Change your clothes. My family doesn't wear jogging clothes to dinner."

Dianne hurried upstairs, stepping over the old tear in the carpet, into her old room.

A framed photograph of Bobbie at fourteen at Mr. Kitchen's Dancing School, hung from the wall. He was standing between two girls wearing white gloves and organdy dresses, a dazed expression on his taut face.

She went into Nannie's room. "The Price Is Right" played from Nannie's television, but she was sleeping.

Dianne tiptoed to the bed, and watched her sleep. Her red hands were folded. Powder was creased in the web of lines on her thinning face and dots of coral rouge on her cheekbones.

On the bedside table there was a jar of lemon drops, and a photograph of Dianne, and the girls. As if sensing Dianne's presence, Nannie opened her eyes, her eyelids flickering.

"Oy. Why didn't you wake me? This lousy medication." She sat up.

Dianne took her in her arms, inhaling the lilac scent on her soft, fading skin. Underneath the quilted bed jacket, her bones felt thin as bird wings. "You look good, Nannie."

"I look lousy," she said with a double shrug. "The doctors don't know what the hell they're doing. Robbers."

They laughed.

Dianne sat on the edge of the bed. She showed Nannie pictures of Sara at her ballet recital. "Sara got a scholarship to New York University, and she can study ballet. In less than a year she graduates."

Dianne chatted about the Samuel West Wing, about her paintings, that she was submitting slides to New York Galleries, and about David Noel's gallery, and how she hoped someday David's gallery would represent her work.

"He's brilliant. He represents artists from New York that no other gallery shows in California."

"So nu?"

"What do you mean?" Dianne said, laughingly.

"Your voice changes when you talk about David Noel. I've read about his gallery in the *San Francisco Times*. He looks like a goniff."

"He's a dedicated dealer. He's the best Nannie, and he's a great collector. He works hard."

"It's up to you, Dianne. You've accomplished a lot. Don't give it away."

"Don't worry, Nannie."

"I worry plenty," Nannie said after a long moment. "Bobbie has no purpose. Your mother spends Max's money like water. Bobbie steals my medications, and runs up bills. Poor Mike is a lost soul. Your mother beat him to a pulp when he was only a little boy. She didn't listen. I don't know what the hell was wrong with her."

They sat in silence.

No matter how you try you can never make the past right.

Dianne watched Nannie fold the newspaper into a boat, her trembling hands carefully creasing the paper. She gave the paper boat to Dianne.

"I always remember you making these boats, Nannie. I'll keep this one."

"Now go downstairs. I'll try to come down later. Your Nannie isn't feeling well."

Max was in the den, watching a football game on television, Max yelling, "Bazooka!' Mother and her new housekeeper Matilda were in the kitchen. Dianne wanted to visit with Bobbie.

She went down the back stairs to the basement, holding her breath from the familiar musty smell of damp.

Bobbie's tool room was once a rumpus room where Dianne and her friends would play *Spin the Bottle.*

The door was locked, and Dianne knocked on it three times. Except from the glow of light that seeped from under the door, the basement was pitch dark. Dianne shivered, remembering the time Bobbie had put her cat Soxy in the washing machine and its head was decapitated. Dianne had sat crying, scrunched up behind the boiler.

Bobbie opened the door. She was struck by his weight gain.

"Hello," he said, giving her a quick wet kiss on the cheek.

"I'd love to see your tool room."

"Come in," he said, holding his arms straight out, as if balancing his pear-shape body. He wore a striped T-shirt, and tan gabardine formal slacks. A rubber apron with huge pockets was tied around his wide waist. He wore a green plastic visor that shielded his sunken eyes.

The room had low ceilings, and it was hot. The one window was shut, and a portable heater was on blasting hot air. The toom reeked from marijuana.

In the center of the room there was a long wood worktable. Beethoven's Fifth played loudly from a small black radio. Next to it was a hot plate, a basket of tea bags, and a cup marked with his name. Expensive compressors, drills, saws, hammers, hung from hooks on corrugated walls, displayed like rare birds. Tiny glass drawers of bolts, nails, shiny and unused, were neatly labeled like rare plants. An expensive tape recorder was on, recording the muffled voices and footsteps from upstairs.

"This is quite a book," said Dianne, looking at a thick black binder with pictures of Doberman guard dogs. There were pages in Bobbie's child handwriting, detailed descriptions of the dog's habits, foods, illnesses, cures. It had required a great deal of research.

"You could publish this, Bobbie. Dog lovers would buy this ... its years of work."

"Guess so." He turned on an electric saw, slicing a thick piece of wood.

"You always loved dogs," she continued, her voice rising above the strident sound of the saw.

He stopped sawing. A darkness like a shadow came over his sad face. "Penny, she was my Doberman. That's her picture," he said, pointing to the photograph in the book.

"Yes, I recall."

"Mother gave her away."

He resumed slicing the wood.

Dianne closed the book. To think that she'd once hated— was jealous of him. He'd been emotionally kidnapped into his mother's house, and never could he get out. He was trapped.

The tool room was his role, his identity.

"What a lovely clock," she said, touching the side of a modern clock set inside a square finished wood frame.

He nodded. "I made it for Mother."

"Mother says she doesn't know what she'd do without you. She's grateful you fix everything."

He shrugged. "That's because Max is cheap. Too cheap to hire anyone. "

He pressed his small mouth. "Max called the police on my boyfriend Mark. He went to jail."

Dianne sighed. "He doesn't understand."

"I have a *plan*," he said, with a lascivious grin.

"You could maybe start a dog business," she said quickly. "Something to get you out of here."

"I'm *plenty* busy here," he snapped, his voice rising. "After I go to the clinic, I polish silver—I go from there." He shrugged. "The other day I made a cake—a nice sponge cake for Mother, decorated it and everything, but she got angry. She said homos make cakes."

"She doesn't understand. I wish you could leave."

"Nannie hoards my headache pills. She hates it here too."

"Bobbie! Dianne!" Mother called, her voice shrill on the recorder. "Everyone is here. Come upstairs."

Upstairs, the relatives sat on chairs arranged at the edge of the living room. Mike hugged her. He wore a jacket with big pockets, and more teeth were missing. "Good to see you Sis. You look swell." His clothes exuded the musty smell of garlic and perspiration.

Mother was at the Steinway, playing Cole Porter songs, and singing *A Million Dollar Baby* in her high baby voice. Dianne sat on the wing chair next to the piano, sipping vodka over ice. A fake fire burned an odd glow in the fireplace.

At the bar, Max made drinks. Bobbie stood off to himself, holding his tape recorder. He stood on his heels, his body slightly backwards, making nasty remarks, and then laughing his Donald Duck laugh.

"Schmaltzy booze, Max," he taunted. He said aloud: "Aunt Zoe's face looks like a bloated mushroom." Mike laughing a rabbit laugh.

Max's granddaughter Myra was screaming in everyone's faces, and then running away.

Aunt Pearl shouted, "Keep the kid quiet!"

As if to upset Mother, Mike bragged about his latest drug "case," and that his "famous" lawyer was "getting him off. "Gotta keep the faith," Mike added, his nervous eyes darting back and forth.

"I keep the faith that your lawyer doesn't spend all my money!" said Max, laughing to no one.

"Let's talk about something pleasant," said Mother, frowning. Mother passed a platter of cheese puffs.

"Nu, Dianne?" said Aunt Pearl with a shrug. "How's our Marjorie Morningstar?"

"I'm doing great," Dianne replied.

"An artist," said Aunt Zoe. "I didn't think she had it in her."

"So what good? After an artist is dead they're famous," said Uncle Maury.

"Still no husband," said Aunt Pearl, with a sigh. "The girl has no luck."

"That rotten Charley," Uncle Maury said to everyone, as if Dianne wasn't there.

"Oy, it's 1978, and the feminist movement made you girls nuts. You'll be alone."

Christopher was running around in a circle trying to catch his rubber mouse. Myra was making Indian warrior screams, and Mike was bragging about his rubber band balls.

"Takes me about five years to make a rubber band ball. I start with one rubber band, and the rest is history. I sell them for five hundred dollars."

"Where he's going he'll have plenty of time to make rubber band balls!" shouted Max, then laughing to no one.

Bobbie held the tape recorder close to Max.

"Mike!" Mother shouted. "Do you have to wear those wooden clogs? They're noisy and they scratch my floors!"

"I like my clogs."

"Real men your age don't wear clogs," she persisted. "They don't wear turquoise beads and pony tails!"

"This time please God, Dianne will find a decent husband,'" Uncle Maury said.

"Please God," said Aunt Pearl.

Mother announced in her baby voice, her hands waving the air, "Dinner."

A stampede went into the dining room. The apricot silk wallpaper was faded, and the dining table was over-polished. Orange Bird of Paradise was carefully arranged in metal frogs inside copper bowls.

At the buffet, the guests served themselves to sliced Roast Beef, Aunt Pearl's homemade noodle koogle, salads, and roast vegetables.

The family ate fast, talking at once about who had died, who was dying, and had filed bankruptcy. The tiny crystal bell was beside Mother's plate, like a prop. Bobbie was obviously stoned. While Mike slipped the silver, and dinner rolls into the big pocket on his loose worn jacket.

My poor family. Everyone is empty—so empty, living unlived lives. They have acquisitions, but no purpose, no structure, and no love.

Later, after coffee, and a too rich dessert, Dianne was alone with her mother in the den. Mother was shuffling cards, getting ready to play bridge. As usual, they were self consciously quiet with each other. Dianne tried to make conversation. "A wonderful dessert. Not like Nannie's lemon pies but the custard was excellent."

Mother shuffled the cards one more time, and then patted the cards, as if satisfied the cards were crisp and clean.

"Blossom Shapiro's daughter met a gorgeous man, Dianne. Now she won't be. *alone*. It's awful for a woman to be ...alone." She patted the cards.

"I'm happy for her," Dianne said.

In a wavy voice, Mother said, "Alyse Birnbaum died. She turned blue. That was it." She sighed, her eyes darting. "Dr. Cohn says my heart is fine." She paused. "Thank God for Bobbie, Dianne. He cleans the house better than Birdie ever cleaned. Brings Nannie her medications." She frowned. "He's fixing the basement floor. It's buckling up--"

"Mother. We need to talk." She waited. Mother frowned.

"We should see each other more often. I want us to know each other before it's too late." Mother blinked. "I only want you to live a normal life." Then as if she had solved everything between them, she went into the living room to play her bridge game.

30

Dianne pulled her burgundy hat over her eyes. It was a dark, rainy night and Mimi Plotkin's new gallery opening was packed with wealthy socialites, art consultants, and curators. Dianne leaned against the bar, admiring a Rothko print of a large black painting with two red bars floating in its center. A quiet torment lay over the painting. A group of collectors were talking about the show.

"The images are so ... so... "

"Expensive," said Harry Nathan.

"We could have bought a Rothko painting. Remember Harry?"

He smoked a cigar. "Once they kick the bucket the art goes sky high. Even the crap prints are high."

Dianne was just about to move away when she saw David. He was talking to a woman with pale angel hair, and wearing a high-tech silver necklace. It'd been over a month since she'd seen him at the pharmacy, and purposely she hadn't been to the gallery.

Quickly, she turned away but he'd seen her, and was coming over to her.

"Hello, Dianne."

"It's good to see you, David. It's been a long time."

"Yes, I know. I've been meaning to call you." He paused. "I have a Schnabel plate painting I want you to see."

"I've been selling my paintings, and, a lot of Bay Area art," she said.

"So I've heard. You're a genius if you can sell schlock to yentas," he said unpleasantly.

"I heard you found a space in Los Angeles?"

He pursed his lips. "It's fabulous, Dianne. LA is where the *major* art is. Here, all the collectors know from are ceramic frogs and prints! The wives of rich men, open galleries, and show junk," he said, looking towards Mimi." He sniffed.

He stood close to her. She wanted to wipe the smudge on his glasses, touch his beard carefully shaped to a point, the rush of curls at his neck. "Can you have a drink?" she asked.

He glanced at his watch. "How about dinner?"

Outside, it was pouring a thick rain. The unpaved streets were filled with puddles. David opened his umbrella, and it made a popping sound. They ran along the dark wet streets to his silver Honda.

"Just move the stuff into the back," he said, getting into the car.

She moved the array of art catalogues, airline tickets, and slides into the back seat, and then she snapped her seatbelt.

He turned on the radio, and then drove into traffic. '*Bewitched, bothered and Bewildered,*" played on the radio, and rain slashed the windows.

As he drove in jerky impatient movements, he ranted about Mimi Plotkins "imbecile show," continuing to complain about the Bay Area art scene; "Jewish Renaissance wives of rich men who think they're dealers will be the death of the art world," he snipped. He couldn't wait to open his Los Angeles gallery, he said.

Dianne thought that he was arrogant and full of himself, but she was in awe of his passion and of his dreams. He was like a young boy running after a ball rolling down a hill and determined to catch it. Even the sound of his velvet voice aroused her, and just sitting next to him she felt breathless.

He stopped the car on 24th Street. He turned off the ignition, and it was suddenly quiet. He touched the side of her face. "Let's go," he said. "I'm starved."

Still raining outside, he opened the umbrella as if it were an annoyance, and held it over his head. Oblivious that she was getting soaked, he walked fast, his box leather purse tucked under his arm. She could hardly keep up with him, rain sloshing around her ankles and soaking her good leather lace up boots.

Inside the restaurant they shook the rain from their coats and hung them on a hook. A long line of people stood inside the tiny brightly lit entrance. Couples drank wine while waiting for their tables. Italian lace curtains hung from the windows, and the small tables were covered in red and white tablecloths. The staff looked experienced and moved fast. The owner said, "I've got your table in the corner."

They sat at a table near the open kitchen where cooks made pasta and moved like rock and roll. The table was so small that their menus touched. David ordered wine. "Make sure the Merlot is room temperature," he said to the waiter. He ordered fried zucchini, garlic bread, and sausage Contadina.

He closed the menu. "That's the one thing I miss about Gloria. She was a phenomenal cook."

"What happened?" Dianne asked, trying to sound casual.

He shrugged. "I wanted children. She had agreed. As soon as we were married she said she couldn't have any." He sighed heavily. "I wanted children more than anything."

Their food came, and they ate, and drank more wine. For the first time since they'd known each other, he asked about her life and about her marriage. She told him about Charley, and then about Donald and the suburbs, the years at art school, and dreaming about becoming an artist. She told him about her daughters and how much she loved them. He listened intently, pouring more wine into their glasses.

"What about you?" she asked, laughing. "I told you too much about myself and I don't know about your past?"

He paused, as if deciding if he'd talk to her about his past. At seventeen he'd gone to design school in New York, sweeping floors in Leo Castelli's Gallery, saving money to buy art, and dreaming of becoming a famous dealer. He got a job designing clothes for Halston. At twenty, he'd married Rene, a very young painter. After she was six weeks pregnant he'd discovered that she was a heroin user. "We had the baby aborted." He looked sad. "My baby would have been twenty-one today."

"What happened to Rene?"

He shrugged. "Somewhere dead in New York probably."

Dianne lit a cigarette. Rain soaked the windows, and the restaurant was warm and cozy.

"You're an interesting woman," he said after a reflective silence. "I like your neurotic energy. You're strange. Wonderful."

"That sounds like my eulogy. I bet you're going to tell me I'm the first Jewish woman you've ever had dinner with?"

He laughed, a deep warm laugh. "I'd like to see your work."

"You wouldn't be interested. I'm a figurative painter."

"I'm interested in everything about you."

When their food came, she was relieved.

David ate quickly, neatly twisting pasta onto a spoon. Between bites, he talked about his dreams of opening galleries in Germany, Rome, to be as important a dealer as Leo Castelli. She loved his mind, and his aura of power.

"Castelli has the most important gallery in New York, Dianne. He has it all---a very young beautiful wife. She's a photographer, and they have a child." He sighed, wistfully. "Youth is everything. I wish I were younger."

"You're forty two. That's young. I'm thirty-eight. What does age have to do with anything?"

"I like your optimism, kid."

They drank espressos in tiny glass cups with lemon rinds floating on top. When she held the glass close to her face, her contact lens steamed up and she blinked against the blur.

"Do you want to come to my house and smoke some dope?" he asked as though it were an expected ritual. "I have some great grass."

"I don't smoke dope, have quickies, or rebounds."

He laughed then, throwing his head back like a wild horse. "You're innocent," he said softly.

He paid the check, and then they left.

Outside, the rain was cold. They hurried up the hill, huddled under his umbrella.

In the car he turned on the radio. *The Autumn Leaves* rose above the sound of the rain pounding the roof of the car. He stroked her hair, his long fingers gently sorting the tangled damp strands. Lightening creased the dark with blue lines, and the windshield wipers swished the rain back and forth along the windows.

"Tomorrow ... they say we're having a storm ..."

"I love the smell of your hair," he said, gently stroking it. "You make me feel young, like I'm in the fifties again. You make me think of Fred Astaire, Ginger Rogers. You're vulnerable ..."

When he took her in his arms she didn't resist. They kissed and she never wanted it to stop. It was perfect, everything she'd imagined it would be. His beard was damp and a strand of her hair stuck to his cheek. She couldn't stop kissing him, deep warm kisses, her tongue holding his, wanting to swallow him. She'd never felt aroused like this. She knew she should run, run fast, but she was burning and nothing but the moment mattered.

"I've wanted to do this for a long time," he said into her mouth.

"Even when we first met?"

"The first time I met you."

"A love affair with me would be a serious thing. "

"I know."

He turned on the motor and they drove into the rain.

They hurried into David's bedroom. He didn't bother turning on the lights and they undressed quickly, their shoes clumping to the floor, and then their clothes.

She slipped off her bra and panties, standing naked, and covering her breasts with her arms, afraid to open her eyes, afraid that the moment would go away and that he would disappear. She put her hand gently on the small tufts of red-gold hair along the center of his narrow chest, hesitantly at first, just touching him, exploring his body, the feel of his pale freckled grainy skin. Then they moved closer, kissing, their bodies rubbing like cats, exploring the feel of new territory.

"I knew you'd be lovely. An odalisque," he said, his fingertips delicately, gently, tracing her body, touching her nipples until they pointed out. Then they were kissing hungry kisses, kissing like they'd never stop, could never part.

She knelt then, as if at an alter, and she licked the tip of his cock, licking the wet, its tiny maze of veins puffed, then keeping it tight in her mouth, keeping him, owning him, sucking away the years she'd wanted him, and then they fell into bed and he went deeply inside her. She pressed him deeper inside her, her body burning with desire, but this was beyond sex, it was as if their souls had touched. They whispered their sexual fantasies about each other, blowing words into their mouths about how much they'd wanted one another, and she wanted to keep him inside her and never let him out, and then she felt the hot tingling, and the orgasm was slow and he was coming too, their bodies trembling until they stopped, and then it was over.

The only clue that time had passed was the stream of pale light shaking along the ceiling. Nothing mattered but that moment together. At last she knew what sexual ecstasy was, and that she loved him.

They lit cigarettes. They lay quietly, enjoying the tingly warm feeling that occurs after wonderful sex. They whispered their thoughts and confessions, the former guile between them, gone. He confided that when he was thirteen he'd had a nervous breakdown, and had shock treatments. His mother had abandoned him and he was sent to live with an Aunt. He became very still.

"My childhood wasn't exactly like Mary Poppins," Dianne said, after a long silence.

He squeezed her hand. "Dianne, I've been very much in love with you for a long time."

She was startled by his confession. She kissed him. "I love you, too," she whispered. "I love you, madly. I loved you the first moment I met you. We're one."

He sighed. "I wish you were the mother of my child. I wished we had met when we were young."

She stayed awake until he slept. She loved lying next to him. The neon green light from the Dan Flavin painting dropped a glow over the bed. It dropped a light on his beard, turning it copper. She didn't want to sleep. She wanted to remember that moment together for the rest of her life. One she knew that could never be duplicated.

The next morning they were eating sausage omelets at Perry's restaurant on Union Street and reading the *New York Times*. Between bites of omelets they kissed. And he whispered, "You know you're beautiful, kid?" She was in a daze. She felt that floaty feeling you feel after something wonderful has happened. The restaurant was busy with hip looking couples. Bartenders wearing red suspenders and white shirts moved behind the long mirrored bar, like they were gliding. The walls were covered with framed photographs of celebrities.

After breakfast, they went to the Museum of Contemporary Art.

Holding hands, they strolled through the rooms, looking at the collections. She couldn't believe this was happening. She was afraid she'd wake from a dream, a beautiful dream. Being with him, looking at art, sharing art was as powerful as their sexual attraction. With him she felt as though she were home. As though they were one person. As he looked at each painting, his arms by his sides, he'd sigh, and then move to the next painting. In front of a Cezanne, like a nun in front of God, he stood still. So still, and there was a quiet reverence on his face.

"Dianne," he whispered, "look at the line. The volume. A pleasure." He sighed wistfully, a faraway expression on his face. He was in another world. His world.

Past noon, when the sun was blooming, they drove to David's gallery. He wanted to show her the Schnabel paintings that had arrived from New York. She sat so close to him she could feel his heart beating. Suddenly David stopped the car on Nob Hill.

"Look at that house!" he said excitedly. He rolled down the window. "Isn't that lovely?" A yearning was in his voice.

"Fabulous," she said, admiring a tall white house with huge bay windows. A 'for sale' sign was on the front.

"The grill work is incredible. The view is perfect," he said, exuberantly. He breathed deeply, as if inhaling its beauty. "Let's go inside."

He ran ahead, his long legs skipping over the wide flat steps, his neck forward. They went inside a large foyer with white marble floors, high, church-like ceilings and the most beautiful art deco staircase. A stained glass dome dropped prisms of light.

"The owner has to liquidate," smiled an agent. She had tiny short curls and large red-framed glasses. Her eyes scanned David's chic suede jacket. "Feel free to look," she said with a smile.

Like a child on a sudden excursion, David ran up the Art Deco stairway, exclaiming about the real brass banisters. "This is what I call a house!" he said. On the top floor they went from room to room, into an Oak paneled library, with floor to ceiling windows, walls of built-in bookshelves, into a huge master bedroom, a massive red tile bathroom and sauna, and two smaller guest rooms.

"Look at that light, Dianne. A pleasure," David sighed, looking up at the glass skylights along the hallway. "A perfect place for you to work, baby. Wonderful rooms for the girls."

He opened the French doors to a large deck overlooking the Golden Gate Bridge. A mist of fog blew like a veil and you could feel the ocean breeze and taste the salt. Seagulls floated in the air, squawking lonely songs.

She smiled at the sudden shine in his eyes. His hair was copper in the light and gold flecks floated in his eyes.

One foot in front of the other, he crossed the room, measuring. "See Dianne, the Scott Burton chair will go here, the Sol LeWitt above the mantle ... I'll open this area, consolidate the three rooms into one. So my collection can breathe. It'll be phenomenal, Dianne. This house will be the most talked about house in California," he said, his voice, as if on a tip of a dream.

"It's beautiful," she said.

"I'm going to put in an offer."

"What about your gallery in Los Angeles?"

"I'll commute," he said, kissing her on the lips.

Breathlessly, they rushed down the stairs.

Two hours later they were at Hill & Company Realtors on Union Street. The realtors fussed over David. In his deep imperious voice and manner he demanded instant service. He made an offer. "Cash," he snipped, dropping his card. He was like lightening. "I want to sell my house as soon as possible," he demanded. While David made phone calls to his lawyer, and then to his accountant, Dianne sat next to him, smoking. She couldn't believe David had changed his life so fast, so drastically, and she felt jealous of his new passion. Quickly, she assured herself that the house had nothing to do with their love for each other. *He wants you to live with him* she reminded herself.

After the Realtor said that the owners were excited by David's offer, the next morning they'd meet at the bank, and begin escrow.

"I want to start remodeling as soon as escrow is closed," David said. He closed his purse. "Baby, it will be a pleasure to get my collection out of the warehouse and hang it in the house." He sighed.

They walked toward the car, the daylight faded into dusk. "Now. Let's see your work."

Dianne unlocked the doors to her studio. She turned on the lights and they made a popping sound. Her canvases leaned along the walls and small Plexiglas boxes dangled from wires. Large triptychs she was working on, of women sitting inside boxes, or lying in meadows, leaned along the walls.

Dianne stood by the doorway, watching as David looked at the work; his hands were slouched in his pockets, a stillness on his face like a secret. As he moved from painting to the dangling boxes, the rubber soles on his loafers squeaked on the paint-splattered cement floor. Gently, his artistic hand touched the edges of a charcoal drawing, like she'd seen him gently touch a flower. Then, as if processing his thoughts, he flipped through a stack of sketches, barely glancing but his quick eye taking in everything. He was used to appraising, and rejecting.

He stood back, looking at the fourteen-foot canvas of a swimmer floating on her back. After what seemed an endless time, he turned to her, a softness on his face that she'd never seen before.

"You will be an important artist," he said with a reverent tone. He hugged her, as if his statement was a sacred confirmation.

Now their love was complete. They were bonded as lovers, and artists. She'd love him forever.

*

31

Escrow closed. David sold his Victorian and began packing his things into boxes. He'd arranged for special movers to move his art to his storage warehouse, until his new house was ready. Almost immediately, he'd hired expensive architects to draw up plans for renovation of his new house. "It's going to be a showplace, baby," he'd say.

She was in love. Her whole world toppled over. It was like every nerve in her body was exposed. The sight of a flower blooming, or the beauty of twilight, would make her cry. He was all she could think about. When she wasn't with him, she wondered where he was, and when she was with him, she anxiously worried he'd leave her. She adored him.

When he was in town they went to art openings, concerts, operas, and the theater. He breathed art. She'd read poetry to him, and he'd show her his designs.

Almost every night, she'd stayed with him, explaining to the girls that she'd met the man she was going to be with for the rest of her life. After they met David, they loved him too. He was good with the girls.

It was six a.m. in the morning, the day David was moving into his new house. The night before they'd gone to an art opening, and then Dianne had stayed overnight with him at his old house. She'd hardly slept. Until dawn they'd made love, then lay whispering and laughing. David was already on the phone to New York, talking to Harriet Korman an artist he was representing, telling her about his house, his deep voice resonating. He sounded happy, and was excited about his new house. Then he was on the phone with Leo Castelli in New York. He spoke about showing Joel Shapiro.

Dianne grabbed her clothes from the chair and went into the bathroom and locked the door. Light poured from the skylight, and David's personal things from the bathroom were packed in boxes. She turned on the shower, glad for the quick stream of hot water, and washing her hair with his shampoo. Then she wrapped herself in a big towel, plugged in David's hair blower, and dried her hair.

She buttoned her shirt and tucked it inside her jeans. Next, she put her things into her museum tote bag. She was jealous—threatened by his new passion: his house. Afraid that he was leaving her. That he would leave her. But quickly, she assured herself that was her neurosis and she was being absurd. She had to stop it.

David was in the hallway, ready to leave. He rolled up a blueprint, and placed a rubber band around it. He wore a navy blue suede jacket and a beige cashmere turtleneck sweater. He looked excited. "It's going to be a show place, Dianne."

She kissed him. Kissed him again. She couldn't get enough of him. "I love you, David. I love you so much."

"I love you too, baby."

"How long do you think it will take to ... remodel?" Dianne asked, carefully.

He shrugged. "A few months."

"It'll be beautiful," she said, trying to sound cheerful.

He looked up and smiled, as if suddenly remembering that she was there. Wistfully, he looked at her, and then he kissed her. "I love you, baby. Know that. I've never loved a woman like I love you. "

They held each other tight. And then it was time to go.

They sat on the steps, in the expanding sunlight, holding hands, until the moving truck arrived. They watched as the movers loaded the truck with David's boxes. An hour later, the movers were ready to go.

"Honey, I'll call you later," David said. He blew a kiss, touching his fingers to his lips and rushed to his car to follow the trucks.

After he drove away, she was feeling suddenly anxious. Everything had happened so fast, and suddenly their course had changed. All her life only parts of her had worked, and now her love she felt for David seemed bigger than she was. She got into her car and drove home.

*

The following months with David were like riding a magic carpet and never stopping. There were highs and lows. He was moody and unpredictable; one moment he was professing great love, and the next he was cold and self absorbed. But she adored him and she thought that at last she found her soul mate. They loved poetry, music, and art. Just the sound of his voice, his smell, the touch of his hand, she felt dazed. As if some voodoo had struck her.

She'd explained to the girls that he was the man she was in love with and would be with, forever. David was attentive to the girls, and had even attended Sara's ballet recital. "If only we had a child," he said constantly. When they'd pass a mother and a child, he'd stop and say wistfully, "If only that was us. I wish you were the mother of my child." At David's urging, she stopped using birth control. More than anything she wanted a child with him. "I never wanted anything so badly, as I want this child," she'd told Dr. Stockford. "A love child," she'd said.

David was everywhere at once. His energy was a bolt of lightning. He hired expensive architects and contractors, and began renovation. "To open the space," he told Dianne. Obsessively, he studied his blueprints, complaining about the contractor's "incompetence." He was consumed with the house, and his art.

He was traveling a lot to Los Angeles, excited about the new gallery space. His emotions were high, on the top, and never in the middle.

Loving David hurt. The deeper she fell in love, the more she worried that he'd leave her---dissolve like Charley had. At times she felt insecure, and was even jealous of David's growing success. They were both high strung, and emotional. Over some small thing, a dropped glass, or spilled coffee, they'd shout at each other, Dianne slamming a door, David throwing things. An hour later, they'd make up, passionately declaring their love. Sometimes in the middle of the night, after a nightmare, she'd wake him, and he'd hold her, listening to her endless fears, whispering, "I love you, kid."

One weekend, she'd gone to New York with David to a Sol Le Witt opening at the Mary Boone Gallery. They'd stayed in So Ho, at Richard Artschwager's loft, and there, Dianne had met famous artists Dianne had only read about. She loved the artists' commitment to their work and their community with each other.

Dining at small Italian Cafes, for hours, Dianne listened as David and the artists talk about art, far into the night. Those three days with David were like entering a world where she wanted to spend the rest of her life.

Her love for David inspired her work, and her paintings evolved into triptychs of women waltzing with shadowed men, their dresses flowing, and their elongated high heels in the air. Her boxes became three dimensional, and evolved with larger themes and secret worlds inside. She made a love box from Plexiglas and lined it with pink satin and filled it with love poems to David, and dried flowers.

He gave her a necklace made of amber. He'd bought it from an artist in New York. "Isn't it lovely? It's you," he'd said.

It was Friday night. They'd been to an art opening. David asked her to stay with him that night. She hadn't seen it in weeks and she was shocked by the gutted rooms.

"The space is going to be *phenomenal,* Dianne."

Sheets replaced the windows and the once beautiful staircase was cut in half. Plaster fell from the ceilings and canvas sheets flapped over the empty windows. Carefully, she walked around workbenches with tools and blueprints, stepping over nails and ladders and cans of paint. David held a flashlight, its yellow light bouncing along the dark. His paintings were crated, and most of his clothes were still in boxes.

The master bedroom, though a mess of boxes, was intact with a bed and a chair and a table with blueprints on it. Dianne was stunned by the excessive demolition of the house, and jealous of his new passion.

He closed the door to keep the room warm. He smoothed the blueprints along a wood table and holding the flashlight above them, he explained every detail. "You see Dianne, here is where the atrium will be, where I'll put the Scott Burton chair, and I'll hang the Jo Baer, the Stella, in the hallway. Wait until you see the Schnabel paintings. Norton Simon has bought three, and John Block is buying several. I put two away myself."

"You have a lot dreams in this house," she said, stroking his beard.

He nodded. "I have measured each room to fit each painting. I consolidated the bigger rooms into the main living room. It's perfect."

"Yes, it's wonderful," she murmured wondering where the girl's rooms would be? Recently, he'd told them that he wanted them to live there and was building special rooms.

He dropped the blueprints on the floor. "Let's go to bed. Let's get warm."

In his bathroom, trying not to bump into the boxes stacked to the ceiling, she undressed, and then folded her clothes. From her overnight bag she took a nightgown and slipped it over her head. She rinsed her face, brushed her teeth, and then trying not to stumble in the dark, she quickly got under the covers.

The heat was off and a small electric heater glowed an orange circle in the dark.

"Your beard tickles," she said, snuggling close to him.

"Keep your hand there."

"I love you," she said, kissing his petulant mouth.

"I love you madly, kid."

He lay flat on his back. Pillows made his breathing "difficult," he'd said.

"David, how are we going to live here, if you're traveling to Los Angeles?"

"I'll commute." His long finger traced a line on the blueprint.

"Would we live in Los Angeles?"

"Dianne, don't push."

He dropped the blueprint on the cover. He looked annoyed.

"Push what? You're the one who talks about living in your house. You told the girls you want them to live here."

"If we have a child, marriage would be essential."

"I didn't mention marriage," she snapped. "And I think it's *essential* that I should sleep home."

He pulled her closer. "I'm sorry, baby. I'm an insensitive prick. I adore you. I want everything with you. As soon as my house is finished, I want you and the girls to live her, with me, forever."

He held her in his arms, murmuring his love for her. She pushed all her doubts away. They existed inside a deep and special world, and they made passionate love.

When Dianne returned home the next morning, the girls were in the kitchen. She wanted to bathe, dress, and go to the studio.

"Good pumbling?" asked Jenny, pressing the iron neatly along a sleeve, holding her long red nails up. She was wearing Sassoon jeans, a purple gauze top, and a green sweatband around her head. "You have a hickey on your neck. You and David are like rabbits."

"Leave Mom alone." Sara said. She was wearing black leotards, and pink leg warmers.

"He's a louse," Jenny said, neatly folding a blouse, and then placing it on the top of a pile.

"It's none of your business," said Sara, glaring at Jenny. "He's artistic, brilliant---arty, like Mom. He's perfect for Mom."

"He's a bastard," said Jenny, chewing bubble gum. "And he'll never marry you, Mom."

"Yes. He told me that someday we'll marry. We'll all live in his house. He wants a child. Would that bother you?"

"Would it bother you, is the big question," Sara said.

*

As the months passed, David traveled to Zurich, Italy, New York, and Los Angeles. He was excited about opening a gallery in Los Angeles. "I'm going to own the state," he repeated. Still, David's house wasn't finished. But the more she worried that he'd leave her, the more she loved him, and tried to please him. It was her insidious neurosis. To protect her anxieties she'd pull away from David, not seeing him for days, or answering his calls. She knew that he too craved the unavailable, and he'd pursue her harder.

As she fell deeper in love, they were inseparable. She couldn't breathe without him. She craved him. Adored him. "If only we had a child," he'd cry. Passionately, they vowed to love each other forever. She couldn't wait until he finished renovating his house. So that she and the girls and David would all live together as one family.

*

32

It was October. David and Dianne were at Mimi Plotkin's dinner party. Her home was a showplace. It was three stories, with tall arched windows facing a view of San Francisco and the Bay.

They sat in the living room, drinking cocktails and discussing the art market. Matisses, Legers, Jasper Johns, Louise Nevelson's Wedding Doors—masterpieces from every period, hung from the walls. Modern white couches, Corbusier chairs, and exotic plants highlighted the art filled room. Mimi, a tiny woman, wore a Jackie O hairdo, her dyed black hair teased high, a flowing white toga, and an emerald necklace. She introduced David and Dianne to curators, artists, and heavies from the art world. David was in his element. He loved wealth, youth, thinness, and perfection. He held court, pontificating about his latest Marden show.

Dinner was announced. The guests sat at a long rectangular glass table set with elegant Asian China and white orchids. Two butlers wearing white jackets, with deadpan faces, served elegant salmon along with tiny roast potatoes, string beans thin as threads and French sauces. Matisse's painting *Dancers* hung next to a massive light painting by Dan Flavin.

Mimi's tycoon husband, a thick man with black dyed hair, told dirty jokes, his dark eyes darting from guest to guest, making sure they were listening. He wore a navy velvet smoking jacket, his hotel crest embossed on the pocket. Linda Branson and her doctor husband, both well-known collectors, raved about their new Schnabel plate paintings they'd bought from David. Muffy Adams, a troll-like woman with teased hair, and wearing an Yves St. Laurent Russian blouse with voluminous sleeves, commiserated with Harry Nathan about their latest art acquisitions. Dianne remembered once going to her office and showing slides of young Bay Area artists and in the middle of the presentation Muffy had brushed them away. "They're not for us," she'd said.

"Warhol is phenomenal," said Muffy's husband, a building contractor who sat on the museum board. "We bought 'Electric Chair' series for a song." He wore rimless glasses and talked in a high, pompous voice.

"Thanks to David, Richard and I bought three Schnabel paintings," said Mimi, smiling at David. "I adore Schnabel's plates ... they're so ... so ..."

"Broken!" quipped Harry Nathan. He puffed on a thick cigar. His face was very red.

"Rodin's penises are ... wonderful," said a pale woman. "They just point at you."

While they talked about their Caravaggio's and safaris and European villas, Dianne thought that they were careless people who used art to enhance their egos; to define themselves.

Mimi flirted with David, and Dianne wondered if he'd had an affair with her? Not only had Mimi bought hundreds of thousands of dollars of art from him, but also there were many times when David had broken dates with her and had dinner with Mimi. "It's business," he'd always explained.

David was pontificating on the glories of minimalism, eloquently talking about Serra, Le Witt, Bochner, Stella, and

Tuttle. Mimi and the guests hung on his every word. He was in his element. He thrived on the wealthy collectors, their rarified worlds, and artists on their way up. To him, success was the only way.

"A quintessential purity," he was lecturing, his velvet voice sliding over fancy phrases, and charming the guests.

Then the talk turned to the importance of collectors. They gossiped about the taxi mogul collector Robert Scull, and how he'd bought all the Abstract Expressionists.

"He and Ethyl bought Rauschenberg and Jasper Johns American Flag series, cheap," said a pipe thin man. Who owned a rare bookstore.

"Collectors are art masturbators!" said Harry Nathan. His cheeks puffed out and his mouth was full.

Harry Nathan monopolized the conversation, telling a long story between puffs of cigar smoke, about how he'd bought several Cornell boxes from Mary Boone in New York. "I have Cornell's up the gazoo. Boxes of schmatas. I have better crap in my basement," he said, blowing a thick puff of smoke.

"David, tell us about your fabulous space in L.A," said Muffy, glancing at Dianne. "Will you and Dianne be living in Los Angeles?"

"I'll commute," David replied to the sudden quiet

As if waiting for her response, they looked at Dianne with sympathetic expressions on their faces.

"Did anyone try the quiche? The quiche is. delicious," said Muffy.

Everyone began talking about their homes in Paris, Faberge eggs, and the right light on their Caravaggio's.

Soon they left.

At midnight Dianne was at David's house. The door to the bedroom was shut so that the heat from the portable heater would stay inside the room. Still unfinished, the gutted rooms were without walls, the beautiful staircase gone and replaced by aluminum steps David had seen in an art magazine.

She was lying in bed, watching David pack for a week in Los Angeles. He smoothed a Cardin tie, held it to the light, squinting his eyes for an imperfection, and then he carefully placed it into his chic suitcase, and snapped the bag shut. Dianne planned to go with him to his opening in a few months.

"I don't care for Mimi Plotkin," Dianne said. "She's condescending. Also, she outrageously flirts with you."

"Don't be silly, Dianne. She's a major collector and client. She's buying incredible art from me."

"She has no understanding of art. To her it's another label."

He pulled off his clothes, and shivering from the cold, he got into bed, pulling most of the covers around him. He turned off the light next to his side of the bed.

The wind blew the canvas sheets that still covered the windows, and the hollow sounds of nails rolling along the wood floors, sheets of sandpaper, and discarded blueprints blowing, were eerie and ghostlike.

Dianne cuddled closely to David's warm body. "So if you're commuting, I'll see you on occasional weekends?" Her voice sounded hollow.

"Don't start, Dianne." He yawned.

"Start what? Start that you say that as soon as your house is finished we'll live together? I'm tired of waiting for you. I don't want to put my life on hold."

"Don't then," he snapped. "Concentrate on your work. You could be so much more."

"I do work. How dare you."

"You waste a lot of time writing in those journals and obsessing about Charley. You create drama so that you can paint. You're gifted and you don't need pain to paint. You haven't reached your potential, Dianne." He sniffed. "You're needy."

"Why is it that when a woman expresses herself, a man says she's needy?"

He sighed heavily. He turned on the light. He sat up, glaring at her.

"Dianne, I'm a busy man. I don't need confrontations and your emotional, neurotic temper."

As if the discussion was ended, he turned off the light, and turned to his side.

She couldn't sleep. She was furious. As if all the months she'd repressed her growing anxieties that David was never going to finish his house and that he'd already moved on, were suddenly true.

"David. Wake up. I don't want to see you for a while. I need time to think and to figure us out."

He didn't answer. The wind made a hollow sound. She knew he was awake.

She got up and grabbed her coat and her purse. Then she hurried through the dark house, stepping over the maze of wires, tools, and workbenches.

Outside a pale moon lit the dark street. Carrying her shoes, and clothes, wearing her coat over her nightgown, she hurried to her car parked in his driveway, and she drove home.

Almost a month later David still hadn't called. Nor had Dianne—as she would have in the past after they'd had an argument—driven by his gallery to see if his car was there or called and hung up when he answered.

She immersed herself in her work, catching up on clients, and spending long hours in her studio, painting. Though she missed David terribly, she felt good about herself, and her decision.

Her body of work was ready to show, she felt. She'd sent slides to New York and Los Angeles galleries. Also, she exhibited her new paintings at a posh gallery, in a group show of bay area artists. She sold *Girl With Gun,* to a well-known collector.

Desperately, she tried to be closer to Sara. But no matter what Dianne did for Sara, Sara maintained a quiet hostility; the same kind Dianne felt with her mother.

Her therapy was important. It was like diving into her soul and staying there for lengths of time, figuring out patterns, dreams, angers.

*

That afternoon she was at her session with Dr. Stockford. For the past thirty minutes she'd been talking about her relationship with David.

"David was right. I am emotionally needy," she said. "Why should I not be? Not to mention that David is emotionally needy, and high strung."

Dr. Stockford remained still.

"I had to break it off. I can't repeat my old patterns… sniveling and pretending everything is great." She paused. "I need him to commit—to fully commit. To tell people that I'm his girlfriend and that we're going to live together and eventually marry. He doesn't say that. He just says that he'll commute."

"What does that word *commute* mean to you?"

"It means temporary. Like he's fitting me in.

"You mean, like Charley?"

She pulled a Kleenex from the box. "I love David so much. I don't want him to leave."

"Leave him before he leaves you," Dr. Stockford said.

"I miss him so much. "

"Maybe you're getting yourself back," he said softly.

As she cried, Dr. Stockford remained still. When the red light flickered on the wall, it was time to go. Wordlessly, she got up and left.

*

33

It was three weeks later. It was midnight and a terrible storm came over San Francisco. An electrical storm had knocked down the wires across the street. She was at the kitchen table, typing pages from her journals.

She typed: *Carol wrote that letter in May 1960. She had to see him. Why? When she was married? Something to do with Carol was the reason he married her? But what?*

When the doorbell rang, Dianne was startled. Quickly she tiptoed to the door calling, "Who's there? Who's there?"

"David."

She opened the door. He stood under the porch light, wearing a burgundy cashmere scarf wrapped twice around his neck. He held his brown leather box purse under his arm like a child holds a toy.

"David, I'm ...surprised."

He sneezed. "I have the flu. The contractors turned off the hot water at the house. The new plumbing isn't installed yet. Baby ... can I sleep here? I'll leave tomorrow."

"You're cold, come in," she said, loving him so much she couldn't breathe.

He held her tight. His beard was damp and he was shivering.

"I missed you, baby. I love you so much."

She took his hand and led him down the creaky hall and into her room. "Get undressed and get to bed," she said. "I'll get you aspirin ... juice."

Like a child given a sudden gift, he smiled, murmuring, "Thank you, oh thank you."

He undressed, his teeth chattering, and got into bed, pulling the covers to his chin.

After she brought him a glass of juice and aspirin, she undressed and slipped into bed, next to him. It was quiet except for the wind howling and the sounds of his coughing and his sniffling.

"I love you, kid. I love you madly."

"I love you too," Dianne whispered. "Now sleep."

They slept in each other's arms, and soon it was only their breathing and the tapping of the wind and they slept.

The next day, David was very ill with the flu. She didn't go to the studio and canceled a client's appointment. She spent most of the day grocery shopping and picking up David's medications, and making chicken soup.

Near evening, the girls came home from their classes. Their faces were red from the wind and their hair flowed down their backs.

"Ssssch. David is sick. He's staying here until the hot water is turned on in his house. He's sick."

"He's Jewish," said Sara, emptying the dishwasher. She was always doing chores.

"When you have your orgasms, tell him to shut up," said Jenny with a yawn.

"Ssssh," Dianne said. "I don't think this is funny."

"Let him pay rent. Mom you work your ass off so Sara can go to New York next year, and now you're bringing the prick trays."

"He's cool," said Sara. "He's helping me find jobs in New York."

Several days passed and David was still sick. Every morning at six a.m, propped by pillows, he'd call New York to talk to the dealers, and artists. After he called his architects and contractors, shouting about their "incompetence," he'd call his new assistant Jason to bring him clothes, tell him what clients to call, his hands plucking the bed covers, and a box of Kleenex by his side.

Dianne carried in a large black wooden tray with a flower and a candle and set it over his lap. When he got off the phone, he grabbed her hand. "You know you're beautiful, kid?"

She smiled. "The girls are home."

He looked concerned. "I should leave." He coughed a bronchial cough.

"You have nowhere to go. Stay here until you feel better."

"The house will be finished soon and then you and the girls will move in with me. We'll marry and be a family."

The phone rang and as if he hadn't just proposed, and planned their lives, he answered it and shouted at some poor workman: "You're incompetent! Fix that fucking water heater or I'll sue you! I'll break your wrists!'

Three weeks later, David was still at Dianne's house. He recovered from his cold but his house was still torn apart and he still stayed with Dianne. His house was near completion he said but generally he was unhappy with the outcome. He'd returned to work but his assistant Joel had dropped off clothes and his personal things that he'd wanted to keep at Dianne's flat.

Sara was officially accepted at NYU, and the following spring she'd audition at New York City Ballet. Dianne had saved quite a bit of money but NYU was a private university and Sara was able to apply for a scholarship. Donald never replied to the letter she'd written, asking if he would help with Sara's college.

It was evening and Dianne unpacked the bags of groceries, assuring herself that David would reimburse her. She put the fresh produce into the refrigerator crowded with David's low-fat foods, yogurts, cottage cheese, and energy drinks. She took out the meat loaf she'd made the day before and slid it into the oven. She lit the old gas oven. David had said that he was having dinner with a client.

Next, she began picking up David's endless newspapers, magazines, and mail that Jason dropped off every morning, stacking them into a pile on the hall table. In the living room, a pile of laundry ready for ironing was on the faded wing chair. His cleaning she'd picked up earlier, hung from a hook in the hallway. So far he hadn't paid for anything.

It was freezing. She dropped fresh logs in the fireplace and lit them with a tall match, watching the flames suddenly rise. Winter was in the air now. Every morning, Mrs. Bianci's lawn across the street was pale with frost.

Dianne went into the bedroom. David's jump ropes that he used every morning were dropped over the chair and the bed hadn't been made. The little pink bathroom she shared with the girls was cluttered with his electric toothbrushes, mouthwashes, and his special retainer. "To keep my teeth in alignment," he'd say. Every morning at six a.m. from bed, David made telephone calls to galleries and clients in the East Coast, his velvet voice low, haggling prices, cajoling, whining, charming.

The next morning when he got up David was packing clothes to bring to his new house. Dianne sat on the edge of the bed, watching. "I want to get my things out of your way. Try to make my house livable."

"I'll miss you," she said.

He looked annoyed. "You need to work, Dianne," he said in a stern tone. "Finish the wax paintings. They're unique."

"We'll get married, you said. I want your baby." She watched him smooth a crease in his jacket. He shook the garment bag a few times, and making sure the surface was smoothed.

"You're not going to use my house as a hotel. I won't allow it," she persisted, trying to keep her voice down.

He looked at her for a long moment. "You're tedious, Dianne. You're also an excellent artist but you're unable to separate from yourself. You regurgitate yourself. You're full of hate."

"Marry me, you said."

He sighed. "If we had a child, marriage would be essential."

"Essential? It's essential that I fuck you, lick your asshole, pop your toes, and listen to your complaints about your house, contractors, and clients. You exclude me from your snotty little world because I'm not twenty-one and thin but you come here after your trips and bring me herpes and run up phone bills. You also owe me money for the groceries, cleaning, medications."

David looked at her for a long moment, a look like a parent has when deciding a punishment for a naughty child. He reached into his pocket and took out the brass key she'd given him to the flat. He held it a second in the palm, as if deciding, and then he dropped it on the dresser and it made a clinking sound. He put on his trench coat and hurried from the room.

When the door shut, she went to the window and watched him drive away. She crept back to bed, her head pounding and pulled the covers over her head. She slipped into sleep.

*

Dr. Stockford advised. "Don't contact him."

"It's been five weeks. I miss him. I love him."

"You love his potential. His power. His artistic side. You mirror each other."

"He's the only man who supported my dreams, who understands me."

"Leave him before he leaves you. You're re-playing Charley's rejection. You've never resolved Charley. You still blame yourself. You set yourself up for rejection. You knew about David."

"It isn't marriage I want from David, it's the commitment. Vows are lies. They don't mean anything. "

Dr. Stockford exhaled a stream of smoke.

"Charley was an emotional idiot. Donald abandoned his children. David is brilliant, talented, exciting."

"Sounds like you want David back."

She lit a cigarette, and exhaled an angry stream of smoke. "The whole mess started with Charley. He's the reason I'm terrified of closeness, and men leave me."

"It started way before Charley," Dr. Stockford said softly. "You ignore what's real, and fantasize the outcomes you want."

"I love David more than anything."

"Exactly why you'd set it up. You knew a long time ago that David had already left you. You pretended he didn't. You set it up. Then you could say he left you too."

"What shatters denial?"

"The truth."

34

"**Y**ou're pregnant," said Dr. Berman.

"Pregnant? Are you sure?"

"Congratulations," Dr. Berman said with a chuckle.

She felt joyful. Suddenly, everything was all right. Her depression over David lifted. Nothing mattered now but their child. "It should only happen," he'd always say.

"How many weeks?" she finally asked.

"Maybe six," he said, writing on a prescription pad. "I need a blood test to confirm your pregnancy. Also you have a heart murmur. You need rest. Care."

"Will the baby be all right?"

"I can't promise. You're pushing forty. But we'll watch you closely." He gave her a prescription and instructed her to go to the lab downstairs. He'd see her next week.

At the lab, she sat on a tall chipped stool. The room was small and airless. The nurse wrapped her arm with a long plastic tube, tapping the crook of her arm for a vein.

"Make a fist," said the nurse, assuming a professional expression on her pale face. When the needle went in the vein in her arm Dianne closed her eyes, imagining the joy on David's face when she told him the news.

The nurse put a bandage on the inside of her arm. Dianne touched the bandage and then she rolled her sleeve down, slowly buttoning the cuffs tight around her wrist.

As soon as she got home she called David's gallery. Her hands were shaking. His assistant Jason said that David was leaving for Los Angeles that evening, and was busy with a client. "It's urgent. Have him call me right away," Dianne said.

Twenty minutes later, David called. "Hello, Dianne," he said in a cold tone. "How are you?"

"David, I need to see you. I need to see you tonight."

"I'm on my way to Los Angeles," he said coldly. "I have important business. I'm opening a show, Dianne."

"It's urgent, David. It's really urgent. I need to see you right away," she said, her voice rising.

He sighed heavily. "I'll pick you up at seven."

Feeling almost giddy, she dressed carefully, wearing the burgundy velvet jacket he loved so much, over black trousers—high heels. She applied make up, and inserted her favorite butterfly rhinestone clip on the side of her hair.

When he arrived, she fell into his arms. She was overwhelmed by love for him. "I missed you, missed you so much," she gushed. He held her tight and they kissed, but it was the unsure kiss lovers have after a temporary break. Assuring herself that everything would be fine, that they were both emotional about the weeks that had gone by without seeing each other, she followed him to the car.

It was raining and a stream of water ran down the car windows. She kept her hand on his leg, assuring herself that the reason he was so distant was because his mind was on his work. Certainly, she was used to that.

He parked the car in front of their favorite restaurant.

Inside the restaurant they were ushered swiftly to the back table where they'd sat so many times, nestled in each other's

332 | Barbara Rose

arms. It was a beautiful room with red-flocked velvet wallpaper and puffy pink roses inside silver bud vases. French waiters with slicked hair, moved like they were on skates. A pianist played Cole Porter songs. His top hat was tilted to the side.

David was cold. He complained that to meet her he had to break an appointment with an "important" client in Los Angeles.

"I'm not in this for my health Dianne. I can't have distractions."

Dianne rolled up her sleeve and held out her arm so that he could see the bandage in the crook of her arm.

He frowned, and looked at her with an irritated expression on his face, as a parent looks at an over zealous child. "So?"

"I'm pregnant. This was my pregnancy test."

He didn't blink, and his hands were in fists. "Are you sure?"

"Positive. Six weeks ... that's why I've been feeling so awful, so moody. I'm sorry we argued. It was my fault. I was needy but it's just that I love you so much. Isn't it incredible?"

His face was frozen. His eyes were averted. He snapped two fingers and a waiter hurried to the table.

"Two champagne cocktails," David ordered. He still hadn't touched her.

Assuring herself that he was in shock and that he was celebrating, she kept her eyes on the piano player until the waiter appeared and ceremoniously poured the bubbly yellow liquid into two flute glasses. A cherry floated on the top. She took a bite, and then dropped the stem in the glass dish. He drank the champagne in one gulp. He didn't look at her. As if he were toasting himself.

"Are you happy?" she asked after a tense silence.

He glanced at his watch. "Get an abortion by Friday. I have a Schnabel opening."

When she stood, she couldn't feel her feet. The room was spinning. She stood there a second longer, watching as David opened the menu. He never looked up, as if she weren't there. As she'd seen him do to artists he was through with and had dismissed.

She left the restaurant, and outside, she got into a taxi, and went home.

At home, fully clothed, she went to bed. She didn't turn on the lights. When the girls came into her room, she told them she had the flu. "I'm going to sleep," she said. "Please close the door."

"Poor Mom," Jenny said, lingering longer.

Sara sighed and closed the door.

A cold rain tapped the windows. All night, she lay awake.

The next morning when the girls came into her room she pretended that she was asleep. When she heard them leave for school, and the front door shut, she didn't get out of bed. She couldn't. She couldn't stop crying. She felt dazed. Her body was tingling, and it felt as though it was dissolving.

Past noon, the doorbell rang. It rang again. Slowly, she got up, and opened the door.

David stood on the porch, the rain soaking him. His hair was disheveled, and his face was white as chalk. She opened the door wider.

Wordlessly, he followed her into her bedroom and she got into bed. He sat on the edge of the bed, watching her. They didn't say a word. Their silence said it all. She knew that he felt pain too. She could feel it, but she also knew that he wanted the abortion over with as soon as possible.

"It's the only way, Dianne," he said after a long while.

"An abortion you mean?"

He nodded, slowly.

"I want a baby, you said. If only you were the mother of my child, you said. You and the girls will live in my house, you said. What is it? Am I too old? Not famous enough? Rich enough? Not thin enough?"

He sighed heavily, as if the world was on his shoulders.

"You need too much care, Dianne. You need more than I can give."

He put his hands over his face then, and he cried. He cried loud sobs, like a child cries at a sudden disappointment. Then as quickly as he'd cried, he stopped, rubbing his eyes with his fist.

"This is a sad thing that's happened to us, Dianne."

"You're an abortion pro, David." You choose your babies like you choose your art. I don't fit the image you want, so you don't want the baby. You destroy your babies as you destroyed your house. I'll decide what I'm going to do, and I'll let you know. Get out."

The expression on his face was stoic, like a punished child, trying to be good.

He kissed her on the lips, and then he left.

When she heard the door shut, she sat by the window, watching the rain. She felt oddly apart from her body, as if she were on the other side of the room, watching herself. Her eyes were wide and full of horror.

David was right. She needed a lot. Never would she raise a child without a father. Never would she put a child through what her girls had been through.

She rocked in the chair, until the pain subsided. And then she got up and telephoned Dr. Berman's office, and left a message. "Urgent," she said.

Fifteen minutes later, when Dr. Berman called back, she told him that she wanted the D&C. "I can't have this child," she repeated, her voice rising.

Dr. Berman sighed. "Based on your heart, the history of heart problems in your family, and your age, I'll do a D&C tomorrow at seven in the morning. Don't eat or drink after midnight today, and be at the hospital two hours early. Come to the office now, and the nurse will take more blood work, and an EKG. She'll make the hospital arrangements. You'll be fine, Dianne."

She bathed, and changed her clothes. And then she drove to Dr. Berman's office.

She didn't feel anything now, not even the rain.

That evening, when she arrived home from Dr. Berman's office, she called David. He answered on the first ring. "Be here at five a.m. tomorrow," she said, coldly. "I'm having a D&C."

"I'll stay with you tonight, baby."

"No. I'll see you tomorrow."

She hung up before she'd change her mind.

She told the girls that she was leaving early in the morning for a D&C. "It's routine," she explained. "The doctor says I have diverticulitis. It's same day surgery. Not to worry. I have to be at the hospital early, but David is taking me."

"Sure he is. He can't wait," said Jenny. She was very tall, and wore bright red lipstick. She had several boyfriends and was on the wild side. She knew what was going on. Dianne knew that.

"Mom, we'll be here," Sara said, looking at her with sympathetic eyes. "You look so sad."

"She's sad because David's a bastard." Jenny hugged her tight.

All night Dianne lay awake, not thinking, not feeling, and staring at the reflection of the moon floating along the ceiling.

She couldn't stop remembering El Paso. She felt guilty, and stupid, and ashamed. Not a day had gone by since El Paso that she didn't think about the baby she had aborted. It was all her fault. Once again she had used bad judgment. She had to stop. Stop her neurotic impulses---denial. The grief she felt was so deep she couldn't breathe.

Soon, it would be light. She couldn't remember, or think, or do anything, and if she did, she knew that she would change her mind and decide to have the child. And she couldn't.

At four a.m. she dressed, and waited by the window in the living room. The house was quiet, except for the sound of the girls snoring. Of all days the storm was worse, and the downpour was heavy. For days she hadn't returned Joe's calls. Nor did she call her mother. No matter what, mothers and daughters sense each other's problems. She sensed her mother would know.

At five a.m, David knocked on the door. He wore his tan trench coat, the belt tied in three careful knots, and his box shaped leather purse under his arm. Dark circles lay under his eyes. He didn't hug or kiss her. She followed him into the car.

"I have to stop at the house," he said, as he jerked his car into traffic.

"We'll be late."

"It'll only take a minute. I have to check a leak."

"This isn't a time to think about your house," she snapped. Even then, he thought about his schedule, his needs, and that moment she hated him.

"Only a minute," he insisted.

He double-parked in front of his house, and ran inside. She sat in the car, waiting and watching the rain soak the car windows. She was merely an appointment in David's busy schedule.

When he returned, he complained about the plumber leaving leaks. "Incompetent," he murmured, recklessly weaving his car in and out of lanes. A forced gaze of sympathy lay on his face.

He parked in the hospital garage. He turned off the motor. She didn't want to go inside. She didn't want the abortion.

"David, last night I dreamed I saw our baby. I held her. We sat in a meadow of flowers."

"Dianne, get hold of yourself," he snapped, impatiently.

"I want to keep the baby. I want to keep our baby."

He pressed his mouth, and he looked nervous. "Dianne. You're upset," he said with a cajoling tone. "It'll be over soon."

"I don't want it over. I want our child."

"You can't. You can't take care of a child. Your work … your children."

"You mean you don't want it."

They sat in silence. Cars drove in and out of the garage. The smell of the car fumes went up her nose.

"Baby, let's go. We'll be late."

Slowly, she got out of the car and they took the elevator upstairs to same day surgery.

A nurse with a heavy face, and averted eyes, asked Dianne to fill out papers attached to a metal clipboard. David stood behind her as she signed her name on the designated lines.

When she completed the forms, the nurse gave her three tiny blue pills inside a tiny pleated paper cup. Dianne swallowed the pills, tilting her head back so the pills would go down her throat.

After that, the nurse told David to sit in the waiting room. Then she led Dianne to a small room. She asked Dianne to undress, and she gave her a warm cotton gown, a paper hat, and paper slippers.

Dianne took off her jeans, shirt, and underwear. She placed her clothes inside a white metal locker. Trying not to remember El Paso, she tucked her hair into the hat, pushing in the curls that always stuck out. She pressed her face closer to the mirror so she could see what she was feeling, but nothing, nothing, only flat dead eyes. Once again she was aborting a human life. Something in her created tragedies. It had to stop.

The nurse then led her to another room, and helped her into a leather chair. It looked like a dental chair, or those chairs in a beauty parlor. Women sat in chairs arranged in rows, knitting, or reading the paper, or sleeping. They waited their turns. Dianne's eyes closed and she imagined a white beach with moons like marbles and soon she felt drowsy.

Two nurses wheeled a gurney and helped Dianne from the chair onto the gurney. They covered her with a warm blue blanket. It scratched her chin.

"It's time, honey. You'll be fine," said the nurse wheeling the gurney down the hall. David, still wearing his trench coat, waited on the end of the hallway, a somber expression on his face. An *Art Forum Magazine* was tucked under his arm. His hands clutched his purse.

"I love you, kid. I'll be waiting."

He kissed her on the lips. His lips were cold.

The gurney was going faster then and Dianne felt as though she was floating in a balloon, her body sagging, a cow's body, repeating silently, *yis kadal, yis kaddash.*

The doors opened with a swish, and then closed with a quick click. Dr. Berman wearing a green suit and mask on his face patted her hand. "Don't worry, Dianne. You'll be fine."

As a rubber mask was placed over her nose, she tried to open her eyes, and then she was lying on smooth grass, the sun touching her face, and the clouds low, and then there was nothing....

By the time she left the recovery room, it was late afternoon. The air was dark, and it was still raining. David held her arm as he led her into the car.

On the way home, she was still groggy. David was quiet and he kept glancing at his watch. He was in a hurry to get to Los Angeles. "So much to do before the opening, Dianne."

At her flat, David helped her into bed. It was still rumpled from the morning. The girls weren't home yet, and the flat smelled of Jenny's Estee Lauder perfume. The wind chimes on the girl's bedroom windows were rattling.

Dianne watched David check the closet. He removed a jacket he'd left behind. He still wore his coat, and his beard was damp from the rain.

"Darling," he said, sitting next to her. "I'd love to have you at the opening, but Dr. Berman says you need rest."

She watched his face for some emotion. Anything. There was nothing, but the impatient look in his eyes she'd seen so many times, when he was in a hurry to meet some artist he was interested in.

"I'll call from LA. The time apart will be good for us," he said with a quick smile. "Time to think about us."

"What about us?" she asked. Her voice was hollow. Faraway.

"To see if we're going to marry eventually."

He stood there a moment, like a polite guests stays an extra minute at a party they want to leave.

He patted her hand. "Got to get to the airport, Dianne. I'll call you."

And then he hurried from the room.

Her eyes were closed as she listened to his fast footsteps, and then the click of the door as it shut. Shut twice. As if he were making sure it was shut.

She closed her eyes and she slept.

When she awoke, Jenny stood by her bed, watching her. Concern was on her beautiful face.

"Mom. Do you want some soup? Sara and I made nice soup."

"I'm not hungry," Dianne said, holding Jenny's hand. "I just need rest-- a night's sleep."

Jenny sighed. "Sara and I hate David."

She sighed again. "If you need anything, wake us. The chicken soup is on the stove."

The next day, Dianne didn't get out of bed. Nor did she want to. For most of the day she slept. She missed her therapy and didn't return Dr. Stockford's calls.

David called from Los Angeles. He was at a producer's party, he said. "A major collector." She heard the happy noise in the background.

"I'm sorry, baby," he said, as if he were checking off a duty from his one of many to- do lists. He promised to pay the hospital bill. He'd mailed a gift, he said.

"The opening is tomorrow, babe. Wish you were here. I love you. I'll call you."

She hung up before he could say anymore.

That afternoon, Federal Express delivered a package. It was from David. It was a stuffed dog with wrinkled black vinyl ears and no eyes, the kind you see in airports. She dumped it in the garbage can.

Three days later, she read in the *Los Angeles Times* art section that he'd had a "smash" Schnabel opening. She stared at his picture; he was wearing a black turtleneck sweater, standing with his gallery assistant Mary Beth, a tall, very thin girl no more than twenty, with arrogant eyes, and lots of black hair.

She recalled David telling her that he'd hired an assistant who was a photographer. "She has attitude," he'd said with a pleased tone. "She can sell art."

There had been so many clues that he'd already left her, but once again, denial embedded into her psyche, she'd pretended he hadn't.

As the days passed, her rage surfaced. The abortion had exacerbated all the emotions she'd ever buried. Her dreams were full of matchbox graves with bloated babies. She mourned the loss of her babies.

As if her body was decomposing, she felt like her limbs were dissolving. To walk, she had to hold on to the walls.

She told the girls she was still sick. She made sure that they kept busy with their schoolwork, and arranged for the girls carpools to drive the girls after school to their activities. She'd been ignoring her mother's calls. So she called her mother and told her she'd been ill with the flu.

"I think that it's that David who makes you sick. I don't like his handshake, or his beard. I knew it, Dianne."

"He has nothing to do with my flu. I'm just pressured."

Mother sighed. "If you need anything Dianne, call me. I'll make a nice pot roast. Bobbie will drop it off."

That day, when she awoke at midnight, she felt depressed. She hated David. He had not only rejected her, but he had rejected her child. Furious, she called Children's Hospital and asked a nurse where the dead babies went? "I need to know," she said. "I had an abortion. I want to know if I can see my baby. Is it in a jar? A jar burial?" she asked. The nurse in an alarmed tone suggested that she call a shrink. "As soon as possible," she warned.

The next morning, Dianne was at the market. She tried to get back to her routine. She finished her grocery shopping and was in line with her food cart. Next to her was the magazine section. On the cover of *Newsweek,* there was a picture of an embryo. There was a feature story about abortion. She paid for the groceries and for the magazine.

At home, she cut out the picture of the embryo, and pasted it to a sheet of paper.

Later that day, she drove to David's house, speeding along the hills. When she saw the 'for sale' sign discreetly tucked along the side of the hedge, she burst into tears.

How long had he been running away? More importantly, how long had *she* known that he was running away?

She got out of the car, and she left the picture of the embryo taped to his door.

That night she fell into a disturbing dream.

The air was thick and damp. She held a gun. She climbed up the side of the box. It was made of papier-mâché and punched with tiny holes. In each hole was a tiny light and they were blinking like stars. She opened the trap door and climbed down the ladder. On the bottom was a tall white chair. She sat on the chair and looked in the trick mirrors she had found in a carnival. It was peaceful in the box. No pain, no sound. She laughed at her face expanding, disappearing. She was dressed as usual in black and wore necklaces of silver and coral.

She aimed the gun at the mirror and pulled the trigger, screaming, "Wake up please, wake up.

*

As the days and then the weeks passed, Dianne's moods and feelings fluctuated from high joy, to sudden despair. One minute she'd be laughing, and the next, just hearing a song that she and David had enjoyed, or seeing a painting he'd loved, she'd burst into tears.

She'd internalized him so fully that even though they weren't together, she felt his presence, heard his sighs, his warm laughter. She heard him in everything she did. When she was painting, she felt him watching her, silently applauding her. Even though she wasn't with him, they were together.

She resumed her therapy sessions, going twice a week. At first the sessions were hard; she'd felt so angry, and hurt. She'd rant, and spew hate. Or she'd cry for thirty minutes. "I'll never feel normal," she'd say. Gradually, the pain transitioned to a calm acceptance of who she was.

Love changes you. No matter what, she'd always love him. Some loves are like that. She knew that she was someone else now. But she was ready for new things.

*

35

It was several weeks later, and Dianne was at her therapy session.

"Last night, David appeared in my dream. He wore chic full trousers and a hat with a thin red balloon stuck in the side like a feather. I popped the balloon."

"The penis promise," Dr. Stockford said.

"Once again, I made myself a victim. Once again I loved a man who didn't love me."

"David loved you," Dr. Stockford said gently. "Until it didn't work for him anymore, he loved you. But he loved you. Know that."

"To him, love is the next painting. Whatever is on the high. He's in love with image. As he says clout, class, youth and beauty."

Dr. Stockford remained still.

"How stupid I was," she continued. "Of course he'd been having an affair with his art groupie assistant in LA. She's twenty something, thin as a thread, and he's forty something. I heard from the grapevine that she's nasty like he is and gives him a bad time. Perfect. He wants what he can't have."

Dr. Stockford jabbed his cigarette into the ashtray.

"Falling in love required emotions I'd never felt or used before. Emotions that I'd kept for my journals. I'm humpty dumpty who fell off a wall."

Dr. Stockford said after a long silence. "He loved your lovingness, your passion, your energy. Your art. "

She watched a stream of light float along the wall then break into dots.

"Dianne, breakdowns are breakthroughs. You held in your feelings all your life, and when you had the abortion this time, all your defenses broke down. I'll help you get through this. I'm going to prescribe sleeping medication. You must rest. Truth broke the wall of denial."

"I need to ask Charley why he married me. I need to resolve Charley."

"It's not Charley you have to resolve, it's yourself," Dr. Stockford said.

"I think the soul is clear and squishy. If it's too cluttered with old regrets and hurts, it won't grow. I need to clear out my soul. It has too much angry debris in it."

The red light blinked on the wall. Dianne put on her Fedora hat, left the office, and went into the fading sunlight.

*

It was near spring. She'd worked hard in therapy, going four times a week, and gradually she'd healed with new awareness and appreciation for herself and her life. No longer did she feel the anger and the raw hurt she'd felt for David. All of that had dissolved and he was now like a photograph she treasured in her album.

Recently she'd read in *Art News* that David had married his assistant Mary Beth Moore in Los Angeles and that they were expecting their first child. Of course it hurt. For days she'd isolated herself in her studio, painting. Yesterday is a bucket of ashes Joe always said, and she was ready to move forward. Loving David had been real. Forever she'd love him.

She'd resumed selling art. But she only saw a few clients now, and spent more time painting and writing poetry. She wanted to save enough money to buy a loft in the country, have dogs and cats and grow vegetables and flowers and ride a purple bicycle with a big silver bell on the handlebar.

Sara graduated with honors from high school, and won a dance scholarship to New York University where she'd study dance and film.

Dianne was taking the girls to the Waldorf Astoria for four days and they would help Sara get settled into her dormitory. Dianne was excited about this trip.

Molly Evans, from the New York Evans Gallery, had called again and offered her a show. Dianne liked the gallery, as it represented new women artists. They agreed to meet when Dianne was in New York.

The Samuel West Wing at the Oakland Museum was having a retrospective of Sam's collection the following year. Joe was helping the museum with fundraising. He'd retired and was living with a lovely girl.

Everything was new.

*

Friday afternoon, shortly before they left for New York, Joe arrived at Dianne's studio. A large photo of Joe and Sam hung above her desk. Photographs of the girls were taped to the walls, along with pictures she'd cut out from magazines---flowers, a child's face, a dog, anything that inspired her.

He stood close to a large painting of a woman sitting on a vast lawn of tiny white flowers. The woman stared beyond. Her skin was painted very white and her black hat covered most of her face. She held a small black gun.

"So interesting," Joe said, looking at Dianne, as if to see into her, and then back at the large canvas. "Her conflict, her pain, the gun, is incongruous to the delicate beauty of the colors, flowers, lyricism, and the paint."

She smiled. "I think that joy has to know pain. Or how can you know what joy is? Or, love?"

"Well, go for the joy now, Dianne. "Put the pain away. Put it into your work. It works in the paintings. Not in your life."

She laughed. "I'm ready. Before I go to New York I need to face Charley, and ask why he'd married me. I need to do this Joe. Not only for myself but for my father."

He looked reflective. "You've probably figured it all out. But if you need to do it Dianne, do it and then let it go. Remember. Yesterday is a bucket of ashes."

That night, she sat at the kitchen table and typed a letter. *Dear Charley. I was married to you once. My name is Dianne Roseman Perlman. I need to meet with you. I need closure. Enclosed is my phone number. 751.5710. Dianne.*

The next day she mailed the letter. Exactly two days later, Charley called.

"This is Charley Berkowitz," he said, just like that, as if it were two minutes ago that they'd seen each other. "I'd be lying if I didn't tell you that so many times I wanted to call you. I read your letter twelve times. You said closure." He paused. "Are you well?"

"Not that kind of closure," Dianne said.

He continued talking stream-of conscious in his light feathery voice: His parents and his brother-in -law had died, and his sister had a nervous breakdown and had never recovered. He'd opened offices around the world. "I'm a workaholic," he repeated. "Once I saw you walking on Van Ness Avenue." He paused. "Tell me about you."

She had two daughters, she said. She was divorced, and she'd graduated from college. She was a painter and an art dealer.

They agreed to meet the next evening for a drink at Ruth Chris Steak House on Van Ness Avenue.

"Six o'clock," he said.

36

Dianne was fifteen minutes early. Her old car was in the Joe's shop, getting new tires so she'd taken a taxi. She was wearing a black pantsuit, high heel black boots, and long silver earrings.

The steak house was dark inside, and the air smelled of scotch. She sat at the very end of the long mirrored bar, so she could watch the door. A television dangled from the wall, and a TV reporter was reciting the evening news about an earthquake in Japan. A tall thin bartender smiled, as if he'd been expecting her.

"Vodka over. Two green olives, please. "I'm waiting for ... a friend."

"Coming right up."

Very quickly he made the martini and placed it on a paper coaster. The drink tasted good and immediately it relaxed her. She drew boxes on the cocktail napkin, feeling suddenly nervous. She'd memorized the questions she'd ask: *Was he married? Why did he marry me? What had happened between our vows and our wedding night? Wouldn't he consummate, or couldn't he? Why did he take her to Hawaii? Where was he really the morning after their wedding night and who had called? Was it Carol?*

"Another vodka over," she said.

Discreetly, the bartender nodded. He mixed another drink and placed it along with a small glass bowl of nuts, next to her napkin.

Slowly, she sipped the drink, her eyes on the Big Ben clock above the bar. Waiters were setting tables in the dining area, and two women wearing pants-suits were at the bar exchanging jokes with the bartender.

The restaurant was different from Charley's usual tastes in elegant French restaurants, and exclusive nightclubs. She remembered when she was dating Charley she'd felt so grownup: the way he'd light her cigarette, open doors, dance as if he were holding a flower. He'd been so gallant, walking on the side by the curb, gently holding her elbow.

Each time the door opened there was a clicking sound, and her heart beat fast. Was it Charley? She watched the Big Ben clock on the wall and it was almost six, and he was never late.

Her hands were damp and she drank the rest of her martini, not caring that she was beginning to get a floaty feeling. But this time when the door clicked and a slight breeze fell into the lounge, she knew he arrived. She felt dizzy, like she'd feel when standing at the end of a cliff, and looking down.

Slowly, she turned. She watched him approach her. He was slender as a weed, his dark hair still thick and banded with silver.

"Dianne, you look great," he said, kissing each cheek, European style.

"So do you," she said, not breathing.

He remained standing, as if he'd wanted to be ready to leave. He nodded towards the bartender. He said: "Cutty Sark over. Another round for the lady."

When their drinks came he raised his glass, as if toasting her. As if he hadn't destroyed her life.

"You look great," he repeated. He sighed, and half closed his eyes. "I can't tell you how many times over the years I wanted to call you. I really did, Dianne. I'd be lying if I didn't admit I thought about you."

"Almost nineteen years ago," she said, her voice drifting. "June tenth, it will be twenty years."

"A mother of two daughters," he said, with a wistful sigh. "That threw me."

"Do you see Dorothy?" she asked. "You were so close."

He shook his head, and frowned. "I had to commit her to a mental institution. I haven't seen her for six years. She's on lithium. When she'd see me she'd get violent, she'd hiss, and swear and foam at the mouth. So I can't."

He sighed heavily. He took another sip from his drink, as if reflecting on what he'd said. He'd always had this habit of pausing after statements. As if they were so important, they needed to be absorbed.

"A few months ago Dorothy called. But I was on my way out. I told her I'd talk to her another time."

He then talked about how great his health was, knocking his knuckles on top of the bar, and glancing at his perfect face in the mirror. He bragged about his daily exercise routine, and that most people couldn't believe he was fifty-two. He owned an airplane, and had recently flown to Hawaii, and had stayed at the Royal Hawaiian Hotel. "It was gorgeous," he said, as if he hadn't been there with her.

"Sounds like your life has been great," she said, looking directly into his blank black eyes.

He looked reflective. "I told my doctor that if I had my life to do over again, I'd want to do it exactly the same way. He was amazed."

"Yes, I imagine he was," she said sarcastically. He was shallow, and incapable of insight. She felt sorry for him.

He paused. "A college graduate... a painter," he said wistfully. "No one gave you credit."

"I was barely twenty."

"Where did you get your talent?"

"Everyone has talent," she snapped, irritated that he was surprised. "My mother was a concert pianist. Nannie was an opera singer, and my father wrote screenplays."

"I didn't know that," he said with forced intensity. He shrugged. "I like to paint landscapes." He paused, as if what he'd said deserved comment. Then he said: "You want to hear something sad?" He half smiled, his eyes searching my face, making sure that he had my utmost attention. "The day before we were married I went to your father's office. Lou, I said. Don't worry about a thing. I'll take care of your daughter the rest of her life."

He raised his glass again and was silent for a moment. As if he had said something profound.

"Can you have dinner?"

She paused. "Yes. That would be nice."

He nodded to the headwaiter. When she got up, he held her arm, and they went inside the dining room.

They were seated at a table in a corner. He opened a satin menu, and as he had when they'd dated, without asking her, he ordered dinner:

"New York for the lady, charred on the outside, medium inside, sour cream on the side...lamb chops for me."

Over another round of drinks, as if he'd had so many memories, he reminisced about the times they'd dated.

"Lou was a man's man," he repeated with a sigh. "How is Bobbie?"

Dianne said: "He's never left home. He's gay, but he's in the closet. Mother hides him. It's really sad."

"If my sister were gay," he quickly responded, "I wouldn't care." He looked away. And then quickly as if covering up his fluster, he chatted about his business, and that his father had been "too frugal," had never trusted his ideas, but how wrong his father had been; he had raised the business from a million dollars to multi-millions.

"Are you married?" she asked.

He shook his head. "No. I've been with Katherine for twenty years, but I didn't want to marry her."

He shook the ice in his glass. "She's almost forty."

"Is she beautiful?" Dianne asked.

"Not as beautiful as you are," he said.

He chuckled. "She says I'm a commitment phobic. We lived together for a short time, but it didn't work out. In ten years, do you know she's never tried to get a job? She thinks I live like King Farouk--"

He was flirting. Dianne could feel it. She remembered his style, his over attentive politeness, little compliments stuck into his boring anecdotes.

Several times he got up to go the men's' room. "Diuretics," he whispered.

When their dinner came, he ate quickly, barely swallowing. While she ate little, trying to absorb his every word, to put her impressions into an order.

"Imagine Charley...if we were in Hawaii now? If we were enjoying each other like we are now?"

He lit a cigarette, looking at her through a haze of smoke. "You had the most gorgeous figure...still do," he said quickly.

"You always made my heart beat. I'd leave your house so aroused I'd have to take a cold shower. "

"Was I a mass of organdy and fluff and dyed to match pumps?"

"Dianne, you were a breath of fresh air," he sighed.

"I always thought there was ... someone else." She laughed.

"Of course, there was Carol," he said.

She held the water glass tight. "So that morning after our wedding night, when you left the airport motel to go to your office I guess you met her?"

"Actually, no. It was business."

"Then why did you end our marriage before it began?"

He shrugged. "It was financial. Something your mother said at the wedding about how I should take care of you scared me."

He frowned, as if searching for an explanation.

"I was a young lad. I needed money. I didn't want my dad to know. "

He pushed his plate away and sipped his drink. "It wouldn't have worked Dianne. Maybe if we lived on a farm in Iowa, away from family...influences--"

"Why didn't you marry Carol?" She pretended to be more interested in her food.

"She was married. We have a son--Andy."

"A son?" Dianne tried to smile. "How old is he?"

"He'll be twenty June eleventh. I can't see him because Carol's husband thinks he's the father. We can't hurt Carol's husband. I can't even put Andy in my will."

As if he hadn't betrayed her, and probably, betrayed Carol, he resumed eating. Dianne sipped her coffee, her mind spinning. Like pieces in a puzzle, the answers were snapping together. His son was the same age as the day he'd told her that he'd made a mistake. She recalled the phone call at dawn on their wedding night, his office emergency—yes, it all made sense. Carol had worked for him, was married, and pregnant, maybe, with Charley's child? Probably, Carol had threatened to tell Charley's father that she was pregnant, and needed money. To keep Carol from creating a public scandal, Charley had probably promised Carol that as soon as he could he'd marry her. So she moved to Chicago with her husband, and waited for Charley. Figuring that as soon as Carol gave birth, Carol's husband would be the legal father, and he'd be free, quickly, to avoid scandal, he'd married Dianne.

Yes. That's it. No wonder Charley's mother wanted to rush the wedding. They knew. They'd all known. Dianne had been their escape.

Dianne opened her cigarette case, and took out a cigarette. Charley leaned forward and lit her cigarette.

"You always had red in your hair. It's still gorgeous." He snapped his lighter shut.

She watched him stir sugar cubes into his coffee, remembering the needle inside the sock. Had he hidden his disease because he was ashamed of it, or was the needle for---drugs?

"How's your diabetes?" she asked.

He looked confused. "Oh, that."

She finished her coffee.

"I'd like to show you my new home," he said. "I live by Coit Tower and I have a spectacular view. I also have a Motherwell painting I'd love for you to see."

"No, thank you Charley. I'm going to call a taxi."

He reached into his pocket and took out a checkbook. 'How are you fixed financially, Dianne?"

"Fine. I'm just fine."

He blinked, as if confused. "I'll drive you home.".

Dianne followed him through a side door to a garage that smelled like fresh paint.

"My crew did a good job on this building," he said.

His black jaguar smelled of new leather. He reached into the backseat and held a large book with a shiny gold cover. "I want to give you this," he said. It was titled, *Successful California Businesses.* He turned on the light.

"Turn to page 214," he said, eagerly turning the pages. One page was bookmarked. "Now read this."

It was an article about how he had developed his father's contracting business into a multi- million-dollar empire in Taiwan, London, and Paris.

"My father would have been proud. He'd never thought I'd do it," he sighed.

"Yes. You've done well." She closed the book. He turned on the ignition, and drove into the night.

The car radio was on and Frank Sinatra sang *Always*. The night was black and the sky dotted with cold stars. The fog was rolling in, and you could see a soft mist of gray filming the dark. He drove slowly, as if stretching out the evening, his long slender neck forward and his slender hands tight on the wheel. One more block and it was over... down the hill, turn left.

He stopped the car in front of her flat and turned off the motor. She recalled that day he'd taken her home, and how smug he'd been.

"It was wonderful, Dianne."

Dianne opened her purse. She aimed the small black gun at his surprised face. She pulled the trigger. Blood splattered on the glass and she could still see the surprise in his eyes, as he slumped forward. And then there were sirens.

At last it was over. The saga was ended, and the story told.

She blinked away her reverie. "Well, good night, Charley. Thanks for dinner, and the ride home."

"Dianne, listen to me. It wasn't your fault."

"I know."

"I'll call you."

"Please don't, Charley."

She got out of the car, and hurried into the house. At last she was home.

As she lay awake, re-playing the night, figuring out every single detail, she realized too that she'd never loved him. They had used each other. She'd used him to be free from her mother's house. He'd used her to avoid scandal, and to please his father. Resolutions aren't possible. Only forgiveness. She was free now.

The shades were open, and she watched a star blinking silver and then slowly diminish into a dot. She closed her eyes and slept.

*

Before she went to New York, she wanted to do one more thing; she wanted to see the house her mother had grown up in; where she was raised by Nannie, her grandparents, and four uncles. In her mother's journal that Dianne had found, her mother had made everything sound so grand, so perfect.

The next afternoon, Dianne got off the bus on Castro Street. She walked along the bumpy narrow streets past candle shops, cafes, tattoo parlors, and bookshops. Everything was alive. She loved seeing men holding hands with men, and women holding hands with women, couples strolling happily and away from the rigid homophobia that existed in other places.

The sky was dark and patterned with thin white lines, and a pink mist hovered over the streets. It'd taken months to trace the address of the house her mother had grown up in and had described in her blue spiral notebook as: *Full of clocks and down pillows and a banister that she had loved sliding on. I grew up in a grand house, with real lace curtains.*

At the Castro Theater, in awe of the Art Deco marvelous theater, Dianne remembered Nannie telling her that at twelve years old, Mother had played the organ for silent films at the Castro Theater.

On a huge billboard the movie *Grease* was advertised. No other theater existed like the Castro Theatre, where the film culture stayed alive. Her mother had written in her journal that after she played the organ, she'd stop at *Nates Deli* across the street, and buy a dill pickle for ten cents.

Across the street, Dianne went inside *Nates Deli*. It was very old, with black and white tile floors, and tall wooden vats of dill pickles. A young man wearing a black rubber apron, stood behind a glass counter displaying cold meats and salads. Photographs of celebrities hung from the yellow walls. Dianne imagined her mother buying the pickle, wrapping it carefully, as she would at home, with waxed paper. Dianne imagined her mother as an eager, gifted child with dreams. What had happened to make her so angry, so cruel?

Feeling sorrow for her mother's lost dreams, she left. Following the address she'd written down, Dianne looked for her mother's house. After walking back and forth, squinting her eyes at the faded numbers on the old plank wood houses, finally, she found it.

It was not the grand house Mother had described, but a wood plank house so narrow it seemed stuck between the laundry and the tattoo parlor. The yellow paint was peeling, and on the windows the lace curtains were torn and half yellow from sunlight and dust. A tall iron gate covered a narrow staircase leading to the front door.

Dianne recalled her mother's descriptions of the Sunday music salons, where she'd play *Shubert's Songs* on the piano, while her Grandmother played the violin, and her mother Nannie, sang. Afterwards, they'd lunch on sausages and pancakes in the shape of balls, with powdered sugar.

Even from the street, Dianne could feel the sadness. Something terrible had happened in that house. Whatever had happened, Mother got caught in some incident, and never got out. Something that she replayed over and over again and finally destroyed her sons.

Dianne shuddered. The story is all in that house. If the story isn't told, then the resolution can't happen. She had to make the tragedies stop. The soul is capable of so many things and is filled with generations of mothers who paved the way for their daughters. Now she had to break the mold and do the same thing.

Dianne picked a leaf from the bush, and decided to walk home.

37

Dianne and Jenny and Sara arrived in New York at the Waldorf Hotel. It was a magnificent hotel on Park Avenue. It brought back memories of when she'd gone with her father as a young girl, on one of his business trips to the Waldorf.

The lobby had emerald plush carpets, high ornate ceilings and dark green velvet drapes on the windows. The air was full of perfumes.

At the desk Dianne registered for their suite. Sara had sent her luggage ahead to her dormitory at NYU and would go there in two days.

The girls were excited. Sara wore a red coat and red beret, and Jenny, her hair streaming to her waist, wore a purple wool jacket and skirt and high leather boots.

A porter wearing a green jacket with gold tassels, and a whistle around his neck, led them to their room on the eighth floor. It was a suite with two double beds and a large white marble bathroom with gold painted moldings.

The girls jumped on the beds, chanting, "We made it! We made it! New York! New York!" Heat hissed from the old radiator, and frost lay on the windows like beads. The steady sound of traffic echoed a mass of horns, and sirens screeched. The room was warm and bright.

An hour later they went to dinner at a Deli up the street. Jenny ate a giant hotdog, and Sara picked at a cottage cheese salad.

Dianne worried about Sara's thinness. But Sara seemed animated and excited about living in New York.

"It's wonderful, Mom. It's where I want to be."

Lucky you," Jenny said, biting her lip. "I'm fuck up Jenny."

"You're not," Dianne assured her. "Stop talking like that. "You'll find your way."

"Jenny, you'll get there," Sara said, holding Jenny's hand.

After dinner they walked along Park Avenue, stopping to listen to the street musicians. From corner vendors they bought cashmere scarves and woolen wonderful hats. New York was so alive, so full of dreams and life and wonder. She loved it.

The next two days were magical. Dianne and the girls took a boat tour around the Statue of Liberty. Jenny took photographs with her new camera, and Sara blew kisses to the statue. Never would Dianne forget the joy on their faces. Afterwards they'd visited New York University, and helped Sara settle into her dormitory. Sara's roommate was a lovely girl from Africa who also was majoring in dance and film. Sara had made her bed with the new pink sheets and warm pink bedspread they'd bought in So Ho. She'd hung Min's needlepoint ballerina on the wall next to her bed, next to a photograph of Margot Fonteyn, and a painting Dianne had painted of the three of them. Her special things from Min were arranged on the velvet cloth next on her nightstand. Then Dianne took the girls and Sara's new roommate to an Italian restaurant and they ate raviolis and drank red wine. Dianne was content that Sara would have a good education and pursue her art.

She prayed that she'd be able to do more for Sara, and that Sara would find peace, and eventually love for her.

The next day, she and the girls took a taxi to the Metropolitan Museum. As the taxi driver drove like a maniac, Dianne and the girls held on to each other in the back seat, laughing, and joking.

The museum was massive with marble floors, a huge double marble stairway, domes, and art from every culture. Dianne spent hours looking at the art. She remembered David looking at a Cezanne, his eyes half closed, and sighing wistfully.

After Sara and Jenny left to go to the ballet studio, Dianne visited several art galleries. At Larry Gagosian's slick and magnificent gallery, there was an exhibit of Cy Twombly paintings. She loved the black paintings with the white hypnotic scribbles and allusions.

At the Guggenheim Museum, she was impressed by a Donald Judd exhibit, admiring his progressions of blocks and bars arranged in a repetition of serial forms and spaces. Especially, she liked a vertical stack of copper bars. At the Museum of Contemporary art she was especially enthralled by a painting of Joan Mitchell. The colors were vibrant, and the paint so sensually thick. The abstract swirling shapes implied the most beautiful gardens. The paintings were full of color and music and emotions. Art is the true language of life, Dianne thought. To paint with emotions, you have to dive into your soul and stay there.

The days went fast. It was the last day and Dianne and Jenny had ordered room service. They ate omelets and drank orange juice and coffee with crème in it. The wind howled outside and there were rumors of a storm coming. Jenny wanted to go to Bloomingdales to meet a friend from home with her family.

After Jenny left, Dianne took a taxi to Sara's ballet studio where Sara was taking Barre. More than anything Sara wanted to dance for the New York City Ballet. That was her dream. Though she'd grown so tall she feared she might not be able to, but she had alternative plans to someday make a film about ballet dancers.

At the studio on West Tenth Street, Dianne rode the rickety elevator to the top floor. Dancers wearing leotards and point slippers, and tiny sweaters, sat on the floor in the hallway, sewing laces on their Pointe shoes, and talking softly. Chopin's Etude echoed from the dance studio, and Dianne went inside.

The studio was a large drafty room. The grimy windows were covered with soot and several radiators hissed puffs of heat. The pale plank wood floor was shiny and slippery.

Dancers sat on the floor, along the walls, watching the dancers take Barre. A woman with a regal face, a pink shawl around her narrow shoulders, sat at the ancient piano, playing Chopin etudes. At barre, the dancers moved slowly, precisely, as if they were in slow motion.

The teacher, a small graceful man holding a stick, moved along the barre, adjusting the dancers positions. In French, he was shouting the positions.

Sara wore a black leotard, and black thick leg warmers. Her hair was arranged in a tight chignon, revealing her very long neck.

Sara moved gracefully, her eyes half closed, as if she were inside a dream, her long slender arm extended into position. Dianne could see that she had something special. Her body was like a poem, gracefully disciplined, and conveying skill, long years of practice, and emotion.

When the music stopped, Sara and the dancers went into the hallway.

After a few moments, Dianne found Sara at the juice bar. She stood in classic ballet position, her feet extended, and her face was flushed.

"You looked wonderful, Sara."

Sara frowned. "I'm too tall, and too fat."

"You're not. You're beautiful."

"Mom, you don't know."

"Let's go to lunch at the Russian Tea Room. And then I'll take you back to your dormitory."

The Russian Tea Room was another world: one of pomp and beauty, with candles, crystal, Faberge eggs inside glass cases, thick ruby carpets, and red booths. Christmas tree lights decorated the festive room, and waiters wearing Russian costumes, glided from table to table. Sara loved it.

Dianne ordered smoked salmon, and caviar. Sara ordered a beet salad. They chatted about New York, and how much they loved it.

"I'll miss you, Sara. I'll be having a show at the Evans Gallery. So I'll visit you often."

"Of course that's why you'll visit me. It's always about your work."

She pushed aside her plate. She'd hardly eaten.

"That's not true Sara. I'd visit you anyway."

There was a tense silence. Sara picked at a beet.

" I worry about your…eating," Dianne blurted.

"Since when?"

"Since always. Please, do you hate me that much?"

. "I've always wanted your attention, Mom. I live in a prison. I can't get out. I'm invisible. I crave your attention, but as long as I can remember, you ignore me. It's always about you, your work, David, Jenny. Never me."

Dianne wanted to die. She wanted to hug Sara, to get back the years she'd been that way.

"More than anything Sara, I want us to be close. It's hard for me. That's the only reason I couldn't. It's never been that I don't love you. Please know this. Please accept all my apologies that I made you feel like this."

"You scare me, Mom. I'm scared that you say you love me, but that as soon as I respond, you'll treat me like I don't exist."

"Sara, please let me try. Again, please let me apologize for all the words I didn't say, for the times I hurt you. Please, Sara. Please try to understand that I love you. Or I don't want to live."

Dianne held Sara's hand. It felt small and dainty. Sara was giving her a chance. She felt happy. For the rest of her life, Dianne would work at her relationship with Sara. Nothing else mattered but her girls.

"I don't want us to hurt each other anymore, Mom."

The next day was the last day. Jenny took the subway to Sara's dormitory. Dianne and the girls made plans to meet later at the dormitory and then they'd go to dinner.

Dianne took the subway to the Molly Evan's Gallery.

At 57th Street, groups of women wearing fur coats, their faces wrapped with scarves, strolled in and out of the rows of galleries, and the book and jewelry shops. Graffiti was painted on the walls along the wide streets.

The Molly Evans Gallery was inside a low industrial building. Dianne went inside, and into the gallery. She took off her hat, and cape. She shook her hair until it fell loose around her shoulders. Immediately, Dianne liked the gallery. It was small. Pale wood floors were highly polished. Skylights dropped natural light along the paintings and photographs.

"Dianne," said a small, woman wearing black and an African necklace. "I'm Molly Evans."

She was maybe in her late fifties. Her silver hair was worn straight to her shoulders, striking against her violet color eyes and white skin. She extended a slender ringed hand.

"Let me show you the main gallery," she said.

Dianne followed Molly into the main gallery to see her current photography exhibit. Photographs of hands closing or opening or clasped. You could see emotions in the fingers, and positions of the hands. It was the artist's first show.

"The artist is seventy-four," explained Molly. "She's made a lifetime study of hands. She captures the subject's soul, by their hands."

"Wonderful photographs," said Dianne. "It's also wonderful that you show her work. Because of ageism, many women artists have been overlooked. Or are known as the 'wife of' such as Lee Krasner, Georgia O'Keefe, and countless others. Especially those artists who are older and never had a chance. I hate labels such as women artists, gay artists. Art has no labels."

Molly nodded. "Let's go inside my office. I made coffee and tea. Or would you prefer wine?"

"Coffee, please," said Dianne, following Molly into a large office.

Molly poured steaming coffee into white ceramic bowl-shape cups. She sat at her large chrome and glass desk and Dianne sat on the gray sofa, facing her desk. Colorful paintings hung from the walls. Plants and books were everywhere. The room was friendly, so different from the rude pristine galleries David had taken her to.

Between drinking her coffee, Dianne related her impressions about the New York galleries she'd visited. "The galleries are slick," laughed Dianne. "As slick as the art."

Molly nodded. "As you know Dianne, I love your work. I've been following it for a while. It's fresh. New. Especially, I like the box paintings." She placed a cigarette into a black holder, lit it, and exhaled a long smoke ring. "The women inside the boxes are---haunting." Molly says.

In your paintings Dianne, you've captured a woman's pain like I've never seen. Your calligraphic line is light, yet strong."

"Thank you," Dianne said. It was exactly what she'd wanted to convey.

Molly continued: "The pain of abandonment is in every door, in every image. I can feel the emotion. "I want to give you a solo show in November."

Molly lit Dianne's cigarette and Dianne inhaled deeply.

Molly said: "I'd like the work shipped to my gallery by

October."

"I would love to have a show, Molly. Thank you."

At that moment Dianne felt complete.

To celebrate, Molly opened a bottle of chilled champagne. She poured the champagne into two glasses. They clicked their glasses, and then drank.

For the next hour, they talked about the plight of women artists, trying to be identified as artists, not as women, just artists. Molly, a ceramist, had used an inheritance from a wealthy Uncle abroad, to open the gallery. She was animated, intelligent, and she knew the art market well.

The day was turning dark. After Dianne and Molly made plans to ship the box paintings, went over terms of the contract, shipping, and when they'd talk again, it was time to go.

"I'll be calling you soon," Molly said, helping Dianne on with her cape.

Outside, it was ice cold, and a haze of blue lay over the darkening sky. The wind was up, and Dianne adjusted her cape around her shoulders. She decided to walk to the corner, and catch a taxi.

"Hello, Dianne." She turned. It was David.

She was taken back. It was one of those moments she'd dreaded, had replayed a thousand times. "Hello," she finally said.

They stood there looking at each other, caught in one of those indelible moments. "I'm surprised to see you, David."

"What are you doing in New York?" he asked.

"Sara is at NYU, and Jenny and I are at the Waldorf. I had a meeting with Molly Evans about my show."

"Great, kid." He sniffed. "I'm on my way to see Castelli. He's waiting at a restaurant a few blocks away." He glanced at his watch.

She nodded. "I read the wonderful article in Art Forum about your Los Angeles Gallery. I'm happy for you."

He frowned. "New York is the place to be, Dianne. The art here is superior. Los Angeles is about freeways, and movie stars. I'm looking for a space here."

She nodded. "Well, I have to get going, David. I'm on my way to meet the girls."

He touched the side of her cheek. A tiny shock made a popping sound. "I think of you ... a lot, Dianne. You know I love you."

She smiled. They held each other close. His beard felt cold against her face.

"Thank you," he said, pulling away and sniffling. He put on his leather gloves, smoothing them snugly over his fingers, over his gold wedding band, until every wrinkle was pressed out.

"Take care, kid. Good luck on your show." He paused, looking at her intently. "You know kid, you're beautiful."

She watched him walk down the street, slumped slightly forward, on his toes, and fussing with his burgundy cashmere scarf. Until he finally disappeared into the crowd and back into his world.

She walked several blocks. At the corner she bought a roasted chestnut. It was hot and tasted charred. She peeled it back until she got the seed and then dropped the shell, watching it roll off the curb.

The wind was howling. She walked faster now, humming

Beethoven's Fifth, as she always would when scared or excited.

The trees were full of spring. On the very edge of a branch, a blue butterfly with transparent dotted wings was shuddering. Suddenly, it lifted up, hesitantly at first, circling the air, and then it took off in flight.

THE END

About the Author

Barbara Rose Brooker is a native San Francisco author. She graduated from San Francisco State University with a Masters degree in creative writing. She teaches writing at SFSU/OLLI and at private workshops and seminars. She steadily publishes her poetry. Also, she writes Boomer In The City, a column for the JWeekly newspaper, Huffington Post, and other papers. Her novels have been published by Morrow, Simon & Schuster, and other presses.

ABOUT THE BOOK:

The Rise and Fall of a Jewish American Princess opens in 1960, and closes in 1981. The story begins with Dianne Roseman's brutal rejection and deception. Dianne struggles to rise from her mother's mental abuse, and generation of women who define themselves by marriage, into her true self as an artist. As she fights adversity, divorce, parenting two daughters, and the changing roles of women, she finds passionate love, and success in the world of contemporary art. The novel is for all women of all generations and cultures and asks questions about marriage and romantic love and women of present and future generations who are stuck in the outdated mores of past generations.

She is working on a new novel. Also, she is the founder of the first Age March in history.

My other published novels:

So Long Princess
The Viagra Diaries
God Doesn't Make Trash
Should I Sleep in His Dead Wife's Bed?
Anyone Can Write
Lazy Dogs Dance